The Uncertainty of Hope

Valerie Tagwira

Best Wishes

Valerie J. Tagwira

The Uncertainty
of Hope

Valerie Tagwira

WEAVER

W

—PRESS—

Published by Weaver Press,
Box A1922, Avondale, Harare, 2006.

Typeset by Weaver Press
Cover Design: Myrtle Mallis
Cover Photograph Dave Brazier, Wide Angle
Printed by Sable Press, Harare

This novel is entirely a work of fiction. The names, characters and incidents portrayed in it are the work of the author's imagination. Any reseblance to actual events or to persons living or dead is entirely coincidental.

The publishers would like to express their gratitude to Hivos for the support they have given to Weaver Press in the development of their fiction programme.

The song 'Wandirasa' is quoted from *Ancient Voices* (published by LusAfrica, France) with the permission of Chiwoniso Maraire to whom we offer grateful thanks.

ISBN: 978-1-77922-063-9

Valerie Joan Tagwira graduated from the University of Zimbabwe's Medical School in 1997. She has a strong interest in health-related and developmental issues that affect women. She is currently studying towards her membership exams for the Royal College of Obstetricians and Gynaecologists while working in London. *The Uncertainty of Hope* is her first novel.

'It began as an exploration in creativity, something that one doesn't practise in the medical field. Then, it became an opportunity for me to explore issues close to my heart … the challenges that women face in their day-to-day lives, and the obstacles that they encounter in trying to make life better for their families.'

In loving memory of my parents

Eileen and Samuel Tagwira

◆ ◆ ◆

CHAPTER 1

Onai Moyo awakened unwillingly from her slumber to the irritating sound of a dog barking continuously in the distance. The racket escalated to an agitated pitch that seemed to grow closer as it grew louder. More dogs in the neighbourhood joined in: barking, yelping and growling. The noise was raucous and broke the stillness of night. Onai felt a spasm of apprehension. This sort of commotion often meant that gangs of *matsotsi e*Harare were out prowling through the ramshackle labyrinth of Jo'burg Lines where she lived with her family.

Her right arm felt like a dead-weight beneath her despite a spasm of sharp pins and needles. She turned over with drowsy indolence and wiggled her fingers to ease her discomfort. Circulation returned in a rush and for a moment the prickling sensation intensified. She opened her eyes. Thin shafts of orange light from the tower light filtered effortlessly through the leaves of the mango tree just outside her window and through the frayed curtain of her bedroom, throwing peculiar shapes on the wall that seemed to cavort in a synchronised manner. *Mimvuri*, happy shadows … she thought sleepily, closing her eyes in an attempt to go back to sleep. She failed.

As she became more alert, she thought again with a sinking feeling that her husband had not yet come home. The absence of loud snores and a pleasant freedom from the stench of alcohol-infused breath told their own story. But still she strained her sleep-heavy eyes in the gloom and reached a tentative arm across the bed. She made contact with nothing, which confirmed her anxiety. Where was he?

At that moment, the rickety metal gate standing a few metres from her bedroom window creaked in a characteristic manner. So he's finally back, she thought with irritation as she fumbled for her wristwatch on the battered cardboard box next to her bed. The upside-down container had staunchly served as her dressing table for almost a year, weathering bedroom conflicts by her side. As she peered at her watch and struggled to make out the time, she heard muted voices and the padding of stealthy footsteps. Tossing her threadbare blanket aside, she stood up.

Cautiously, she drew the curtain sideways a fraction, and out of the corner of her eye caught a flurry of movement. Two figures crept past the mango tree and disappeared into the shadows towards the kitchen door. So, tonight, they were the burglars' chosen ones! Her heart knocked painfully against her rib cage. The sound transmitted itself to her ears in a subdued, pulsing beat.

'God help me please,' she offered a heartfelt prayer. She knew how daring burglars ordered people to remain quietly in bed while they ransacked their homes. With the new breed of malicious intruders, assault was no longer a remote possibility. She was certain, moreover, that her loudest screams would not coerce her neighbours out of the safety and comfort of their homes. Nobody in their right mind would risk their lives by coming to her aid. Not at this time of night. So, apart from her children, she was well and truly alone.

She swore under her breath at her absent husband. *Uripiko nhai Gari?* Where are you Gari?' Her mind sharp with fear, she realised that she had just a few minutes to spirit her children to relative safety. She moved silently and instinctively through the darkness into her daughters' bedroom. Sixteen-year-old Ruva and fifteen-year-old Rita were both awake, which was a relief, though not surprising given the clamour that the dogs were still making. She half-dragged them out of bed and shoved them into her bedroom. Ignoring their surprised questions, she hissed at them to be quiet. Exchanging confused glances, they obeyed. She then tiptoed into her son's tiny bedroom next to the kitchen. Amazingly, ten-year-old Fari was fast asleep. She placed her hand over his mouth and gently woke him up. Clearly startled by this intrusion, he struggled and hit out before he heard her reassuring whispers. Mother and son moved quickly into the main bedroom.

The family huddled in a tense, quivering group in the corner of their sanctuary. Profound fear hung over them as they listened to the muffled sounds and imagined their home being desecrated. Rita, the neediest of Onai's children, leaned closer towards her and sought out her

2

hand with a trembling, clammy palm. Onai took the shaky hand in a firm grip and drew the terrified girl closer.

She closed her eyes and thought about their black and white television, by far their most prized possession. It stood with imposing presence on a wrought-iron stand, easily dominating their poky sitting room. Without seeing it, she knew that it had gone. 'Maybe it will be the only thing they get away with because it's so heavy,' she dared to hope. She wondered if the burglars had knives. Or a gun. The idea made her shudder. She circled her arms around Rita and drew some comfort from the softness and warmth of the young girl's body. Again she swore at her husband for leaving them so defenceless.

After what felt like the longest ten minutes of Onai's life, the faint noises quietened down and the back door closed with a barely perceptible click. Next, the gate creaked and sighed. A flood of relief washed over her and the tension in her body slackened. The intruders had left. Rising from her crouching position, she groped for the light switch and pulled hard on the string. The sudden brightness was almost like a physical blow. Fari looked dazed. Rita was shaking violently. Ruva's mutinous face showed a fiery but impotent anger. Onai felt a moment of self-reproach. She could not protect her children from the life they were destined to live.

As if on cue, the family moved silently and resolutely into the sitting room. Their television which had withstood the ravages of time had gone. *Sekutamba chaiko.* Just like that. Rita and Fari perched on the edge of the old armchair, wordless still. The silent disappointment on their faces only added to Onai's sense of despondency. Of course, she would never be able to replace the set. Not in a lifetime. Without doubt, they would miss their weekly highlight, the Nigerian Movies of the Week which provided an intriguing concoction of Christianity and witchcraft. Nor would their evenings be the same without the suspense of a *Studio 263* episode. Thankfully, their black Supersonic stereo still stood on a woven reed mat in the corner. She lifted it off the floor and placed it carefully on the wrought-iron stand. *'Pabva gondo pagara zizi,'* she mused, somewhat inappropriately, then dismissed the thought. For that elevated position, the stereo was surely a poor replacement.

For a room that had just been burgled, everything else looked startlingly normal. Not that there was anything else that would have stirred the burglars' interest. The noticeably small room was further dwarfed by four shabby blue armchairs, well past their prime. The wobbly wooden table stood where it had always stood, right at the centre of the room, looking as lopsided as ever.

Onai's eyes moved up the blue, streaked wall. Her two picture frames, embellished in gaudy imitation gold, still hung on either side of the cheerfully corpulent Humpty Dumpty clock. 'Humpty Dumpty sat on a wall ...' her thoughts wandered, seeking escape and remembering of all things, Fari's favourite rhyme. She stopped herself irritably. The clock appeared to be smiling at her, eyes twinkling, features seemingly alight with joy. She removed her gaze from the illusion of its happiness.

Ruva whirled round to glare at her. '*Amai*, where is *baba?* Look at the time. It's three o'clock, *Amai!* He should have been here to protect us. Why isn't he here?' she railed, her soft adolescent features contorted by resentful anger.

Onai looked at her and flinched from the intensity of her rage. '*Mwanangu*, just like you, I don't know where he is. We're safe now. Let's go back to sleep, *vanangu*,' she said in a mother's calm, gentle voice. Inside, she was seething. For a moment, she felt an irresistible urge to slap her daughter really hard, but with no small effort she suppressed it. She thought of uttering some belittling remarks about Gari, but again she restrained herself. She would never admit openly to her children that their father was a blatantly irresponsible man. What purpose would it serve, except to further erode the flimsy fabric of Gari's relationship with his children?

Tactfully, she ignored the increasingly familiar look of condemnation on Ruva's face and shepherded her offspring back to bed. She checked the lock on the back kitchen door and was dismayed to find it badly broken. Getting it fixed would cost no less than five hundred thousand dollars. *Veduwe, nhamo haibvi pane imwe chokwadi ...* poverty bred even greater poverty. There wasn't much more that the pittance she grossed as a vegetable vendor could accommodate.

Resignedly, she tried to hold the broken lock together with a piece of thick wire. It did not work. She tried harder. The wire dug into the roughened skin of her palms. Finally, she managed to hold the door at a slightly crooked slant. The twisted wire offered no protection. She shut her eyes tightly and drew in a slow, deep breath, bravely willing herself free of another cloud of misery which was threatening to suffocate her.

Fortunately, the barking dogs had quietened their rowdy chorus. The swift transition to tranquillity was a bit strange, but comforting all the same. Maybe the burglars had retired to bed, well pleased with their spoils for the night. Maybe they had shifted to more lucrative targets. Whatever the case, Onai did not really care. The fact that they had gone offered a welcome reprieve. She slipped back into the familiarity of her bed but found no further solace. The sheets had become very cold and sleep would not come. She lay on her back and shivered as she stared vacantly at the bleak, corrugated, asbestos sheets which roofed the house. She rolled and turned, restless and unable to get comfortable. At last, curling up into a tight foetal position, she lost herself in a muddle of sad thoughts.

Gari was not an easy man to live with. Over the years, she had worn herself out just trying to conceal proof of his violence. As a model of perseverance, nobody could have done better than she had. If and when she failed, it was never for want of trying. Despite this, she did know that her endless, effusive explanations no longer convinced her neighbours. Her episodic facial bruising and blackened eyes had ceased to be material for speculation because they all knew precisely what was happening. However, the cocoon of pretence that she had woven around herself had become her armour. It was the one thing which held the frail vestiges of her dignity securely in place. There was nothing else she thought she could do. She was, after all, only a woman. How could she fight against fate?

Only recently, her daughter, Ruva had tried to talk to her about how the situation caused her distress. Onai had skilfully steered the conversation to less precarious ground. She had made it clear to her daughter that discussing her father was taboo. And anyway, what could one discuss with a mere sixteen-year-old about the delicate intricacies of love and marriage to an obnoxious man?

She thought of Katy, the one woman in her life who deserved to be called her *sahwira*, her best friend. Just the previous day, Katy had said to her, 'Onai, I just cannot understand why you don't want to leave Gari. Do you want us to take you out of this house in a coffin? Huh? *Asi chii nhai?* Why are you holding on?'

'For my children, of course. Please let me be, Katy. Gari will change. He's just going through a difficult time at work. There's a rumour that the company may move to South Africa because it's losing money here. I know he'll change as soon as things get better for him,' Onai had said, trying to breathe conviction into the words as she spoke them.

Katy had laughed. It had been a high-pitched, mirthless sound of disbelief. 'The rumours about the Cola Drinks Company only started last month. Gari has been like this for years and years. You have to stop making excuses for him,' she had replied firmly, her husky voice rising with annoyance, while expressions of irritation, compassion and tenderness flitted across her face in quick succession. Onai had chosen not to answer. Katy had broken the awkward silence with a different approach, 'You deserve better than this, *sahwira*. What about your self-respect? Have you lost that as well, Onai?'

'If what I'm doing for my children shows that I have no self-respect; then, yes, I've lost it – or maybe I did so when I decided to become a mother,' she had responded stubbornly, unsure of what exactly her friend had meant.

Katy's rejoinder had been sharp and sarcastic. *Mashura chaiwo!* I can't believe what you are saying. If you want to do something for your children, why not leave Gari and remove them from this mess? What do you think this is doing to them?'

Onai had responded with a deliberate, dismissive shrug. Within, she had been silently begging her friend to reassure her that she was doing the right thing for her children. But predictably, Katy had given up and left in an ostentatious sulk. Onai knew she would be back and it would be as if they had never argued. The little dents in affection and small rifts between them never went beyond transient inconveniences. But despite being such good friends, she did not really expect Katy to understand her position. Their lives were different, and their upbringing even more so.

The knowledge that her mother did understand was a constant source of comfort. MaMusara's own marriage to Onai's late father had been very troubled. But she had stayed for the sake of her children and because marriage was not something that one could just walk away from. 'Once you get in, you stay. *Kugomera uripo chaiko mwanangu* ... no matter how hard it gets. Always remember that a woman cannot raise a good family without a man by her side,' MaMusara had declared, obviously keen to instil similar values in her daughter.

Onai had listened attentively, acknowledging that if her mother had left her father, she might have ended up living on the streets with her two young brothers, reduced to a life of begging and petty crime. Or worse. So, in the same manner, she stayed and felt extremely proud that she was able to do so for her children. This was the essence of a true African woman ... perseverance in the face of all hardship, especially for the children. One always stayed for them.

For the third time that night, the gate creaked and moaned. Onai's reverie was instantly broken. She got up with weary acceptance. Peeping out from behind the threadbare curtain, she chastised herself for not switching off the light earlier. Whoever was out there would probably notice her shadowy outline against the window. Gari's large frame lurched into view and staggered towards the front door. His trench coat caught on a protruding branch of the mango tree. He lost his footing and stumbled against the shack housing their sole lodger. He cursed loudly and rattled the front door, clearly annoyed at finding it locked. Surely he can't have lost his key again, Onai thought to herself and sighed miserably.

'Mai Ruva! Open the door, woman! *Iwe mukadzi iwe!*' he bellowed in an angry voice. Fearing that he would awaken her children or disturb the neighbours, she obeyed immediately. There was no need to expose everyone so openly to her marital disharmony. Gari loomed in the doorway and walked into the cramped sitting room with an unsteady gait. He brought with him the heavy odour of stale beer and a whiff of a nauseatingly sweet perfume. The nicotine-stained fingers of his right hand were curled possessively around the slender neck of a brown bottle of Castle beer.

She looked at him incredulously, taking in his crumpled clothes. The front of his shirt was emblazoned with bright red smudges. Lipstick! Her heart contracted painfully. His zip was undone and the edge of his shirt was offensively sticking out of the fly. She did not have to think too hard to imagine what he had been up to. His shoes were encrusted with what looked suspiciously like a thick layer of vomit. And Fari would have the thankless task of cleaning the shoes in the morning!

'Imi, baba vaRuva! Where have you been? Do you know that we were burgled?' she asked him, her face burning with resentment. Gari gave her a brief, glazed look and swayed drunkenly. He placed the beer bottle on the table with surprising care. Struggling out of his trench coat, he threw himself clumsily onto her favourite armchair. It creaked in protest beneath his weight. His face was a spectacle of incomprehension. He looked like a contemptible caricature of the man she had fallen in love with all those years ago whose memory now held the surreal quality of a dream. He gave a complacent burp and stared at her again through bleary, red-rimmed eyes.

Onai shook her head, disgusted and angry, aware that in this state, she would not be able to get through to him. His brain was lost somewhere inaccessible, in a foggy faraway place. She trembled with the rage that was bubbling within her and felt her self-control slipping away, a dull pounding setting off behind her eyes. She leaned on the wall. It's solid coolness steadied her and seemed to ease the throbbing in her head.

'I said we were burgled, baba vaRuva. They took your precious TV. Get this into your thick head,' she said with intentional carelessness. There was more silence and yet another vacant stare. She detected something on the whites of his eyes, a tinge of yellow that she had never noticed before. It gave him an odd, rather sickly look which only added to her mounting repulsion. 'Damn you straight to hell *baba vaRuva. KuGehena chaiko,'* she cursed him heatedly, trying to goad him into a response, temporarily overlooking the fact that she might provoke him into a very public fight. Still, his unfocused eyes stared through her and past her. She might as well have been invisible. Shrugging with a sudden nonchalance, she gave up and walked back into the bedroom. There was nothing to be gained by trying to talk to him. It was so much wiser to try to get some sleep. He reeled into the bedroom after her and rasped through drooling lips, 'You bitch! Where is my TV?'

So, finally, his mind had registered something in the real world? The joy of pleasant surprises … *mashura chaiwo!* Onai bristled and glowered at him. 'I told you, the burglars took it,' she said in a low, urgent voice, now desperate to minimise the noise.

'Liar! What burglars are you talking about? You think you can fool me, don't you? I say no! I am the one with the brains, not you. You gave my TV to your boyfriends. You whore! *Uri hure!'* he slurred through thick lips, his bloodshot eyes gleaming triumphantly.

Onai felt dispirited and fatigued. If the situation was not so ludicrously sad, she would have liked a good laugh. But this was not the way things were going. More annoyance, yes, and maybe a few tears as well. But, at the very least, she would not get any sleep. She knew the routine well enough. Once the matter of her imaginary indiscretions came up, there was always hell to pay. Fortunately, the more drunk he was, the less likely he would be able to inflict serious injury upon her. But still there would be no sleep and that was a real nuisance. She badly needed a rest because she had to get up early to collect her fruit and vegetable orders for the market. She could certainly do without this.

He hovered threateningly at the edge of the bed and continued slobbering, 'You liar! I'm going to teach you a lesson … a really good lesson. Do you hear?' He shook his hairy fist for emphasis, and with astonishing vigour for one so obviously drunk. She stared back at him, greatly annoyed, but confident and unafraid. There was hardly anything he could do to her in that pathetic state. His burly physique and an inborn penchant for aggression were the only advantages he had over her. In contrast to him, she was totally in control, very clear-headed and agile.

He took a drunken lunge at her with a clenched fist. A surge of fear crushed her earlier confidence. She quickly backed away and cowered against the wall. His fist caught her directly over the right eye. She registered a multitude of glittering stars and tried without success to scramble off the bed.

He grabbed her nightdress and tugged hard. She lost her balance and fell headlong. The floor rose swiftly to meet her and her brow made exquisitely painful contact with the concrete door-stop's sharp edge. Blood poured out of a deep cut above her left eye. She screamed and curled herself up in pain.

≈≈≈

Ruva rushed into the bedroom and took in the scene. Her mother lay on the floor, a stream of blood-stained tears ran between her fingers as she held them protectively over her face. Ruva's alarmed gaze shifted to her father. He was lying at an angle across the bed, already blissfully lost in a drunken slumber. His mouth open, he was discharging thunderous snores and his feet were dangling carelessly over her mother's curled form. Her eyes filled with bitter tears. Her heart ached, and a hopeless pain filled her chest.

She dropped to her knees next to her mother and shook her shoulder tentatively. '*Amai*, are you all right?' she asked. '*Amai?*' her voice shook. There was no answer, apart from a few pathetic moans and a subtle movement of the head, which could have been a nod, Ruva was not sure. She stood up slowly.

Clearly, her mother needed to get to hospital. Getting an ambulance out would be time-consuming and probably impossible. Because of the fuel shortages, the local service had become unreliable. The running joke was that if you called an ambulance, it would take a couple of days to crawl to your house, and by the time it arrived, you might just have taken your last breath. Laugh as people might, the reality of the situation was that some lives had been lost through such delays. The more reliable, modernised Medical Air Rescue Service required a cash payment upfront. Ruva knew that her mother did not have the cash.

Maiguru, mai Faith was her only hope of getting her mother to hospital. If *maiguru* could not do so, she would at least let her use the phone. Once again, Ruva found herself disregarding her safety and sprinting into the wintry darkness, up 50th Street and around the corner into 49th Street.

Anger and despair burned inside her, as they always did after the fights. Anger with her father for his violence, anger with her mother for allowing the situation to continue, and despair because there was absolutely nothing she could do about it, except sprint up the street to *maiguru's* house after each fight, shrouded by darkness, hounded by imaginary shadows, and fearing for her own safety. So familiar was the route that she could have run it with her eyes closed. She climbed over the low fence into *maiguru's* yard and banged hard on the door.

Katy stirred into unwilling consciousness and strained her ears. She thought she heard banging on the front door, then she recognised Ruva's voice calling out her name. She gave a heavy sigh and sat up with reluctant apathy. Her husband snored softly and made a movement with his right hand, but continued sleeping. She pushed the bedclothes aside and pulled a dress over her head. Her bare feet made contact with the cold, cemented floor. An involuntary tremor coursed through her body.

She flung the front door open to find her friend's panicky daughter on the doorstep. She knew instantly that Gari had been at it again. With a flash of annoyance, she wondered what it would take to make Onai accept that she had to leave Gari.

'Sorry to wake you up, *maiguru! Amai* is hurt. I think … I think she has to go to hospital. Please, *maiguru*, help me,' Ruva snivelled almost incoherently through a flood of distressed tears.

Katy knew right away that it was serious. There was no time to be indecisive. 'Get her ready. I'm coming shortly,' she said firmly to the

11

distraught girl and went back into the bedroom.

John was already sitting up in bed, looking groggy and annoyed. 'Don't tell me it's Onai and Gari again?' he said in a voice thick with sleep.

'Sorry, *mudiwa*. Yes, it's Onai and Gari again,' Katy replied, feeling too drained to rush robustly to her friend's defence as she usually did. A strong desire to crawl back into bed enticed her. But she merely sat down at the edge of the bed and cupped her right jaw with her hand. No, she could not creep back into bed. Her *sahwira* needed her. She looked up and held John's eyes hopefully.

'Well, this time I'm not going out there to stop their fighting. They are adults. Let them solve their own problems,' John spoke abruptly and disengaged his eyes from her expectant gaze. Drawing the soft duvet tightly around his body, he turned over and faced the wall in an explicitly dismissive gesture.

'I think this is serious, John. Ruva said Onai is hurt. She needs to get to hospital.' Her response was grave.

'*Saka?* So what?' John grunted and laughed without cheer. He rolled over and faced her. 'Am I now supposed to provide an ambulance service for Onai? Why can't Gari take his own wife to hospital or call an ambulance for her? Why me?' he asked unnecessarily. The reasons were obvious to both of them.

Katy sighed and supported her head with both hands, her right foot tapping restlessly on the cold floor, while a nerve on the right side of her face twitched. Her husky voice rose in pleading tones. 'Please listen to me. You know that Gari will not take Onai to hospital. You also know that the ambulance service is unreliable. Onai has nobody else who can help her except us. Ruva is a very sensible girl. She wouldn't have called us if it wasn't serious. Please, *mudiwa*, will you?' she begged, her voice now shaky. She was close to tears.

The imminent tears did it. John gave in, but without enthusiasm. He heaved an irritable sigh and got out of bed. Very slowly. 'All right. Get her out to our gate. I'm not coming with you to her house. If I come face to face with Gari, I tell you, I'll lose my temper and beat him up,' he said gruffly. Katy grabbed a jersey and made a hasty exit before her husband changed his mind.

≈≈≈

John finished dressing hurriedly, his mind running a mental tirade against Onai and Gari. Taking Onai to hospital would be a reckless misuse of his hard-earned petrol. As a cross-border haulage truck driver, he was often away from home. On this occasion, he had wasted three of his five leave days in a long queue in Harare city centre, just to get a measly fifteen litres of petrol. Now he would have to waste it on Onai! Still upset, he reversed his car out to the gate where the women were waiting under the harsh glare of a tower light. Onai was a shivering bundle emitting low, piteous moans. One side of her beautiful face was horribly swollen. Her normally flawless, dark skin was marred by bruising and swelling. A blood-stained piece of mutton cloth was tied crudely across her forehead. As he helped her into the car, John felt no compassion at all. He had been through this too many times before. Obviously, she did not have the self-esteem to value her own life. What a waste of such a beautiful woman … what a terrible waste, he thought to himself.

Turning to Ruva, he said, 'You're going to school in a few hours, aren't you?' She nodded mutely and trembled in the biting chill of early morning air, her arms overlaid with goose pimples.

'We'll take care of your mother. Go back home,' he ordered brusquely. She looked at him with big apprehensive eyes, obviously reluctant to leave. Katy took her arm and elbowed her towards the corner into 50th Street. Then she climbed into the car and sat on the back seat with Onai, holding her in an embrace. The two women were silent as John drove them to the hospital. The car's headlights were out of focus and most of the tower lights were faulty, at best giving off flickers of inadequate light. As a result, the vehicle kept dropping into outsized pot-holes that John would have otherwise avoided. The twenty-five-year old Datsun 120Y jerked, spluttered and coughed as they left Mbare and drove towards Beatrice Road.

Two buses, which had been involved in an accident near the broadcasting corporation complex the previous evening, still stood abandoned, encroaching dangerously into the road. John swore and tried to negotiate his way round them. Brakes squealed loudly as he came to a halt at red traffic lights. Suddenly, three men materialised out of the darkness and started hitting the car. They shouted noisy obscenities and tried to wrench the doors open. The two women huddled together and stifled frightened screams.

John panicked and tried to spring the car into motion. His right foot pushed the wrong pedal. The car jerked and stalled to a complete stop. He finally managed to re-start the engine and took off just as one of the thugs picked up a large stone and threw it at his window. The stone missed its target but skimmed noisily over the boot. The car struggled up the steep incline towards the hospital, threatening to stall more than once. There was no other sound apart from Onai's soft whimpering. John made a silent vow. This was the last time he would ever do this.

≈≈≈

When they arrived at Casualty, one of the night nurses led Onai to a stark little room, which was dimly-lit and extremely cold. 'You're very lucky. You won't have to wait very long because we have enough doctors covering tonight's shift. And that, my dear, is very unusual,' the nurse said cheerfully and beamed a smile at the wounded woman.

Onai gave a slight nod, unwilling to make any effort to talk. Speech would only worsen the pain threatening to tear her skull apart. The nurse made her comfortable on an examination couch. With deft movements of her soft hands, she checked Onai's pulse, blood pressure and temperature. She gave another bright smile. 'All normal my dear. The doctor will be with you shortly,' she said, before leaving the room.

Onai lay on the examination couch, shivering violently as she waited for the doctor. Her face throbbed and her head pulsed with waves of pain. She tried to block it out by closing her eyes, but unable to bear the sudden feeling of being alone in the dark world of her misery, she re-opened them immediately.

After a short while, a tired-looking doctor came in and mumbled an introduction that she did not grasp. He was a dour little man who wore wrinkled scrubs. His eyes were red and puffy. One side of his face was covered in a graphic cobweb of sleep marks. He took a brief medical history from her. In her mind, Onai formulated some careful responses to avoid implicating Gari. 'I walked into a door ...' she started, then stopped because the pain had become unbearable.

The doctor fidgeted with his pen and looked at her impatiently. 'Go on. I don't have all night,' he said abruptly, his face creasing into a frown. In disjointed sentences, Onai explained how she had accidentally hit her head against the bedroom door in the darkness, while looking for a light switch.

The doctor gave her a look that told her he didn't believe her, but he did not probe further. He shook his head in a distracted manner and wrote something on a card. During the examination, a black stethoscope dangling from his front pocket swung worryingly close to Onai. He ignored it. His gruff manner hinted at a deep longing to hurry to bed. After he had finished his speedy examination, he said, 'You will have to be admitted to hospital because you need observation for your head injury. I will suture the cut on your forehead and request a skull X-ray.'

'Thank you, *chiremba*,' Onai mumbled with a heady sense of relief. The hospital stay would be a welcome break from the demands of her life, as well as from Gari's abuse. Maybe just for one day she would savour sweet freedom and enjoy a carefree existence. Just for one day she'd be able to surrender herself to the care and ministrations of others. Strong feelings of maternal guilt forced her to block out thoughts of her children. For was she not abandoning them?

The doctor laid out a suture pack and called a nurse to assist him. 'There is no local anaesthetic,' the nurse explained to Onai. 'So you have to bear with us. I will hold your hand'.

Onai nodded, unprepared for the agony that followed. She moaned and bit back a scream as the needle cut into the skin on her forehead. Her head jerked involuntarily. The instrument in the doctor's hand slipped and dropped to the floor with a loud clatter. He cursed.

'*Shingai Amai. Shingai.* It will be over before you know it,' the young nurse held her hand and encouraged her to endure the supposedly short procedure. She was wrong. Onai cried silent tears and kept rigidly still, trying hard not to offend the doctor who seemed to think that she was being difficult. Finally, the procedure was over. She almost howled with relief. She accepted some tablets from the nurse and took them immediately, gulping down some water through a tight throat.

Katy and John wheeled her to the ward on a rickety wheelchair. It creaked and wobbled along a dim corridor, and round the corner towards a lift which took them up to Female Surgical Ward. In the lift, Onai had the strangest feeling of being in a coffin, so bare and desolate-looking it was, with walls that were rusting in parts and the paint peeling. She closed her eyes and leaned backwards, gripping the armrests on the wheelchair. She was happy to arrive in the ward.

As Katy and John turned to leave, Onai gripped Katy's hand. She opened her mouth to speak. Her jaws felt heavy and stiff. She croaked, 'I'm so sorry for getting you out like this. I'm sorry that we were attacked. But thank you very much my friend. *Ndatenda sahwira*. I don't know what I would do without you.'

Katy replied soothingly, 'Onai, don't worry about anything. Just concentrate on getting better. I will ring the hospital tomorrow morning to check how you are doing. I can't come back today because John returns to South Africa this evening. I have to pack for him. That flighty daughter of mine is visiting this afternoon as well.'

Onai observed a subtle flicker of pride in her friend's eyes as she made reference to her daughter. Faith had left high school with excellent grades. She had gone straight to university. Which mother would not take pride in a daughter who was studying for a degree in law? Stifling a rush of envy, she cleared her throat and swallowed. It still hurt. 'Please tell the children not to worry about visiting me after school. It won't be easy for them to get transport here and back home.'

'I will do that, *sahwira*,' Katy replied and gave her a quick hug. Onai's heart brimmed with gratitude. However, she had a disquieting intuition that Katy's patience was bound to wear out eventually. It was just a matter of time. She had no idea who she would turn to when that fear became a reality. Her mother lived in another world. The kind of support which she offered kept Onai sane, but she needed so much more. She needed Katy for the practicalities of surviving life with Gari. And for surviving life in Mbare. She would be lost without her friend.

≈≈≈

Dawn was breaking as they drove back to Mbare, darkness easing into daylight. Already, the roads were lined with people making an early start to work. For most, the prevailing transport problems, coupled with inability to pay the ever-increasing fares, meant an hour or more walking to work.

'How many times must I point out something so obvious? Your friend must leave Gari. One day he'll do something really serious,' John said. 'Like killing her,' he added gravely.

Katy attempted a laugh. It rang out, shrill and artificial. 'Don't be so pessimistic John! Nobody is going to kill anyone.' She was not willing to admit yet again that she shared exactly the same concerns. Onai's predicament was now a well-debated and well-worn topic. There was absolutely nothing new to say.

He made a slight movement with his shoulders. 'I hope I won't be saying *takambozvitaura* one of these days.' His voice was heavy with cynicism.

'Don't worry. I will talk to her again soon. The biggest problem is that she explains away everything that Gari does. I am not sure why. I suspect she loves him,' she replied, wondering if at last she had stumbled upon the most logical explanation for Onai's attitude. Nothing else seemed to make sense.

He frowned and raised his eyebrows. 'Really? To me, the idea of anyone loving Gari is absurd. *Asi*, I'm not a woman. Even at the best of times, women can be very irrational. Well, maybe except you, *mudiwa*.' Suddenly, he inclined his head towards her. His face broke into a smile.

Katy exhaled with relief. The tension was broken. She said thoughtfully, 'If only there was a way for Onai to earn enough money to buy a house of her own and take care of her children ... I'm sure she would leave him.'

He cast another sideways glance at her and laughed. 'Be serious, Katy.

17

This is Zimbabwe. A poor woman will always be a poor woman. *Hazvichinje!*' After a moment of contemplative silence he continued, 'Onai will never own a house. She is an unemployed dressmaker who works as a vegetable vendor. How can you even imagine that she could buy a house? Where would she get the money from?' Katy stared back at him and did not answer. He was right. The notion of Onai ever owning a house was ridiculous.

'And by the way, that was the last time. Can you imagine what would have happened if those thugs had managed to open the doors? *Taifaka?* We could have died,' he said quietly, as if suddenly overcome by the wonder of realisation.

She looked away, partly blaming herself. Yes, it was time she had a serious talk with her friend. In the past, she'd tended to be almost overly cautious and fearful of exposing the secret place where Onai kept her deepest emotions hidden. Next time, she'd have to be more direct. Brutally direct. It was time for things to change before the violence spiralled into something worse. Soon it might be too late for anything to change. As Onai's *sahwira*, she had to do better. Onai deserved better.

The rest of their drive back to Mbare was made in complete silence.

CHAPTER 2

At four o'clock that afternoon, Faith's boyfriend, Tom Sibanda picked her up from the Swinton Hall of residence at the university and drove her to her parents' home in Mbare. He smiled wryly and commented that driving through the high-density suburb was always a great challenge. Faith nodded sympathetically.

They were both acutely aware of the unwritten but readily enforceable road regulations peculiar only to that part of Harare. You were not allowed to drive faster than fifteen kilometres an hour; neither were you permitted to blow your horn at the throngs of pedestrians strolling casually down the middle of the road. You had to slow down respectfully and allow them to step aside at their own relaxed pace. Blowing your hooter could result in you receiving an onslaught of vitriolic abuse and having your vehicle pelted with stones; or worse. It did not take much to provoke sufficient public ire resulting in one's car being overturned. So Tom drove at a leisurely pace, taking great care to avoid offending the teeming crowds of careless pedestrians.

Faith turned towards him, smiling for no particular reason, except that she felt happy to be with him.

'Are you still going to the UK, Tom?' she asked, raising her eyebrows.

'Yes, sorry, I meant to tell you. I fly out next Friday. Got no choice. I wish you could come with me, though.' His voice was touched with regret. He laid a warm hand on her thigh in an intimate caress. She revelled in the feeling of being desired.

'*Asi chii nhai?* Are you joking? How would I explain that to my mother? I won't even speak of my father!' She gave a low throaty laugh. Going to the UK with him indeed! Maybe in her wildest dreams.

Tom countered mildly, 'My love, this is 2005. And you are a sophisticated young woman of twenty-four, not a child. '

'Try telling my mother that. The curse of being an only child … My mother still treats me as if I were a babe in nappies,' she said smiling. He laughed. After a brief silence she continued, 'But do you know how difficult it would be for me to get a visa? I don't think I would get one at all. I definitely fit the British Embassy profile of a person who would disappear into the London crowds as soon as the plane landed … another illegal immigrant, another young Zimbabwean, poor, unemployed and with no economic ties to my own country. Seems to me their general assumption is that everyone is just waiting to become an economic refugee!'

'Mmm, I know what you mean, but there's no harm in submitting an application. The worst they can do is to refuse it.'

She nodded. 'Maybe sometime after my finals. Right now, I'm too preoccupied with my exam preparations. Why, I'm not even sure that I know exactly why you're going this time? Is it about the flowers?'

'Yes, I must find a market abroad. I'm sure you can appreciate that running both the farm and the shop is becoming impossible because of the shortages of … well, virtually everything! I must somehow earn some foreign currency. Otherwise everything is just going to fall apart.'

Faith nodded. For the majority of people, life had deteriorated. It felt as if everything was indeed on the brink of falling apart.

Tom continued. 'Just to show you how desperate the fuel situation is … the one service station that had petrol and diesel yesterday was asking for payment in US dollars.'

Faith was incredulous. '*Shuwa?* That is so unfair! Only a handful of people earn foreign currency, and most of them expats. What is everyone else expected to do? No wonder the public transport situation is worsening. I wonder where all this is heading, whether we have a future at all …' her voice wavered and trailed away.

Tom looked at her, amused. 'Of course we have a future. Don't take things so seriously or so personally, Faith. *Iwe neni, tichagara mushe.* You and I are going to be just fine.'

She frowned but did not answer, knowing that he had deliberately misunderstood her. Of course, she had not just been talking about the two of them. Unlike Tom, she had been surrounded by deprivation, squalor and poverty for most of her life. While within her own family it had been a bearable kind of hardship, today's reality was something else.

After a while she asked, 'Going back to the foreign currency issue …
as a new farmer, aren't the banks supposed to give you preferential
access?'

'Huh!' Tom snorted. 'Don't be so naïve, Faith. That's just something
that's announced on the news – or something that you'll read in the
papers. In reality, it just doesn't happen. I can't name a single bank that
has had foreign currency readily available for clients in the last five
years. Even if you attend the RBZ foreign currency auctions, you
would be lucky to get anything at all, unless you have a child going to
university overseas. I don't bother going anymore. I don't know what I
would do without the black market.'

He frowned and swerved the car to avoid a group of dust-coated
boys playing football in the middle of the road. They scattered in all
directions with the boisterous excitement of young, township children.
Faith gasped and looked back at them. They were laughing and waving
cheerfully at the car. Two little girls were furiously skipping by the roadside. Their ropes were going so fast that they were almost invisible.
Dust peppered the air in a faint cloud around them. She shook her
head, then smiled to herself. The children's excitement struck a deep
chord. She remembered the years when the same streets had been her
playground. In their own way, they had been wonderful years.

Tom continued, his voice now faintly subdued, 'I wish I had just a little bit of optimism about my trip to the UK, though. Our economy
doesn't do much to inspire investor confidence. I hope this won't be
one wasted trip. As it is, the ticket has eroded my bank balance.'

'*Usashushikane kanhi.* Don't you worry. I hope everything will work
out for you in the UK,' Faith replied cautiously, unable to think of anything more reassuring to say. The export business was too far removed
from issues with which she was more conversant. They turned into
Jo'burg Lines and stopped by the corner, at a safe distance from her
parents' house. Passers-by threw openly curious glances at them.

'Is your mother still trading at Mbare Musika?' Tom asked. Faith nodded. He lowered his voice in a playfully exaggerated manner, 'And is she
still dealing in foreign currency?'

21

Faith bit the inside of her lower lip and smiled, a small, guilty smile. She nodded affirmatively again. *'Asi,* I'm sure she's at home today. She skips the market whenever father is about to go away.'

'I think you should warn her. She will have to stop dealing, at least for a while. The police are going to be arresting anyone they catch selling foreign currency on the black market,' he said seriously.

Faith saw the sombre expression on his face and felt a flash of annoyance. 'Don't be so hypocritical, Tom! If it weren't for people like my mother, where would people like you get the foreign currency that you seem to need so much?' She managed a mocking smile.

He did not look offended. 'You know I'm only trying to help. I don't want your mother to be arrested, that's all. You should tell her that the market places are going to be closed and all illegal structures like those shacks in your parents' yard will be knocked down,' he responded in the same solemn manner.

She looked at him sceptically and laughed. *'Haurevesi!* Surely you don't mean that! Half of Mbare's population lives in shacks. Where would they all go? And if the markets are closed, these people would starve!' she exclaimed, peering at him suspiciously. 'How do you know all this anyway?' Her voice was challenging.

'Sorry, love, I can't tell you how I know, but it's really going to happen sometime soon, possibly in the next two weeks.'

She stared at him with a mixture of bewilderment and antagonism. Always cognisant and protective of her roots, she possessed a fierce loyalty to people like her mother and the rest of the disadvantaged people of Mbare. At that moment, she felt furious with Tom, who seemed to be threatening their livelihoods from his lofty perch in society. She turned away slightly and held him off with both hands when he leaned over to kiss her. He tickled her and grinned. She did not smile back. She pulled a carrier bag full of second-hand clothes from the back seat. They were her cast-offs which she wanted to give to *mainini* Onai's two daughters.

'See you in an hour, then', she said coldly, then immediately regretted it. Wasn't he the love of her life? She gave him a weak, unconvincing

22

smile and jumped from the car in a lithe motion.

'Don't be late. I have a Consumer Council board meeting this evening,' he reminded her. She waved and walked away without so much as a cursory backward glance, keen to maintain the impression that she'd always given him. Loving him didn't mean that she was a push-over. Illogically, her niggling worries about Tom and his farm were starting to resurface, more strongly than ever. Why couldn't things be either black or white? Why did there have to be so many shades of grey?

≈≈≈

Tom was unruffled by Faith's outburst. He knew they would make up all too soon. In fact, making up was something to look forward to. He watched her as she sauntered off on incredibly long legs, appreciating her voluptuous body, and her neat micro-extensions resting on the promising curve of her firm bottom. He took time to admire the woman he loved mingling with the crowds of Mbare, until she disappeared from view.

For a while, he remained parked by the roadside, a dreamy look on his face. He recalled how a chance meeting had developed into the most stable relationship that he'd ever had. In her final year at university, his sister Emily had been a sub-warden in the Complex Four Residential Hall. Faith, then in her second year, had been living in the same hall. When Tom first met her, she'd been in his sister's room, assisting with plans for a fund-raising variety show.

Faith had stood out with her infectious enthusiasm about their little project. But what had struck Tom most was her resemblance to Nyaradzo, the one woman he had truly loved. As usual, his memories of Nyaradzo were tainted by feelings of regret. There was no valid excuse for the way he'd treated her. An uneasy feeling settled in his chest as he imagined the daughter that he'd probably never see. His mother would be deeply disappointed in him if she ever found out.

Shifting his thoughts from Nyaradzo, he remembered how angry Emily had been when he'd asked her about Faith. 'She's just a sweet, innocent girl, Tom, so hands off!' His sister had snapped. 'Just let her be, will you? She's not your type.'

'And what's my type, beloved sister?' he had asked teasingly, trying to humour her and feigning ignorance about her scathing inference to 'his type'. Back then, he'd had a reputation for being a ladies' man. His sister's open disapproval hadn't daunted him. His fascination had grown with the realisation that unlike most of his previous conquests, Faith didn't seem impressed by his wealth or his famed charisma. He'd enjoyed the thrill of the chase, wooing her persistently for a year during which, much to Emily's disgust, he'd had another failed relationship.

Under Emily's disapproving scrutiny, he'd finally started a relationship that promised something real. To his relief, Emily had eventually concluded that this time he was serious. However, still viewing the young woman as her protégée, she watched him like a hawk. As if Faith needed anybody to protect her!

'Where is your loyalty anyway? Are you forgetting that I'm your brother?' he'd often protest whenever Emily reproved him for some misconstrued misdemeanour. She just couldn't or wouldn't believe that he'd changed, and was no longer the cruiser that he'd once been, but Tom knew for certain that he had. For the first time in his life, he dared to think about settling down. Already, most of his friends were married with children, and at thirty-five, he certainly wasn't getting any younger. As his wife, Faith would be a real asset, and a partner in every sense.

A beggar, walking slowly up the street, came into view. The clothes covering his body were a mass of brownish-grey rags which seemed to be weighing him down. For a fleeting moment, their eyes locked but the man quickly averted his gaze in the furtive manner of a thief. Or a very dishonest person. Tom's stare followed the man. Something about his bearing looked vaguely familiar, almost as if … He stopped himself. His friend was dead. He shook himself.

He would go to the nearby shops where he'd wait for Faith. He had at least an hour to kill. The late afternoon air had become slightly warmer and his throat felt parched. 'Maybe I'll have a drink while I wait,' he thought to himself. 'With luck, I might just stumble across some ice-cold Coca Cola in one of the shops. Even a newspaper.'

≈≈≈

As she'd expected, Faith found her parents at home. Both seemed pre-occupied. For a moment she wondered whether they might have quar-relled, then she brushed the thought aside. She'd never seen them fight-ing and she doubted she ever would. Her mother greeted her and con-tinued bustling between the ironing board and her father's open travel-ling bag. It was almost full. She sat down on the low armchair opposite her father.

'How's university?' he asked dutifully. His smile was a bit distracted and he spoke as if he was slightly out of breath.

'University's fine, *Baba*. I'm busy studying for my final exams now. Which means I can't stay long,' she added apologetically.

Her mother glanced at her with suspicious eyes, and protested loudly, 'But you've only just arrived. Stay for a cup of tea at least.'

'Sorry, *Amai*. I didn't mean that I would leave right away.' Faith felt a pang of guilt. Time at home had gradually paled into insignificance. Lately, her world seemed to revolve around Tom and her books. Her conscience niggled her. She had to make more time for her parents. She quickly made some Rooibos tea for herself and her father. She liked the brand of tea which he brought from South Africa especially for her. They drank leisurely while they talked. 'What's the remaining balance on your fees Faith?' her father asked.

'Fifteen million dollars, I think. I'll have to let you know. Students with outstanding balances won't be allowed to write examinations,' she sighed, remembering how she'd turned down Tom's offer. Her mother had always stressed that she should never be indebted to a man, except in marriage. 'And not even then,' she'd laughed.

Smiling, her father reassured her, 'Don't look so worried. I'll do everything possible to pay up. There's no way you're going to miss out on your final exams! Just let your mother know what the balance is, and we'll see what we can do.'

'I will. Thank you. *Baba*,' she said and turned to her mother, 'I've brought some of my old clothes that I want to give to Rita and Ruva. Is *mainini* at home or is she at the market today?' she asked.

Her mother shook her head and clicked her tongue irritably. *'Zviripi?*

She's in hospital again. Third time this year.'

Faith was appalled. She placed her tea cup on the table and stared at her mother incredulously. '*Zvakare?* I can't believe that it's happened again. Can't you do something *Amai? Babamunini* should be arrested. At least that's what I think,' she said heatedly.

Her father agreed. 'I know *mwanangu*, but at the end of the day it's up to her. He cannot be arrested unless she reports him, and I don't think she will report him. We try to help but it is not as easy as you might think. You can leave the clothes with me. I will take them to her house when she comes out of hospital.'

'But this can't be allowed to continue. There has to be something …' Faith said pensively, shaking her head. Much as she wanted to help, she felt helpless. What exactly could she do about the situation? It was inappropriate for her to say anything to her *mainini* directly. That part would have to be played by her mother. She toyed again with the idea of specialising in women's rights when she completed her degree in law. That was probably the only way she could make a meaningful difference to the lives of abused women. She decided to discuss the matter with a lecturer who had become her mentor, a woman who was clearly passionate about women's rights.

But for her *mainini*, an urgent solution was needed. By the time she became a fully-fledged lawyer, it would probably be too late. At this rate, her *mainini* might be permanently maimed by then. Or they would have long since buried her.

Talking about *mainini* Onai dampened the general mood and caused the conversation to falter. Faith found herself close to angry tears. Why should a woman allow herself to bear so much at the hands of a man? Her own husband? Had his act of paying bride-price reduced her to nothing more than a possession? Faith just could not understand her *mainini*. If she ever married Tom, she would not allow herself to be his doormat. Never!

Suddenly, her father switched to the issue of food shortages and perennial queues. 'I think I'll smuggle some groceries for you from South Africa. I might even bring extra to sell to the neighbours, and some cosmetics for you to sell to your friends at the university, Faith.'

Guilt stirred. It weighed on her that her parents were doing this mainly for her education. She asked with concern, 'Why don't you just bring groceries up to the R1500 legal limit? Won't you get arrested if you're caught smuggling?'

'My daughter, the legal limits are not important. How else do you think we can raise your university fees and set aside money to start building? The line between what's legal and what is not, has never been as blurred as it is now. *Hakuchina*. Don't take this law business too seriously. You're not yet a lawyer. Neither are you a police officer, so let me be,' he teased her, then conceded ambiguously, 'But I suppose you're right, though who really cares? We're only trying to survive, like everyone else. I've a lot of friends working at the border post so there should be no problems. And I can always bribe those who are not my friends. You'd be surprised by what some grown men at the border post are prepared to ignore for as little as a packet of sugar or flour!' he laughed with enjoyment.

Faith found nothing comic in her father's remarks. The food situation was getting worse every day. She struggled to identify the crucial point when their lives had become one big obsession with obtaining food, and making sure that meagre groceries stretched as far as possible. She wondered why they had not seen it coming, for she acknowledged the signs had all been there. They had just chosen not to see them for what they really were. Back then, there had been comfort in denial. False comfort.

Her mother was frowning as she folded a crisply ironed shirt and placed it in the bag. She spread out a pair of trousers with quick, impatient movements and pressed hard with the steaming iron. She seemed to be transferring her frustration onto the ironing board. It groaned under the force of her movements.

Faith sighed and glanced at her watch. It was time to go. Tom would be waiting. She said a hurried goodbye to her father. As she walked out to the gate with her mother, she mentioned what Tom had said about the impending market closures and demolitions of shacks.

Katy was openly disbelieving. She cautioned her about repeating such alarming hearsay. *'Iwe!* Such dangerous gossip! Remember, you never know who might be listening. Just be very careful,' she reprimanded her crossly.

≈≈≈

When she told John about it later, they had a good laugh. It was probably just another absurd rumour that the university students had invented in order to stir up trouble. John said, 'You know there is nobody better at causing public unrest than that rowdy scholarly lot who imagine that they know better than everyone else.'

Katy nodded, remembering the nineties, a decade when students had engaged in endless demonstrations against a multitude of issues ranging from police brutality, human rights, media freedom and of course the contentious issue of their loans and grants. For several years, the university students had been known as hooligans. John said he thought it was a name which suited them perfectly. 'I hope Faith will be all right among all those hooligans,' he'd often said, as he did so again.

Katy laughed. 'That's if she is not one already! But don't worry, she'll be fine. We have brought her up well and she has a sensible head on her shoulders.' She did not mention Tom. The idea of Faith being involved with a man would have probably distressed John. He was that kind of father. She zipped up the travelling bag and made herself comfortable next to him. His face was scattered with the beginnings of an untidy stubble. She felt a rush of affection and nuzzled against his ear.

'We've spent so little time together. I still can't believe I wasted three days just waiting in a petrol queue. I think I must try and smuggle some petrol from South Africa when I come back this time.' He looked pleased by the brilliance of the idea, as if it had just struck him.

Katy drew back violently and looked at him with wide eyes. 'What is it with you and this smuggling business? If this was only about groceries, I would say yes. But petrol? Where would we keep it?'

'Maybe in the empty shack at the corner of the yard. It should be all right out there.' He was casual and non-committal.

'But, *mudiwa*, that's very dangerous. That shack is made of wood.

Zvakare, it's too close to the other shacks, including our neighbour's. Remember what happened at Maya's house a few weeks ago?' John shook his head and scratched his chin. 'No? I think you were in South Africa then. Her lodger was selling petrol from his shack. God knows how he came to have it in there. It caught fire and all the nearby shacks were burnt to the ground. A small baby died in that fire, John. I don't want to take that kind of risk. *Handidi ngozi pano!* I will not put our lodgers' lives in danger,' she stated firmly.

He stroked her back and smiled at her. 'Don't worry, *vadzimai*. We will be careful. Do you want me to spend all my leave days in a petrol queue again next time? Huh? And think of this ... we can always sell petrol for as much as a hundred thousand dollars a litre. Just imagine the profit we could make! These are hard times. We must do everything possible in order to survive, *vadzimai*.'

Katy opened her mouth to protest, then she hesitated. John only called her *vadzimai* when he wanted to assert his authority as her husband, in his own subtle way. Normally she was his beloved ... *mudiwa wake*. She sighed. 'I know that we have to survive. But at what cost? I'm just worried about safety, that's all,' she said, yielding slightly. She did not want to insist and start an argument. Not when he was just leaving. And she did have an obligation to obey her husband. She had always been mindful of the fact. That was one of the reasons why their marriage was a success, and one of the reasons why John had stood loyally by her side when his mother had insisted upon him divorcing her.

'Why did my son have to waste *roora* on a barren woman? A full bride price and no children!' Katy's disappointed mother-in-law had moaned repeatedly to anyone who cared to listen. More painfully, spiteful mutterings had found their way to Katy, conveyed by female relatives who could not resist the appeal of gossip. At one time, her barely post-adolescent sister-in-law, who had given birth to four children at an astonishing speed, had said with glee, 'She said maybe you're a man. She said how can a real woman have such a husky voice? Or such a straight, board-like body? No breasts, and no hips to speak of!'

Katy had borne the comments and the spite only because John had stood by her. Her quest for motherhood had gone on for five protracted, disappointing years, then Faith arrived, but there were no further pregnancies. And still, John had stayed. Considering that men loved the idea of a son, that said a lot about how much he cared. Katy knew her place, so she changed the topic. 'What time do you have to get to the depot?'

'Six o'clock. Kundai is coming to pick me up in a short while. I should be leaving Harare by seven. Did you understand my instructions about the foreign currency deal?' he asked her.

'I think so. You said this assistant commissioner of police, Mr Nzou, is coming to collect the two thousand US dollars tomorrow at six o'clock. He will give me twenty-five thousand Zim dollars for every US dollar. That will make fifty million dollars,' Katy said, feeling proud for remembering the details with such precision.

'Correct. Let's be careful with the money because it has taken me two whole years to save it up. We must pay the balance on Faith's fees and the remainder should go down as further payment for the Mabelreign stand. Hopefully, that will leave us with a modest balance. Once the stand is paid up, we should start building. You and I will leave Mbare yet,' he declared with firm resolve.

'I know we will. But why deal with a police official? You will find me languishing in prison when you come back!' she joked, though her voice was tempered with genuine anxiety.

'Don't worry. I know this man quite well. He's very desperate for foreign currency because his business depends on imported goods. Cheer up, *mudiwa*.' Katy stared at him silently, her earlier reservations now back in full force. One of the masters of *sungura*, Marko Sibanda, had sung about these things: *Matsotsi haagerane* ... there was absolutely no honour among thieves. While dealing was necessary, it was still not legal. Neither was it safe. So how could John be so sure? So confident?

'The best thing about dealing with Nzou is that if we are ever threatened with arrest, he will protect us. We're now in this together,' he continued reassuringly but Katy remained unconvinced. Her usual transactions did not exceed two thousand South African rand at a time.

Besides, she had never had a police official for a client, a very senior one for that matter.

A strident car horn blew outside. 'I think Kundai is here. I have to go,' John said, as he slung his bag over his right shoulder and picked up the packed meal with his other hand.

Katy walked him to the gate and waved him off. Later, she half-watched the news as she tidied up her cluttered sitting-room. There was a report about more HIV awareness campaigns being launched to target high-risk groups. The reporter gave a list of vulnerable groups. It included long-distance truck drivers. She felt her heart sink, right down to the pit of her stomach. What about John? While she trusted him, one could never be sure about how men behaved when they were away from home. She knew enough about HIV to feel very unsettled. One encounter with an infected person was enough to destroy several lives. She remembered Onai's twin brothers and other people whose funerals she had attended. She found herself needing to sit down at once.

Staring at the television, she listened intently, but the newsreader had already moved on to another story. A fleet of buses had just been brought into the country from some place with an obscure name. They were expected to ease the crippling public transport problems. Katy had doubts about that. How would that be possible when there was hardly any diesel in the country? Maybe she had missed the bit which explained that fuel would soon be flooding in.

The next item was about a collapsing banking corporation. There was nothing new there. It was the third bank to collapse within a year. She listened with fascination as the story unfolded. The youthful, flamboyant bank managers and their girlfriends were reported to have flown regularly to England to watch soccer matches at the bank's expense, their idea of job perks! It was beyond belief to imagine that the whole thing had gone unnoticed for so long, right until the bank had collapsed. She switched the television off irritably. Would there ever be any good news?

Sitting down to a lonesome evening meal depressed her a little. These were the times when she envied Onai with her three children. It would

31

have been so good to sit down to supper with a family surrounding her, numerous beings to fill the house with activity, laughter and love. But she only had Faith, who was now too absorbed in her studies and her relationship to bother coming home, even for the odd weekend. And a husband who, as she had just been reminded, was in a high-risk group for contracting HIV.

Well, life was like that, she mused. One could never have it all. *Uye misi hainaki yese.* Life would never be uniformly good. But there were things which one could do without – like HIV. But then, HIV had broken out of the mould of stereotypes to become everyone's problem. It was no longer something that happened to other people. She sighed.

CHAPTER 3

A few hours after Onai had been admitted, cleaners invaded the ward, armed with buckets, mops and detergent. The strong, astringent smell lingered long after they had left. It was a smell which reminded her of death, though she was not sure why. Her day passed in a blur of a severe headache and neck pain. All the while, she fretted about her lost earnings at the market. It would be exceedingly difficult to make up for her losses. In four months' time, she would have to pay school fees for her children again. That meant a three-million-dollar bill in addition to the rest of the household costs. She dared not think about the textbooks that she still had to buy for Rita; a sweet and loving child who seemed to find school such a struggle. Nowadays, just a single book cost three hundred thousand dollars, and at the rate prices were rising, it would be double that in four months' time.

She summoned up nostalgic memories of days when schools had provided all the textbooks required by their pupils; a time when a school fees' invoice meant nominal charges for people in difficult circumstances like her, and a time when the words 'social welfare' had held a meaning of sorts. It all seemed so long ago, almost as if it was just an illusion her fretful mind was conjuring up to erase the ugliness of reality.

Of course, Gari would not lose any sleep over the situation. According to him, his financial responsibilities did not go beyond paying the council rates. And as he had often pointed out, she should be grateful that they could live in the house that had belonged to his parents. The reasonably good salary which he earned as a section manager at the Cola Drinks plant was reserved for his bingeing, and only God knew what else. Onai was not even sure how much he earned. The only time that she had dared ask, she had been threatened with immediate divorce. A threat that had promptly extinguished her smouldering curiosity.

She did know, however, that one of Gari's colleagues in a similar position owned a house in Belvedere. How she wanted to live in a place like that … what she would give to have a spacious home with a garden full of flowers. But, of course, it would never be. Belvedere was way out of her reach. It was a suburb where luckier people lived. She was destined to live in Mbare, and it could not be more different.

She tried hard to think of something pleasant, but couldn't. A conversation between two women at the opposite end of the bay broke into her thoughts. A woman in a bright yellow dress was saying very loudly and officiously, 'I am telling you, it's true. If you want the nurse to dress your wound today, you have to wash your old bandage and put it out to dry in the sun. Do it now while the sun is still shining. Otherwise it won't dry.' She leaned on her drip-stand and tapped the bag of clear fluid with a long, bony finger which tapered into a fingernail of almost similar length. 'See this drip here? My husband bought it for me yesterday. There is nothing for free, here. And that includes bandages. *Zvemahara futi? Zvakapera zviya!* I am telling you, you have to wash that bandage.'

The other woman's face was a picture of disbelief. 'That can't be true. They always use new bandages. They did so when my child was admitted. I'm going to find the nurse. I'll ask her,' she replied curtly and wobbled off towards the nurses' station, her back rigid with annoyance.

The woman in the yellow dress shrugged and said to her retreating form, 'Suit yourself. I know because I've been here for a week. I have to wash my bandage every day.' She pushed the drip-stand aside and walked slowly back to her bed by the window through which sunlight filtered into the ward.

Onai drew her thoughts back to herself and wondered if she too would have to wash her bandage when the time came for her dressing to be changed. Would the nurse at least help her take it off? She lay back on the hard mattress and wondered if hospital standards could have really deteriorated so far. Maybe the woman was wrong.

As the day progressed, she felt the bleak atmosphere of the hospital smothering her natural resilience. During the afternoon visiting-hour, there were eruptions of loud wailing from some people who had come in to visit their relatives, only to find them dead. The grief-stricken lamentations flooded her with fresh memories of her twin brothers. She did not need constant reminders about the fragility of life. It was enough that with AIDS on the rampage she attended, on average, one funeral every other week.

The hospital meals were deficient and tasted as bland as they looked. She hardly ate any of the food, preferring to drink water instead. Never before had she appreciated the capacity of plain water to quench both thirst and hunger.

The terribly thin woman whose bed was next to hers offered to share the meals brought in by her husband. 'Please have some of this. I can't finish it. If I keep it, it will only go bad,' she spoke in a barely audible voice; her large, strangely luminous eyes were her only feature that held a genuine glimmer of life.

Onai initially declined the offer, mortified by the idea of taking food from someone who looked so obviously needy. But in the evening, she clapped her hands with a gratefully resonant sound and accepted the food. She was dizzy from hunger and the hospital taps were now almost dry. *'Maita henyu vamwene,* I'm so grateful,' she smiled as she thanked her neighbour who returned her smile. It was such a sad, tired smile that it seemed to mirror her own thoughts, and for a moment she felt an indefinable connection with the woman.

≈≈≈

Gari knocked off from his late shift and walked from the Cola Drinks premises to Mbare with Silas, a friend and loyal drinking partner who worked as a general hand on Gari's floor. It had not been a good day at work for either of them. The managing director had circulated a rather abrupt memo confirming previous rumours: because of persistent losses, the company would soon be moving most of its operations to South Africa. The management would hold a meeting with all the employees soon. For Gari and Silas, the memo spelt doom. They suspected that announcements about job losses would follow in a matter of weeks.

'Do you think they might take some of us down to South Africa?' Silas asked anxiously. He fidgeted uneasily with the straps of his worn satchel and pulled them tighter. One strap broke. His anxiety levels rose. It showed on his puckered face.

Gari looked away, shaking his large head doubtfully. 'I don't think that they will take any of us down south. But who cares? Let them close the company. We'll get recompense and start our own businesses,' he answered in a voice that held little conviction.

He stopped to light a cigarette then took a long, leisurely pull. Almost immediately, a burst of smoke made a conspicuous exit from his mouth and nostrils. '*Ndinopika neguva raamai vangu vakafa,* I swear by the grave of my dead mother, this is all happening because of the sanctions imposed on our country,' he said viciously, shoving the matchbox into his pocket. He kicked at a stone with his right foot. Pain shot through a corn on his little toe. He cursed himself. It was time to get a new pair of safety shoes.

Silas looked confused. He sought an explanation from his friend. '*Bhururu,* I've heard about sanctions many times on the news. They said that the sanctions are something to do with travelling bans on important people. How can that cause our company to have money problems? How?' he asked. Gari took an impatient pull of his cigarette. He was in no mood to educate Silas about sanctions, so he remained silent.

Silas went on worriedly, 'You talk about starting our own businesses, but where would we get the money from?'

Gari's annoyance increased. Why was Silas questioning him as if he had the power to miraculously solve the country's problems? Everything was bleak. He was aware that interest rates for bank loans were very high. They were also adjusted regularly to keep up with inflation which was said to be running above six hundred per cent. In any case, very few people would ever qualify for a bank loan. The repayment conditions were impossible to comply with. National funding for small-scale enterprises had declined to almost nothing years ago. So, raising the finance was nothing but a dream. He pulled on his cigarette again and exhaled. The dream went up in smoke and dissipated into the light breeze of early evening.

'Cheer up Silas! *Tiri varume,* we are men. We must not panic like a bunch of women. We will face the problems when they come. No use worrying now. It won't solve anything,' he said forcefully as they stopped to cross an intersection on Rotten Row. He'd lost interest in both the conversation and in his half-smoked cigarette, which he stubbed out fiercely and placed back in the packet. This kind of talk was too depressing. The whole thing was an outright threat to his manhood. What would happen to him if he stopped earning a regular salary?

Silas looked at Gari and smiled. He spoke with sudden brightness, 'You're right. Let's wait and see what will happen.' He hit Gari playfully on the back and asked with a mischievous glint in his eyes, '*Ko* 'small house' *yakadii?* How is the new Missis?'

Thinking about Gloria lifted Gari's spirits considerably. 'Small houses,' the new euphemism for mistresses, were the best thing to happen to a man. Spending some time with Gloria was guaranteed pure bliss because Onai was not at home. She had been taken to hospital in the early hours of the morning by that interfering mad woman, Katy. Well, he would make the most of this opportunity. Some chances only ever came once. He made up his mind to spend the night with Gloria.

Thrusting his hands deep in his pockets, he licked the dryness from his lips. 'Small house, *ndizvo*. Gloria is the most exciting woman I've ever been involved with.' His thick lips parted into a proud, wolfish smile. He gave a low whistle and kicked playfully at another stone. Again, it hurt. He cursed himself and slowed down to a limp.

'Are you sure Onai won't find out about Gloria? Her shack is only at the top of Jo'burg Lines. You know these women. All they do is gossip. What if Onai hears something about you and Gloria?' Silas sounded concerned.

Gari stopped and replied slowly and carelessly, '*Ndezvake izvo!* That's her own problem. I really don't care if she finds out. If she can't live with it, she's free to go anytime'.

Silas raised his eyebrows doubtfully. 'I still think you should have someone a bit further from home. Like that girlfriend you had a couple of years ago, that Sheila from Highfields. That's what you need, a small house in a place as far away as Highfields or Glen View. Your wife will never find out.'

'I told you, I don't care if she does. Anyway, guess where Sheila is living now?' Gari held his sides and laughed uncontrollably.

'Kupi? Ari kupi Sheila? Where is she?' Silas was curious.

'She is now my lodger, you know ... in the shack.' Gari laughed harder. 'Remember that crazy lodger I had ... that teacher who thought he was so educated? The one who kept saying he knew exactly how to solve the country's economic problems?'

Silas nodded. Both men remembered the young schoolteacher, an intense, almost fanatical man who had kept them entertained at the beerhall. He'd been bursting with bizarre ideas about how the country should be managed. Many of his suggestions had been close to what most of the beerhall regulars considered barefaced treachery. It had not taken long for him to earn a reputation as an 'enemy of the people'. *Mutengesi chaiye*. Word had it that he had fled to the UK to seek asylum, like so many others before him.

Gari continued, 'Anyway, when he left, Onai introduced Sheila as our new lodger the following week. I was shocked but Sheila just pretended that she didn't know me. I don't think she'll say anything to Onai. She's been living with us for about six months now,' he said, looking relaxed and unperturbed.

Silas shook his head. It was clear that he did not approve of Gari's behaviour, but his friend did not really care. He had Gloria. What more could a man want? The two men parted with a promise to meet up for a beer the following day after work.

≈≈≈

Gloria sat on the edge of the bed in her poorly-lit shack and waited for Gari. The wooden shack was a small, confined space with a very low ceiling. It was just the right height for Gloria, but definitely not for Gari, who had to stoop. There was no proper window, save for a high, incredibly small aperture covered in plastic sheeting; thick but translucent. The opening allowed in a dull sliver of twilight, barely illuminating the room. Only the exquisite bed-linen in deep, luxurious reds, lent colour to the room. Gloria's friend had brought her the linen from Botswana as a special favour. According to her, shades of red worked wonders on a man's passion.

A grey suitcase stood forlornly in one corner, just below an assortment of clothing that was hanging loosely from coat-hangers. In the other corner was a primus stove, a clutter of cooking utensils and a few groceries. Various other items peeped from under the bed, as if seeking out additional space.

Gloria had worked herself up into a blistering temper. She had spent a fruitless day in Harare city centre, waiting in a mealie-meal queue. Violent rioting had erupted as soon as the delivery van arrived. The police had been called to restore order, which they had effected with indiscriminate force and sadistic delight. She had received several baton-stick blows before managing to break away empty-handed from the melée. She was still smarting from the encounter. Hearing that her previous partner had died of an HIV-related illness, just that morning, did not help matters. Fear and anger wrestled with her sanity.

Gloria had no illusions about her own HIV status. She was shrewd enough to realise that it was just a matter of time before the inevitable happened. She did not want to die a lonesome death on the streets of Mbare, or in a ditch somewhere, as had happened to some of her dearest friends in the profession. She needed a man to call her own, a man who would look after her when HIV laid its claim upon her.

It was payback time for all the men to whom, for so little money, she had given so much pleasure. Gari would have to pay the outstanding dues for all of them. He would have to marry her. It was obvious that she would not get anyone better. The rest of the men had a tendency to disappear with astounding speed whenever she mentioned marriage. But Gari was different. Clearly devoted, he struck her as someone who would stay. So he would have to do. As a second wife, she would have special treatment anyway. Being a 'small house' was definitely the way to go. No relationship could give a girl better security or more comfort. Gari's wife would be no problem at all. With any luck, he might even be persuaded to divorce her. She knew just how she would persuade him when the time came.

≈≈≈

When Gari arrived at Gloria's shack, his dreams of an evening of pleasure in her arms were promptly thwarted. He found her in an unexpected rage.

She fumed and hurled accusations at him. 'You only want to use me. You just come here to sleep with me and you don't even care that I live in a miserable shack. If you love me as much as you say, why don't we just get married?'

Despite her anger, she looked beautiful in the soft candlelight. Still, that did not lessen his worries. This disagreeable side of Gloria's nature had not been previously revealed to him. It was far removed from the sweetness of the girl who'd caught his eye ... a girl whose unbridled passion matched no other ... a girl who spoke and acted as if she'd been born to please men. He pleaded with her while trying to buy precious time. 'Calm down my sweetheart. We have to talk seriously about this and make proper plans. Please? We can't just suddenly get married.'

His attempts to appease her were in vain. She continued with her tongue-lashing. 'What plans do you mean? The only plans I will make with you are plans for marriage. I want a satisfactory answer, *izvozvi!*'

He was further alarmed by her increasingly riotous display of anger, which switched to tears and feminine sniffles without obvious reason. He doubted that any man would consider marrying a prostitute, but he still wanted more of her, so he cajoled her with all his sweetest words.

While marriage to her had never crossed his mind, it was extremely flattering to know that she loved him enough to consider being his second wife. His very own 'small house'. He imagined having exclusive rights over her. The idea was becoming more appealing by the minute. He decided to give it some serious thought, later on. For now, there was no harm in promising her the best that he could offer.

'Just give me a month, *mudiwa*. One month is all I need to get rid of Onai so that I can make you my wife. Please,' he pleaded, and wiped away her tears.

In a lightning change of mood, Gloria switched on her most alluring smile and gave him a deep kiss. 'For you, my darling, I will wait,' she said in those seductive tones which never failed to rouse a stirring in his groin. 'How was your day at work?' she asked and draped her arms around him, her manner back to the sweetness with which he was more familiar.

Gari heaved a sigh of relief. The storm had passed. He told her of his concerns. 'The company might be relocating to merge with its South African branch. We haven't been told what is going to happen to us. I'm very worried.'

Gloria listened attentively and tried to comfort him. 'You are an important man in the company, Gari. They won't just discard a section manager. I think they will give you a job in South Africa. Or a very good retrenchment package.' She sounded very confident.

Gari's fears lessened somewhat, as he listened to her soothing words. 'Thank you, my dear. I feel better already.' He felt comforted, which was all a man needed. Gloria simply smiled and continued massaging his neck with hands that felt incredibly soft.

He tried to take off his shoes, and winced. The corn on his right little toe was still sore. Gloria took off his shoes carefully and planted playful kisses on his feet. She pulled a bottle of Johnson and Johnson's baby oil from under the bed; she had nagged him to buy her the expensive oil the previous month. Sprinkling a few cold drops on his feet, she massaged them with smooth, efficient movements. Gari closed his eyes. He allowed himself to enjoy the relaxing sensation while they made light, flirtatious conversation.

Once again, he was reminded of how being with Gloria had changed his life. She listened to him and made him feel important. Onai did none of those things. She was only good at complaining about money, groceries, and clothes for the children. She made him feel like a failure, and starved him in the bedroom. But not his Gloria. She was a girl who could satisfy practically all his needs. When he was with Gloria he felt like a real man. Almost like a king. Maybe taking her as a second wife was not such a bad idea after all.

≈≈≈

The man lay under a small, dried-out viaduct and shivered. He had arrived at his regular sleeping place to find his pile of newspapers missing. One of the street children had probably stolen the whole lot. Without his newspapers to keep him warm, it would be a long, cold night. This was turning out to be one of the worst days of his long two months on the streets. Hunger gnawed at the pit of his stomach.

Earlier, he had passed by Mai Ruva's house to beg for food but she had not been at home. Her younger daughter had asked him to wait while she looked for something to give him, but the girl they called Ruva had stormed to the door and slammed it shut in his face. A quick rummage through the neighbourhood bins had yielded nothing. Maybe the dogs beat me to it today, he concluded miserably. He thought again of Mai Ruva and wondered whether she had travelled. He worried about her a lot. In the two months that he had known her, he had seen her a couple of times with bruises on her face; bruises that could only have come from being assaulted, possibly by a man who could well be her husband.

The man shivered again. His thoughts wandered dreamily to what he often thought of as his past – and it was; the past that was inexorably linked with the future to which he would proceed when he had purged himself of the guilt festering within him. With that one, very brief instruction, he had destroyed everything that had mattered to him; so he'd resolved to live out this extreme act of contrition. People often talked of *kutanda botso* – a ritual undergone if one wronged one's mother beyond the point of verbal apology. But he was doing this not for his mother, but for the wife he'd loved; the woman he still loved so much that it hurt. In an attempt to cleanse the remorse that weighed him down, he'd modified *kutanda botso* for himself; he would beg and accept public humiliation as an act of contrition.

By night, under the protective cover of darkness, he allowed himself to grieve. He was determined that nobody should witness his anguish. It was private, and he had to endure it alone. However, by day he roamed the streets openly; accepting with cheerfulness the disdain of those he met. Begging for food was a vital element of this self-styled ritual that he had to endure.

None of his family and friends knew where he was, and he liked it that way. He had walked away from home with nothing but a few million dollars in his pocket, which even now were strapped to his waist in a small money-bag. He had managed to hold on to it because all he'd needed were old newspapers and scraps of food, and he could get both from bins or from Mai Ruva. In any case, using the money would have amounted to cheating. It would have defeated the whole purpose of his mission.

The brief encounter with Tom had shaken him. That had been a really close shave. Two months down, he thought, just one more month more to go. Oh Edith, I'm sorry, he cried silently as he shivered in the cold. When sleep finally overcame him, it was not his pregnant wife who filled his vivid dreams, it was Mai Ruva. She was offering him a morsel of sadza.

CHAPTER 4

The next morning, a young female doctor came to review Onai. Her eyes reflected such a profound but condescending sympathy that Onai felt like shedding tears for the mess that her life had become. She was only thirty-six years old, but she felt like a tired old woman ... one still far from the end of her long journey.

She wondered irrelevantly how such a beautiful young girl could be a qualified doctor. Perhaps, she was an inexperienced student gaining some hands-on experience and taking advantage of the gap left by doctors who had flocked to the West. The girl wore an elegant cream dress that flatteringly outlined the contours of her supple body. Her striking freshness seemed almost obscene on the cheerless ward with its derelict furniture and discoloured walls.

In Onai's opinion, her style was not appropriate for someone looking after patients. Men would be distracted from the crucial matter of recovery; women would be consumed with envy – not a healthy emotion. Onai's model doctor was a stern-featured older man in a white coat, possibly balancing a pair of glasses on his nose. *Chiremba vakuru chaivo*. A real doctor, not this girl. She did not inspire confidence. Onai struggled to hide her displeasure. As the young woman bent over her to inspect the wound on her forehead, she was just able to make out the name on her I.D. badge – Dr Emily Sibanda. So she must be a real doctor, Onai thought.

The doctor asked for more information about her injuries and gently tried to find out if there had been any abuse. 'My colleague who saw you yesterday suggests that you might have been assaulted. Please, Mrs Moyo, if you are experiencing domestic violence, it is important for you to report it. Don't be afraid. Help is available for people in situations like yours,' she said kindly and laid a warm hand on Onai's stiff shoulder. The older woman turned her head to the wall, trying to put an invisible, but protective barrier between herself and this prying young woman.

'There is no situation and there is nothing to tell.' she responded with atypical frostiness, her lips tremulous. She turned back and looked boldly at the young doctor, instantly resenting her for her apparent confidence. Her life was obviously brimming with promise, even in such harsh times. It was not a life that Onai and her children would ever experience, no matter how hard they worked or how high their aspirations.

The doctor made a quick entry into the medical notes, and then regarded Onai pensively. She tried again, a little more forcefully. 'I don't know what you're afraid of, but I can refer you to an excellent support group with whom I work. They will take care of you and help you through, whatever …' her voice faded away. 'But whoever is doing this to you should be reported to the police,' she spoke with the self-assuredness of youth, her warm eyes starting to burn with impatience.

Subdued, but not yet ready to be forthcoming, Onai repeated her implausible story about how she had walked blindly into a door while fumbling in the dark during a power cut. Load-shedding was a regular occurrence in Harare. There was really no need for the doctor to doubt her. But it was clear that she did. Disappointment marred her pretty face as Onai emphatically denied that there was any violence in her home.

'In Casualty, we see many women brought in with assault injuries. A good number have repeated admissions, with injuries just like yours. I'm disappointed that so many women appear to be in denial when we could help them. I suspect that you are too. Remember, you are not alone, Mrs Moyo. I'm a woman like you, *vasikana;* I'd be happy if you allowed me to help you.'

Onai felt a ridiculous urge to burst out laughing. Yes, the doctor was a woman, anyone could see that. However, there was no possibility that the two of them could ever compare experiences. Their lives were worlds apart.

'I'm not in a violent marriage. I have a loving husband and I don't need any help from you. Why are you telling me all this? It has nothing to do with me.' She was obstinate. She didn't quite know why: was it fear of the unknown, fear of what Gari might do to her, fear that such an admission suggested failure? Or was it simply that the doctor seemed so self-assured, and it was against all her instincts to submit to a woman so young?

Finally, the doctor appeared to yield. 'Anyway, if you think of something that you want to disclose, feel free to speak to Sister Mashava,' she said, pointing towards a woman in a green uniform who was giving instructions to two nursing students.

Onai did not respond. The doctor sighed wearily and shifted her focus back to the injuries. 'The cut above your eye was sutured quite well. It should heal with no complications. The stitches will have to come out in three days' time. You won't need a daily dressing. Painting it with Betadine will do the trick. Just remember to keep the area clean. Your skull X-ray looks OK. I am still waiting for my senior colleague to examine it. If he agrees, you should be able to go home later this afternoon,' she said as she walked towards the door.

Onai murmured, 'Thank you.' She was suddenly overwhelmed by a familiar depression – the knowledge that people would always blame her for her circumstances. Why couldn't they understand? She did not want to be coerced into revealing things which had the potential to destroy her marriage. She would not be able to bear the shame of being a divorced woman. How could she possibly face a world that despised divorcees; looked down on single mothers? Marital status was everything. It did not really matter how educated or otherwise skilled a woman was. A woman's worth was relative to one man, her husband: westernised values about women surviving outside marriage held no authenticity *mumusha*. In her whole extended family, nobody had ever had a divorce. She would not let herself be the first.

Her mind wandered back to Gari. Was he thinking of her at all while she languished in hospital? She doubted it. He had not even visited her. But then, she had not really expected him to.

≈≈≈

Emily walked over to the tiny sink in the corner of the ward. Pressing the valve, she impatiently waved her manicured hands under the tap. Not a single drop of water resulted. The hollow pipe echoed jarringly across the quiet ward.

Sister Mashava called, 'There is no water, *chiremba*. Last night there was a trickle but there hasn't been any water since early this morning. They are repairing a burst pipe behind the hospital.' She walked over to the sink and held out a bottle of methylated spirit.

With a dry half-smile, Emily gratefully accepted the acrid purple spirit and splashed her hands liberally with it. Its coldness stung. She turned to Sister Mashava, 'I keep asking myself why I don't move abroad like so many of my colleagues, and I can't find the answer, or not one that makes sense.'

'No, *chiremba*. Don't ever think that way. I could have gone as well, but people need us here. If everyone goes, who will look after the patients? Please don't go. It might not be very obvious to you, but we are making a difference. Things will get better one day.'

Emily shook her head. There were no easy answers. She knew the nurse was offering her comfort and support. She had used the same words herself. But could one make a difference without medicines, without water, and when the authorities appeared not to care?

Sister Mashava gave her a bright, practised smile and walked back to the nurses' station. Emily's eyes followed her, then turned to the woman she had just reviewed. Mrs Onai Moyo was sitting hunched forward on her bed, her hands cupping her face. Emily was sure the woman was in an abusive relationship. One did not get such injuries from walking into a door. Why wouldn't or couldn't she speak out? Soon, she'd probably be just another tragic statistic, and there was nothing Emily could do about it. Glancing at her watch, she realised that she was running late for her locum at the Avenues Clinic. Blast – her petrol tank was almost empty. She'd have to call her brother, Tom, as soon as she finished the ward round. Maybe he'd be able to source some petrol from one of his dealer friends.

A week previously, the engine of her car had been damaged by petrol she'd bought on the black market, because she didn't have the US dollars that the service stations now required. The fuel had been tainted, the mechanic told her, 'probably mixed with paraffin or water'. Emily had been shocked. What would people do next to make quick money!

She wondered if it was need or greed. Probably the latter. Nowadays, there was just too much criminal activity taking place … people, it seemed, would do almost anything to make a quick buck. Dirty money. She was also beginning to lose faith in her mechanic. Whenever she took her car in for a service, it came back with one or two new problems. She hoped he wasn't switching her relatively new car parts for old ones. It had been known to happen.

She decided not to take any more costly chances. She would no longer buy petrol from people's cluttered backyards or smelly kitchens. If she couldn't get fuel through Tom or from a proper service station, she would just walk. But how would she get to work, when public transport had become so erratic? She wondered if her friend Ben would help.

With another sigh, she moved on quickly to the next patient, a woman whose fractured femur was just not healing – a woman so ravaged by AIDS that she would probably die from the condition before her leg healed. She had wanted to be a doctor to heal the sick, now all she seemed to do was preside over the dying …

≈≈≈

That morning, Katy hurried to the market. She was running late because she'd overslept. She skirted the main bus terminus, located next to the market, and the most prolific hub of activity in Harare, a place where everything moved at a frenzied pace. Not only could one catch a bus to anywhere in Zimbabwe, but also to South Africa, Botswana, Zambia and sometimes even further afield.

The air was thick with the noise of blaring horns, rumbling engines and impatient shouts. Rowdy touts jostled aggressively and competed for passengers. Physical fights among the unruly young men were not uncommon. Occasionally, groups of family travellers found themselves pulled forcefully in different directions by the youths. The Mbare terminus was also a permanent haunt for Katy, and her constantly mobile business rivals, who hawked roasted groundnuts, sweets, cigarettes, fruit, sticky buns and drinks to departing passengers.

The market seemed louder and more crowded than usual; it had the feel of a month-end's hustle and bustle. It was a place where one could buy anything from fresh fruit and vegetables to love potions, live goats, foreign currency, cannabis, coffins and second-hand car parts (of sometimes dubious origin). Colossal sums of money changed hands during both legal and illegal deals. This was the distinctive flavour of Harare's largest market place, Mbare Musika

Katy sold her vegetables while keeping a vigilant eye out for the familiar faces of her regular foreign currency customers. She made two surreptitious trips to the stinking toilets next to the bus terminus, where money exchanged hands rapidly and furtively under cover of the heavy stench. Around noon, she packed up her box and left for home where a quick call to the hospital informed her that Onai was waiting for a doctor's review, pending discharge. Katy asked the nurse to let her friend know that she would be coming to see her. From home, she proceeded straight to the hospital.

≈≈≈

At lunch-time, Onai's headache had subsided. Her X-ray report was reviewed by one of the senior doctors. Everything was normal, so she could go home. The nurse taped a piece of dry gauze over her wound, and said she could take it off when she got home. 'But remember,' she said, 'keep it disinfected with Betadine.' Onai nodded gratefully although she had no expensive disinfectant at home. Dabs of salt water would have to do. She fingered the hospital bill, which the stern ward clerk handed her. 'You have to make the payment at the cashier's office within thirty days, or …' He let his words hang, leaving her to imagine the worst. One million dollars … the small print on the flimsy white slip of paper seemed to menace her with their size.

She thought of telling him there and then that she did not have the money, but his intimidating manner stopped her short. She wondered what would happen if she didn't pay the bill. Would the hospital have her arrested? Or send someone to confiscate her property! With the TV gone, what could they take anyway? Her old armchairs? The stereo? She didn't know. She folded the slip of paper into tight little squares, which reflected her mood, and thrust it viciously into the depths of her pocket. Anger towards Gari flared for a moment as she made her way out of the ward. In a just world, he would have been liable to pay this bill. But no, fairness was an alien concept, at least within their marriage.

She sat on a hard bench just outside the ward and waited for Katy. The strong, nauseating smell of detergent lingered, clinging tenaciously to her clothes. Hospital life buzzed around her. It was business as usual. A shrouded metal coffin was wheeled past, so were several trolleys bearing comatose patients and, after a while, a man in blood-soaked clothes. He was lying on the stretcher at an awkward angle as if he had multiple fractures.

Her thoughts transported her away from inflated bills and depressing realities. Maybe the letter from Nhembe Factory would be waiting for her at home. They had told her at the end of the interview, that she should expect a response in a week, and that was eight days ago. Perhaps, at last, she would begin dressmaking; a job she loved and for which she had been trained. Just maybe. The small possibility gave her something to look forward to. Her pulse quickened.

She took a deep breath and exhaled. It would be good to be back with her children. She indulged herself in the pleasure of thinking about them while she waited for Katy. Hopefully, her *shamwari* would arrive soon, as promised. She did.

'*Hesi vasikana!* You look much better, Onai. I'm so happy to see you,' Katy exclaimed and gave her an embrace. She stood back and appraised her, 'They must have looked after you really well.'

Onai laughed and said dryly, 'They do their best, I think. Thank you for coming, Katy. I am well, thank you. I would feel even better if it wasn't for this.' She dug into her pocket and waved the bill at Katy.

Katy read the amount in amazement, then she said, 'You're lucky. At least they're letting you go without paying. Do you know, they used to detain patients until they paid the bills? No cash, no discharge.'

Onai was surprised. Surely that could only mean that the final bill would be even higher. 'Really?' she asked.

'Really,' her friend replied. 'Like prisoners *pa*Chikurubi!' They shared conspiratorial laughter as they walked through the hospital doors.

CHAPTER 5

It was a typical afternoon in May, the weather was crisp and chilly. The wintry sun hung in a flawless blue sky, but the air was devoid of any promise of warmth. The two women chatted as they strolled out of the hospital gates and walked down to a bus stop next to the sprawling post office. Both took great care to avoid discussing Onai's assault. The only reminder was the stark white gauze strapped to her forehead.

They approached the crowded bus stop eagerly, bracing themselves for the jostle for seats. Commuters milled about, anxiously awaiting transport. As Onai and Katy had feared, there was no direct transport to Mbare. Unruly touts for the few emergency taxis were shouting for commuters to the city centre. It was too long a distance to walk, so the ET operators could charge very high fares.

Onai shook her head. 'This is unbelievable. People are profiting from the fuel shortages. They know we've no choice except to pay their high fares. Why must we go through the city centre in order to get to Mbare? The direct route is not half the distance to the city centre!'

Katy answered cynically,. 'So that you can pay the fare twice, my dear. They make their money that way. This is life, Onai. Who was it that said a clever bird uses other birds' feathers to build its nest?'

Onai didn't answer immediately. It was true. There was no shortage of people trying to make profits at every turn, regardless of whom they crushed or cheated in the process. 'Sometimes I have the feeling that we are slowly turning into a nation of thieves,' she said, in a melancholy voice.

Katy threw her an odd look and laughed. 'What a thing to say, Onai! We're not. Goodness, I should take you back to hospital so the doctor can take another look at your head ... the inside, that is!'

'But Katy, *shuwa,* I can't be the only one to see that the situation is getting out of hand. I only hope the authorities are aware of what's happening and will intervene so that the shortages and ridiculously rising prices will become a thing of the past.' Katy looked at her and laughed again.

The two women decided against a bus to the city centre just in order to find connecting transport to Mbare; it simply doubled the expense. Such luxuries they could not afford. Instead, they chose the long walk home, which would cost them nothing, apart from their time and energy. They had both in abundance, but a determination to reach home in the shortest possible time put a lively spring in their steps. They shared township gossip and companionable laughter as they walked through the bustling Southerton industrial area. Within half an hour, they were crossing Beatrice Road into Mbare.

Onai took in her surroundings with fresh eyes. She admitted to herself that this was not the place where she wanted her children to grow into adulthood. Her encounter with the young doctor had given her a thought-provoking glimpse of what life could be for her own daughters. It had left her feeling strangely disturbed and dissatisfied. She thought with envy of Katy's only child who had managed to leave Mbare and was now at university. Indeed, the future looked bright for Katy. But it seemed that for Onai and her children, there would be nothing beyond a life in the slums. The idea of leaving Mbare was the substance of impossible dreams. She replied to Katy's chatter distractedly, looking around her as if she was seeing the area for the first time.

Mbare was a high density township that had absolutely no redeeming features to speak of. The degree of overcrowding was spectacular. As the tasteless joke went, one could not reach out an arm without touching one's next-door neighbours – and in their beds, too. A multitude of tiny houses were stacked against one another making an intricate maze of carelessly planned streets. This housing itself was a colonial inheritance; then it had been considered suitable accommodation for the township dwellers. Overcrowding during the war and since independence had only made matters worse. Contrary to people's expectations, the services had deteriorated. Matapi Flats were a perfect example. The dilapidated tower-blocks dominated the flawed Mbare skyline. They stood defiantly, almost regally, overlooking the squalor of the surrounding shanty town.

Innovative homeowners had haphazardly added extra rooms to the 'main houses': a variety of shacks, resourcefully constructed from wood, asbestos, metal sheets, and in a few cases, colourful plastic sheeting. These were rented out to families of desperate job seekers who'd drifted to the irresistible lure of the big city's bright lights, or the elusive promise of work. Both Katy and Onai were proud owners of such shacks. It was not unusual to find among them a scattering of vegetable plants that families used to supplement insufficient diets. The food shortages made it crucial for anyone with a few square metres of space to become instant, small-time farmers. Cabbages were a popular favourite, by virtue of their bulk. A few criminally-minded people had been caught out with solitary cannabis plants growing robustly among innocent vegetables.

The two women turned into Jo'burg Lines, happy to be finally home. They stopped briefly just outside Katy's gate. 'Onai, I'll see you tomorrow. I'm expecting a big client this evening. You will be all right, won't you?'

Onai beamed and fiddled with the gauze above her eye. 'Yes, I'll be all right *shamwari yangu. Ndinotenda.* Thank you. I will see you tomorrow at the market. I hope to be up early, so I can collect my previous market orders as soon as VaGudo drives in.'

Katy frowned suddenly and scratched a spot on her right cheek. She looked worried. 'I'm sorry Onai, I don't know how I could have forgotten to tell you something so important. I really meant to do so as soon as …'

'What is it?' Onai interrupted impatiently, eager for her friend to get to the point.

Katy sighed. 'There's a rumour that the markets are going to be shut down sometime soon and we will have to destroy the shacks because …'

Onai's eyes opened wide. *'Chii?'* she interjected in a small, shocked voice.

'Faith heard from her boyfriend yesterday that the markets are actually going to be demolished, as well as all the shacks …' Katy explained with troubled uncertainty. She had wavered between panic and disbelief since first hearing the … what was it? News? Gossip? Information?

She wondered who else had heard, but no one had mentioned anything to her; and yet, Faith's boyfriend had connections … now, speaking about it, gave the rumour a reality that she'd prefer not to acknowledge. What could they do, anyway?

What Katy had just told her, made no sense at all to Onai. She gave a hollow, strained laugh. 'But that cannot be true. I mean, where would all the people who live in the shacks go? There are thousands and thousands in Mbare alone! How does Faith know all this anyway?' she asked, bewildered.

'As I said, her boyfriend mentioned it to her. He is Mr Tom Sibanda, … you know? He has a lot of powerful friends, so I guess that's how he heard this rumour.'

Onai shook her head and frowned. Katy had only told her that Faith had a rich boyfriend. Beyond that, she knew next to nothing about the man. The actual significance of his name was lost on her. Whoever he was, it struck her as unfair that he should know so much about something which would impact negatively on her own life.

'He's the one who took over that farm in Norton … the one where flowers are grown. At least, you must know about that, Onai. It was on the news only two weeks ago as a success story of the new indigenous farmers,' Katy stated knowledgeably and a little proudly.

Onai still felt puzzled. Unlike Katy, she did not like watching the news. There was never anything on it that was faintly relevant to the realities of her life, nothing that she found remotely helpful. It was quite possible that she had missed that particular report.

Katy went on patiently, her attention now focused on Faith's boyfriend, Tom Sibanda. 'He owns the farm in Norton which was once owned by that farmer, Mr Johnson who …' she suddenly stopped in mid-sentence and shifted awkwardly on her feet.

Onai remembered the story about Mr Johnson with great clarity. It was not something that anyone would be comfortable talking freely about. The unfortunate farmer had died after being brutally assaulted in his home. Amid great speculation, his family had fled the country soon afterwards. Three years previously, the issue had been much discussed. But why would Faith be associating with a man who owned a farm with such a dreadful history? 'Are you sure Faith is all right? I mean, are you sure it's safe for her to have a boyfriend who …' Onai caught herself, slightly shocked by what she'd been about to say.

Katy gave a tight little smile which failed to soften the hard look in her eyes. She reached out for her sturdy metal gate and leaned against it. 'I think Faith is OK. Tom Sibanda was not involved in anything that happened to Mr Johnson and his family. Surely, Onai, you must remember that the incident involved a burglary that went wrong.' Her words were convincing but her face told a different story.

Burglary that went wrong? Onai wanted to ask Katy if a burglary could ever be described as having gone right. But the words stuck in her throat. She swallowed anxiously.

Katy gave a wide smile but her face looked strained. 'Anyway, I think it's all groundless gossip, I mean about the shacks and the markets. Things like that don't just happen. It's mischievous people who want to cause trouble and disturb the peace who spread such malicious rumours. I wouldn't be surprised if all of it is coming from the university. You know how those students are always causing trouble. I'm sorry for mentioning it in the first place. Don't worry yourself, *sahwira*,' she said in a more convincing tone.

Onai grabbed hold of the reassuring words and held them fast. She felt a weight lifting from her shoulders. Yes, of course, such things would never be allowed to happen. Just imagining the upheaval was deeply unsettling. She found comfort in disbelief.

She said, 'I think you're right. Look at all the gossip we hear that never amounts to anything. For many months now, people have been saying that real money will soon replace these bearers' cheques, which are now so frayed that they're falling apart! It's also said that our money system will be changed so that we won't have to buy everything in hundreds of thousands and millions of dollars. But nothing has changed. Everything is just getting worse.' She laughed almost hysterically. 'I never thought that in my lifetime, I would be a millionaire. *Inini chaiye miriyoneya!* But look at me!' She laughed again and gestured majestically,

'I must be among the poorest millionaires in the world!'

Katy nodded. 'I'm happy to see you smiling again, *sahwira*. And you're right. People often say one or another thing will happen. Who knows … *zuva raizobuda kubva kumavirira chaiko! Pakati peusiku chaipo!*'

Onai laughed harder. The sun would never rise from the west, and certainly not at midnight. Maybe Faith and her young man were wrong. They had to be. Katy asked her to send Ruva to collect a parcel from Faith. Onai thanked her again. The two women parted good-naturedly and went their separate ways.

CHAPTER 6

Swinging her small bag, a song in her heart, Onai walked on briskly and soon turned the corner into 50th Street. She slowed down on meeting the ever-smiling vagrant who spent his days roaming the streets of Mbare. Nobody knew his name, but people had taken to calling him Mawaya because it was suspected that he was mentally deranged.

The man occasionally stopped by her house to beg for something to eat. Quite frequently, she had spotted him competing with stray dogs for rare bits of food from people's bins. Nobody could afford to throw away anything that was remotely edible, nowadays. These were lean times and it showed. Both Mawaya and the neighbourhood's stray dogs looked like walking skeletons. Mawaya's cheek bones jutted out like twin peaks on his gaunt face. Onai had no doubt that under his mass of rags, you could count the bones of his ribcage.

He looked delighted to see her, almost childishly so. Clapping his hands in a feverish manner, he said, '*Maswera sei, mama?* Anything for me today?' There was a hopeful spark in his eyes.

'Not today, *mukwasha*. Next time, I promise,' Onai responded with a smile. This seemed to be enough for Mawaya. Extraordinarily white teeth showed themselves in a gleaming smile, and in marked contrast to the greyness covering him from head to toe. He clapped again, whistling to himself, as he ambled up the street. Onai watched him go, wondering what had happened to bring him to this pass. Everyone had a life story, even this genial vagrant with his permanent smile.

She turned and walked towards her home. The stench hit her before she saw the rivulet of raw sewage meandering across the road. The pipe had burst again. She stepped daintily over the thin stream, wondering how long it would take before the pipe was repaired. It was just too close to her house, and Fari liked playing in the road with his friends.

She found the interior of her house remarkably neat and quiet. The broken latch on the back door had been fixed. She gave it a small test shake. It held fast. Good. Ruva had probably looked for someone to carry out the repair. Involving himself in trivial domestic chores, such as mending broken doors, was not something Gari would dream of doing. There would, of course, be a bill to pay.

On the battered cardboard box next to the bed, she found a letter addressed to her. The bold typescript on the envelope appeared official. It could only be the letter that she'd been waiting for ... the follow-up to her job interview at Nhembe Factory. She tore open the khaki envelope with eager, shaking hands. Her pulse raced and her eyes ran down the page. Then her heart sank: she had not secured the job. She wondered why. The interview questions had been straightforward enough. She had completed the practical task long before any of the other candidates.

'Well done,' one of the male invigilators had mouthed at her. She had been under the impression that she'd done well. Maybe it was the way she had been dressed. True to form, with borrowed garments; the suit that Katy had lent her had hung loosely on her slender frame. She shook her head. It had to be something else. Could it be because she had not known anyone on the interview panel? Should she have paid a bribe? She had no answers.

She turned the page over with trembling hands. The letter was concluded in the same detached style: she had not worked for two years since completing her Diploma in Dressmaking, and this had counted against her. Onai was dismayed. The words had a painfully familiar ring.

She wanted to scream indignantly, *'Ndiri shasha pakusona!* I am so good. And I have been working. I sew clothes and uniforms for my children, and sometimes for my neighbours for a fee! You should see how beautifully my patchwork covers the holes on my children's faded clothes ... that's my work ... so I'm working!' Abruptly, her thoughts switched to past tense. Well, she had been working. That is, until Gari had thrown her very old, but still functional, sewing machine against the wall in a fit of rage. It had been damaged beyond repair.

She stroked the rough surface on the wall where the impact had left a graphic labyrinth of cracks. For three months, she had done no sewing at all. She missed the soft caress of fabric in her hands. She missed the reassuringly solid smoothness of her old machine. She missed it so badly that her fingers tingled.

With her machine gone, her earnings had dwindled to what she made from vending. Inevitably, their life had worsened. It hurt that her two years of deprivation, while attending her dressmaking course, now counted for nothing. She had suffered beatings because Gari had seen her decision to go to college as wilful defiance; a deliberate challenge to his authority as a man. The suffering had not ended there. Her mother had sold five of her six cows to help pay for the fees and the practicals. Her children had walked to school barefoot. They had worn threadbare uniforms. For that, they had borne the brunt of their friends' taunts. But Onai had been optimistic enough for all of them. Refusing to admit defeat, she had juggled her vegetable vending and her dressmaking lessons with remarkable dexterity. And, at the end of it all, she had triumphantly passed her finals.

Now, all she could think was that she was worse off than before. She had still not managed to buy even a single cow to repay her mother. She tore up the offending letter and threw it in the bin.

Lost in thought, and with distracted, automatic movements, she made herself a cup of sugarless tea. How terribly she missed its sweetness! There had been no sugar in her house for two whole months. Her craving was like an ache. Just thinking about the sweetener made her mouth water.

≈≈≈

She went to sit on her front doorstep, facing Sheila's shack. A light afternoon breeze fluttered the edges of the yellow plastic sheeting which formed the shack's windows. It was still only May, but the weather was considerably colder, especially at night. With the plastic sheeting already that frayed, cold air would enter the shack. And Sheila had a small baby. Onai accepted that she would soon have to replace the plastic sheeting with something thicker and more protective.

She stretched her legs lazily in front of her and enjoyed the peaceful afternoon, slowly sipping the hot, bitter drink. It gently warmed her insides, and as the warmth spread to her limbs, her mood lifted.

'*Matomati, mazai pano!*' The piercing, energetic chant of a street vendor, peddling tomatoes and eggs, cut through the near-silence and disappeared. Tomatoes, Onai thought with yearning. Her market stall had become a priority for whatever few tomatoes she could lay her hands on. Raising money took precedence. Eggs were just one more luxury which had disappeared permanently from her family's meals. Tomatoes and eggs. Luxuries.

Suddenly, Sheila's loud, racking coughs emanated from the shack and broke the noon silence. A grubby baby girl crawled cautiously out of the shack and looked apathetically at Onai. Her eyes were like pools sunk deeply within her skull. Sparse wisps of hair covered a scalp festooned with ring-worm. Her undersized vest was stretched tightly across her abdomen. She wore a dirty-brown nappy that looked no better than a rag. Emaciated limbs seemed to stick out from her distended belly, which accentuated her thinness.

Onai watched the child crawling slowly towards the vegetable patch and held her breath, willing her to stop immediately before she trampled on the cabbage nurslings. Amazingly, the little girl stopped right at the edge of the patch. Onai exhaled. The nurslings were safe. She scrutinised the baby keenly, clicking her tongue with disapproval. Really! Sheila ought to look after the child better, or at least keep her clean; though it was possible that a single mother suffering from AIDS might not cope with a baby – and it was most likely to be infected as well.

A large black *chongololo* crawled slowly in front of the hapless infant. She watched it with sudden fascination and then reached out a tentative arm to grab the insect, raising it to her lips as it curled around her hand. Onai jumped up and snatched the squirming millipede out of the baby's tight grasp. The child immediately started wailing, wounded at being deprived of her quarry. Sheila flung open the door of the shack and picked up the crying toddler. She sat her squarely on her bony hip with soft soothing murmurs before she turned to greet Onai, choosing not to make reference to her hospitalisation. That way she could let her landlady hang on to some dignity. Without intending to, she fixed her gaze on the dressing above Onai's eye, then hastily withdrew her eyes in embarrassment.

Onai ignored her discomfort. 'Are you not at the flea market today, then?' she enquired, smiling broadly.

'No, I had to take the day off. I went to the hospital again to try and register for HIV drugs,' Sheila replied, a sad look in her eyes. Her gaunt frame drooped, despair seemed to weigh on her shoulders.

Onai looked at her troubled face and felt her pain. 'Any luck this time?' she asked softly.

'No. I've been put on a waiting list. They said they're not taking on new patients at the moment. There's no money to buy the drugs. I was not surprised at all. *Chii chitsva?* Things never change. Except to get worse.' She gave a brittle, sarcastic laugh.

'That's strange. I know somebody who got registered only last week. Are you sure about that?' Onai was certain that Sheila was mistaken.

'That's what the man told me. Maybe I need to be connected to somebody important. Perhaps sleep with someone … a man. That is what I'm good at, isn't it?' Again that derisive laugh and a widening of the listless eyes. 'It's madness! We hear there are drugs donated by the UK or America, but when you want to register, they say they have none. Last week I saw someone selling the drugs at Market Square. He wanted five million dollars for a month's supply! Never mind how he came to be selling the drugs on the street. Where would I get five million dollars from?' her voice rose by several octaves, startling the fretful baby into a loud burst of whimpering.

'I'm so sorry. I wish I could help you Sheila, *vasikana*. Why don't you go back and check next week?' Onai asked, feeling ill at ease, and desperate to say the right thing, knowing full well that her suggestion was of no value.

'No point going back next week. Ha ha! They said I must try next year. *Hakusi kupenga ikoko?* It's madness! I'm sure to be dead by then. They don't care. So why should I care?' she gave a humourless snort.

Onai was at a loss for words. This flippant candour was just a mask. She could see right through it. Behind, lay a terrified, vulnerable, young woman whose health had deteriorated visibly in recent months; and she had a disturbing, brassy cough which Onai occasionally heard from her own bedroom at night.

Sheila patted the gurgling baby's back absent-mindedly then said, 'You know what, Mai Moyo? When I was a prostitute, I didn't care about catching HIV. I thought I would die from hunger, anyway. *Kusiri kufa ndekupi?* As a prostitute, I could at least die with a full stomach. Now that I know I will die of AIDS, I think dying of hunger is far much better. If I could have another chance …' her voice shook.

Onai was aghast. She could not keep up with the younger woman's train of thought. Sheila's hurt and confusion were almost palpable. In that awkward moment, she was unsure how to encourage her to be strong without sounding unsympathetic. Why was living with the results of one's life choices always so hard?

Sheila continued speaking, her voice now tearful. 'Who will look after my poor baby when I die? I'm not strong enough for any of this.' She waved her hand in an expansive gesture. Fat tears welled up in her sunken eyes and ran freely down her cheeks.

Onai took her emaciated hand gently in hers. It was floppy, almost lifeless. She spoke kindly, 'Sheila, you are not dying. *Usataure mazwi akashata kudaro.* Do not speak such words. It's May now, only seven months to go before you start getting the drugs. Be positive, all right?'

Sheila gave a smile which fleetingly smoothed the edge of despair from her haggard features. For only a split second, she looked as hopeful as any young woman should be. 'Thank you, Mai Moyo. You are so good to me. There was a time when I thought you would ask me to leave because I have AIDS. I'm so thankful that you gave me lodgings when nobody else would. My own family have disowned me.' She was once again close to wailing.

Onai gave her an encouraging smile and replied, perhaps a shade too brightly, 'Don't worry Sheila. *Zvichanaka chete.* Everything will be all right. You are welcome to stay here for as long as you like.'

Of course, she knew that when Sheila became very ill, she would have to leave. But where would she go? The thought filled her with remorse but there was nothing she could do about it. She could not take on the added responsibility of looking after the young woman, or her baby. Her back was close to breaking from the burden of cares in her own life.

Sheila looked at her and nodded gratefully. She bent over and went back into the shack with her agitated baby.

Onai walked back into her house. She glanced up at the smiling Humpty Dumpty clock on the wall. Ill-defined thoughts frolicked in her mind about Sheila and the clock. The clock's shiny, plump face portrayed happiness, good health, and something else which Sheila would never have because ... The delicate thread broke. It was almost five o'clock. Her children would be back from school shortly.

CHAPTER 7

It was the end of yet another busy day in meetings. Assistant Commissioner Nzou was tired. His secretary had already left. Lazy cow! He scowled as he unlocked one of the drawers at his desk, pulled it open and took out thick, tightly-bound wads of bearer cheques. This was the currency that had been in circulation for about two years. Initially, the not-so-durable notes had been introduced as a temporary measure to alleviate crippling cash shortages. However, they seemed to have become a permanent fixture within the routine transactions of the mainstream economy.

The commissioner thrust one hundred and twenty-five million dollars worth of the cheques into a satchel. It was time to go to Mbare to collect some US dollars from Mrs Nguni. He hated having to deal with women. They could never be trusted to keep a secret. *Vanhu vepi vasina hana?*

He threw a full-length leather coat over his uniform and left his office. The building appeared deserted. Everything felt ominously quiet, though there would, of course, be a flurry of activity in the main part of the station. Ignoring the silence, he ran down the stairs with youthful buoyancy and strolled out into the car park, deciding not to drive his brand new Mazda 6, given to him by the force only two weeks previously. It would make him too conspicuous in a place like Mbare. He selected, instead, the older Santana which was reserved for his exclusive use. For this mission, he wanted to be invisible, if that was possible. Whistling happily, he eased himself into the car and reversed out of the gate, waving condescendingly at the guard. *Mahobho.* 'What a job!' He thought.

As he drove to Mbare he reflected on his consultation later that evening with a spiritualist in Kuwadzana. Tsikamutanda had undertaken to formulate a strong charm that would smooth his course towards a more senior post and bring prosperity to his ailing business. Nzou speeded up. The spiritualist disliked clients who arrived late, throwing his tight schedule into disarray. He had a large clientele and was almost always fully-booked. Nzou could not afford to miss his appointment with the great man. Tsikamutanda's Chipinge origins suggested phenomenal potency, both as a spiritualist and a herbalist. Could a man be more gifted? Nzou doubted it.

Promotions had become notoriously elusive. One could forget educational qualifications and work experience. Instead, one needed to pull the right strings, grease the right palms or procure a little ancestral help. Bribing one's way through the ranks was also becoming harder, the more senior one became. Bribes had become infamous for not working, if it happened that someone else offered a larger amount of money. On the other hand, sometimes the panel had no interest whatsoever in taking bribes, which had come as a complete surprise to Nzou during the last round of promotions. Whatever the case, it was a gamble, but a very necessary one all the same. You were damned if you didn't, and with various degrees of likelihood, you were damned if you did.

The most noteworthy challenger for Nzou's target post was rumoured to be consulting a powerful Malawian spiritualist. Well, Tsikamutanda was rumoured to be even more powerful. Why else would he be charging for his services in foreign currency? Nzou had run a meticulous check on his credentials. The man had an excellent track record. There would be no embarrassing incidents like the one involving that businesswoman from Gweru. She had been defrauded out of the foreign currency she had paid to a spiritualist, who had purportedly agreed to fly three mermaids from London! She'd been made to believe that the young fish-women would revive her grocery business. Mermaids! Nzou snorted with contempt and shook his head, wondering what depths of desperation and stupidity had entangled the woman in a ruse of such implausible proportions.

Nzou grinned happily and gently passed his right palm over the bag of bearer cheques. Soon, he would have the required foreign currency. He sincerely hoped that the charm would work. He'd been stuck in the same position for years with no immediate prospects of promotion. Being passed over several times had punctured his pride and humiliated him. Besides, his business was showing signs of floundering from a constant diversion of funds. So, this time, the charm had to work.

He impatiently blared his horn at a woman whose car was moving slowly in front of him. 'Make up your mind, you brainless idiot,' he mouthed. Did she want to drive? Or did she want to park her car right in the middle of the road? *Chii chitsva? Vakadzi!* Women were such bad drivers. If it was up to him, they wouldn't be allowed on the roads at all.

He made an impatient clicking noise with his tongue. She was probably driving at that speed because her tank was near-empty. The fuel shortages had resulted in a new type of driver. Crawlers, he called them; crawlers coaxing their cars forward on the remnants of their fuel. He hated them with a passion. If they didn't have petrol, why didn't they just park their vehicles and stay at home? He hooted again and tried to overtake the woman. He failed and swerved back into his lane to avoid oncoming traffic. The driver behind him blasted his horn angrily.

This was the worst time of day to be driving across the city centre. Throngs of pedestrians crossing the road at random, made things no better. Neither did the emergency-taxi drivers, who drove as if their fathers owned the roads. One would think that given the shortages, there would be no traffic at all. But no, it was still there, including the crawlers he hated so much. The black market was obviously thriving.

Irritably, he slowed down like everyone else. As soon as he turned up the car radio, Tuku's powerful voice belted out some well-known lyrics, '*Shanda mwana, shanda nesimba. Ndoishandira mhuri yangu vakomana.*' Yes, that's what it was all about. Working hard, and for him, doing everything possible to secure his children's future. Pulling deals would always be part of it. Even with all his benefits at work – most of which were self-conferred – the money was not enough. Their salaries were pathetic, and the cost of living too high.

His Santana crawled on through town. At this rate, it would take him all of forty-five minutes just to reach Mbare. Resignedly, he sat back, a frown of annoyance on his face.

Just as she was closing her bedroom window, Onai was surprised to notice a man stooping stealthily into Sheila's shack. He was carrying a plastic bag bulging with what looked like groceries. A much older, stouter figure, he was nothing like the young man who'd been hanging around Sheila in recent weeks. Onai shook her head. Some lessons went unlearnt, but the price was very high. For the man's sake (and his wife's sake, if he had one) she hoped that he was Sheila's relative. Something about his furtiveness told her that he wasn't. *Varume!*

She went into the kitchen and set about making a less than modest evening meal for her family. The shortages meant that what she laid on the table was always the most basic food, just passable as a meal, and usually sadza and boiled cabbage. There wasn't even a drop of cooking oil to fry the cabbage. Neither were there any tomatoes to add a little colour and taste, so the cabbage would be soggy and pallid. What a difference some oil would have made, she thought ruefully, then decided to count her blessings. At least she still had some seasoning. She smiled. How bizarre that salt should count as a blessing!

Gone were the days when availability of such food products had been a matter of course. Her son, Fari, had spent the previous Saturday in a queue for cooking oil, while the girls helped her at the market. He had returned home empty-handed, dust-covered and exhausted, but bursting with exciting, hilarious accounts of skirmishes with the riot police. His propensity for enjoyment, even when he came away from the long queues with nothing, constantly astonished her. But then, he was only a child, and childhood was like a shield. The grim realities of life did not hurt so much within its relatively safe confines.

Meat was now a dream. With some luck, they would have a braai of sorts on New Year's Day and make a grand entrance into 2006. Seven months might just be long enough to save for a sumptuous barbeque. Yes, she would make sure her children had some meat either at Christmas or New Year. So vivid was her imagination that she could almost see the bliss on Rita's face at such wanton extravagance. *Nyama yekugocha!* Certainly, this was something to look forward to. Rita possessed the delightful knack of adding value to every small pleasure.

Drawing her thoughts back to that evening's meal, Onai stirred the pot of sadza and realised that the thick paste would be scarcely palatable. The maize meal currently available in the shops was the worst she had ever known. Gari would be upset. She would not be surprised if he angrily swiped the food off the table with his large hairy arm, in a gesture that diminished the effort it had taken to make sure that it was there at all. It had happened before. It could happen again.

Just after five o'clock, the children arrived and with a welcome raucousness, breaking the tranquillity and her stream of sad consciousness. Greeting her happily, they were clearly relieved to see her back. Neither Fari nor Ruva seemed happier than Rita. As usual, she followed Onai around, clinging to her at every opportunity, as if she was afraid that she would be taken away again. She was the only one who looked with concern at the gauze above her eye, touching it tentatively, and asking if it was painful.

Onai shook her head. 'No, not any more. Don't worry. I'm fine.'

Ruva gave her an awkward glance before placing her books on the small kitchen table, and sitting down to do her homework.

'Who mended the door, my dear?' Onai asked her quietly.

'VaHondo repaired it yesterday. He said it's for free,' Ruva replied as she flipped the pages of her large atlas. She looked up and opened her mouth as if to say something else, then she stopped.

'Remind me to go over to thank him and his wife this evening,' Onai said.

'I don't think he is there today, *Amai*,' she mumbled, returning her eyes to the book.

Fari had one question. '*Mhama*, are we going to queue for a new TV on Saturday?'

Ruva retorted disdainfully, 'How stupid to think that people will queue to buy TVs! Shops are full of them. They're covered in dust because nobody can afford them. Your head is too full of queues. And water!'

Onai's voice was sharp, 'Ruva, how many times do I have to tell you not to speak to your brother like that?'

Ruva glowered and looked down at her small pile of books. She tapped the table with the end of her Eversharp pen. Onai spoke to Fari in a softer voice, 'We're not buying a TV any time soon *mwanangu* because there is no money.' He looked crestfallen.

'Good thing too,' Ruva was quick to say. 'Maybe some people whose names I won't mention will study instead of watching *Gringo* or *Studio 263* all the time. Maybe for the first time they will not be position thirty-five in a class of forty.' She gave Rita a meaningful glare. Rita mumbled something inaudible and looked away, her expression both guilty and piqued.

'Do I really have water on my brain, *Mhama?*' Fari asked earnestly.

'No, you don't. Your sister was just teasing you,' she answered. Fari's relief was visible. He jumped up exultantly, hitting out at the air with his right fist. Ruva scowled at him.

'Now, go and take off your uniform,' Onai told him. Within minutes, he was out with his hyperactive, perpetually dusty friends, who were waiting for him by the mango tree.

Onai shouted after them, 'Mind the burst pipe. Don't play near the sewage!' So swift was their noisy disappearance that it seemed as if they had not heard her at all.

Yes, life was back to normal. Later, they would eat their insipid evening meal in good spirits. Then they would wait for Gari to come home. Maybe he would arrive before they all went to bed. Onai was not sure if she wanted him to return early in case she found herself under the undesirable obligation of intimacy.

Her biggest failure as a wife lay in refusing Gari his conjugal rights … unless he agreed to use condoms. In a rare moment of rebelliousness, she had told him clearly no condoms, no intimacy. She felt a twinge of guilt, then immediately forgave herself. What was a woman supposed to do with a philandering husband when the risk of HIV infection was so real? So real that everyone in a relationship was at risk?

While she had no hard proof, her instincts and a host of tantalisingly suspicious incidents told her that there were other women in his life. It would have been reckless to gamble with this evidence. She was consumed by a burning desire to stay alive for her children, and stay alive she would. So she made sure that there were always condoms in the house. However, her stance had cost her a great deal. The escalating beatings were ample testimony of Gari's reaction to her defiance. According to him, condoms were what a man used when he thought of sleeping with a prostitute, not with his own wife for whom he had paid a grand total of ten cows and an expensive coat for her father, as *marooro*.

In recent months, she had taken to collecting free female condoms from the family planning clinic at Spilhaus, just a stone's throw from Harare Hospital. Female condoms were a blessing. She had been pleasantly surprised by the freedom they gave her. They made her feel more in control of her sexuality and definitely less vulnerable to Gari's demands. During his various degrees of drunkenness, he often failed to notice when she had a condom on. This meant that the fights about him wearing a condom were less frequent than before. What a relief it was that on most evenings he was drunk, almost to the point of paralysis! One of her worst fears was that soon enough, the situation was bound to explode in her face.

How lucky Katy was to have a husband who obviously loved her … a husband who seemed to be faithful, and who lusted after her earnestly as if they were still newly-weds.

≈≈≈

A Santana police truck crawled up 49th street in the gloomy shadow of falling darkness. It pulled up just outside Katy's gate with a hissing sound. A few of her lodgers were sitting by a fire outside their shacks. They stared towards the gate with curiosity. A mysterious figure clad in a full-length coat and a jaunty cowboy hat sprang energetically out of the car and swaggered into the small yard.

The lodgers all knew of their landlady's shady foreign currency dealings on the black market. They whispered among themselves. Was she facing arrest? This could bring excitement to an otherwise dreary evening. Their landlady was a good woman and they all liked her. But anything that promised to break the monotony of an existence fraught with constant hardship was always welcome. Their single inquisitive gaze pursued the man to the front door.

≈≈≈

'Pindai,' Katy responded to the knock on her door. A very tall man entered the sitting room, appearing to stoop as he did so. He introduced himself as Mr Nzou. They shook hands and exchanged perfunctory greetings. He explained that he had come to collect the US dollars as arranged by her husband, two days previously. He smiled at her and immediately made himself comfortable on the low chair nearest the door, stretching out his long legs in a relaxed manner, and displaying a pair of impeccably polished brown shoes. Katy could almost see her reflection in them. She wondered if a police recruit or a prisoner had done the polishing.

She noted that Mr Nzou was a handsome, well turned-out man. The fine leather coat perfected the picture of affluence. However, the fancy cowboy hat balanced on his head looked rather superfluous. An appendage often worn by the new farmers, she wondered if he'd been given a farm. And why was he wearing sunglasses at dusk and in the house? Maybe it was a feeble attempt at disguising himself? But why bother since he'd already given her his name? She looked at him suspiciously through narrowed eyes, almost expecting him to whip out a pair of handcuffs and arrest her on the spot.

He gave her another confident smile; obviously he was more at ease than she was. Nervous tension seeped out of her body. Her shoulders relaxed and she sat back in her chair. Maybe he was all right.

To her utter relief, the transaction went smoothly. Mr Nzou counted out the notes with the proficient ease of someone used to handling large amounts of money. No handcuffs were whipped out as she had feared. The deal was concluded with surprising transparency. At the end, he signed her little receipt book and printed his name in full – John's little idea. Proof of transactions with this man could be very useful one day.

As he got up to leave, and nervously scratching her right cheek, she ventured, 'Mr Nzou, can I ask you something?'

'Chii?' he asked, now impatient to be gone. It was almost time for his appointment with Tsikamutanda.

She drew in a deep breath. 'Is it true that the markets and housing shacks are going to be demolished next week?'

Nzou was momentarily stunned. His feet propelled him back into the house. It was a purely reflex action. Perplexed thoughts raced through his mind. How had this shanty-town woman come across such highly confidential intelligence? Certainly, there would be demolitions to clean up the towns and drive out criminals, including some unscrupulous foreign currency dealers who were running the country's economy aground. The currency situation was now chaotic; almost a circus. Its effects on the country's economy were now more apparent than ever. There was a sense of urgency. Drastic measures needed to be put in place without delay.

Of course, the whole procedure would be above board and well within the limits of the law. It was expected to be formally announced soon. Early leakage would only cause misunderstanding and disorder, possibly inciting violence and warning the very criminals who were meant to be flushed out and arrested. There were obviously some treacherous moles in high places who had leaked the information. It was time for damage control.

Quickly regaining his composure, he smiled. 'That must be the most fictitious thing I have heard in years! *Manyepo chaiwo!* If something like that were to happen, I would be among the first people to hear of it. Do you know what the problem with you women is? Too much gossiping, heh? Nothing to do, heh? You obviously have too much free time on your hands. Your husband should stay at home and keep you busy with activities that are more productive and enjoyable than gossiping,' he said flirtatiously, while looking at her very intently.

Nzou was aware of his effect on women. It appeared as if Mrs Nguni was not immune to his charms. Looking flustered and giggling like a young girl, she bit her lip shyly, and said, 'It's something I heard yesterday. I didn't really believe it.' Her husky voice was low and breathless. She was almost whispering.

'Good. You are a wise woman not to believe such things. We are business partners now. I would have told you if it was true. So you can tell your friends that it's all lies,' he asserted.

She thanked him and walked him to the gate.

≈≈≈

The lodgers looked on with a good measure of astonishment. They had been so sure that the police official had come to arrest their landlady. Obviously, they had been wrong. Interesting. Maybe she was having an affair, one of them whispered, lacing his suspicions with allusions of intrigue. Married women were not invulnerable to the temptation of affairs, especially when they had husbands who were constantly away from home. They assented cagily and nodded. The possibility shook them. Mr Nguni would be devastated. He obviously loved his wife.

CHAPTER 8

Next morning, the vegetable vendors stood in the open space next to the market and waited patiently for VaGudo's delivery. His overburdened truck squealed to a halt in a cloud of dust. He was right on time. That was one thing they liked about him; he was always prompt. A large, blustery man with a vibrant personality, VaGudo's hands were continually in motion, their liberal gestures harmonising with his gregarious personality. His facial features were sunk in rolls of fat that gathered themselves into three chins at the front of his neck. His stomach seemed to fall in folds over his belt. For his customers, the man was all pleasant smiles and cheerful remarks; for his assistants he seemed only to have acid words. The three young men scuttled about like frightened rabbits and served the customers at great speed.

Onai felt a spasm of despair when she realised that the prices had again gone up considerably. She held out some spinach and complained that the price was almost double what she had paid just a week previously.

Katy spoke up, 'Yes, VaGudo, how come all your prices have gone up and you didn't even warn us? *Sei?*'

He crossed flabby arms over his chest and gave a deep laugh that seemed to spring from the depths of his enormous belly. His three chins wobbled. *'Veduwe!* It is very unfair of you to say that.' He winked at Katy. She stared back at him and waited for an answer, refusing to be wooed by his practised charm. Onai looked on hopefully.

He shrugged, 'I have to raise my prices so that I can also make a living. I need petrol to drive out here. And now fuel, when you can get it, costs up to one hundred and twenty-thousand dollars per litre, though the official price is still only fifty thousand dollars. Just think about it. Besides, the shops increase their prices without warning every day. So how come you expect me to make an announcement on Radio Two? Or should it be front page in *The Herald? Kana muKwayedza?'* His eyes twinkled.

Katy laughed. She no longer looked particularly bothered. 'I'm just shocked by your prices. The money that I had budgeted is not enough to buy what I need for my stall today because you have increased all your figures,' she said. The other vendors nodded and murmured in agreement.

Onai dared to ask, 'Can you please go back to the old prices? Just for today? Please VaGudo,' she requested earnestly. Unlike Katy, this was no laughing matter for her. Years of raising her children on next to nothing had made her meticulously thrifty. They had taught her the importance of striking a good bargain. Every single dollar counted. Rita's textbooks would have to be bought by Monday, the teacher had said. It had been an ultimatum.

VaGudo shook his head in exasperation. He rolled chubby hands over his stomach and launched into a convoluted justification of the price hikes, while the vendors begged him for lenience. They had families to feed.

He shook his head again. '*Ndiudzei,* am I the one with no family to feed? Life is very unfair. Very, very unfair. How can a hapless man like me win when a group of aggressive Mbare women have ganged up against me?' Nonetheless, he looked like a man who was enjoying himself, as if haggling with his customers was one of the highlights of his day. Eventually, a satisfactory compromise was reached. The vendors were happy. When VaGudo left, the truck was empty. His three assistants, now spread-eagled in comfort at the back of the truck, waved goodbye.

≈≈≈

Katy and Onai crossed over into the hectic market to prepare for the day's business. They dusted off their stalls and spread out their fruits and vegetables. In no time at all, business took off. In between serving customers, the vendors shared gossip about where to find certain groceries. Of particular interest were maize meal, flour, cooking oil, bread, sugar and soap. They shared valuable wisdom about how to stock up on foodstuffs and make them last as long as possible.

Out of the corner of her eye, Onai occasionally observed her friend talking to potential foreign currency buyers. On one occasion, Katy sneaked off to the nearby toilet to close a deal, leaving Onai to mind her stall. There were just too many street children loitering in the market. Their restlessness and stealthy glances gave away their mission: the perfect moment to pounce, grabbing fruit, or anything else that could be resold in town at a higher price.

The day progressed just like any other; the atmosphere saturated by vendors gossiping or negotiating earnestly with prospective customers. The few who had televisions engaged in enthusiastic chatter about *Studio 263*, the most popular TV drama of the day. Onai learned of the sibling rivalry between Joyce and the beautiful Vimbai. She heard of a married woman's extra-marital affair, and of the fictional dealers whose glamorous lifestyles could be nothing other than romance in a country like theirs, or so she thought. Without a TV, she had nothing to contribute. However, she listened avidly to the entertaining discussion.

As the day passed, babies strapped to their mothers' backs became restless and hungry. A serious wailing contest commenced, punctuated by soothing maternal noises. Now and then, the occasional bleat of a goat or the cluck of a chicken could be heard. At the end of the day, instant mob justice was meted out to a hungry young man who had dared to steal a banana from one of the stalls. This was Mbare Musika.

As Katy waved to Onai, she shouted out a reminder. 'Don't forget to send Rita and Fari to queue for bread at the Supa Superstore. There'll be a delivery shortly.' Onai thanked her and waved. She had enough money to spare for at least one loaf of bread.

≈≈≈

Two hours of evening study had been enough. Faith sauntered out of the library with her friend, Melody. They walked down the steps leading from the entrance and crossed over to a notice board just outside the Great Hall. Faith took some Stiki-Stuff from her satchel and secured the fluttering edge of a notice. Out of curiosity she read it: 'Hurry, hurry, hurry! Special offer for Medical students: Two copies of Clinical Anatomy by Snell for sale. Brand new. Imported from the UK. Not available in the campus bookshop. Only three million dollars each. Call 091.260.435.' She turned away, disinterested. Boring subject.

Ridiculous price. A tenth of a whole semester's fees just for a single textbook! It was madness.

She murmured to her friend, 'Can't wait for the exams to begin and end. I hate the atmosphere around Great Hall during exam week! Great Hell! It does feel like hell you know.'

'I don't know why you complain about exams, Faith. You're always one of the top three, so quit moaning!' Melody ribbed her, not without a hint of admiration. She peered at another notice, 'That's the Tuku show that I'm going to with Chanda on Saturday. Are you going as well?'

'No. Tom is off to the UK tomorrow. I think I'll go to Mbare and spend some time with my mother,' Faith replied, shaking her head. She scrutinised the notice board again, looking for bargains relevant to her degree programme. There were none. 'Pity. I would have wanted us to go as a group,' Melody replied.

They moved away from the board and strolled companionably towards Swinton Hall. They passed a few groups of students clutching books, others drinking beer – was beer not illegal on campus? – and loving couples clinging to each other. Just outside the residence, some young male students, who could only have been first-years, hovered near the car park, obviously on the look-out for girls. They whistled enthusiastically each time a female passed. Much to their delight, Melody performed a mock catwalk saunter, and the two girls laughed as they entered Swinton together.

'Come up to my room. My room-mate isn't around today,' Melody suggested. Faith nodded. This was the perfect opportunity to raise a matter that had been bothering her. Passivity and silence had their own way of making things worse; of sustaining the deterioration of situations that might otherwise be salvaged. She took a deep breath and followed Melody up to her room on the first floor.

Her friend immediately switched on her cassette player, selecting a tape by Chiwoniso. Faith put her books down on a desk and pulled out a chair, mentally blocking out the song, '*Wandirasa*'. The words were such a poignant expression of a woman's anguish. How difficult the condition of women could be. She seemed to know so many women facing difficult choices, in addition to having to work through her own.

Turning to her friend, she said, 'Mel, you did tell me Chanda was married, didn't you? So what's between the two of you? '

Melody smiled coyly. 'What about us?' she replied, sounding deliberately vague.

'Married men will promise a lot, Mel. But they never leave their wives for their girlfriends. This man will turn you into his 'small house'. You could end up with a broken heart …'

Throwing her head back, Melody laughed, careless and unperturbed. 'You're so funny, Faith. Don't worry, I know how to look after myself. I've thought about all this, you know. I'll be all right.' Serenely, she began to sort out the laundry on her bed, folding her clothes and packing them into the wardrobe, while tapping her foot in time to Chiwoniso's sweet *mbira* rhythms.

Faith looked doubtfully at her friend. It was inconceivable that a girl like Melody could become intimately involved without the stirrings of emotion and without the risk of pain. Or could she? Chiwoniso intruded. '*Wandirasa, wandirasa, wandirasawo* …' It was a woman's plea. Words that could cut Melody like a knife. 'You have left me …' The silence between them grew. Melody continued shaking her body in time to the tune, playful and untroubled.

'And what does Chanda say about your relationship?' Faith asked finally, raising her eyebrows questioningly.

'Mmm, he's said he'll stay in the marriage because his children are still young, and need some stability,' she shrugged, swaying her hips gently to the next song: '… and every woman has known dark hours … when she is full of doubt …' Doubt and uncertainty; corrosive agents that ate away at women's belief in themselves. For no reason at all, Faith found her thoughts flitting to *mainini* Onai. What were her doubts? What fears had stopped her from liberating herself from her abusive husband? Had Melody also simply shackled herself to Chanda out of fear of aborting her degree programme, or did she really love him? Were they using each other? She didn't like to think this of Melody, her friend, whom she was sure would be easily hurt. But she was also still free; this made her situation very different from Onai's. Her *mainini's* predicament was worse because she had children, and she was of a different generation, one still very influenced by culture and the demands of family. What was it that her lecturer had said of the older generation: 'Women over forty simply expect to be beaten or abused.'

The fragile strands of her thought were severed by Melody's voice '… he's said he'll leave when the children are older. I know he's lying but it doesn't bother me. Right now, I'm getting what I want. One day I'll find a decent man to marry.'

Faith shook her head. The conversation had taken a surreal turn. Did Melody really live in an emotional world so different from her own? 'He's a married man, Mel. He's the one who's using you. Why don't you just let him go? He's forty-five, after all. He could be your father. Get somebody your own age, for goodness sake. Somebody single.'

Melody stopped dancing and wagged a finger at her. 'Now, don't start preaching to me. How come it's bothering you, all of a sudden?'

'Well, I … because I didn't know …' she faltered. She hadn't at first realised that Chanda was married. When Melody had told her, the words had been spoken so casually, they might have been just another of her jokes. She should, of course, have guessed. Why had she been so naive? Had she assumed he was widowed, or had she simply not thought about it?

Melody pulled up a chair and sat next to her, looking intently into her eyes. Faith averted her gaze. 'Faith, this man paid my university fees for this semester, and he has pledged to do this until I graduate. Unlike you, I still have another year at university. He buys me clothes, groceries, and gives me money for food. Now tell me, which twenty-two-year-old single man could do all this for me? Besides, most of them have no experience and no manners.'

'What about his wife, though? Don't you feel any guilt for destroying another woman's marriage?' she asked rather fearfully. She was afraid Melody would think she'd gone too far. But still, one woman ruining another. Why? Didn't women have enough problems already?

Melody laughed and tossed her head, clearly not taking Faith seriously. 'I haven't done anything to his wife! I'm not the one who told her to become a 'dot.com' in the UK. You tell me what she's doing there, leaving her husband and children, visiting them only twice a year … risking her marriage to chase the pound. How foolish is that?' She was impertinent and candid in condemnation of her lover's wife.

Coming from Melody, the words seemed disconcertingly out of character. Faith shook her head. This was not her Melody. What had happened? 'The fact that his wife is in England doesn't make it right. What's happening, Mel? This is just not you …'

'Don't be so self-righteous, Faith,' her friend interrupted brusquely. 'Do you think this is what I wanted for myself? This is what I have to do, not what I want. For the first time since I came to varsity, I haven't had to scrounge and get by on one meal a day … or have you passing me your left-overs. For the first time, I haven't had to worry about which of my pompous relatives I should approach to beg for money, only to endure lectures about how they are struggling as well. For the first time in months, I haven't spent sleepless nights considering whether I should become a prostitute to finance my studies …'

Faith was appalled. She felt blood draining from her face. 'You're not serious. You wouldn't think of prostitution …' As she said the words, she realised how stupid and naive she sounded, and yet she was genuinely shocked. How could she and Melody have been friends for so long. It seemed she didn't know her friend at all.

'I would … or rather … I have thought of prostitution. If you knew anything about real poverty, you wouldn't blame me. If you want to blame something, blame the economy for forcing me into a corner.' The young woman's nostrils flared with indignation, revealing anger just beneath the surface. 'Yes, blame the economy for forcing me into a corner.'

Chiwoniso's mellow voice, now rich with hope and joy, paid a lover's tribute to the child, Tamari, urging her to be brave and optimistic in the promise of a new day. Would Melody wake up to the dawn of a new day? What if AIDS got to her first?

Faith swallowed. 'I'm sorry, but aren't you concerned about the risk of HIV?'

Melody bristled. 'I'm not stupid, Faith. I do protect myself, you know. There are condoms, condoms and more condoms. Just stop judging me! You don't know what it's like! I'm not blessed with good parents who are foreign-currency dealers. Or a rich, unmarried boyfriend. I told you, if you want to blame something … someone … blame the economy for forcing me into a corner.' Her voice continued to rise, angry and defiant.

Faith hung her head. Why hadn't she realised the depth of her friend's problems? Melody was always bubbly, cheerful and kind. She didn't deserve this. Nobody did. But what about choices? Did the economy really dictate individual choices to this extent? A lump lodged itself in her throat. 'Your brother …?' she made one last, feeble attempt.

'My brother earns five million dollars a month. He spends half on transport, to and from work. He would go old and grey before he saved the amount that I need to get through one semester. Whether you like it or not, it's Chanda … or I join the ladies of the night who haunt the Avenues. I'm going to become a lawyer, Faith. Whatever it takes.' She gave her friend a steady look. A cynical, half-smile playing on her lips; her anger had waned, but a hint of sadness lingered between them.

Faith sighed. There seemed nothing left to say. 'I think I'd better catch up on some sleep. I stayed up late last night.'

'You do that,' Melody replied and gave her a genuine smile, light-hearted, once again. 'And stop worrying about me and Chanda. I know what I'm doing. Are we friends or not?'

Faith looked at her and despite herself returned her smile. It was impossible to be upset with Melody for any length of time. Two years had cultivated and nourished their friendship.

'Friends,' she quietly affirmed. Gathering her books together, she bade her friend goodnight and walked out to the sound of Chiwoniso's *Chaminuka*, an accolade to their eminent forefather. The lyrics inspired reflection. 'If Chaminuka was alive today, he would have wept for the daughters of his land,' Faith thought. 'Blame-the-economy-for-forcing-me-into-a-corner.' The phrase that Melody had used to absolve herself echoed in her mind merging into one long ominous echoic phrase that could not have contrasted more strongly with Chiwoniso's lyrical lines.

She thought of her mother engaging in unlawful foreign-currency dealing to put her through university, and build a dream home. She thought of *mainini* Onai struggling to raise three children within an abusive marriage; of Melody, trading her innocence for university fees and groceries. How far was she from promiscuity? She thought of *mainini* Onai's lodger, Sheila, a self-proclaimed ex-prostitute whose fear of hunger had been greater than her fear of AIDS. Even she had niggling suspicions about the man she loved, and his farm. Hadn't the promise of security been an initial attraction? Was Melody right in saying, 'Blame the economy for forcing ...'

She thought of all the many Zimbabwean women flouting socially and lawfully acceptable norms to fend for their children. Women wilfully shackling themselves to unsuitable men, because life offered nothing better; or so they'd concluded. She thought of all the women who yearned for some kind of freedom; women who were too afraid to seek it out, or embrace it. Chaminuka would definitely have wept for the daughters of Zimbabwe. Yes, that beast called 'the economy' had a lot to answer for. Something burned deep within her. Maybe working with the disadvantaged was where her calling lay. She recognised that she had choices, and determined to make them wisely.

CHAPTER 9

Katy sat in her kitchen with a cup of tea. Over the previous few days, both her husband and daughter had enquired after Onai. Replying simply that she was doing her best to help, had seemed inadequate, and Katy felt slightly uneasy. Gari had a reputation for womanising and violence, and she was well aware that both could kill her friend. She really needed to make a concerted effort to persuade Onai to leave her husband, if her conscience was to remain clear. She knew the conversation would be difficult, as it had always been in the past. Onai was very prickly and defensive about her marriage. Who could blame her? But Katy was her best friend, and she made a firm decision to try and break through her friend's defensiveness. Sipping her tea, she did not look forward to the encounter.

And, indeed, when she raised the subject, on their way back from the market, Onai was annoyed and resentful. 'This is not the time to be discussing my marriage,' she said coldly. She increased her pace, weaving through the crowds, driven by anger and frustration against her friend. What options did she have? Her *pata-patas* pounded the dusty road, raising more dust, a fine layer already covered her legs.

'There will never be a good time, Onai. We haven't had a chance to sit down together since you came from hospital, and yesterday you turned down an invitation to come to my house for a chat. This is the time that we have. Suitable it may not be, but we must talk … You have to leave Gari. I care about you. What do you think this is doing to me, *sahwira*? What do you think it's doing to your children?' Katy asked patiently, adjusting the box of vegetables on her head. She was as determined as she was patient.

'I've told you before. Leave my children out of this,' Onai snapped. She was tired. It had been a long day. Did Katy not realise that she worried about her situation every single day, but could see no way out other than to stay with Gari? If she left, he would never pay maintenance. She'd be even worse off. 'And where do you propose I should take my children? Huh? Have you gone that far with your plans to rearrange my life?' Her voice rose. People turned to look at them.

Katy touched her on the arm. 'Slow down, *sahwira*, I'm out of breath. No, I'm not making any plans to rearrange your life. But if you leave Gari, we can think of a way to take care of your children. I promise, I'll be there to help you.'

Onai shook Katy's hand from her arm and said frostily, 'I keep telling you, it's not as simple as you make it sound.'

A disembodied tyre appeared from nowhere, and ricocheted into Katy, faltering on its precarious journey, and landing in a dry flowerbed by the roadside. With an annoyed click of the tongue, Katy dusted down her dress; then stared at the little boy who'd sprung forwards to retrieve the tyre. He glanced briefly at her, his eyes round with fear.

She shouted, *'Iwe mwana iwe!* What do you think you're doing?' The child did not answer. He disappeared into the house opposite, as fast as his short, chubby legs could carry him. Katy placed her box on the ground and made as if to follow him, but Onai pulled her back and said, 'Let's go home. It's not worth the trouble.'

Katy sighed and picked up her box. 'Yes, of course, you're right. *Saka, nyaya yedu* ... but what do you want me to do for you Onai? I'm really worried ...'

'Nothing!' She pursed her lips defiantly.

They walked on in uncomfortable silence, then lingered by Katy's gate. 'It is a bit cold today. Why don't you come in for a cup of tea, *sahwira?'* She was cross with herself, perhaps she'd chosen the wrong time to broach this difficult subject, but no time was a good time.

'No,' Onai replied turning away, so that Katy would not see the tears in her eyes. She hated it when they had disagreements; that the arguments were mostly about her marriage made her feel worse. Turning to Katy, she held out her hand, then dropped it to her side. Her voice shook, 'I'm sorry for being abrupt with you, Katy. I know you care, but please understand, I can't leave Gari. I just can't. I will see you tomorrow. I have to get home ... the children must be back from school by now.'

Katy nodded sadly. 'See you tomorrow. Any time you want a cup of tea … I still have sugar.'

The thought of tea with sugar was tempting, but Onai waved good-bye. She wanted to be alone; she needed time to think, she told herself, although thinking would not change a thing. Hadn't she been thinking of nothing else, all these years? She was so tired of thinking; she was tired of everything. Life had always been a struggle, but no single year had been as hard as 2005 was fast becoming.

≈≈≈

As she approached her gate, Onai caught up with her neighbours, Hondo and his wife. The man's real name was Mr Ngozo but everyone called him Hondo because he'd fought in the war of liberation. His war-veteran status had earned him respect in their community, and his warm personality had endeared him to many. A big, muscular man, Hondo was pushing a cart full of luggage; his small wife had an out-sized satchel on her back. They stopped and exchanged greetings with Onai.

She said, 'I didn't know that you were away. I came by several times to thank you for mending my door, but the boys didn't tell me that you'd travelled.'

Hondo chuckled, slightly short of breath. Fine drops of perspiration lay on his brow. 'I gave them strict orders not to tell anyone that we'd gone away. With all these burglaries, it's not safe for people to know that there are no adults at home. Had you been at home when we left, I would have asked you to keep an eye on the boys as well. Perhaps they've been going to school unwashed and in dirty uniforms!'

'I'm sure they're fine. Peter passed by to pick up Fari on his way to school this morning. I must say he looked very smart,' Onai commented and looked inquisitively at their luggage: all the bags and boxes crammed onto the pushcart. Curiosity got the better of her, and she asked as they walked up the road together, 'Are you coming from *kumusha?*'

'No, from South Africa. We went to buy some goods for resale … anything to raise a bit of money. Otherwise, we won't be able to pay school fees for our children next term,' Mrs Ngozo explained, adjusting the heavy satchel on her back. Onai nodded. She still hadn't worked out how she would raise school fees for her three. Most of the time, she didn't even want to think about it. But she would have to face reality soon.

Mrs Ngozo looked at her closely and said, 'You have nice, thick hair Mai Ruva, though it could do with a bit of straightening.' Onai laughed and shook her head. 'I've brought quite a few relaxing kits. You must come and buy the Dark and Lovely one,' her neighbour added insistently.

Onai said she might, but she knew she wouldn't. Hair-care was pure extravagance. There was just no need for it. She observed the friendly couple with growing envy. They looked and worked like a solid team. At that moment, their obvious unity made her feel the inadequacies in her own marriage more acutely. What had gone wrong? Why couldn't she and Gari be like this? She wished he hadn't refused her permission to apply for a passport. Raising money for school fees did not have to be so difficult. With a passport she could simply go to South Africa to buy goods for resale. She would simply have joined Katy on one of her rare trips across the border.

≈≈≈

On arriving home, she found Sheila loitering by the gate with a young woman. The girl was short and light-skinned, her face open and friendly, her smile as radiant as her yellow floral dress.

Onai noted that Sheila looked happier. Her customary aura of sadness appeared to have lifted. Her skin had a faint glow, and in the past week, her bursts of nocturnal coughing had grown less. She looked … alive. 'Mai Ruva, meet my friend Chenai,' she said to Onai.

The older woman greeted the girl politely. She was really in no mood to stand around chatting to Sheila's friends. She had escaped from Katy and still wanted to be alone with her thoughts.

Sheila said, 'We've been working together at Union Avenue flea market but Chenai got a job at Simba Stores in Parktown two weeks ago.'

Chenai giggled. *'Asi chii nhai Sheila?* Is that a job? I spend my days dusting shelves and checking that everything is priced correctly. At the rate prices keep going up, my hands are now sore from changing price tags every few days … no, make that every few hours!' With peals of laughter, she spread out her supposedly sore hands: they were delicate and feminine with strikingly varnished red finger-nails.

Sheila smiled indulgently at her friend. 'At least you have a job to go to! My employer wants to fire me from the flea market because I have a cough! Maybe she thinks I have TB. Have you ever heard of such a thing?' She laughed hard as if she had made several jokes in quick succession. Her friend joined in. Onai stood there uncomfortably, failing to identify anything worthy of such laughter, and feeling increasingly uneasy in the company of the two young women.

Sheila's laughter stopped abruptly. She faced Onai and said, 'Chenai was just telling me that they had a delivery of sugar and cooking oil late today at Simba Stores. They're going to be selling it tomorrow. I've enough for myself. Why don't you send the girls to queue in the morning?'

Sugar? Cooking oil? Onai turned to Chenai with growing interest and found herself warming to the smiling girl. She peered at her. 'Really? Thank you for letting me know. I need both. Ruva can see to the market stall tomorrow. I will go to Parktown myself. Thank you, Sheila. Thank you, Chenai.' She turned to enter her house, leaving the two younger women still hovering by the gate, their conversation punctuated by more laughter.

The children hadn't arrived back from school. She wondered why, then she remembered. It was the day for inter-school matches. She felt a stab of remorse for not taking an afternoon off. She should have gone to watch Rita playing netball. But Rita would understand. She always did, unlike Ruva, who had been a noisy, attention-seeking baby and had grown into an equally demanding child. Now, at the cusp of womanhood, she was only a little better. But maybe that wasn't such a bad thing, Onai thought. Life was not kind to weak women and Ruva had the makings of a strong one. Unlike herself, Ruva was bound to do well.

In the kitchen, she uncovered a bowl and inspected the sugar beans that she'd soaked in water that morning. Now soft and engorged, they would be easy to cook. Boiled beans and sadza would be a welcome change from their usual fare of boiled cabbage and sadza. The children would be pleased. One of these days, I'll buy rice and chicken for them, she thought decisively as she switched on the two-plate stove and prepared to start cooking.

After a while, the front door creaked open. 'Mum, your *mukwasha* is here!' Ruva's voice called out.

'Who?' Onai shouted back, not sure whom she meant, but happy that her children were back.

'Rita's husband is here. Mawaya. I think he has come to collect his wife,' Ruva called out again, her voice loud and belligerent, obviously spoiling for a fight with her sister.

'Shut up, Ruva,' Rita responded crossly to sounds of a scuffle. Onai smiled to herself. Rita had earned herself the unenviable status of being called Mawaya's wife: she made sure he never left empty-handed if her mother was not home when he came begging.

'It's Mawaya, Mum! Rita's husband!' Fari sounded as if he was enjoying himself.

'Shut up, Fari!' Rita ordered, close to tears.

'Children, children, behave yourselves,' Onai scolded as she walked into the sitting room. The girls immediately stopped grappling with one another. She glanced outside, and sure enough Mawaya was hovering nervously by the door.

'*Maswera sei ambuya?*' he grinned awkwardly. 'Anything for me today?' He clapped his hands politely, as he always did.

Onai looked at him. He pulled at her heartstrings. No human being deserved to live a life begging for food on the streets, competing with stray dogs. It was such acute debasement of a man's dignity; of anyone's dignity.

A smile, which always seemed incongruous under the circumstances, split Mawaya's face. For one dizzy, illusory second, she saw past the rags. The beggar possessed surprisingly white teeth and generous, almost feminine lips. His were not the teeth of a homeless beggar. I must be going mad, she thought at once, wondering to what levels of indecency she was sinking. Is this what growing estrangement from my husband is doing to me? Admiring a man? And a beggar, of all men?

She dragged her thoughts forcefully back to the matter at hand and gave him a positive answer. '*Chaizvo mukwasha.* I do have something for you.'

Ruva opened her mouth as if to protest. Onai shook her head and walked into the kitchen. She returned with a wrapped-up lump of cold sadza, left over from the previous night. 'Here is a little sadza. I'm sorry I have nothing to go with it.'

The sincerity of Mawaya's gratitude was almost painful to behold. 'Sadza! Thank you, *ambuya.*' He clapped vigorously and ambled off, unwrapping the package with eager hands. Within the few minutes that it took him to reach the gate, he was sinking his teeth into the lump of cold, stiff porridge.

Onai's husband arrived just as Mawaya left. A heaviness immediately descended upon the house. The children stopped chattering and hurriedly greeted him.

'What was that man doing here?' Gari sounded furious. Onai hesitated, unease gripping her. This was not supposed to happen, certainly not in front of the children. Why couldn't he have returned as usual, long after they had gone to bed? It was not right for them to witness his rages. Almost as if they'd picked up a silent signal, the children sidled into the kitchen.

'I said, what was that man doing here?' Gari angrily asked Onai again.

'*Maswera sei baba va*Ruva? How was your day at work?' his wife made a vain attempt to deflect the looming argument. Her heart thumped, its sound filled her ears; her body prickled with apprehension.

Gari pointed an accusing finger at her. 'Don't play games with me, Mai Ruva. What was that man doing here?'

'He was asking for food. I gave him some leftovers.'

'Asking for food? And you let him into our home? Are these not the scum who burgled my house a week ago?' His voice shook with anger, and he raised his arm as if to strike her. Onai cowered and looked away, expecting blows. None came. She turned back to look at her husband, surprised. His arm had dropped to his side.

Within that moment of unexpected relief, she discovered the

courage to spring to Mawaya's defence. 'He didn't come in, he only stood by the door. I don't think he's the one who burgled the house. He's a harmless …'

'Shut up! What do you know about him being harmless? Is he your boyfriend, then? Feeding beggars with my food! Am I Father Christmas? You complain about groceries, yet you give away my food to beggars! How dare you?' He raised his arm again.

Onai's fear swiftly and surprisingly transformed itself to anger. She decided to stare bravely at him, silently daring him to hit her. She was overcome by an impulse to shout back and tell him that the food she had given away was not his. He hadn't bought any maize meal in almost a year, yet he still expected to eat! The words of anger did not make their way past her lips. The sheer effort of restraining her rage and humiliation seemed to stop her tongue, almost choking her. Gari scowled and sat down.

Silently, on trembling legs, she returned to the kitchen to finish making supper. Her children immediately asked for permission to go to *maiguru* Katy's house to watch *Studio 263*. She allowed them to do so. It was better to have them out of the way. The sight of his children was like a catalyst, which fuelled Gari's anger. If it wasn't her, it was them.

When she finished cooking, she placed food for them both on the table. He threw one painfully brief, dismissive look at the plateful of beans that she had taken such care to prepare, shoving it aside without a word. Out of his trouser pocket, he took a packet of biltong and made a great ceremony of laying the pieces of dried meat on a plate, almost as if he was counting them out.

While Onai ate sadza and beans, her husband noisily chewed biltong and sadza. The silence between them was suffocating. She cast covert glances at the plate of dried meat, hoping that he would at least offer her a small piece. But of course he didn't. Her mouth watered. So great was her craving that as she ate more of the beans, they seemed to acquire the flavour of biltong. Slowly, the ache of longing receded. At the end of her meal, she took a long drink of water.

≈≈≈

Faith pushed her books aside and switched off the desk lamp. It was eight o'clock, just the right time to take a break from studying. Her head felt tight from three hours of concentration. Preparing for exams was always stressful, accompanied as it was by headaches, loss of appetite, and a nervous tingling in her stomach.

She wondered if Tom's plane had landed. He should have arrived in the morning, but he still hadn't rung. Another quick call to his mobile went straight to voice-mail. She let the recorded message play right through to the end; filling her head with his deep baritone voice. It was the closest she could get to him; she missed him terribly.

She stared at her face in the mirror above the sink and groaned quietly. Tension was taking its toll. Her forehead was spotted with pimples. Vanity made her wonder what Tom would think. She wanted to look her best for him. Always. She stared at her face again and resisted an urge to squeeze the bigger blackheads. Squeezing would only leave dark marks that not even the best shade of Black Opal foundation would conceal, and would take months to fade. She wished she had smooth, clear skin like *mainini* Onai's. It was obviously wasted on her. She didn't seem to care about her appearance at all. The luxury of natural beauty!

Faith squeezed out the residue of toothpaste from a badly twisted tube. As she brushed her teeth, she thought of Melody, still running around with Chanda. She'd seen them together earlier that evening. Chanda had been charm itself, but it had seemed so affected, so pretentious. He was a middle-aged man trying with ludicrous desperation to act the part of a young man. What disappointed Faith most was that Melody had looked so at ease with him. Their previous discussion had yielded nothing. Faith sighed and rinsed out her mouth with tap water.

Suddenly, a soft knock sounded on the door – three sets of sequential beats, the code that she shared with Tom. She opened the door and flew into his arms.

'I'm so happy you're back! I was worried. How are you? When did you arrive? Why didn't you phone?' She shot the barrage of questions at him without waiting for an answer.

He laughed, 'Slow down, Faith, I'm not a machine! Too many questions, too quickly! We landed three hours ago. Sorry for not ringing earlier, I had to go home first. The flight was delayed for five hours at Gatwick ... something to do with fuel. Ridiculous isn't it? The long arm of poverty is stretching all the way to London! And then, as if to add insult to injury, our direct flight became an indirect flight.'

'*Sei?*'

'Well, we made a detour via the DRC. A VIP had to be dropped off there. I must say I wasn't surprised, though it has never happened to me before. But it was annoying to say the least. If ever there is a next time, I'm switching airlines. Anyway, I'm finally here. All in one piece.' He laughed, clearly happy to see her, then he transferred a lightweight bag from his shoulder to her bed. 'For you, my sweet.' She moved to open the bag, but he pulled her into his arms and dropped onto the bed, sitting her on his lap.

'Not now, *mudiwa*. You can do that when I leave. Just talk to me. I've missed you, you know. Surely, that parcel cannot be more important than me,' he teased and snuggled his head against her neck.

'Of course not!' Faith retorted. She put her arms around him and asked, 'So how were your meetings?'

Tom explained that they'd gone better than he'd anticipated but the final outcome had been disappointing.

'Why?' Faith asked, with a stir of discouragement.

'They're no longer very keen to go into a joint venture because of the economic situation in Zimbabwe, plus the difficulties of accessing and handling foreign currency.'

'Oh, I'm so sorry,' Faith said, feeling his disappointment. She knew how much effort he'd put into developing costly catalogues and carrying out market research. Out of the three possible companies, Blooms.com had been his best bet.

'How about the maize? Since you harvested so much last year, can't you export some of it, and earn foreign currency that way?' she suggested helpfully.

He grinned. 'When the country is starving? Do you ever read the paper, Faith?'

She shrugged. 'Big *No.* I guess I've become too sceptical. Nothing you read seems to be true.'

'But you must read the paper,' Tom said firmly. 'You have to know what's going on around you. Haven't they taught you in Law School that as a lawyer you'll need to be well-informed about current affairs?'

'But I don't want to read the paper, because …'

He raised his hand. 'No. That doesn't matter at all. I'm sure you're discerning enough to sift what you read. Paradoxically, nowadays, you get so much more out of reading everything than not reading anything. Be selective, my dear. Anyway, back to maize … exporting it is illegal; I'm surprised you didn't know. Maize has to be sold to the Grain Marketing Board; national reserves, and all that. I'm just holding out for better prices, but I doubt they'll go up much, if at all. In fact, I think I'll be forced to sell very soon, settling for a loss, which considering everything else, is all a load of …'

She gently placed a hand over his mouth, 'No swearing in my presence.'

He laughed. 'Sorry, *mudiwa*. About UK, there is still a little hope I think. The director of Blooms suggested we have another chat early next year. I don't think he'd say this if it meant nothing at all. I'm quite happy to wait. In the long run, it will be worth it. Like when I get married to you.' His eyes danced.

'You're so arrogant! Who says I want to marry you?' she exclaimed, pleased all the same.

'I do,' Tom said with great confidence. Faith couldn't stop smiling. Getting married to Tom wouldn't be bad at all, as long as the timing was right.

'Let's drive to Vic Falls tomorrow, sweetheart. We'll be back by Monday,' he suddenly suggested, snaking his arm round her waist.

'That sounds great. I've never been there. But I have a mock exam next Friday. And my revision lectures …' Her initial enthusiasm faded as she remembered all that she'd set herself to do.

He interrupted, 'Think of it this way. You'll only miss one lecture on Monday, if we set out early tomorrow morning. Please, Faith? I've a surprise for you, you know.'

'What?'

'If I tell you now, it won't be a surprise, you funny girl. But I promise you, it's going to be wonderful,' he answered mysteriously. He pulled her up and close to him, wrapping his arms tightly around her, swaying in a slow simulated dance.

'And diesel for such a long trip?' She groped for another possible impediment. She really needed to study.

'Leave that to me, *mudiwa*. Am I not the man? Please say yes,' he said, looking into her eyes.

Her feeble resolve crumbled and her knees went weak. 'OK, OK, don't suffocate me.' She wriggled in his arms, making a pretence of struggling to breathe. 'I'll come with you, but on one condition,' her voice held an inflection of happiness like music.

'Anything for you, my dear … if I could give you the sun, I would …' Tom's eyes danced. Faith almost believed him.

'I don't want the sun. I'd melt. A few stars will do for me, thank you.'

'A few stars it is then, *Mambokadzi*. I just need a few days to work out how to harvest them from the great sky above.'

She collapsed giggling. 'Stop it, stop it, Tom. Fine, I'll come with you, but only if Emily comes too.' She hadn't seen Emily recently, and if her mother asked, a chaperone would be a good thing. But if Emily wasn't busy at the hospital, she was always chasing one locum job or the other.

Tom released her from his arms and laughed in his infectious manner.

Faith interposed, *'Iwe,* what's so funny? I like Emily and I think it'd be great to invite her!'

'Good luck,' he replied. 'My sister has no time for such foolishness as a weekend break. 'Remember! She's a doctor!' As if that explained everything.

'So?'

'Well, show me a few fun-loving doctors who can distance themselves from their work. They don't exist, Faith. Emily and I are a different species, I'm afraid.' He gave a mercurial smile. 'During my time at varsity, I couldn't stand medical students. Books and more books, was all they talked about; seasoned, of course, with grisly stuff about

94

dissecting cadavers and the like. Give me a beer-guzzling, nose-picking UBA any time. That's my comfort zone!'

'You're joking!' Faith exclaimed.

'Definitely not. I was a most faithful, devoted UBA. I spent my days and most nights at the Students Union, diligently consuming Bollingers or Castle and ogling pretty girls!'

'But you hardly drink!' she laughed. 'Can't you be serious for a minute? Please? I think we should invite Emily, if only to save her from herself!' She glanced at her watch. It was almost nine o'clock. 'Do you think she's still awake?'

'When I got home, mum said she was still at the hospital, so yes, I think she's still up.' he replied.

Faith rang Emily's mobile. As it turned out, Tom was right. There seemed to be no room for frivolity in Emily's life. 'I'm leaving Harare at five in the morning. I'm off to Nyanga for an AIDS workshop. Let's try lunch at Avondale next week. Sorry, Faith. Bye.' Her voice was brisk and businesslike, without the faintest hint of regret despite her 'apology'. She merely sounded as if she was in a great hurry.

'Don't worry about Emily. I want you all to myself, anyway,' Tom said 'I'll see you at seven o'clock tomorrow, *mudiwa*. I'm so tired, I don't know how I'll get to Darwendale tonight.'

Faith felt her heart plummet. 'It's late. Why don't you just sleep in Mount Pleasant?' she asked him.

'I need to attend to a few things at the farm before we leave tomorrow, and I want us to set off early. So may I please have your kind permission to go tonight, Madam?' He was teasing her again.

She smiled, wondering when she would feel brave enough to ask that question about the farm, the one question that would certainly anger him. She wasn't afraid of Tom. Her reluctance came out of a fear that he would only confirm what to her was a foregone conclusion. This would be sure to play havoc with her conscience, and that would be life-long – if they got married. The thought made her heart flutter again.

Foolish woman, she reflected later, I'm no better than Melody. One moment I want a career, independence, to do something for the community, something for women, and the next, I'm weak-kneed at the thought of marriage.

Tom's surprise had better be good, if she was going to lose so much time. She would have to make up for it next week.

≈≈≈

The children were asleep and Gari had retired to the bedroom. Onai sat on her sofa and half-heartedly tried to mend the trousers of Fari's uniform. She surmised that if she sat up long enough, he would fall into a deep sleep, and not bother her when she went to bed. There would be no heated arguments about condoms. Even better, there would be no progression to fumbling about with the slippery sheaths. Best of all, Gari would not assault her tonight.

She inspected the pair of trousers again and wondered if she should just throw them away; the bottom had huge holes on either side. Both knees were threadbare. In just a matter of weeks, they too would be gaping holes. She sighed, admitting to herself that a patched uniform was better than nothing. She wouldn't throw the trousers away. No, she'd stick to her original plan and patch up the holes.

She carefully cut pieces of fabric from Fari's older uniform that no amount of patchwork could restore. Slowly, she stitched on the patches, thinking how much easier and faster the job would have been if Gari had not smashed her sewing machine. A blaze of anger rose within her, but it subsided as fast as it had arisen. Time was a great teacher. She was learning that being angry with Gari was pointless. It only ate away at her, filling her with bitterness, and sometimes self-loathing, because staying with Gari was a conscious choice. She had to take the consequences.

After she'd finished with the trousers, she started making adjustments to the dress that Katy had given to her. It was almost new and she liked its colour, pale-blue. A little while later, the neighbourhood dogs started barking. The clamour continued in fits and starts. *Matsotsi* were probably out again. This time she did not feel any anxiety because Gari was at home. Tonight, the responsibility of protecting the children and the home would not fall to her. His presence made her feel almost cared for and sheltered. She turned up the stereo to drown out the noise of barking. Steve Makoni's voice rose, singing the touching, melancholic *Handiende*. An abused woman was making a vow that she would not leave her marriage. She would stay for the sake of her children. Onai's resolve strengthened. She felt less isolated. There were probably others out there who shared her views. Steve Makoni would not have written a random, meaningless song. She listened attentively to Radio Two playing all the yester-year greats from Marshall Munnhumumwe, James Chimombe, Leonard Dembo and of course Tuku. She revelled in sweet nostalgia for those years, remembering a time when life had held such promise, when there had been so much to look forward to.

A full two hours later, her task was completed. She crept into bed as soundlessly as possible and lay as far as she could away from her husband. For what seemed forever, his loud snores kept her awake. She listened resentfully, tossing and turning. Finally, exhaustion triumphed and eased her gently into the land of dreams where life did not hurt so much.

CHAPTER 10

Saturday was a perfect day for the drive to Victoria Falls. The morning was cold but sunny. The weather forecast had promised a warm day. Tom picked Faith from Swinton Hall at seven o'clock. Some students, both male and female, threw glances in their direction. Faith sensed envy in their looks. She clung possessively to Tom's arm as they walked to the car park. She felt pride at being the woman by his side. She placed her small bag at the back, noting that there were fuel containers next to his bag. What if they had an accident? Everything would go up in flames. Worse, they could be burned to death! She pushed the thought from her mind. They were not the first people to travel with containers of fuel in their car.

'We have to stop by the supermarket to pick up some drinks. We'll go to Simba's shop in Parktown. I asked him to reserve some Coca Cola for us.'

'OK. Parktown it is, then,' Faith replied as she clambered into the Nissan. She waved at Melody who was walking up the small incline towards the library. She felt a twinge of guilt for abandoning her books.

'I still can't believe Emily would choose to go to an HIV workshop instead of coming with us. She attended a similar workshop only recently,' she complained, still feeling slighted that Emily had turned down the invitation.

'*Ndi*Emily *iyeye*. These things are close to her heart. I wouldn't worry if I were you. Did I tell you she now does voluntary work for Kushinga Women's Project on Thursday afternoons? I have a feeling my sister is on a big mission to save the world, and save the world she will,' Tom said lightly, as he reversed out of the parking lot, obviously not bothered. 'Besides I want you to myself, and I'm not sure that you need Emily's protection!' He laughed.

But Faith was pre-occupied. If Emily had links with Kushinga, she might just be the person to help my *mainini*, Mai Ruva. 'I wonder if she could help my mother's closest friend,' she said aloud, 'that's if I can drag her to the centre.'

Tom threw her a quizzical glance. 'Faith, people who need help don't have to be dragged anywhere. They actively look for it,' he said reasonably.

She retorted, still pre-occupied, 'That's easy for you to say. What do you know about being a poor woman? You're a rich man!'

'Sometimes, I get the strangest feeling that both you and Emily would prefer me to be a woman,' he muttered. 'Unless you want me to find you petrol, take you out to dinner or drive you to the Falls!' Faith laughed.

As Tom turned off the main road into the shopping centre, he swerved to avoid cars that were lined up in a petrol queue, and protruding quite dangerously into the road. He turned left into the parking space next to Simba's shop.

'*Maiwe, maiwe!* Just look at those crowds. I wonder what they are waiting for today,' Tom said, as they looked at the throng outside the supermarket.

As he parked the car, Faith observed a long queue of mostly women and children standing listlessly in the morning chill. It meandered from an auxiliary side-entrance and along the length of the building, to disappear abruptly around the corner. Amazingly, she spotted a few smiles here and there. Some women sat on a patch of dry grass next to the parking lot, evidently already tired. Maybe they'd been there since the crack of dawn. Riot police stood strategically by as if they were expecting chaos, whatever the crowd was waiting for.

Tom grinned, 'In Zimbabwe, it's not only death and taxes which are certainties. You can add queues and riot police to the list!' Faith refused to be drawn. Not long ago, she had had to queue for her mother, and she remembered the endless, boring hours, the anxiety that the product would run out by the time it was your turn, and the anger you felt when someone jumped the queue, as touts did all the time.

Together, they by-passed the long, patient queue, making their way to the rear and then slunk into the shop through a back entrance normally used by staff. They did not expect to be questioned, because Tom was the shop-owner's friend.

Faith felt guilty. All at once, the Coca Cola that had been reserved for them seemed trivial and superfluous when the majority of people were going without basics. These people were spending hours just waiting and waiting, without any assurance that they would get whatever they were waiting for. And here she was, strolling into the shop with Tom to pick up Coca Cola of all things! It was so wasteful. She battled briefly with her conscience, then decided to enjoy herself. Guilt was a wasteful emotion in its own way.

The cans had been put aside in six-pack cartons, all ready for collection. Tom placed them in a cooler bag while she paid. It took her several long minutes to count out the twenty-thousand-dollar bearer cheques and confirm the total amount of five hundred thousand. She inclined her head towards the side entrance and asked the till operator, 'What are they waiting for?'

'We're going to be selling sugar and cooking oil shortly.' Then, dropping his voice into a hoarse whisper, he said, '*Sisi*, do you want some? I can get you two kilograms of sugar, if you give me four hundred and fifty thousand dollars. Or two litres of cooking oil for seven hundred thousand. It won't take long. If you wait for me at the back of the shop I can arrange a deal for you very quickly. *Hazvidi hope*.'

'No thanks,' Faith said abruptly. She registered his disappointment. Of course, the real prices were nowhere near that. The man just wanted to make money. Well, she would not be exploited. She walked over to Tom and they sauntered out of the shop, this time through the front entrance, carrying the cooler bag between them and smiling at some funny remark that Tom had made. The mass of people swayed, still waiting with the practised patience of Zimbabweans.

With a start, Faith spotted her mother's friend. *Mainini* Onai was standing in the queue with her daughter. Faith wanted to stop and greet them, but her legs felt as if they were being propelled forwards by an invisible force. At that moment, and in Tom's company, she felt too embarrassed to acknowledge Onai and Rita as being a part of her life.

She stared at them, then averted her gaze as she passed to the opposite side, trying desperately to avoid meeting *mainini* Onai's eyes. She noticed that Rita was barefoot. Her legs and feet were covered in a layer of red dust. Her *mainini* wore a pair of faded Bata canvas shoes; a little toe on either side stuck out of each shoe through a conspicuous hole. And their clothes … Faith guiltily ceased her examination and then, because she could not resist it, threw them a backward glance.

Thankfully, *mainini* Onai didn't seem to have noticed her. She was listening with rapt attention to something that Rita was saying, smiling broadly and gesturing emphatically with her hands. Faith was struck by how Rita was growing to look very like her mother: beautiful too … with a loveliness that overcame her shabby dress.

As they stopped by the car, there was a sudden uproar of voices. Faith turned. The crowd had surged forwards and a scuffle had begun at the side entrance. Riot police immediately moved in to subdue them. Faith spotted Onai and Rita untangling themselves from the chaos and running away. The confusion was spreading fast towards the car park.

Tom grabbed her arm and thrust her into the car. 'Let's get away from here.' He ran round the car, clambered into the driver's seat, started the engine and drove off at great speed.

Nothing would stop them from going to Victoria Falls.

≈≈≈

Early in the morning, Nzou and the dealer stood in a parking space just outside the carport of his home. The police driver sat in the Santana. Nzou did not want him to overhear the conversation. As usual, his wife had not come out of the house. He did not want her involved either. He was in a bad mood. He felt cheated. The dealer who routinely smuggled electrical goods across the border for him was obviously becoming greedier. Initially, he had promised clearance without duty. The arrangement had worked perfectly for several months, but recently, the man had taken to randomly surprising him with extra charges. How uncomplicated it would have been if he could cross the border with the goods himself! But for now he had to let somebody else take the heat at Beitbridge, especially when his promotion was so close.

The wiry little man whined, 'Ask anyone, *shefu*. It's getting harder each day to pass through, especially with electrical goods. My friend was off sick, so I had no choice except to pay duty.'

Nzou clicked his tongue. 'I'm tired of it all. If you keep doing this, I will find somebody else to deal with,' he snapped.

The threat found its mark. The little man shuffled nervously on his feet and whined again, 'Aah, *shefu*. I'm sorry. I promise, next time I will communicate better with my good friend at customs.'

Nzou did not answer. He still felt angry and cheated. Bitterly, he handed over five thousand US dollars to the man and inspected the factory receipts. His police driver came out to transfer boxes from the dealer's truck to the Santana. The dealer apologised again; Nzou nodded silently. He had to send a message. The man drove off in a hurry.

'It's not very far to Kwekwe. I want this car back before nightfall. No diversions to Zhombe or wherever it was that you were seen last time.'

The driver looked pained. He pulled at the peak of his cap and hovered. 'Yes?' Nzou asked impatiently.

'Diesel, *shefu*. The fuel is low,' he mumbled sullenly.

'Why are you telling me this now, when I told you a week ago that you'd be going to Kwekwe? Don't we have fuel at central station? Just get it from there,' Nzou said. His dog frisked excitedly around him. He nudged it away with his right leg.

The man stroked his beard uneasily. 'Yes, diesel is there, but I think I've gone there too often. Remember, we got fuel when we went to Chipinge two weeks ago, and again when we went to Kwekwe last week. They want to know why I keep coming for diesel when you mostly use the Mazda. The man who questioned me is the one on duty today.'

Nzou was annoyed. 'Who is this person who dares to question my fuel requirements?'

'The new guy … Muronda,' the driver mumbled.

Nzou went into his house to phone the depot. In a very brief conversation, he instructed Muronda to fill his driver's tank with diesel.

Returning to the waiting Santana, he ordered, 'Out with the goods!' The driver looked at him in confusion. Nzou felt exasperated. Why was this man so slow? It was surprising that he could drive a car at all.

'I said, unload the car. If people are going to question you, then I'd rather you didn't take my goods to central station,' he explained less brusquely.

'But that means I will have to drive back all the way here and …'

Nzou interrupted, with renewed impatience, 'Exactly!'

Wearily, the man unloaded the boxes and drove off.

Nzou sighed. He'd run out of all his foreign currency, thanks to that greedy dealer. While he guarded his boxes and waited for the driver to return, he used his mobile phone to contact three more dealers. No one had anything to offer him. As a last resort, he called Mrs Nguni. Her husband was still away and he hated having to deal with a woman.

≈≈≈

Katy was about to make a later start than usual, when the phone rang. She heard Mr Nzou's voice when she picked up the receiver. A dealer at heart, she was pleased to hear from him. His voice was friendly. 'How are you Mrs Nguni? I'm just calling to find out if you have any US dollars that I could buy from you?'

Her heart leapt. 'I'm well, thank you, Mr Nzou. Actually, I don't have US today, but I should have a thousand tomorrow,' she replied. John had just phoned to tell her that he would be sending over one of his colleagues with some money. The timing was perfect. She detected pleasure in Mr Nzou's response, 'That's very good. If possible, I would like to collect it at around six tomorrow evening.'

The deal was sealed at a rate of twenty-five thousand Zim dollars to the US. Katy smiled. It would be one of her easiest transactions. Despite her contentment, vague doubts remained. How had John managed to amass so much money so quickly? He's a man, she comforted herself, he knows how to make a good deal.

As she packed her box in preparation for the market, she wondered if Onai, who'd gone to Parktown at daybreak to join a food queue, had succeeded in obtaining anything.

Reaching Parktown at the crack of dawn had been a futile exercise. Chaos and disorder had aborted sales of much needed basics: sugar, oil, soap. Riot police had ordered everyone away from the queues and the premises. Onai and Rita walked home empty-handed and dejected. On the fringes of Mbare, the older woman suddenly decided to walk to the city centre. She did not want anything particular, but she felt the desire for an hour alone to briefly experience an existence that was not related to anyone else; to exist unfettered, not as a mother or a wife, but simply as herself.

Turning to Rita, she said, 'It's still only half-past nine. I think I'll walk to town.'

'Why, *Amai*?' Rita asked, a look of surprise on her face.

Onai invented a reason. 'I just want to see if I can get a bar of Key soap from OK. We're down to the last bar. You go and help Ruva at the market.'

Her daughter looked at her anxiously. 'Can't I come with you?' she asked plaintively. 'I don't want to go to the market today.'

Onai shook her head. 'No, the walk is too long for you and I have no money for a combi.'

'I can walk too, *Amai*,' she pleaded.

'No. I think it's better if you go home. If Ruva is delayed at the market, you can start cooking. I might be late getting back, especially if I have to join any queues in town,' she said decisively. Rita nodded reluctantly and they parted.

Onai turned and walked all the way to town. From Speke Avenue, she wandered towards First Street. She let herself idle, her thoughts remarkably far away from soap or groceries. She passed a beggar just outside Clicks. Blind, he was singing a Bob Marley song to a guitar that he played beautifully. But generosity seemed to have deserted the city centre that Saturday morning. The plate by his side was empty. Onai had nothing to spare for him either, but that did not stop her from enjoying his singing.

Reminiscence engulfed her. Her brothers had loved Bob Marley. She remembered how as teenagers in Chiwundura they had enjoyed listening to his music on their decrepit, battery-powered *wairosi*. How their mother had complained about them wasting money on batteries! But how, despite her complaints, she always had money to spare for them. When had pleasure departed from life?

Opposite Clicks, a shirtless man was walking on a tight-rope, and then swinging around in impossible balancing acts. Fascinated crowds pressed closer. Onai joined the spectators. Out of the corner of her eye, she spotted a smartly dressed young man dipping his hand into an unsuspecting woman's handbag as she was engrossed in the lively street entertainment. The man's eyes locked with Onai's. Silently, he raised an index finger and passed it across his neck. Onai got the message. Speaking out was not safe. When had it ever been?

She left hurriedly and moved on past Intermarket Bank, surprised to see the long queue weaving its way out of the bank and down the street. She remembered Katy mentioning a fresh crisis of cash shortages. Glancing further up towards CABS, she spotted an even longer queue. She was no stranger to queuing, but the sight of bank queues was more than a little unfamiliar. Her CABS account had long been closed due to insufficient funds. Her current bank was made up of three Lactogen tins which inhabited a spot under her bed, safe, she hoped, from Gari's eyes. She recorded her deposits and withdrawals meticulously in a little pocket book. Worthless money. Very soon she would have to get a bigger 'bank'. Possibly a large box that she would hide in the girls' room.

As a child, she'd exchanged stories with friends about how in Zambia one needed to fill a wheelbarrow with money, just to be able to buy a loaf of bread. Though she'd never been there, she'd repeatedly told the story as if it was something she knew to be fact. It certainly felt as if they were heading in the same direction and would soon fill wheelbarrows with money, just to buy a loaf of bread. She recalled with mild amusement how during the 2003 cash shortages she had to bribe a bank teller with ten thousand dollars, just so that he could reserve the cash that she needed from her own account. Katy had laughingly said, *'kutenga mari yako'*. How dire the situation had been then! They had never imagined it could actually get worse.

The beautiful clothes in Topics Store caught her eye as she walked on along First Street. When she thought of buying anything, she thought of Power Sales, Number 1 Stores, or the Chinese shops, nicknamed *zhing-zhang* stores. The latter, which had sprung up all over the place, carried affordable clothes and shoes, but ones which invariably fell apart in record time. So with that jaunty sarcasm with which the poor have always kept their end up, their products were referred to as *zhing-zhangs*, because they never lasted more than a couple of weeks.

Onai hung around at the entrance to Topics, briefly intimidated by the atmosphere of sophistication within the shop, and by the sweet perfume that wafted towards the entrance.

She gathered her courage and entered, thinking to herself, 'Who knows, I might shop here one day. Even better, I might even make clothes for them.' Dreams, dreams. Almost immediately, a smartly dressed young woman materialised by her side, 'How can I help you today, Madam?' she asked briskly.

Madam? Onai was momentarily speechless. 'I'm just looking,' she mumbled at last.

The assistant nodded, but kept behind her, ostensibly in readiness to help. Onai had the distinct impression that this undue attention was not out of genuine consideration, but because the girl regarded her as a potential shoplifter. So close was she, that Onai could feel her breath on the back of her neck. She felt crowded. A heightened awareness of her own shabby clothes overwhelmed her. Her desire to admire the beautiful garments withered under the assistant's hawk-like scrutiny. She walked out indignantly, head held high. They could keep their shop if they didn't think she was good enough to shop there.

She continued her languid stroll up First Street. A street child grabbed a bottle of Coca Cola from another pedestrian. It all happened so swiftly that the woman could do nothing but stare speechlessly after the grubby child. Shaken, Onai walked into OK supermarket. A quick inspection of the shelves told her that there was no Key bar soap: neither was there cooking oil, sugar, flour, bread or any other essential items that shortages had made so elusive. Basics were supposed to be readily available.

There was no other reason to linger in town, but Onai had no desire to make her way back to Mbare. She savoured the time alone, and was refreshed by the break from her day-to-day life. She decided to walk up to Africa Unity Square to admire the jacaranda trees whose beauty she'd always loved, and to browse among the art and craftwork stalls on the periphery of the square. Arriving, she was disappointed to find no flowering trees, no purple blooms forming a thick carpet on the road. In fact, the majestic trees were almost without leaves. How could she have forgotten that it was winter? She knew the trees only bloomed in summer.

She found her eyes unwillingly drawn to artificial flower arrangements for funerals on a stall directly in front of her. Two crucifix arrangements in blue caught her eye. They were identical to the ones she'd laid on the graves of her brothers. Abruptly, she turned away and walked home, overcome by the power of memory.

≈≈≈

Tom had driven fast, and they had arrived at Victoria Falls in the late afternoon. They checked into the Elephant Hills Hotel. Room 601, immaculately furnished in heavy oak, was inviting; the ethnic print curtains softly echoing the warm colours of the room. Shafts of sunlight poured through the large windows. Looking through them, Faith just caught sight of the shimmering waters of the Zambezi.

Just before sunset, they drove to the waterfalls, buying highly priced disposable raincoats at the entrance. Tom insisted they would need them. Nothing had prepared Faith for the grandeur of the Falls. Untamed, the Zambezi River whirled and cascaded in huge waves over the edge of the great rocky drop, before billowing back in thick clouds high in the air. Faith felt minute droplets cascading over her face.

Tom shouted above the roaring noise. 'Let's see as much as we can before it gets dark. If you mind getting wet, we may have to avoid some of the views. The spray can get quite heavy further up.'

Faith was too excited to bother about getting wet. 'Oh, I don't mind, as long as we can keep the camera dry,' she answered, clicking away: pictures of the Falls and of Tom against the stupendous background of water and the glowing sky. Working their way up, they took more photographs from different angles, stopping now and then to kiss and laugh in the light spray. By the time they left, they were well and truly soaked, despite their raincoats.

Later, they danced Saturday night away at the Kingdom Hotel's night club. Faith was impressed by the beautiful layout of both hotels, but remarked on the surprisingly low number of guests. 'Isn't it peak season then?' she asked Tom.

'Not quite. It's winter after all. But you're right. Hotel occupancy is generally low nowadays. That's Zimbabwe for you, my dear. Our negative publicity has suffocated tourism. Besides, most Zimbabweans can't afford to stay in these hotels. They tend to take day trips or stay in the smaller lodges and camping sites which are more affordable.'

Faith nodded. 'It's a shame. This is such a beautiful place. People don't know what they're missing!'

'I don't think it's about people not knowing what they're missing. It's just a Zimbabwean problem. The Falls themselves continue to attract tourists, but many now prefer to view them from Livingstone on the Zambian side. Business is thriving there, while many of our lodges and hotels are almost empty. South African tour operators are also including trips to the Falls in their tour packages. In essence, this means that fewer and fewer visitors view them from our side. And for many tourists, only here for a day, whether they're in Zambia or think they're still in South Africa, is neither here nor there.'

'What a shame,' Faith murmured.

'Well, my dear, as in any business where the stakes are high, the tourist industry is cut-throat! Whoever offers the best all-round package and delivers the goods, stands to get the best deal! We have problems, sure, but it doesn't always help when we assume that every visitor is rich, or deserves to be fleeced, simply because they come from Europe. Do you remember my friend, Dick? He saved for years to make a trip to Zimbabwe.' Faith nodded, her mind drifting. It was too beautiful an evening to have a serious discussion about the highs and lows of tourism.

The young couple drove companionably back to their hotel for the night.

≈≈≈

The two lovers started off Sunday with an early morning swim. Initially reluctant, Faith was surprised to discover that the water was not cold, just pleasantly cool. After breakfast, they opted for a safari run by one of the local companies. Later, Tom said they should return to the Falls for one last look before driving home. As they stood against the background of thundering water and smoking mist, he held her close to him and said seriously, 'I love you, Faith. I'd like us to get married later this year.'

Faith looked up at Tom, who was smiling down at her. She was conscious of feeling a moment of pure joy. She was loved, wanted and accepted for herself. She knew too much about Tom not to be aware that he could have his pick of marriage partners.

'Yes,' she said, quietly. How could it be otherwise? She smiled with happiness, 'but give me just a little time to think …'

'What is there to *think* about? We love each other.' Tom sounded more puzzled than hurt.

'Yes, Tom. We do. And I do want to be your wife … but …'

'No buts please,' Tom smiled. 'I've driven you all the way to the most beautiful place in the world to ask you to marry me, and now you're saying *but* …' He laughed and Faith laughed with him.

'Just a few days,' she said, 'Not to say "No," but to think … my parents, my exams, my career …'

Tom smiled indulgently. 'Have I ever said that you shouldn't work, shouldn't have a career? Why, I want a wife who is independent, and having a lawyer to advise me as well …'

'But sure, if you want a few days, you have a few days. I'll be waiting.' He was confident of her answer. He swept away her worries. He kissed her. 'Don't worry, little one. There's nothing to worry about. Nothing that can't be sorted out.'

Faith felt a huge surge of love for him. How many men would be so kind, so understanding? That he loved her, and wanted to marry her, seemed overwhelming. For some time, she had felt sure that their relationship had developed into something more permanent, but now that Tom had actually proposed, she felt both overjoyed and not quite ready. She looked up at him and smiled. Holding hands, they walked slowly back to the hotel.

≈≈≈

Tom didn't like talking very much when he was driving, preferring to listen to music and focus on the road. So Faith had plenty of time to think.

She wasn't sure about her father, but she knew her mother would have reservations about Tom. That he was eleven years older than herself, that he was rich, and they were not. Katy would be suspicious and proud. Her father was more a man of the world. He would be proud too, but he would be proud that such a man wanted to marry his daughter. Nonetheless, he was the one who had really encouraged her to work for a while before thinking of settling down. And she wanted to help them with the stand in Mabelreign. They had invested so much in her education. Now it was her turn to help them. Would Tom really allow her to work? His sister Emily was an independent woman; Tom was not afraid of independence in women, indeed he liked it. She would talk to him, as soon as the exams were over, just to make sure there were no misunderstandings.

She knew Tom had had a previous relationship, well at least one that had mattered very much to him; and though she had none of the details, she knew that he felt responsible for it going badly wrong. Now she was the one to benefit. Closing her eyes, she allowed herself to think that all would be well.

The car swerved to avoid a large pothole and she opened her eyes. Bush, veldt, nothing but dry land and trees. Did she want to live on a farm? Farm? All her submerged suspicions came back. With an impulsive abruptness that surprised and frightened her, she said, 'Tom, did that farmer have to die so you could get the farm?'

She saw him stiffen with surprise. His hands tightened on the wheel. He gave a short laugh, more like a bark. He said slowly, his eyes focused on the road, 'Oh my God! I was right all along, then. I've always detected your reluctance to accompany me to the farm, or even to talk about it. What do you think I am, Faith? If it's been bothering you, why haven't you said something before?'

Faith's face burned with embarrassment. He was right, she should have asked him before. But anxiety had held her back. She hadn't even intended to ask the question now. It had just burst out, like a child, she thought angrily. She mumbled, 'I thought I should know, especially if we are going to get married.'

He said quietly. 'I bought the farm, Faith. I have the title deeds at home. I'll show them to you as soon as we get to Harare. This is the wrong time to be discussing this. Do you mind?' His face was fixed stonily on the road.

'I'm sorry. I didn't mean to offend you.' Faith knew she sounded stupid. Now she had spoiled everything, on this day of all days. She stared out of the window, twisting her hands in her lap.

Tom switched off the music, his favourite track, Oliver Mtukudzi's *Bvuma*, and they drove on in silence.

CHAPTER 11

The next Saturday started off like any other winter's day in Mbare. The sky was a clear blue, with not a single cloud in sight. The air was still and chilly, and continued to be so for most of the day. Later on in the afternoon, a few police cars went round announcing by public address system that people living in shacks had to pull down their homes by the following day. Informal traders and unregistered small-scale businesses were also required to dismantle their premises and close shop, with immediate effect. The same applied to stall-holders at all market places.

The cars delivered their message while in motion. Only a handful of people heard the crackling bursts of transmission through to completion. Out of habit and characteristic apathy, even fewer bothered to listen. What was the point?

Onai did not hear the message at all. She was busy celebrating a notable achievement with her children, in their small kitchen. Their day spent waiting for bread and sugar at Mbare shopping centre had been very rewarding. They had left the food queues with two litres of cooking oil, four whole loaves of bread and two kilograms of sugar.

Rita was the most excited. Onai realised that her daughter had not stopped smiling from the moment she reached the front end of the long queue where the shop attendant had stood with a forbidding and slightly superior air. Rita had proudly received a two kilogram bag of refined sugar and a loaf of bread in exchange for two hundred and twenty-five thousand dollars. Onai and Ruva had each managed to buy a loaf of bread. Miraculously, Fari had secured two litres of cooking oil. As an afterthought, Onai had asked Rita to go into the supermarket to get some Sun Jam. She had found only one bottle on the shelf, the last. It had been their lucky day.

Onai looked again at her daughter's animated face and felt her heart swell with a sense of maternal protectiveness. Rita was too childlike and unworldly for her age. With those feminine curves already beginning to complement an attractively innocent face, she would have to watch her very carefully.

She wished her younger daughter was more like Ruva, who often displayed a maturity beyond her years. Ruva's fierce independence, which occasionally bordered on aggression was quite reassuring. As a woman, such a quality would take her far in a society which in Onai's opinion was unfairly dominated by men. She smiled at her children's happy faces and said regretfully, 'We don't know when we will be lucky enough to get more sugar. Let's try and make this packet last for at least two months. Only one teaspoon of sugar per cup of tea, and nobody is allowed more than one cup at a time.'

The happy smile vanished from Rita's face. She looked wounded. 'Only one cup at a time, and one spoon of sugar for a whole cup! That's so unfair. We've been queuing for hours!'

Onai understood her feelings completely. Her children had lived for such a long time without having any bread, or sugar with their tea. For weeks on end, breakfast had consisted of black, sugarless tea and salted maize-meal porridge. She knew that Rita hated porridge with a passion. She watched her wiping the table with excessive vigour, her mood dampened by what must have sounded like unreasonable sugar restrictions.

She decided that she couldn't afford to be lenient where groceries were concerned. Times like these called for stringent rules. Knowing her daughter's weakness for all things sweet, a weakness so like her own, she wagged an admonishing finger at Rita's doleful face, 'And no dipping wet fingers into the sugar. If I find as much as a single grain in your bedding, there will be no more sugar for you, dear girl,' she said in her firmest voice.

'Aaah, *Amai!*' Rita protested loudly against the injustice of her mother's accusation. Her siblings burst out laughing, amused by her mortified indignation.

Ruva frowned and asked her mother, 'Aren't you tired of this kind of life, Mum? Why can't we just walk into the shops and buy what we need, like we used to? Are we always going to be queuing for food and never getting enough?'

Onai looked up at Ruva's troubled face. Her heart lurched. Poverty had robbed her children of the carefree, fun-filled existence that all children deserved. Even she had enjoyed as much, despite growing up in the rural areas. Life had been good; even very good.

She forced a smile and answered her daughter, 'What a question, Ruva! Of course, things will be all right soon enough, though I really can't say when.'

Ruva insisted, 'But *Amai*, how can you be so sure that things will get better? What if they get worse?'

Rita shrugged, rolling her eyes dramatically, unimpressed by her sister's persistent questions.

Fari had a brainwave. 'I'll ask my maths teacher. She's very clever. She knows the nine-times table. I think she knows everything,' he said seriously.

Ruva snapped at him, her voice filled with scorn. 'Your teacher knows nothing about when things will change … if ever they do. I bet she doesn't know anything beyond your silly nine-times table!'

Onai was ready to tell Ruva off, but Fari didn't look bothered. 'Maybe *baba* knows. I will ask him, if he comes in before I go to sleep,' he said hopefully.

Ruva cackled sarcastically, 'Ask who? Do we ever see him? Fari, you are so stupid! I'm really getting worried about you.'

'Ruva, I will not have such language in this house. What an awful thing to say to your brother. And I will not have you making those comments about your father.' Onai reprimanded her daughter sharply. Ruva shrugged with all the nonchalance of female adolescence, a sage expression on her young face. Picking up the newly acquired bottle of Sun Jam, she scrutinised it with narrowed eyes, before passing a damning verdict. 'This bottle-top is very dusty. I bet it's been sitting on the shelf for months. I'm sure the jam inside is rotten. *Kuora chaiko!*'

Onai felt a wave of disappointment wash over her. She'd been so looking forward to having the bright red Sun Jam spread thickly on a slice of bread. She'd wanted so much to fulfil her craving for the sticky, satisfyingly saccharine Sun Jam … a childish craving, but nonetheless one of those little things which made life sweeter.

'What do you mean it's rotten? Aren't we going to eat the jam now?' Fari demanded crossly. He thumped the table hard. It vibrated.

'Too fussy. Too fussy and too bossy,' Rita muttered mutinously, obviously sharing her brother's fears.

'It's rotten. It must be. Just look how dusty this bottle is. People don't have money to buy jam, that's why! *Amai*. Don't let Rita choose the groceries ever again. She'll only get mouldy stuff. There's too much rotten food on the shelves these days.' As Ruva gave her expert opinion, she looked at Rita with disapproval. 'I bet this bottle is filled with bacteria,' she concluded forcefully.

Rita and Fari glared at her. 'What's bacteria?' Fari asked anxiously.

Ruva shrugged. 'Why must I explain everything? Ask your clever teacher.'

Onai ordered her to open the bottle before they all died of curiosity. Ruva did so with some difficulty, screwing up her face in disgust. A horrible smell pervaded the small kitchen. Onai grabbed the offensive item and inspected its contents. Her heart sank at the sight of the moulding, rusted jam. Firmly, she placed the container in a plastic bag and threw it into the outside bin. Ruva was duly criticised by her disappointed siblings for spoiling everything as usual.

Through the din that her children were making, Onai heard the indistinct boom of the mobile public address system and sighed inwardly. The council was probably announcing more water cuts. Possibly electricity cuts, too – or was it ZESA who was supposed to announce those? Maybe it was the council issuing another stern warning about the mountains of uncollected refuse, which frustrated home-owners had dumped unceremoniously in open spaces. She smiled to herself at the absurdity of it all. What difference did their announcements make anyway? Countless times, Mbare had been plunged into darkness with not so much as a warning; countless times, they had woken up to dry taps, and her unhappy children had slouched off to school hungry and unwashed.

Rubbish had gone uncollected for several weeks now because of the fuel shortages. Dumping was no longer an issue about irresponsible alternatives, but the only way to avoid swamping backyards with malodorous garbage and swarms of persistent flies. She frowned again. There was no point in paying attention to any of the announcements. They really didn't make any difference to anything.

≈≈≈

Katy did not hear the police announcements, either. She was at the university complex in Mount Pleasant with her daughter. She had received a rare invitation to lunch in the senior common room. Mother and daughter had an important matter to discuss. Faith had just told her about their recent trip to the Falls; that Tom had proposed and that she had more or less accepted. He intended to start the traditional marriage proceedings sometime before the end of the year.

Her daughter seemed happy but Katy had mixed feelings. 'That's not what I had in mind for you, *mwanangu*. It's always better for a woman to graduate and experience some independence, giving herself time to mature before marriage. What's the hurry? If he loves you, he will wait. Besides, your father and I have been looking forward to you helping us build our new home once you start working. Why not wait a bit?'

Her mother's sensible words echoed her own feelings. Faith placed her fork down and answered quietly, 'I'll talk to Tom again because I understand what you mean. I've been thinking about all these things; I'd also like to be single and independent for a bit. Waiting for another year seems a sensible idea to me, too.'

Katy nodded, then gently asked her daughter, 'Are you sure he's the right person for you, my dear?' Thinking of an earlier discussion with Onai about Tom and his farm, she felt a mild uneasiness. Would Faith be all right with this man?

'Of course he's the right person, *Amai*. I'm sure you'll like him once you get to know him. I only have to convince him to wait a while,' Faith replied contentedly, her eyes bright. 'After all, we've known each other for almost two years now. I know he's older than me, and we're very different in some ways, but it's as if these differences create a balance. I'm not sure I'd want to marry a man who was just like me. It would be so boring.' Her eyes twinkled.

116

Katy was relieved to hear that Faith had given the matter so much consideration. She would bide her time. If Tom was serious, she would begin to know him better through the marriage negotiations. It had worried her that there was such an obvious discrepancy in wealth between the two families, but now that Tom had proposed, she felt this anxiety lift somewhat. Clearly he was not a snob; and neither had he simply been using Faith, taking advantage of her youth and vulnerability, something which seemed to happen far too often these days.

'I'm very happy for you, Faith,' Katy smiled, remembering her own happiness when John had proposed. She'd definitely made the right choice for herself. She hoped her daughter would be just as fortunate. University had changed Faith from a gawky, insecure schoolgirl to a confident young woman. Katy was proud of her. She would be able to hold her own and a year's independence would increase her maturity.

So they sat in the SCR and ate their lunch, unaware of the public announcements being made in Mbare. Smiling with mutual satisfaction, they discussed Faith's future possibilities with gratified caution.

As she made her way home, Katy felt a lightness and peace that she had not felt for a long time. John, she reflected, would be pleased too, as long as the Sibandas did everything according to custom. He was very proud of his daughter, and would see her moving up in the world as natural and right. If Faith could work for a year first, and help them with their stand, that would be an additional blessing. By the time of the wedding, maybe they'd even be living in Mabelreign. Faith had seemed fairly confident that Tom did not want a wife who was just going to sit at home. She reflected on how traditions changed, and not always for the worse.

She also wondered what Onai would say when she told her. She'd have to be tactful, not only because good fortune was not always best discussed when someone was having such a hard time, but because her friend had seemed to know more about Tom's background than she did herself; at least more than had appeared in the press.

≈≈≈

Gloria jerked violently and held her head up as she lay in Gari's arms.

Gari was jolted from his sated doze, 'What is it?' he murmured, before he heard the sharp, crackling bursts of a public address system. He did not register any distinct words.

'I heard something. They're going to destroy the shacks!' Gloria said in a panic. She was distinctly alarmed, immediately fearful of looming homelessness. Gari didn't really take in what she was saying. He just wanted to sleep. He closed his eyes and dreamily continued stroking her. She pushed him aside in a sudden show of aggression. 'That's it! I told you I need somewhere decent to stay. Did you hear that? They said the shacks are being destroyed. You have to do something now! There are a lot of men out there who would do anything for me, you know.' The threat was not subtle.

Gari tweaked the disorderly strands of his shaggy beard worriedly. 'Of course, I will. Soon, my dear. But I think you heard wrong. Nothing is going to happen to your shack.'

'Forget the shack! I just want you to rent a house for me,' she replied petulantly.

Gari suddenly felt tired. Gloria's demands were escalating. This was not what he expected of their relationship. He attempted to whisper loving reassurances into her ear. 'I'll get you a new place once we're married. You're not about to become homeless. I really think you heard wrong, *mudiwa*.'

Gloria was adamant. 'I did not! I know what I heard. The shacks are going to be destroyed. Just be quiet and listen!'

They listened. They heard nothing, except the high-pitched sound of voices singing a popular children's song from the street. '*Shiri yakanaka unoendepi? Huya, huya, huya titambe. Ndiri kuenda kumakore ...*' The song about a beautiful bird was spectacularly out of tune. The mobile public address system had passed.

Gloria persisted heatedly, 'I know what I heard. You will have to get me a room. Today.'

Gari tried to pacify her. He knew what would work: hints about marriage had changed the balance of their relationship significantly. It was a change which he found very agreeable. There was a lot of pleasure to be gained from promising wedlock. He whispered tenderly, 'We're going to get married soon. I just need a couple of weeks to get rid of Onai. Please. I promise. Nothing but the best will do for you, my beautiful Gloria.'

She latched on to his sweet promises and pulled him closer. Gloria had a strong, shapely back and Gari appreciated the enticing things which she did with it. He decided firmly that he would spend the night in her shack. The alternative was for him to go home, but there was nothing to gain from doing so. He stayed with Gloria. The public announcement was promptly forgotten.

≈≈≈

Most residents only caught snatches of the announcement, as they went about their daily business. What they heard, they received with concern, which rapidly switched to scepticism and amusement when they discussed the matter with their friends and family. There was no way any such thing would be allowed to happen, especially in Mbare; after all, the township was the bedrock of the informal employment sector, the largest in the whole country. It was also home to thousands.

In a few quarters, grossly distorted versions of the announcement were shared with rising tension and anxiety. Word was that the army would descend on Mbare with armoured cars and guns to shoot anyone who resisted the demolitions.

By evening, alarm and uncertainty had spread. A handful of people began packing their meagre belongings and prepared to dismantle their homes the following morning, fearful of breaking the law. Others looked on contemptuously, wondering aloud where this panicking lot hoped to go with their young children, when the nights were now so cold, so unforgiving.

That night, the Mbare population was more restless than ever. Twilight quickly turned to night, and darkness fell like a thick blanket. It brought with it a tangible sense of apprehension; an uncertainty that was as dark and oppressive as night itself. In the ominous silence, even the barking dogs were quiet. The night prowlers had stayed indoors to contemplate the bleakness of an uncertain future.

As it happened, by the time they went to bed both Onai and Katy had still heard nothing. The next morning, Mbare was back to its usual frenetic bustle. It was as if there had been no announcement at all. The reality brought by the new day was that they had to press on with their day-to-day business in order to survive.

CHAPTER 12

The door into the poky sitting room was ajar, allowing in bright shafts of wintry sunlight. The rays illuminated the room and picked a dazzling reflection off the cement floor, cold still from the unpleasant night chill of winter. Sitting on her tattered blue armchair behind the door, Onai held her head in her hands.

Her extremities were frozen and aching with the cold. Anxiety and lack of sleep certainly did her no favours. A headache was stealthily advancing behind her eyes. She saw stars and dark spots. Nausea held her on the brink of vomiting. Even though it was a long time since her last severe headache, she was certain that in no time at all the pain would escalate into a blinding crescendo. The symptoms were all there.

Her husband had not come home, again. Although this was the second time within the short space of a month that he had stayed away overnight, she felt a strong sense of foreboding without quite knowing why. Vaguely, she wondered if she should file a missing person's report at the police station. However, she lacked conviction that any of the officers would take her seriously. She could almost see the ugliness of their noisy amusement about how she was making a mountain out of a molehill. She could imagine their derisive dismissal. It wasn't as if Gari had been away from home for several days. It was only a single night, hardly worth getting oneself into a state of panic.

She pictured them telling her what she knew already. So many men spent nights away from home without telling their wives. It was a man's prerogative to run his household as he wished, with no allegiance to any rules, especially those dictated by a woman. Her husband was no exception. He was, after all, a man, no less so than the next.

But still, one could never be absolutely sure. Gari tended to return home in the early hours of morning; rarely did he stay out all night. She wondered if she should check the hospitals and mortuaries. He might have come to a violent, inebriated end. For a moment she felt horrified, covertly ashamed by the readiness with which she embraced the possibility of widowhood. In that transient moment, the darker side of her nature felt a glow of liberation. His death could not harm them.

Her forehead creased in concentration as, tired and over-anxious, her mind, almost obsessively, turned over a range of gruesome possibilities. Maybe he'd been run over by a car as he lurched home blind-drunk. Maybe he'd been mugged and left for dead, as sometimes happened to drunks staggering home from the beer halls. She tried to pull herself together. It was unlikely. Much more likely was a thought that she dared not entertain. She shoved it firmly to the back of her mind and in exasperation ran frozen fingers through her Afro.

Her head was throbbing and she was close to vomiting. She got up and went into the bedroom to look for some Paracetamol. Behind the door, lay a pile of Gari's dirty clothes. They reeked of cigarette smoke and stale body odour. She picked up the small Paracetamol container and rattled it close to her ear. Opening it, she was disappointed to find only a few pumpkin seeds that she had meant to plant when the rains came. She grimaced. There was no way she could go to the market with a migraine. She had to get some pain-killers, but where from?

Being Sunday, the clinic would be closed. The prices of everything in the nearest dispensary were greatly inflated. She could do without paying two hundred thousand dollars for a box of twelve tablets. Two hundred thousand dollars equated to the price of four loaves of bread. Buying Paracetamol would be an unjustified extravagance.

She sat down on the tatty armchair and gingerly placed a wet towel on her forehead. Its coolness had a mild, soothing effect. She glanced up at the Humpty Dumpty clock, annoyed at the plump, grinning face. There was nothing to smile about. She realised that she was already very behind schedule. It was well after nine o'clock. Trading at the market would have started, and she would have missed out on early morning sales, which tended to be brisk at weekends.

'Heyi, Onai,' a loud voice rudely interrupted her thoughts. She looked up with feigned pleasure, a wan smile on her face, and saw Maya, her larger-than-life neighbour blocking the doorway. The room immediately became darker. Her bulky, frame resting on its disproportionately thin legs,. looked as if she might topple over at any minute. Onai resisted an urge to stretch out her arms to catch her. But, of course, no such thing was about to happen.

'Good morning, Maya. How are you, and what brings you here so early?' She tried to hide her displeasure at this unsolicited imposition of such a large and unwelcome presence.

'Huh! Some welcome for a beloved friend! I've been in the rural areas for two weeks and that's all you can say?' Maya snorted with mock disbelief, then broke into unjustified peals of noisy laughter, her whole body one delighted mass of heaving flesh.

Onai hoped she would not make matters worse by having to run to the bathroom to vomit. She felt as if her head was being tightened by screws. Then, a familiar wave of irritation swept over her. Maya was a truly unsavoury character. She was the worst gossip in the neighbourhood. As sure as the sun rose and set, Maya would have detailed knowledge of one or another scandal. Maybe that was what being childless did to a woman. Maya's flagrant disregard for other people's privacy and the tenacity with which she spread rumours had culminated in several notable disasters in their small community. For that reason, she was unpopular among both men and women.

The only person who seemed to appreciate Maya was her timid husband, Mazai. He was something of a laughing stock, among the men, anyway. Who did not know that in Mazai's home Maya ruled the roost? Why, the other day he had been spotted doing the dishes at the outside sink. Doing the dishes! That alone spoke volumes about him, and paid fitting tribute to the woman he'd married. Onai sighed again. Just her luck to have Maya descend upon her so early in the morning, and on a day when she was feeling so grim.

'I'm just surprised that you are not at the market already, that's all. You usually beat us all to it,' Onai responded as best she could.

'*Iwe!* I just got back late last night! How can I be at there already? Anyway, forget the market, *shamwari*. There are more important issues. I simply had to see you. I have important news for you. But I must say you look terrible. What's wrong?' The self-satisfied expression on her face belied any real concern. Her ample bosom wobbled, a quivering mound of soft flesh. A restless fly floated around her head in a continuous circular motion. She waved an irritated hand but missed her target. The fly continued to hover just above her head. She clicked her tongue crossly.

'I have a terrible headache. The clinic is closed and I have no Paracetamol,' replied Onai, screwing up her eyes. The light hurt as the migraine slowly but remorselessly took possession of her head. She wished she could sink into oblivion ... anything just to relieve the pain.

Maya looked on dismissively. 'Listen, I came to tell you something. But tell me first, is your husband in? Are your children in?' she enquired, dropping her voice to an exaggerated whisper. She threw herself clumsily on the armchair opposite Onai, and it creaked pitifully under the massive assault. Onai felt a moment of panic ... her best chair was about to disintegrate right in front of her eyes.

Her alarmed gaze slid down to Maya's spindly legs, which the woman had stretched out on the cement floor, inadvertently kicking the table as she did so. Onai's box of fruit and vegetables, packed and ready for the market, vibrated dangerously. With surprising agility, Maya flung out a flabby arm and steadied the box.

Relieved that the vegetables had not fallen all over the floor, but puzzled by the questions, Onai took a deep breath and replied wearily, 'No, the children are not here. They left for church ages ago. Gari is not in, either.'

'Good,' Maya stated with obvious satisfaction. She continued, 'You have to answer this truthfully. If you found out that Mazai was having an affair, would you tell me?' She stared at Onai, her eyes shining and oddly expectant.

Onai frowned, and replied in a small guarded voice, 'I think so.'

'How about this,' Maya continued relentlessly, her face intense and lascivious, 'If I found out that Gari was having an affair, would you want to know?'

Onai felt beleaguered. She nodded mutely, silently praying, 'Please God, don't let her say what I think she's going to say.'

'I'm sorry to be the bearer of bad news, Onai,' Maya said with smug haste, looking far from being sorry. 'I'm sure, after all, that you must have suspected that something has been happening. Gari is having an affair with Gloria, that floozy who has been through so many men that she herself has lost count. Mazai told me so last night. The two lovers left the beer hall together. Mazai says they were all over one other,' she sighed with the complacency of complete gratification. Then, interlacing her chubby fingers and resting them on her enormous bosom, she looked at Onai's face intently, almost as if expecting to find a glimmer of appreciation.

Onai stared back at her in shock. A silent scream filled her head and another wave of nausea washed over her. Any other woman but Gloria, please! By Jo'burg Lines standards, Gloria was the most infamous of prostitutes. Once ensnared, no man had been able to resist her wiles. She discarded them only when she no longer had any use for them – usually after she'd spent all their money and wrecked their marriages.

Recently, one of her previous boyfriends had died of AIDS. The story doing the rounds was that Gloria was HIV positive. How on earth could Gari do this to her? How could he be so irresponsible? Onai was appalled at the enormity of the consequences.

Maya appeared oblivious of the effect her news was having on Onai. Fine droplets of saliva flew from her mouth, 'You know what men are like. Some of them are no better than dogs on heat! There's only one thing on their minds, day and night! I've always told you that you're too soft with Gari. Look at my Mazai. He enjoys his beer, yes, but he knows I will not tolerate any nonsense about other women. But your Gari is the limit! Throwing himself at that slut. Why, everyone knows she has AIDS and ...'

'May you kindly leave my house, please?' Onai interjected tersely, stopping Maya in mid-sentence. Her neighbour stared at her, astonished by such a deliberate display of ingratitude. The nostrils of her squat nose flared with fitting indignation.

'Get out now!' Onai said in a voice of steel.

'Hey, hey, I was ... I was only trying to be helpful,' Maya stammered, getting up and leaving in an unceremonious huff, banging the door loudly behind her. The sound reverberated through the quiet house, simultaneously drowning Onai's anger and intensifying her migraine.

Her rage ebbed, leaving her completely deflated. She got up, thought of going out, then changing her mind, slumped onto the chair, weeping.

It was all right to have unconfirmed fears and real concerns. It was even all right for Gari to assault her. What was not all right was to have her suspicions validated so graphically, and to have a real name and a real face thrust firmly into the picture. A beautiful face like Gloria's … Gloria who was quite likely to have AIDS …

The threat of HIV hung over her like a hangman's noose. There was no guarantee that Gari would not force himself upon her without a condom one of these days. She wondered if he had been using condoms with Gloria. The risk of infection was now very immediate and the thought of it terrified her. What would her children do without a mother? The thought led to renewed weeping.

For a moment, she felt a manic desire to run screaming through the streets to Gloria's shack at the top of Jo'burg Lines. Confronting her would be the one sure way of putting a stop to all this madness. Only one thought stopped her. Gari was probably still with her, if he'd really spent the night in her shack. No matter how upset she was, she could not risk provoking his wrath. Maybe they would spend the whole day closeted together. Or possibly go to the beer hall and drink the whole of Sunday away. What was she going to do? No realistic alternatives presented themselves. She felt a deep, almost hopeless, resignation. What could she do but accept whatever life pitched at her?

Her blurred gaze took in the box of fruit and vegetables: a pathetic sight that represented the loss of a day's earnings. There was no way she could go anywhere near the market, even if her migraine lifted. By now, Maya would have told everyone about her marital humiliation. The idea shook her. Perhaps they all knew already. Katy obviously did-n't, otherwise she would have used it as yet another reason why she should leave Gari.

Hurt and shame threatened to suffocate her. She found her rosary beads and held them in her hands above the pain in her chest. She closed her eyes and said a desperate prayer. Was she being punished for missing church on so many occasions … for being such a casual and occasional Christian? But, how could she have gone to church? The need to make a living for her children had been much greater than the desire to spend her Sunday mornings in prayer and worship. Somewhere along the line, the core of her faith had disintegrated. She could pinpoint the day when the process had begun: the day her twin brothers had died within hours of each other.

≈≈≈

There was no transport at the bus station. Not even a single emergency taxi was in sight. A few stranded commuters milled about anxiously. Maya decided to walk to the market. In any case, it was not that far. She balanced the large box of fruit on her head and clutched a small hand-bag with her right hand. Cursing under her breath, she hurried through the dusty streets of Mbare, still immensely offended. Her cheeks burned with humiliation at the way Onai had treated her. How dare she? Fury spurred her on. She walked with incredible speed for one so obviously overburdened and overweight.

Despite the cold weather, she was sweating and out of breath by the time she'd walked round the bus terminus and crossed over into the market-place. Not speaking to the other women whose stalls were close to hers, she prepared for the day's trading. She laid out the apples that she had brought from Nyanga in angry little rows, and rapidly counted out her change of $500 and $1000 notes. She tied up the larger denominations with an elastic band and buried them beneath her bosom. Almost all the other vendors had arrived and business appeared to be well under way. Immediately next to hers, Onai's stall looked conspicuously bare.

≈≈≈

Katy had slept late after quarrelling with John on the phone. She couldn't understand why he wasn't coming back home for his leave. It had never happened before. She woke up late and got to the market at the same time as Maya. She groaned inwardly when she saw her. So she was back! They'd had a good two weeks in her absence; a refreshing period free of malicious gossip. She noticed that Onai had not arrived and wondered why she was late. She'd been looking forward to telling her about Faith and Tom.

'Good morning Maya. How was your trip *kumusha*?' said Hannah, the gentle soul who owned the stall opposite Onai's. Her subdued expression appeared to match her shapeless brown dress.

'Good morning, Hannah,' Maya replied tersely, obviously upset about something. Pulling out a handkerchief from her pocket, she wiped a film of perspiration from her piqued face.

'Have you heard the news?' Hannah whined, obviously not for the first time, sounding on the brink of tears.

'What news?' Maya asked, her face lighting up with inquisitive enthusiasm. Katy looked on, wondering what this was all about. She hid a smile at Maya's avid curiosity. It was obvious that nothing was more fascinating to her than a little delectable gossip.

'Well, just something on the news today, I didn't quite get it because I was rushing out. Something about the police arresting people in market-places and confiscating their goods. I'm sure we'll be next,' replied Hannah, seemingly defeated at the prospect of this inevitable calamity.

'And why is that?' Maya asked impatiently. Katy's heart skipped a beat. Was this what Faith had been talking about? But Mr Nzou had assured her that it wouldn't happen. Had he lied to her?

Rhoda, a small, bird-like woman in a garish yellow print chipped in with a lengthy, eloquent speech. 'I'm surprised that you girls don't know about this. The police went round yesterday announcing something about a clean-up operation, which will involve closing some markets and demolishing shacks that are not in good condition. Of course, they were not talking about this market. Can you imagine the largest market in the country being shut down for no good reason? So everyone is here as usual. The proper clean-up operation is supposed to demolish shacks which are not suitable for people to live in, and to rid market places of illegal traders, criminals who deal in foreign currency.'

She felt very pleased at being the most well-informed, and turned to stare malevolently at Katy, before whispering something to Maya. The two of them burst out laughing.

Katy ignored them. She stood aloof and silent while confused conversation swirled around her about the imminent demolitions. She wondered whether she should believe what they were saying. And where was Onai?

Maya swept condescending eyes over the group of nervous women and declared, 'I don't think they'll close this market. We've been here for years and years. The council is well aware of our business.' Inclining her head in Katy's direction, she said sarcastically, 'I don't know about those who dabble in illegal foreign currency deals. Maybe that's who they're after.' There was a ripple of laughter.

Again Katy pretended that she had not heard. Indifference to barbed comments from these women always seemed to work. Eventually they grew bored and changed the topic to something more salacious. She bit her lower lip and wondered with growing unease why Onai was late. It was so unlike her. In the rest of the market, men and women stood in tense groups, nervously sharing the bad news.

Suddenly, bicycle tyres screeched to a halt in a cloud of dust. 'Good morning, ladies,' shouted Paul, the shoe-repair man who spent his days in a makeshift workshop just in front of the big Superstore, next to the market. He flashed a toothless smile, looking incredibly jovial. The bright red cap worn back to front was in marked contradiction to his advanced age.

From his neck hung a huge cross which proclaimed him as an elder in the new Bible Followers Church. He shot a cheerful, lisping stream of questions at them. 'Why are you still here? Haven't you heard the news? Haven't you heard that the police are out in full force?'

Katy, like the rest of the vendors, looked at him wordlessly, somehow comprehending but choosing the false security of denial and disbelief. Their self-appointed spokesperson, Maya, said nothing, staring at him blankly.

'Anyway, you have to remove your goods immediately because the police are out in a big way. As soon as I heard, I left church and came here. I have taken all my materials and shoes home. I might as well tell you that they have teargas canisters and thick baton sticks in case you want to try anything funny. Who knows if they don't have guns as well? Leave now while you can take your vegetables. If they find you here, they will confiscate your goods and goodness knows what else they are capable of …' Despite the urgency behind his lisp, he still managed to look as happy as he always did. Not even the bad news that he was sharing could wipe the toothless grin from his face.

Having more to hide than the rest of them, Katy gathered her stuff hastily and packed up her box in preparation to leave. Looking around furtively, she pulled a wad of South African rands from her pocket and tucked them into the box, just beneath a small mound of blameless tomatoes. She dropped her change accidentally and bent down to pick the fluttering bearer cheques. Maya's scornful gaze turned and rested on her, before shifting irately back to Paul.

'Grow up *va*Paurosi! Why do you have to spread alarm with false stories?' she asked him angrily. The women next to her hovered. They looked as if they would gladly comply with whatever she decided.

Paul shrugged and gave another one of his game but shockingly pink smiles. 'Well, it's up to you, ladies. But these guys really mean business! Don't say I didn't warn you. See you!' Waving, he rode off in another cloud of dust and impressive screech of tyres. Katy balanced her box on her head and hurried off. She had to find Onai.

≈≈≈

Just after Paul had left, a police truck filled with armed riot police arrived. They spread quickly and efficiently into the market to address the groups of traders.

A clean-shaven, suspiciously young policeman was apparently in charge; he might have been pulled out of a high-school class that very morning. Smiling politely at Maya and company, he said, 'Good morning, ladies. I'm afraid I have to ask you to leave. This area is not properly designated for your business. May you kindly remove your goods?'

Maya's voluminous dress billowed. She quickly rearranged the folds with agitated hands, and with nostrils flaring, she gave vent, 'Now: look here young man! You can't just …'

'With all due respect, madam, this is not an issue for discussion. If you have any grievances, or need to know where you can continue to trade, you have to go to the municipal offices to obtain a licence. You will be assigned a proper, hygienic place to conduct your business.' The policeman spoke calmly and confidently, unruffled by her regal display of anger. He sounded as if he was reciting a well-practised speech. 'We will be back in an hour or so. If you are still here, I'm afraid we won't be able to help you.' He swung a pair of handcuffs as if to emphasise the point.

A few other riot policemen in semi-military attire, armed with baton sticks and teargas canisters, preened and paraded their weaponry before the traders. Their shining black boots gleamed menacingly in the wintry sun. Handcuffs dangled carelessly from their waists, overt symbols of their supremacy. Their whole demeanour hinted at restrained savagery.

They did not speak, but their forbidding glares conferred great weight on the softly spoken words of their baby-faced colleague. Without much further ado, the grand, authoritative entourage sauntered back to the truck and drove off in thick swirls of dust, to issue further harsh warnings to other traders.

≈≈≈

Their worst fears for the day realised, the market stallholders had no choice but to do as they had been instructed. How would they make up the day's lost earnings? How would they survive until they were able to resume trading? These were the questions on everyone's lips. For the majority, the market had been their sole source of livelihood. It had been bad enough before, but this new calamity would remove their only means of supporting their families.

Maya felt offended and hopelessly out of control. She did not like this one bit. She had to get home quickly and listen to the news herself. Surely things such as this could not be allowed to happen. Someone, somewhere up there had probably made a massive blunder and would soon be apologising profusely for disrupting the smooth

131

pattern of her day at the market.

Hannah whimpered querulously, 'Where is Onai, *vasikana*? Someone ought to tell her about this.' She turned to Maya, 'Katy has gone. You're the only other person who lives near her, Maya. Could you pass by her house in case Katy doesn't?'

'No, I don't think so,' came the mean response. Hannah shook her head, bewildered.

'Well maybe she didn't come in because she has heard about this on the news,' Beady Eyes in a gaudy, floral print suggested helpfully, small eyes glinting. 'Onai would never miss a day at the market for no good reason. It seems she needs the money even more than the rest of us.'

'How wrong you are!' Maya said viciously under her breath as she packed her fruit back into the padded box. She longed to feed them the juicy news about Gari's affair, but this was not the moment; everyone was distracted, and she'd prefer a good audience. Loudly she continued, 'I really don't know. I can't pass by her house because I have to get home so I can listen to the news. 'She can stew in her own juice,' she thought, 'What do I care?'

All of a sudden, a brilliant thought struck her. What if they stood their ground? Nobody had a right to come and boss them around. She paused a moment and then announced loudly, 'I think those officers were bluffing. Who do they think they are? Let's stay here and see what they'll do. I would very much like to smash that boy's face in. The little upstart!' A few voices twittered in nervous amusement. A few more murmured in agreement and the affirmation swelled as Maya's stance won more widespread approval. What else, after all, could they do? Maya beamed proudly. This was more like it. She was back in control.

Beady Eyes enthused, 'I love running battles with the police. I'll never forget the thrill of overturning a police car during the 1998 food riots! I can assure you, it was great fun. You just have to make sure that you don't get killed!' A mood of hilarity took over, as empowered at the idea of challenging uniformed authority, excitement spread among them.

The notion of engaging in a bit of violence was suddenly quite appealing. It filled the restless crowd with ripples of unruly excitement. It would be the perfect outlet for all their anger and perennial frustration. A sizeable number of women and young men decided to participate.

≈≈≈

Mawaya stood in a queue in one of the terminus toilets. He needed a quick wash-down. The stench of human waste was overpowering, but he resolutely waited his turn at the sink. Just as he opened the tap, there was a burst of loud, angry voices, blaring hooters and the sound of running feet. He recognised the wail of a police siren. In alarm, he covered himself up and rushed out of the toilet to see a throng running from the market towards the shops.

'What's happening?' he asked a man who was pushing his way past him.

'Police,' the man said in an urgent voice. 'If you know what's good for you, just disappear. *Shayikwa!*' Mawaya could recognise danger when it confronted him. He turned hastily, only to find himself being pushed back towards the market. Riot police had appeared from the opposite direction, herding the crowds away from the shopping centre. A spate of looting had started. At the periphery of the market, he struggled to break free from the pandemonium.

The ground was a sea of burst, broken and crushed fruit and vegetables. He slipped on a banana peel and stumbled, grabbing at a woman in front of him. She screamed and lashed out. The child on her back cried pitifully. Rocks, fruits, vegetables and other objects flew in the air as angry people hit back at the police, who were assaulting them and launching tear-gas canisters into the air. Gasping for breath, Mawaya tore himself free, his eyes streaming.

Already, roads were being barricaded with boulders by irate residents and traders. It looked as if the police would be overpowered, being obviously outnumbered. Mawaya limped hurriedly towards Matapi Flats, shocked by the violence he'd just witnessed. The last time something like this had happened had been in 1998. Then, he had narrowly missed being run over by a car as he'd escaped from police who were indiscriminately shooting rubber bullets in the city centre. He abhorred violence in any form and wanted to get as far away as possible. He would try to make sense of the situation later. Beyond the stadium, he sat on the ground, leaning against a sagging fence. He wondered if the time had come for him to return home. Doubts about the purpose and logic of his stay on the streets of Mbare surfaced. Nothing could ever bring his wife back. Nothing. What was he doing amongst this madness, when he could be in the safety of his home, or his office? For the first time, he questioned his own sanity. Were they not right in calling him Mawaya?

≈≈≈

The market-place resembled a battleground, as the traders were caught up in a spate of violent protests and looting. The riot police threw teargas canisters into the crowds and beat down the protesters with sturdy baton sticks.

Beady Eyes found herself in handcuffs. She was led roughly to a waiting police car. Shocked realisation engulfed her. These were not the 1998 food riots. This was 2005, and her dream of a morning of fun had been brutally squashed. She would not be overturning a single police car. Instead, she would most likely have to serve time in jail.

A teargas canister landed at Maya's feet and dense fumes overcame her. Her eyes stung and tears flowed from her eyes. As she struggled blindly to get away, she received several hard blows to her head and chest. She gathered her flowing dress and ran from the blitz as fast as her large frame would allow.

Hannah thrashed about through the confused, panicky mass of people and screamed until she was hoarse. Her aching legs carried her from the scuffles and she collapsed in a ditch next to the bus terminus. Getting home would take her several hours.

By afternoon, more riot police had descended with a vengeance on the market. The people had to pay for daring to launch a counter-attack on police officers. There was no going back. Assistant Commissioner Nzou crawled past the market in a new, unmarked Mazda. He stopped the immaculate vehicle a safe distance away. Through large designer sunglasses, he regarded the chaos with cool detachment. 'Not bad for a day's work,' he thought, as he appraised the continuing clashes. 'Not bad at all.' Stalls and illegal structures were being pulled down or torched. Confiscated goods were being loaded into police trucks. The number of arrested criminals was rising. He wondered how much foreign currency had been confiscated … because if he played his cards right, he could profit hugely. All things said, the operation had gone smoothly. The country had to be rid of the crawling mass of maggots, all bent on destroying the economy. At the end of this exercise, the former 'sunshine city' status of Harare would surely be restored. This was the objective of the exercise. He wondered whether this would give rise to recommendations for a promotion. So far, Tsikamutanda's charm had done nothing for him, although he wore it around his waist everyday, as instructed.

CHAPTER 13

Katy hastened home, her mind heavy with a sense of premonition. She had to find out exactly what was happening, without any distortion or hearsay. As she hurried through the streets, she observed a general restlessness that had not been apparent earlier that morning. It seemed as if there were police officers everywhere and everyone seemed to be in a hurry to get somewhere fast. She collided full-on with a man, just as she was approaching Jo'burg Lines. The box on her head teetered. She grabbed it with both hands to stop it from toppling to the ground.

'Would you look where you are going!' She snapped angrily then recognised the offender. It was one of her lodgers. 'Why, it's you Themba! Are you trying to knock me down or what?' The flustered young man looked down in embarrassment.

He stared at his feet and mumbled, 'I'm so sorry Mrs Nguni. I was just coming to the market to get you. There are policemen at home and they would like to see you. *Izvozvi.*'

Panic gripped Katy. Her heart missed a beat. So she had been finally caught out! They must have found out about her foreign currency deals. Fear squeezed her heart in an icy grip. The risk had always existed, but she had never imagined the police would actually come after her. How had they found out? Could they have been informed by one of the women at the market, who were so plainly jealous of her? She wouldn't put it past Maya to do something like that.

Katy felt very frightened and alone. John would have known how to handle this situation. Why had he decided to cancel his leave at the last minute? Would the assistant commissioner come to her rescue? She thought of turning back and losing herself in the thick crowds of Mbare. They would never find her. She could change her name, shave her head and start wearing the flowing white robes of *mapositori*. She could gain weight, use a skin lightener or … she stopped herself. Who was she fooling? There was nowhere to run to.

'What do they want?' she asked Themba, feeling faint with trepidation.

'They're knocking down your shacks. We had to throw our belongings out into the open. They also want to see the plan for the main house. If the extension is not on the plan, they've said that they will knock down the extra rooms.'

For some reason, this sounded much worse than her original fears of being arrested. She stared at him doubtfully. 'You're joking. They can't do that.'

'But they can. They have already knocked down a lot of shacks and a few houses along the street, including that tuck-shop at the corner,' he responded miserably.

Katy was incredulous. She shook her head continuously; not willing to believe what she knew to be true. 'All right, let's go home. I have to see for myself what this is all about.'

Themba took her box and led the way as they hurried home. Along the road, they met more groups of anxious people carrying bags and transporting items of furniture in pushcarts. The sight unsettled Katy, but she could not stop to ask any of them what had happened or where they were going. She had to find out what was happening at her own house, first.

On arrival, she was shocked to find shards and splinters of wood and asbestos where her three shacks had been standing only that morning. The bulldozer was just reversing slowly back onto the road. It had flattened a portion of her fence and the flower-bed in its wake.

Police officers stood by her gate, giving an impression of being poised to pounce at any moment. Her lodgers and their families stood next to their belongings. They were visibly shaken. Two energetic toddlers jumped up and down on one of the beds. Their vigorous excitement caused piles of kitchen utensils to fall to the ground with a loud clatter. Their cross mother unsuccessfully tried to restrain them. Resounding slaps rang out, followed by a chorus of loud wailing, as the children clambered off the bed.

A short, swarthy policeman approached Katy. He looked confident and authoritative. 'How are you, Ma'am?' he asked off-handedly and went on without waiting for an answer. 'I understand you're the owner of this house here? As you can see, we've bulldozed down all your shacks.'

Katy noted that there was no hint of apology. But then, why should there be? Clearly, she was on the wrong side of the law. The man waited a moment, as if to let her absorb his report of an action so obvious. He continued, 'We announced yesterday that you should pull down your own shacks, because they're illegal, but you didn't do so. So we had no choice but to bulldoze them ourselves.'

Katy could only look at him in stunned confusion. A nerve twitched in her right cheek. So the women at the market had been right! Why had she not heard the announcement? Besides, Assistant Commissioner Nzou had given her his word that no demolitions would take place. She started, 'There must be a mistake. Mr Nzou, the assistant commissioner, he said … Mr Nzou …' she stammered helplessly. The police officer's eyes seemed to light up in anticipation of what she was about to divulge. Her voice weakened and she clammed her mouth shut. What was the point?

She looked around her again and wished John was by her side. She turned to the officer. 'But why? Where are all these people going to go? What about their property?'

He looked totally unconcerned. 'They can go wherever they came from … I really don't know. Maybe they will be resettled,' he said carelessly, shrugging his shoulders.

'But where? And when will that be?' Katy persisted with her questions, still feeling as if she was in a dream.

'Dear lady, don't take me to task, all right? I'm only doing my job. I should be asking the questions and you should be giving me answers. I see you have two extra rooms added on to the original house. Can I see your plan, please?' he asked her roughly, with sudden briskness.

Katy went miserably into her bedroom. She rummaged through John's drawers and found the required plan. She unfolded it, then handed it to the frowning man who, scrutinising it, gave a satisfied grunt.

'This is in order. You see, this is what it should be like. As long as you're doing what is required of you, there is no problem at all. OK gang! We're out of here,' he called out to his counterparts. 'Bastard!' Katy swore silently as she watched him and his entourage swaggering next door where the routine began all over again.

Feeling as if she'd been unwillingly conscripted into a terrible dream, Katy spent the rest of that morning helping her lodgers and neighbours to move their possessions to Tsiga Grounds, where displaced families were gathering to seek refuge and mark out their territories in the open space. It was a pathetic sight. By late afternoon she realised with guilt and regret that she had been so engrossed in her own crisis that she had completely forgotten about Onai.

≈≈≈

After Maya had left in a sulk, Onai decided to try and sleep off her headache and her misery. Mercifully, she sank into a deep, dreamless slumber. She slept so soundly that she did not hear her children when they returned from church, around one o'clock. Fari burst into her bedroom and woke her up. Her groggy mind could not make sense of what he was excitedly shouting about the police. Ruva called out from the sitting room to say she had to come outside quickly.

Just at that moment, she heard the deafening blare of a car horn, amidst the shouting of furious voices. Wondering anxiously what the uproar was all about, she walked unsteadily to the gate, where her children were standing. Sheila came out of her shack to join them. As they watched, a bulldozer rolled into view, followed closely by two trucks full of riot police. They stopped at Maya's house, at the corner of 50th Street.

Within minutes, her lodgers had started emptying their shacks and throwing out their belongings. There was a lot of shouting and angry gesticulation. Maya's voice rose above the rest, fuelled by rage. Her husband appeared to be cowering behind her, evidently not saying much. Anything else would have been a great surprise.

From where she stood, Onai could not make out what was being said, but she could tell that tempers were running high. After about half an hour of frenzied activity and heated exchanges, the bulldozer edged towards the empty shacks. Homes collapsed spectacularly under the massive assault. Everything was flattened; only a pathetic layer of wreckage remained. Curiosity got the better of Fari and Rita who sped excitedly towards the centre of confrontation without heeding their mother's angry calls to come back at once.

Onai frowned, trying desperately to make sense of what was happening. Sheila turned to her, her voice an agitated moan, 'I heard about this yesterday, but I didn't believe it. What am I going to do?'

Onai stared at her. 'What do you mean you heard about this. Why are they destroying those shacks?'

'You mean you don't know!' Sheila's tears stopped abruptly. She started laughing manically. 'You really don't know? Someone told me that the police went round announcing that the shacks should be destroyed. They also said something about the market being closed. My baby was fretful all of last night and I didn't get any sleep. I've been sleeping and haven't been out today, so I don't know what's happening out there. Didn't you go to the market today?'

Onai shook her head quietly, overwhelmed by this unexpected chain of events. She wondered why Katy had not bothered to warn her. What was going to become of her family? She could not even afford even a single day of lost business. Losing today's earnings was bad enough. If the market was closed, how would she survive further losses? And where was Gari? What a disastrous day this was turning out to be!

'Did you hear anything about this yesterday, Ruva?' she turned enquiringly to her daughter.

The girl shook her head, 'No. We just saw a lot of policemen everywhere, when we left the church.'

Sheila's troubled voice broke in, 'They're getting closer. I think I should empty my shack.'

Onai glanced across to the commotion at the house next to Maya's. She agreed in a flat monotone, 'You're right. I think they'll be here soon. We must empty your shack.'

Sheila strapped her agitated baby tightly to her back in a sudden show of bravery, and they began working mechanically. Outside, they heard more angry voices, running feet, the sound of crashing mortar and now and then, the distant sound of sirens. The atmosphere was saturated with fear, anger and uncertainty. While they had all yearned for change, this could not be further from what they'd anticipated. How could anything improve after this?

In a short time, Sheila's property stood in a disorderly pile under the mango tree. The two women watched the drama unfolding next door, and awaited their own fate. A feeling of resignation united them.

Rita bounced back to tell her mother that she would be required to show the plan for the house extension. Onai went indoors and pulled the faded document from Gari's tattered suitcase. She silently thanked her dead parents-in-law for having been shrewd enough to meet council requirements on extensions.

In no time, it was her turn. A flustered officer approached her guardedly. Taking a deep breath, he greeted her, *'Maswera sei, ambuya?'* He waited for a reply. Onai ignored him. 'I see your house has two extra rooms, in addition to the original plan for this area. Do you have the plan for these additions?'

'Yes.' Onai replied curtly, then with a flourish she handed him the required document, which she had been holding in her sweating, trembling hand.

The man inspected the house, and then pored closely over the plan before handing it back. 'Everything appears to be in order.' His expression showed obvious signs of relief. He turned and looked pointedly at the shack, then at Sheila's paltry belongings standing in a solitary pile under the mango tree. A pink blanket failed to adequately cover the shambolic array of all her worldly possessions: a paraffin stove, blankets, a sleeping mat, clothes, a wireless and cooking utensils. The man raised his eyebrows and pointed towards the shack with his foot, saying, 'I'm afraid that has to come down, *ambuya.*'

Onai looked at him coldly, and in silence.

'We have a bulldozer, but it can't get into your yard. Gate's too small,' he said almost regretfully. Onai continued to stare at him with silent hostility. He went on evenly, 'If you don't want us to bulldoze through

141

your fence, the option is for your husband to dismantle the shack.' He looked around expectantly. Obviously, there was no husband in sight.

Still, Onai said nothing. 'Or we could torch it,' he suggested helpfully, as if offering a better alternative.

All Onai could think of was that their bulldozer would trample her little vegetable patch. If they torched the shack, the searing heat would wilt the vegetables. The defenceless plants were still very young and delicate. She suddenly saw splashes of red; then a cornucopia of stars and black spots. Her migraine hovered, with an onslaught of pain. Her chest felt heavy with the effort of restraining her anger. One day, my chest will explode, she thought. Very coldly, she said, 'I will do it myself.'

The officer stared at her, openly surprised. He laughed contemptuously. 'I really think you need a man for a job like this.'

She stared back at him and shouted, 'I said I will do it myself!' With a start, he backed away slightly. He shook his balding head, scratching the receding hairline in exasperation, and walked towards the riot police who were waiting expectantly across the road, ready to stifle any disturbances.

Onai stormed indoors and grabbed Gari's axe from behind the kitchen door. She planted her feet firmly next to the shack and concentrated. She willed all her energy and anger into her arms and gave a mighty swing. The sharp edge of the axe descended on Sheila's former home with a deafening crash. The sound of collapsing wood gave her a deep, strangely satisfying feeling. She was in total control. She swung again and again; tearing, breaking, trampling with her feet and swinging the heavy axe over and over again.

Her neighbours and other people walking along the road stopped to stare at her as she attacked the shack. The riot police edged closer. Sheila and the children looked at her in alarm. Onai ignored all of them. She did not care. She was a woman possessed. She struck a forceful blow against all the Garis of the world and against everything that threatened her existence. She groaned and swung the axe into a higher, wider arc. She felt droplets of sweat on her face, coalescing around her eyes and nose, and mingling with her bitter tears. Her headache now forgotten, she pressed on with the sole mission of destruction.

She cried about her miserable life with Gari. She cried about the food shortages. She cried about the market that had been closed, leaving her without a livelihood. Out of the corner of an eye, she glimpsed Sheila's forlorn, hunched figure and wept for all the people who had suddenly become homeless. She cried about the poverty that had left her crushed and hopeless, about everything that rendered her powerless, everything that held her bound in chains …

The rise and fall of the axe continued with rhythmic precision. The force of her blows caused the wood on the axe handles to splinter, piercing her palms. She did not feel it. She was beyond physical pain.

The officer walked away, still shaking his balding head, mocking her, 'I've had enough of these deranged township women. I made a mistake. I gave this woman too much credit. The ones who look composed are always the craziest.' Onai heard the words floating towards her, as if in a dream.

'Tomorrow, we will be next door. I don't like the look of the man peering from across the fence,' another officer was saying. They were probably talking about Hondo, her neighbour.

Another voice laughed and said, 'Let's have a good breakfast before we tackle that one. I hope my son, who joined food queues this morning, has managed to find at least a loaf of bread, so that I can have a good breakfast. Maybe my wife will fry an egg for me.'

With these words, Onai rested the axe on the ground and jerked her head towards the man. So these people were human, they had wives, they had children? How very surprising! The man who hoped to eat an egg for breakfast signalled to the rest of the officers, and they walked up the street to their parked truck. The bulldozer inched down the street behind them. Their day was over.

≈≈≈

When the shack was no more than a mass of broken wood and her rage was depleted, Onai sat slumped on the ground, weeping. Ruva and Sheila vainly tried to persuade her to go indoors. Katy found her sitting dejectedly under the mango tree. She took her hand and led her into the house, away from the neighbours' prying eyes. Her friend's arrival made Onai feel slightly better and less isolated in her grief.

She told Katy about Gloria and wept fresh tears. Katy was horrified.

'I'm so sorry, Onai. I didn't know. What are you going to do?' Onai just shook her head because she had no idea. Then, just as she had expected, Katy asked her, 'On top of everything else, isn't this a good enough reason for you to leave Gari?'

Onai suddenly started laughing, almost hysterically. 'With all that has just happened, how can you even be asking me this?' When Katy did not answer, Onai attempted a murderous joke. 'Maybe I should get a machete, hack the pair of them into little pieces and feed them to the dogs!'

Katy looked worriedly at her. Onai was quick to say through her tears, 'Don't worry. I'm not mad. But how I wish I was! How I really wish I was, then I could do anything and nobody would hold me responsible.'

Katy took her hands and said softly, ' My heart is breaking for you, Onai. *Ndiri kurwadziwa*. I will never be at peace until you are free of Gari. Just leave, *sahwira*.'

'It's not as simple as that, Katy. How can I leave in the midst of all this? Where would I go with the children? I wish … I wish … ' Her voice wavered and she began to weep again. Katy sat with her on the bed and held her silently. At that moment, there was nothing more she could do or say to alleviate her friend's pain.

≈≈≈

Ruva stood by the gate with Rita. Twilight was descending upon the city. Sheila remained stooped unhappily next to her property. She said to Ruva, 'I have nowhere to go. I have no idea where I will spend the night.'

'I don't know where you can go, *sisi* Sheila.' Ruva secretly hoped that her mother would not offer her a place to stay in their house. She had her reasons. She glanced at Sheila's baby suckling vigorously from a floppy, desiccated breast. The baby was hungry and dissatisfied. Now and then, she stopped suckling, and giving a frustrated whimper, grabbed the withered breast tightly with her tiny hands as if to squeeze some more milk out of it.

Ruva enlisted Rita's help and they covered up Sheila's possessions with some plastic sheets. Just for that night, everything would be safe out in the open. Just for that night, the thieves would probably not steal anything. They would be too preoccupied with the important matter of finding somewhere to sleep; somewhere to store their spoils.

When Onai came out of the house and offered Sheila room to sleep, Ruva was disappointed. Pulling her mother aside, she hissed fiercely, 'Mum, are you sure that *sisi* Sheila can sleep in our house? She coughs a lot. What if she has TB? You can't put her in Fari's room. We will all catch TB.'

Her mother gave an annoyingly conciliatory smile, 'Don't worry. We will see about getting her somewhere to stay tomorrow morning. She can't sleep in the open with the baby. Besides, the nights are so much colder now.'

At the mention of the baby, Ruva relented with good grace. She was, however, surprised when Sheila turned to her mother and said, 'Thank you, Mai Moyo, thank you very much. I just want to say I'm sorry about everything I've done. You, the one person who has shown me so much kindness, but I ...' she started weeping.

Ruva glanced at her mother, who also looked surprised. 'What is it Sheila? What is it? She laid a hand on Sheila's shoulder.

The girl would not explain. She just cried harder and repeated her apologies. Ruva noted that her mother did not press her. Instead, she told her daughter to take Sheila and the baby into Fari's box-like room. When the complicated sleeping arrangements were sorted out, Fari was consigned to the sitting room. He would sleep on the floor on a reed mat. He said he didn't mind; he would lie on his back and watch the smiling Humpty Dumpty clock until he fell asleep. It was clearly a fitting end to a day that for him had been a singularly exciting one.

'When I grow up I want to become a demolition man. Or a policeman. Which one is better, *Mhama?*' he asked.

Ruva scowled at him. Her mother said she didn't know.

'Can I be a policeman and a demolition man at the same time, *Mai?*' he continued, innocently.

'Will you shut up, Fari!' Onai barked, much to Rita's surprise. Fari withdrew and ran from the house, a look of hurt in his eyes. Her mother sighed wearily, and sat down. 'Can you make a pot of tea for everyone, Ruva?' Her daughter nodded and put some water on to boil.

≈≈≈

Later at home, Katy sat alone, thinking about what had happened, and wondering how much further things would deteriorate. She hoped John would call. He didn't. When the phone rang, it was Faith, calling her from the university. She sounded anxious. '*Amai*, are you all right? I've been studying all day in my room and I've only just heard about what's been happening out there. Do you want me to come home?'

Katy sighed. 'Thank you for ringing. I'm all right. Terrible things have happened today, *mwanangu*.' As Faith listened and clicked sounds of disbelief, Katy described the events of the day.

'But Mum, they can't get away with this. Somebody has to be accountable. It's winter … people will be sleeping in the open and in makeshift shelters. What about the children? How long will they live like that?' She sounded outraged.

Katy was quick to say, '*Mwanangu*, mind how you speak, and take care who you utter such things to. It is not your place to be so forthcoming with open criticism. I'm just grateful that nobody I know was injured today.'

'Well, I think having such sentiments makes things so much worse than speaking out does …'

'*Iwe* Faith, why are you so stubborn? Trust me, this is a serious matter. You can say what you like to me, but not to other people, as I'm sure you know very well. And don't worry about coming here. I'll be all right'.

Faith protested, 'But *Amai*, you are all alone and …'

Katy was firm. 'No. There have been some clashes with the police today, so it's not safe. Neither is it necessary. You have your exams to prepare for and you can always visit next weekend.'

'Only if you promise to let me know how you are each day …'

Katy laughed. 'Are you mothering me now?'

'I can't help worrying, Mum.'

'I know. Thank you Faith, and goodnight. But remember what I've said. Be very careful and don't go about saying things that might get you into trouble.' Her daughter agreed reluctantly, but she was clearly unconvinced.

≈≈≈

At the top of Jo'burg Lines, the clean-up operation brought a new dimension to Gari's dilemma. The demolitions had caught him unawares as he lay in Gloria's shack, his mind befuddled by a raging hangover. He had been rudely disturbed by the arrival of riot personnel. After the shack had been torched, he'd had no choice but to force himself out of his stupor, and take immediate action. He'd spent the rest of the afternoon running around, desperately trying to find an affordable room to rent for Gloria.

Some perspicacious, if selfish, homeowners realised at once that they had an opportunity to make a great deal of money. Within a matter of hours, the rentals in Mbare had quadrupled to one million dollars a month for a single room.

The room that Gari finally secured for Gloria was a great improvement on her shack. However, the expense was a very sore point. He reluctantly paid the five hundred thousand dollar deposit, and agreed to bring the rest of the money the following day. As soon as Gloria was installed, he left quickly, still reeling from the sheer extravagance of having to pay so much money for just one room. His desire had also been fatigued by her steady stream of complaints.

The atmosphere at home was not much better. On his arrival, his children immediately fled from the sitting room and disappeared into the kitchen. He did not mind. The less he saw of them, the better. Every time he looked into their eyes, he sensed accusation. He hated the feeling, because he was not doing anything wrong. He had grown up with a father who was hardly home, but he'd turned out all right. So, why did they give him such accusing glances?

He acknowledged Onai's narration of events with a few grunts. He just couldn't be bothered. He was too tired even to make any objections to Sheila's presence in his house.

≈≈≈

The evening meal was eaten without enjoyment and in grave silence. Onai wondered if she should later question Gari about why he had not returned the previous night. Although she was emotionally exhausted, she also wanted to ask him about Gloria, but his silence had firmly set the tone for the evening. She wouldn't be able to question him, even in the privacy of their bedroom. She watched him with bitterness while he devoured sadza and cabbage, as if he had no cares in the world. She half-expected him to pull some biltong out of his pocket, but he didn't. Surprisingly, he ate all the cabbage. It was indeed a day with a difference. A painfully different day.

By the time she had done the dishes and gone to bed, he was fast asleep. The discomforting combination of her troubled thoughts and his loud snores kept her awake for half the night. She burned with self-contempt, loathing herself for her weakness. Why had she not gathered enough courage to ask him about Gloria? Conflicting emotions disturbed her tired mind. All at once she felt a strong need for Gari to hold her, to tell her that he loved her and everything would be all right. There was a void within her that needed to be filled. Lying next to him, she felt so alone.

≈≈≈

Elsewhere in Mbare, people whose homes were still standing opened their doors and squeezed in displaced families. Overcrowding, and sleeping on kitchen floors, was not an issue. That day, human compassion was manifested at its best among those who knew the meaning of poverty.

CHAPTER 14

The next morning, Gari left for work as usual. The children went to school and left Onai helping Sheila to pack her belongings into large plastic bags and woven sacks. She had still not explained her strange apology and Onai decided not to think any further about it. By mid-morning, Katy had joined them. They carried Sheila's property to Tsiga Grounds where several displaced families had set up improvised homes out of plastic bags and poles. With the aid of poles, scrap-metal and plastic sheeting, Katy and Onai fashioned a crude shelter. It was hopelessly inadequate but there was nothing better on offer for Sheila and her baby. Thanking Katy and Onai for their efforts, she crawled in with her baby and her belongings.

When Onai got back home, she found the demolition team in a heated confrontation with Hondo, her neighbour, the war veteran. He was gesticulating and shouting irately at the riot police about their lack of respect for people who had fought in the war to liberate the country from the British.

However, they did not appear to be paying much attention to what he was saying. His lodgers also seemed to have realised that their landlord's war-veteran status did not make them immune to the demolitions. They proceeded to empty their shacks speedily. In no time, the two informal dwellings in Hondo's yard had been devoured by raging flames. Clouds of thick, grey smoke rose into the air.

Hondo had to be restrained from attacking the officer who had torched his shacks. 'I will shoot the whole lot of you! Do you know who I am? Do you know whose sidekick I was during the struggle? You're going to be very sorry. If you don't leave now, I will shoot you. I swear by the graves of my dead comrades.'

The spectators whispered uneasily. Nobody was sure whether he had a gun or not, but it was obvious that they all wanted to avoid any violent incidents. A young man tried to reason with him. Hondo spat a thick globule of saliva onto the ground next to the youth's feet. His show of contempt could not have been clearer. 'How dare you come here and destroy my property? Do you know who I am? Do you know that I fought for this country? Do you know anything?' he repeated angrily.

'Those shacks were illegal dwellings. That's why we've torched them. Now stop wasting my time and show me the plan for your main house. We don't have all day,' an older, more authoritative officer replied in a cold, hard voice. His approach was brutal.

Pain twisted like a knife in Onai's heart. She knew how hard Hondo and his wife had worked to extend their house. His war-vet pay-out had helped, but they had had to raise more to complete the process of building and furnishing. The extension consisted of two small rooms which were separated from the main house by a neat little veranda and a low side wall.

Hondo looked undeterred by the officer's ruthless manner. 'You don't understand what I'm saying, do you? I said, I fought for this country. I said, I risked my life for this country. Is this the reward that I get? Who are you to come here and destroy my home? My house has been standing like this for more than ten years. I built it with my war-veteran pay-out. Why do you want to see plan now? You can go to hell, the whole bunch of you!' he said furiously with a volley of expletives. Onai had never seen him so upset.

'Look here, mister. Everything that you're saying is not relevant, not at all. This is not about the liberation war. If there's no plan, we have to bulldoze down these two extra rooms.' The officer replied and signalled to the demolition team to start their work. The engine roared to life and the hideous bulldozer inched forwards.

'I know who sent you! You are all British puppets; sell-outs, the whole bunch of you. Are you listening to me? I said I fought for this country!' Hondo continued raving. He did a mad little dance and burst into a popular war song which made reference to the blood that had been spilt to secure his beloved country's freedom. *Zimbabwe ndeyeropa baba! Zimbabwe ndeyeropa remadzibaba!*

Onai's apprehension rose as she watched. Premonition hung heavily in the air. Something really terrible was going to happen. Hondo and his wife had always been good neighbours; she wished she could do something to avert the imminent disaster, but her mind was blank.

As the bulldozer edged closer, Hondo raised a ladder and clambered up to the roof shouting loudly, 'Over my dead body! Over my dead body!'

The officer did not look impressed by Hondo's hysterics. He glared at him coldly, 'Come down at once. The walls will collapse and you will only get injured.'

But Hondo paid no attention. He continued shouting wildly. 'Over my dead body!' Onai looked with sympathy at his wife who was sobbing brokenly, and begging her husband to get off the roof. He ignored her.

The officer gave a second, impatient signal for the demolition process to begin. Concrete blocks and asbestos sheets fell with a resounding crash. The noise seemed to jolt the rebellious Hondo back to reality. He acknowledged defeat and leapt off the roof. He looked stunned as he watched the house, which had embodied his dreams, falling down. There was no way to save any of the furniture in the two rooms that were being reduced to rubble.

His wife stood helplessly near him, sobbing in the confusion, 'My goods from South Africa are in there! Please stop. My goods are in there,' she pleaded and held out her hands to the officer in charge. He ignored her. Onai walked over and held the distraught woman in an embrace, pulling her as far away as possible from the collapsing bricks and clouds of dust.

When the work was completed, the remaining rooms stood in the early morning sun looking crooked, casting an irregular, unhappy shadow over the ground. It was only a figment of Onai's imagination. Shadows had no capacity to feel or show human pain. The demolition team left for the next house in the line without a backward glance.

One of them suddenly turned back and walked back. He stood at the gate ... at a safe distance from Hondo. He shouted, 'Make sure you get rid of all that rubble, otherwise you'll be getting a fine from the city council.' Nobody gave him any sign of acknowledgement.

Hondo's loud, heart-rending howls of grief filled the morning air. 'Why?' he declaimed, being emasculated and publicly humiliated in the worst possible manner. Was this the reward for his sacrifice? How could this happen to him of all people? Flinging his hands in the air, in a heartfelt display of anguish, he cried out again and again: 'Why? Why? Why?' Nobody could answer him. Onai listened to the cautious whispers amongst the spectators. They did not know what it really meant to have fought in the war of liberation; so, despite having also lost their homes, they could not fully identify with the sheer magnitude of his pain.

Suddenly Hondo got up and staggered towards the remains of his flattened gate. He broke into a sprint, screaming wildly as he ran up 50th Street. Somebody said, 'Leave him. Don't follow. He's so angry that he might attack you.'

A few of the riot personnel who were loitering along the road looked on and laughed derisively. 'Be a man! You will get over it,' one of them shouted after him. His colleagues laughed. Yes, he would have to stop acting like a woman, and just get over it. 'He shouldn't have extended his house without a plan in the first place,' they said.

≈≈≈

Onai did her best to console Hondo's distressed wife, and spent most of the day with her. By nightfall, Hondo had still not returned home. Later that evening, Onai accompanied his wife to the police station to report him missing. A very stressed police officer simply told them to go back home and wait. He added, 'There's no need to worry. He's probably at a beer hall somewhere, drinking his sorrows away.'

The two women exchanged glances of disbelief and anxiety, returning home unwillingly and without much hope.

The next morning, Hondo's mangled body was discovered on the railway tracks by children walking to school. The train's wheels had sliced him across his torso and abdomen. His head was untouched. Those brave enough to look at his face reported that he seemed strangely peaceful, almost as if death had brought him a good measure of the calm which had eluded him in the last hours of his life. No foul play was suspected. It was generally accepted that the events of the previous day could have driven him to suicide, especially as he'd always been a highly-strung man with a tendency towards political fanaticism.

≈≈≈

Onai temporarily forgot about Gloria when she found herself caught up in Hondo's funeral. Inevitably, the gathering of mourners spilled over into her small yard. To her own ears, it sounded petty and callous to keep asking them not to trample on her young cabbage plants. So, by the end of the first day of the wake, there was no vegetable patch to speak of. The count of her losses was rising steadily. Gari also got himself actively involved with the funeral preparations, consulting with the other men about what would constitute a suitable burial for Hondo. For a while, the tragedy that had struck their neighbour appeared as if it might draw them closer together.

Hondo was buried three days later, on a cold winter morning. The graveside speeches reiterated that strife was for the living; Hondo had gone to a better place; a place where he would surely find rest. He was a great man who'd fought for his country with remarkable bravery. He deserved only the best in the next life. His widow was generally thought to be a very fortunate woman. At least she and her children still had somewhere to live. A lot of people had become completely homeless. So, she was very lucky indeed. It was time to move on.

CHAPTER 15

The aftermath of the first stage of the demolitions left no one in Mbare untouched. Elsewhere, they continued in a similar manner. Homes and livelihoods were lost, almost as if on impulse. Mbare was the worst affected, by virtue of its levels of overcrowding and social deprivation. People were constantly on the move with their families and possessions, just looking for open spaces in which to erect makeshift shelters. It did not help that the police were persistently on the lookout for any such illegal dwellings. So the nomads continued on their difficult journey in the unremittingly cold weather; miserable, hungry families who'd lost all hope of a future. Bedding and food brought in by well-wishers and church communities could not suffice for the scale of their loss.

The cold weather did not make their plight any easier. The very young and the elderly came down with chest infections and swamped the Casualty Department at the local hospital. They were attended to by overworked doctors who sent them away with prescriptions, because there were no medicines in the hospital. With most families having lost their source of income, raising the hundreds of thousands of dollars required for an average prescription was impossible. So the slips of paper ended up in dustbins, or as rubbish on the roadsides; anywhere but in the pharmacies where they should have been redeemed.

The prevailing strife mirrored Onai's personal life. Having Katy's full support didn't do much to bolster her uncertainty about the future. Foremost in her mind, with no income at her disposal, was the issue of feeding and clothing the children. Not being able to pay school fees didn't have the same urgency.

This would have been the best time to talk to Gari. Surely, he would appreciate that with the market closed, she could no longer cater for the children's needs. However, he had become quite slippery, and was spending less time at home than ever. If her husband wasn't dead drunk, he returned so late that it was impossible to discuss anything with him. Onai found it inconceivable that he had so much money to spend on drink, and nothing to spare for his children's groceries.

Faith's sensitivity touched her. The girl had again brought a dress for Ruva. Before she left, she said, 'If there's anything I can do to help, please let me know, *mainini*.'

Thanking her, Onai had nodded and smiled.

'Anything at all, *mainini*,' she'd said again, almost as if she had something specific in mind. But she'd left without saying anything further.

≈≈≈

In addition to Hondo's funeral, there were three other funerals in Jo'burg Lines that week. The saddest was one for two toddlers who'd died instantly when the demolition team erroneously moved in without checking whether there were people inside the targeted shack. Not only had the parents been left homeless and impoverished, but also childless and grieving.

One woman's bloated body had been found floating in a ditch overflowing with raw sewage. Nobody had any idea how she had died. Those who knew her, said she might have died of grief, because she too had lost virtually everything.

Another woman had committed suicide by taking rat poison, when both her tuck-shop and her shack were demolished within a few hours of each other. With no home and no means to look after her six children, life had ceased to hold any meaning. As the story was told, death had been almost a quick and easy escape. Her children, including a one-year-old toddler, joined the homeless throngs on Tsiga Grounds. A lot of children stopped going to school because the very notion of sitting down in class to concentrate on lessons seemed pointless, when they were homeless and starving.

Families continued to map out new territory in open spaces as more and more people had their homes destroyed. There were occasional aggressive incidents about encroachments over vague boundaries. Theft was rampant and the loss of property continued. There was no clean water and no sanitation facilities at Tsiga Grounds. It was soon clear that the camp was a health hazard.

At the end of that week, riot police swooped down on the camp at dawn, and rounded up the wretched vagrants. They bundled them into army trucks, with whatever of their few belongings had survived the demolition and theft. Word was that they would be taken to a holding camp on a farm just outside Harare. Their newly-constructed makeshift homes were razed to the ground in a scene poignantly reminiscent of the initial demolitions.

Onai and Katy sadly waved Sheila goodbye. Could life get any worse? What would the holding camp be like for the young woman and her baby? As far they knew, there were no dwellings there. Just a week of sleeping out in the open had already ravaged Sheila's health; her cough was worse, her eyes lifeless pools in a face worn with fatigue. She now had the familiar, skeletal appearance of a victim of full-blown AIDS.

The vagrants would live in tents and temporary shelters, which, somebody said, were worse than the shacks that had been destroyed. Onai wept silently. Life seemed meaningless. There was no point in trying, because trying made things no better; it only intensified the sense of loss.

'Sheila was a fighter, *sahwira*. But now … she is like a lost soul. How on earth will she survive with her baby in tow?' she asked Katy, without really expecting an answer.

Nevertheless, her friend responded, 'I doubt she'll make it. The fire has faded from her eyes.'

Shelia's destiny seemed too cruel. Was destiny to blame, even if one had to submit to it?

≈≈≈

Unbelievably, after a few days, more families had started to re-group at Tsiga Grounds. Onai didn't know where the new arrivals were coming from. Clearly, the situation was spiralling out of control.

Mawaya was one person Onai hadn't seen since the start of the demolitions, and she asked Katy if she'd done so. Her friend shook her head. 'No, but the way police officers are rounding up people, he might be in hiding, or in a holding camp.'

'I hope not,' Onai smiled sadly.

'Why are you smiling?' Katy was curious.

'Promise you won't laugh … it's just that I miss seeing him around,' Onai said sincerely.

Katy laughed. 'Are you mad, Onai?'

'Go ahead and laugh. It's true. There was something about him, his smile …' She spoke unconvincingly, unable to find the right words to express how exactly she had felt about the beggar. It was nothing to do with feeling sorry for him, or having any sort of protective instinct. She couldn't tell Katy that Mawaya had given her a sense of stability; one that came with knowing that there were people worse off than herself, who still found something to smile about. She tried to express herself, but gave up as Katy simply continued to laugh, unable to see the point her friend was trying to make.

So she quickly changed the subject by asking after John, who Katy hadn't mentioned for a while.

Her friend did not answer immediately. Then, slowly, she said, 'I really don't know what to think about John.'

Onai was surprised. 'Why?"

'We've been quarrelling on the phone because I'm not sure why he didn't come home for his leave. The other day he was in Beitbridge. Now he's in Jo'burg. I asked him why, and all he said was something vague about business. *What business?* It's something that I don't know about, and he just won't tell me.'

'Maybe, he has a good reason. I'm sure he'll explain everything when he comes home.'

'And when will that be? After his leave, he normally does another long trip, so he won't be back any time soon. As it is, I'm running out of rands. I might have to cross the border to sell more of those expensive upholstery covers, so that I can get rands for my regular clients. I don't know if I'll be able to afford as many sets as I would like from the shop in town. The lady who used to supply me at reasonable prices had her business closed last week. I wish I was good enough to sew them myself,' Katy sighed wearily.

'Don't read too much into why John didn't come home. I'm sure he has a good reason. Why don't you ask Faith to come and spend some time with you?' Onai suggested.

Katy shook her head. 'She's too busy with studying for her final exams. I don't want to disturb her.'

Onai nodded. 'But you have to stop worrying Katy. Please.'

Katy's voice was bitter. 'How can I not worry? With everything that's happening, I need him here with me; and I want him to be honest with me. I wish these men were worth all the trouble they give us!' She gave Onai a sideways glance and asked, 'Have you talked to Gari about Gloria yet?'

Onai shook her head. 'No, I haven't. But I will. Very soon.' She meant it.

≈≈≈

Faith was feeling a bit overwhelmed by her revision schedule. When she wasn't studying, she thought about the unresolved issues between herself and Tom. Sometimes they seemed as nothing, at others – especially when she was tired – they seemed insuperable. Sensibly, she resolved to postpone any serious discussion until after she had completed her exams. On the one occasion when they discussed the demolitions, they had quarrelled.

Faith told Tom that she thought what was happening was illegal. He initially made no comment then he said it was tragic and quite unfair.

'Unfair?' Faith's laugh was clearly not an expression of joy. She spoke vehemently. 'How can you call the operation "unfair"? It's a gross abuse of humanity. People are now homeless and destitute. Just over a week ago, they all had roofs over their heads. They were earning a living from self-employment. They had dignity, they had self-respect. Can you honestly sit here and tell me that this can be described as *unfair?*'

Tom laughed uneasily, wondering why Faith was so passionate about the issue. Her family had only lost three shacks. The market closures could not have affected them to any great extent because her parents obviously got higher returns from their foreign currency deals.

He felt that her point of view was in some way, out of order. 'Faith my love, you shouldn't be saying things like this.'

'But why not? That's how I feel, Tom. Don't forget that I grew up in Mbare. I know how hard life is for those families. Have you been to Mbare recently? Have you seen how people are suffering? Have you?' she asked, suddenly close to tears.

Tom shook his head. He had not been to Mbare since the demolitions started, but he was aware of how people's lives had deteriorated. He also knew that Faith had a tendency to care deeply about those who she perceived as vulnerable. It was one of the features he loved about her, but now he wished she didn't care so much, or take things so personally. It wasn't as if he didn't care about people's suffering. He did. It was just that he wanted to get on in life. He had done well so far, and he knew too well how the wrong word and at wrong time or in the wrong place could set one back. One day, he hoped, people would be able to express their views more freely, but that time wasn't now, and he was damned if he was going to jeopardise his new farming venture with a few emotional opinions. He searched for something positive to say, 'What did you notice about the city centre when we went out today? Tell me, *mudiwa.*'

She looked down at him and dried her eyes. 'I know what you're getting at. I've heard it enough on the news. But do you really believe it when they say that the streets are cleaner, and the city more beautiful? There are just as many potholes as there were before; just as many broken street lights and broken street signs; just as many neglected buildings, and so much rubbish everywhere. Why, only yesterday, you were complaining that driving across town is now very risky because most traffic lights don't work. I have eyes and a brain that works, you know!'

He pulled a face. 'Well, aren't you full of facts! Have you been keeping stock of everything then?' He laughed in an attempt to lighten the mood but she only stared silently at him.

He tried again. 'Well, I still maintain that being in town is actually more enjoyable now. You were able to eat your ice-cream freely when we walked down First Street, without fearing that a street kid would snatch it from you. You didn't get pestered by vendors who wanted you to buy cigarettes ...' He laughed.

'So I suppose you'd call those flower vendors, opposite Meikles, on licensed stalls, "vermin"! It was a beautiful site. A tourist feature! I've already told you. I have eyes and a brain that works. You can't coerce me into your way of thinking. No, no matter how many ice-creams you give me!' Finally, she smiled.

'I've no intention of doing any such thing,' he grinned. 'But, seriously, Faith, I'm just trying to make you see things from a different point of view. One thing which may not be obvious to you is that crime has also gone down, not only in town but in Mbare, too.'

Faith made a sceptical sound. 'Don't believe everything you hear. Ask me. I was at home two days ago. Thefts in Mbare have become worse because people are so desperate. So many homeless people have had their belongings stolen while sleeping in the open. A good number of homes have been burgled. You can't convince me on those grounds.'

Tom said patiently, 'But look at how people used to live … those shacks in Mbare weren't fit for human habitation. I'm sure you know that houses are going to be built for all the people who were displaced. And those will be so much better than the shacks they were living in before.'

'I understand what you're saying Tom, but it doesn't change the fact that right now people are suffering. The shacks might not have been fit for habitation, but are the holding camps and the streets where they live now, any better? They are not! The promise of a house in the distant future does not ease these people's pain. My mum went to four funerals in one week because …'

Tom interrupted her, 'It's the pattern of history, my dear. Whenever radical changes are effected to improve society, there is always someone who suffers. But in the end, whole communities do gain the benefits. Think of wars of liberation, Faith … people die, people suffer … but in the end …'

Faith became angry again. 'How can you assume that? Would you dare say that to the mother who lost two toddlers when their shack was destroyed? Is this a war situation? It's all very well for you to speak like this. Sometimes, I get the feeling that you're too far removed from reality. You don't spend days in food queues or go to bed on an empty stomach. You only have to make a phone call and people fall over each other to give you what you want. Why are you so defensive, anyway? Is it because you're privileged and you have that farm? Ordinary people have rights too!'

Tom shook his head in exasperation. The conversation was slipping out of control. 'Who defines those rights and who defines what violation is? These people are going to be resettled in new homes, Faith. Isn't that good enough for you? Don't you think people who were renting out shoddy shacks were abusing human rights? As for being privileged, I can't help being who I am! And what does my farm have to do with this, anyway?'

Faith glared at him. 'How come you got the land that belonged to that farmer whose family was almost killed? I've tried to ask you before but you always block my questions!'

The young man sighed wearily, regretting ever starting the conversation, 'Yes, I do block your questions because I had nothing to do with what happened to Mr Johnson and his family. What are you implying, anyway? I bought the farm, Faith. I thought showing you the documents would be enough, but I was obviously wrong.'

She shrugged sullenly and swallowed hard, glaring at him. 'That land must have been worth … billions. It's in a prime farming area. Where did you get the money from?' she demanded.

Despite himself, Tom suddenly laughed. 'You're such a breath of fresh air, my dear. I like the idea that you don't know how much I inherited from my father. There's no danger of you loving me for my money. I've never had that security in past relationships,' he teased her, trying hard to diffuse the tension.

'That's what you say about *your* farm. But there are people out there who own farms simply because somebody died,' Faith said stubbornly.

'Fine, but so what? What has that got to do with you and me? I don't want to be drawn into discussions with political undertones … matters where we have no hard facts, issues based only on hearsay. In fact, I'd be happier if you stopped talking like this. I love you, but you're treading on dangerous ground,' he concluded quietly.

Faith shook her head. 'I can't promise you, Tom. I can't. I haven't done or said anything wrong. Who will speak for the voiceless, if we all let fear crush us? I feel for these people. I really do.'

Tom felt a heaviness in his chest. Faith could be very headstrong. That was fine because he liked the idea of a woman who could stand up for what she believed. But now her opinions were exasperating, to say the least. And her obsession with his farm was even more annoying; it showed a downright lack of faith. But he loved her. So he took her in his arms and said, 'Faith, we're getting married some time in the future; and I'm looking forward to raising a family with you. However, for me, politics is a no-go area.' He paused, took a deep breath, and went on, 'Listen, my dear, for your sake and mine, don't do or say anything dangerous. Please. You never know who might be listening, and we have our own lives to live. Let everyone else watch out for themselves. The risks are not worth the sacrifice. Please?'

Faith continued to shake her head. 'But ...' she started. He did not let her continue. He held her tightly and kissed her. He could not believe that their biggest quarrel had been over the demolitions. For goodness sake, the demolitions had nothing to do with them! In the midst of it all he was sure of one thing. Faith was an intelligent girl and soon enough she would understand that there were boundaries. Sadly, it was possible to violate some limits without being aware of it until it was too late. Life was like that.

CHAPTER 16

The changes at home and the prevailing air of resignation shocked John when he returned from South Africa. He'd heard snatches of information on the news. However, the reality went beyond anything he could have imagined, and blighted his prospects of an enjoyable leave. At his company's depot on Seke Road, his supervisor assigned Kundai, one of his colleagues, to drive him and his goods to Mbare.

They passed through the town centre to deliver a sewing machine that John had brought on order. His potential customer was a man who ran several market stalls at the Union Avenue flea market. The two men were astounded to find the place deserted, the entrance chained and the few empty stalls that remained covered with a thick layer of dust. John's customer was nowhere to be seen; neither were all the other traders or their clients, who had made the market a hive of activity.

The face of Harare had changed drastically. There was no sign of the street kids who had spent their days loitering on pavements: begging, rummaging through bins and sometimes being a general nuisance. There were no vendors at street corners inviting city strollers to buy cigarettes, bananas, sweets or pens. Even the belligerent, self-appointed car attendants, whose presence was a normal feature on Harare's streets, had disappeared.

John rang his customer's mobile phone number, only to receive a clipped message, 'You have dialled an incorrect number.' He was very disappointed. He was certain there'd be no sale. He'd expected to make a profit of at least fifteen million dollars from the machine, money that was supposed to go towards paying for their Mabelreign stand. Shaking his head dejectedly, he asked Kundai to take him to Siyaso Industries where he had to deliver some polishing bricks. These had been ordered by a man who specialised in making granite tombstones, a flourishing business with the AIDS pandemic, when everything to do with funerals had become a potential money-spinner – enterprising entrepreneurs had soon discovered that it was possible to make huge profits from another's misery.

Kundai frowned, and said doubtfully, 'I'm not too sure, but I think Siyaso is one of the areas that was closed down.' Looking around restlessly, he rattled the car keys, obviously not keen for further diversions *en route* to John's house.

John raised his eyebrows in disbelief. 'Why would Siyaso be closed down? Surely that's not possible. Let's go.' Kundai made no effort to respond, but looked pointedly at his watch.

Their drive to Mbare was made in uncomfortable silence. As it turned out, Kundai was right. Instead of a thriving market area, they were confronted by piles of rubble. There wasn't a single worker in sight. A few children frolicked energetically among the desolate ruins, visibly delighted at finding a new haunt of such expanse and fascination, perfect for games of hide-and-seek and *mahumbwe*.

John was bemused. For years there had been a thriving home industry at Siyaso. It had been the backbone of informal employment for the men of Mbare, a place where they had been making a profitable living for their families. Several of his friends had owned carpentry workshops there. The last time he'd driven past, there had been rows of well-crafted furniture on display outside the workshops. Now there was nothing, apart from the heaps of debris and some frisky children. Envying their apparently carefree existence, he wondered what had happened to his friends. Losing both his major customers was a huge blow.

From Siyaso Industries, the two men went straight to Jo'burg Lines. John's thoughts of Katy were fraught with apprehension. He knew that she would ask him why he'd not come home earlier, and she would demand an answer. But one thing was clear, he could never tell her, because she would never forgive him.

≈≈≈

Katy was so relieved when her husband arrived that her anger immediately evaporated. Anxiety about possible police raids had worn her out. She had lost weight from worrying and not eating well. Faith had been no help at all. On the three occasions that she had visited her, she had been unusually withdrawn, only responding to her mother's anxious queries by declaring vehemently that she was fine. Katy doubted it. Her fears about Faith's possible pregnancy were growing; she hoped fervently that it was only the stress of preparing for final examinations that was upsetting her daughter.

'I suppose it's a good thing that I decided not to smuggle in some petrol,' John said. 'With the shacks gone, I wouldn't have had anywhere to store it!'

Katy shrugged. 'Yes, a good thing because I never wanted to store fuel in the shacks. Anyway, the petrol you left in the car should still be there, unless somebody drained the tank one night,' she replied, as she helped him to unpack.

'*Shuwa?* Would anyone do that, *mudiwa?*'

'Of course. You wouldn't believe what people are doing in order to make enough money to survive. Thieves regularly steal petrol from parked cars, if they have a means of draining it out. And if our tank is empty, don't buy petrol on the black market. I hear it's being mixed with paraffin and God knows what else. Even water! It's better to spend days queuing in town than to buy fuel from these dishonest vendors.' Tskk. She clicked her tongue.

John sighed and fondled his beard. 'I used to hope that life would improve. Now, I just don't see how it can. The vendors were only trying to earn an honest living. What else can people do when there are so few employment opportunities?' He spoke slowly and deliberately, as he unpacked a box of groceries, separating out the few items that Katy had listed for Onai and her family. 'Is she still with Gari?'

Katy looked at him and laughed. It was a short, rather sad sound. 'What do you think, John? Of course, she's still with him. And before you ask, yes, I did try to talk to her, but there's been so much happening since you left, we've all been preoccupied. Anyway, she doesn't want to hear. I think she's afraid to leave Gari.'

John shook his head, 'I agree. I don't think she will leave him, but you must keep trying. One day she might thank you for opening her eyes.'

Katy nodded. This affirmative gesture was in marked contrast to the doubt she felt.

From a large box John took out a sewing machine and placed it carefully on the table. Katy's eyes opened wide. 'What a beautiful machine! How much did it cost?' She stepped forwards and ran her palms over the instrument, stroking its smooth, glowing surface.

'Four thousand rands. Too expensive if you ask me, but I didn't mind because I thought I had a guaranteed customer. Now I don't know if I'll be able to sell it at all.'

'It looks like a very good machine. I'm sure it will sell really fast.'

'I don't know about that. It was an order for someone who had a stall at Union Avenue flea market, but I arrived there only to find the market closed. I can't even get through to the man on the phone, so I guess I'm stuck with this,' John shook his head wearily. He sat down and gripped the armrests on his chair, head tilted onto the back rest.

'*Mudiwa*, I'm sure we'll get a buyer sometime soon. You can try advertising in *The Herald*, if their rates are affordable.' Looking wistful, Katy added softly, 'I wish I was as good as Onai at sewing, then I could make use of this machine.'

'It might be a good idea for you to attend a course, once we finish building in Mabelreign. Then you could start your own business. Just think about it. I really don't want you vending again, even if the market is re-opened.'

'Oh John, you're talking of finishing building when we haven't even started! Remember, we still have to pay the balance on the stand,' Katy exclaimed, shaking her head.

'I'm sure we'll be able to pay up very soon. We can't start building this year but we will next – once the rainy season is over. I told you a long time ago that you and I will leave Mbare.' her husband gave her an unexpectedly self-assured smile.

≈≈≈

Onai arrived at that moment. She was tired and somewhat breathless from her long walk. Her throat felt uncomfortably dry and she had a slight headache. There was a dull throbbing in her ankles and she needed to sit down. As usual, trying to get transport from town had been a futile exercise. Empty-handed after failing to get the mealie-meal, which she'd set off to look for early that morning, she'd joined the throngs of weary pedestrians trudging back to Mbare.

She greeted John and Katy distractedly, her eyes fixed on the sewing machine. The sight of it made her heart heavy with longing. Her fingers tingled. If only she could afford a machine like that, her life would improve. Numerous possibilities flooded through her mind. None of them included Gari.

'*Shamwari,* what do you think about that?' Katy's overly bright voice jolted her back to the present. She started and dragged her entranced gaze from the sewing machine.

'I'm sorry. What did you say?' She gave a tight, embarrassed smile and shifted awkwardly in the armchair.

'I was just telling John that it might be a good idea for you to give me some dressmaking lessons. Who knows what we could achieve with this machine?' Katy spoke enthusiastically, glancing at her husband, as if seeking his approval.

Onai stared at her uncertainly. 'Well, I'm not sure whether I'd be a good teacher. I've been out of practice since …' she stopped in mid-sentence. Now was hardly the time to remind them about how Gari had smashed her sewing machine against the wall. Remembering that incident still hurt and she knew what they both thought of Gari.

Katy seemed to understand. She shrugged and said, 'All you need is a bit of practice and you'll be back in top form. *Uri shasha.* Just because you haven't found a job doesn't mean that you are not good. *Ndiyo Zimbabwe yedu* and jobs are hard to find, that's all. It will be all right again one day.' She made it sound simple but her words were no consolation. To Onai, it was a mantra that seemed devoid of meaning.

John chipped in. 'Anything is worth a try Mai Ruva. In time, you ladies can even rent a shop in town for your business. There are lots of buildings in the centre where self-employed tailors are making a killing.'

'Most of them were closed last week, I'm afraid. The tailors were evicted,' Onai's voice was as flat and tired as she felt.

'Why?' John asked sharply, surprise widening his eyes.

'*Haiwa!* You haven't seen anything yet. It was on the news – there were criminals operating in those buildings. The police claimed to have made a few arrests. For show, I'm sure. They told us that some people were found selling *mbanje*. However, I wonder if anyone will arrest *baba va*Jimi, that soldier who sells *mbanje!*' Katy elaborated with flippant sarcasm. John just shook his head, his expression simultaneously cynical and confused.

'Sometimes, I think it's all a horrible dream. You must go and look at the main Mbare market and at Siyaso Industries,' Onai said to him.

'I know what you mean. I drove past the site on my way home. It all seems so … so … unreal. Personally, I think the suffering will overshadow whatever benefits are supposed to come out of this.' He shook his head again.

'*Asi tashaya nyaya here?* Isn't there something else we can talk about? What can we say or do to change anything, anyway?' Katy asked irritably.

'There is nothing we can do,' Onai answered in the lifeless voice of one for whom hope has ceased to exist. In the long run, acquiescence was less traumatic than nurturing meaningless optimism in a situation that only seemed to grow worse every day.

She was, however, grateful and surprised by the gift of groceries from her friends. She clapped her hands, thanking them profusely, then left for home.

Feeling a bit sorry for herself, while despising herself for her life choices, she walked on. Once again, her thoughts drifted to Gloria. Jealousy and anger against the woman who had captured her husband's heart consumed her. For a brief, insane moment, she wished she could just stop living. An overdose of malaria tablets would be fool-proof, as had been shown countless times before. Didn't they say, '*Vakafa vaka-zorora!*' The dead were resting and nothing could impart such freedom as death.

She had never contemplated suicide before. The thought frightened her. Was she going mad? And what would happen to her children if she died? She hurried home, eager for the strength of resolve that they always gave her.

≈≈≈

John refused flatly to detail any of his responses to Katy's probing. She still wanted to know why he had not come home over his last leave days. Why did she doubt his explanation that he had volunteered to make extra trips between Beitbridge and Johannesburg? After all, they needed the money. She sensed he was holding something back, and it bothered her.

What her husband did not tell her was that he had slowly established a lucrative business that involved smuggling girls and women across the border. In their acute desperation, females were soft and pliant, men tended to be demanding and more difficult to manage; and, if that was their attitude, John had no compunction about wishing they might fall prey to the Limpopo's crocodiles.

To many poor and struggling people, crossing into South Africa provided the only solution, an escape from poverty-ridden Zimbabwe. They did not think beyond that. John knew precisely where many of the women would end up – in brothels, on the streets, or in badly paid domestic service: the only ways guaranteed to keep a vulnerable, jobless woman fed and clothed. Occasionally, this awareness pricked his conscience, but never enough for him to reconsider his activities.

One needed to have supporting paperwork, an invitation, and a thousand rands worth of travellers' cheques before a South African visa application could be approved. Well, he could smuggle women across the border for just half that amount, sometimes even without passports. He had identified a network of like-minded immigration officials whose only requirement was a hundred rands per head. It was unbelievably easy money. His new venture was one in which there were no losers, and he was quickly gaining a reputation for reliability.

Knowing that Katy would not approve, he maintained his silence though his guilt made him impatient with her persistent questioning. 'Why, anyway, should I have to endure her anger when I am doing it all for her and Faith?' he reflected sourly. So he was a little relieved when his wife finally gave up and walked heavily to the kitchen. It was time for her to prepare supper.

After their evening meal, eaten in silence, they watched the eight o'clock news. There was a report about criminals who'd been arrested for selling foreign currency on the black market. Thousands of South African rands, US dollars, Botswana pulas and some British pounds had been confiscated from the alleged criminals who were said to be working with local and international 'Enemies of the State' to sabotage the country's once vibrant economy. In John's mind, his own alliance with Assistant Commissioner Nzou made the report a farce. For his contribution to the black market, the official could well be described as an 'enemy of the state', as could John himself.

So many 'criminals' and so many 'enemies' for such a small country, he mused. Guilt rose, floundered, and was held at bay. It was a question of survival of the fittest, and John had every intention of being among the survivors. 'Ndini ndingazvidii,' he thought unrepentantly.

A young policeman stood proudly under the glare of television cameras. Next to him were boxes of confiscated cash. Smiling broadly, he pointed out the different currencies, explaining at length how expert intelligence had been used to capture the dealers.

John wondered how much of that currency would end up stashed away in the young officer's pockets. Being in the business for so long had made him sceptical of the law and its operatives. He knew that a different set of rules and varying degrees of protection existed for particular groups in society. Fortunately, for the right price, that protection could be extended to people like him. All that was required was willingness to part with money and astuteness at making the 'right' connections.

'I keep worrying that we will be next. I've had a horrible sense of premonition since last week,' Katy said uneasily. She stared at the television with a stony face. Her voice shook, as did her hands which were unnecessarily adjusting the folds of her skirt.

John got up and sat next to her. 'You're just imagining things, Katy. Of course we won't get arrested. Remember, we're now connected to people in high places,' he said glibly, trying to reassure her.

It was as if she had not heard him. She insisted, 'It's quite possible that somebody will sell us out. I don't know if it's safe for us to have all those rands here. Do you know that new laws state that the police can just come in here, whenever they like, and turn the house upside-down without a search warrant?'

His voice was cold and calm. 'I do know.' Some of her anxiety seemed to seep through to him as he held her hands. Thinking of the wads of cash under their bedroom mattress, he said, 'I'll have to phone Mr Nzou tomorrow. He hasn't contacted me about the money. Do you think we should hide it somewhere less obvious?'

Katy nodded. Husband and wife lifted a display cabinet in the sitting room. They shoved the incriminating rands under the carpet. With the wooden cabinet back in position, nobody would guess that they had secreted five thousand rand's worth of notes under their floral carpet.

≈≈≈

Faith's finals were about to start, as were Melody's third-year exams. Both women were so absorbed in their revision that time together had become a luxury. Faith had not been spending much time with Tom, either. While he'd understood that she had to study, she felt deeper concerns about the relationship that would need to be addressed once she finished her examinations. Now, she just wanted to focus on her work, and Tom could easily become a distraction. Her mentor, Mrs Gava, had been very supportive during revision sessions. Faith's confidence had received a much-needed boost. She had begun to picture herself as a qualified lawyer with a strong interest in women's issues – just like her lecturer.

As she hadn't seen Melody all day, she decided to go up to her room for a quick chat. She found her still in bed, looking dishevelled and miserable. Her eyes were red and puffy. Before Faith could say anything, she announced abruptly, 'I broke up with Chanda today.'

Faith felt an immediate stab of pity, followed, in quick succession, by a wave of relief that Melody had finally ended a relationship which had no future, and anxiety that her friend would drift into the arms of yet another married man. It was possible. There was no shortage of married men in search of cheap thrills with younger women; and Melody's financial needs had not suddenly vanished with Chanda's disappearance. Shocked by the speed of her assessment, she reached out to touch her friend, but Melody drew back.

The girl threw her an odd, defiant look as she burrowed deeper under the faded university bed linen. 'Aren't you at least going to ask me why it's over? Aren't you going to take pleasure in gloating, since you warned me?' There was a hostility in her voice.

'Of course not.' Faith retorted. 'I guess you don't realise how much I care about you. Yes, I warned you, but I'm certainly not going to gloat. You must be so miserable,' she concluded sympathetically.

Melody was immediately contrite. Tears trickled down her cheeks, 'Sorry ... You were right. I don't know how I could have been so foolish. I've never been so humiliated in my life as I was this afternoon.'

'Whatever happened?'

Melody shook her head and brushed away a tear. 'His wife ...'

'Yes?' Faith prompted, her heart pounding.

Melody blew out her cheeks dramatically, 'She's back from the UK. She turned up at lunchtime, breathing fire. For a moment, I thought she was going to give me a thorough beating.'

Faith was aghast. 'How did she find you? Who told her?'

Melody gave a strangled laugh. 'She has a relative, a student here at UZ ... she's the one who told her about me and brought her here, to my room. The wife slapped me and called me a prostitute. I was so ashamed, Faith. She told me that she was leaving Chanda and that I could have him, but that he would cheat on me as well. Apparently, she's been working very hard, doing double shifts, sending him money to build their home, and so on. But he hasn't built a thing. He must have spent some of the money on me, and another girl from the teachers' college. Who knows if he didn't have a third girlfriend? I can't believe the bastard was cheating on me!'

Faith shook her head. 'Did you really expect him to be faithful to you, when he was cheating on his wife?'

Melody looked at her, peeved. 'Don't be so damn judgemental! He told me he was faithful to me and, yes, I did trust him. He was good to me.'

'Well, you shouldn't have trusted him,' Faith snapped.

Close to tears again, Melody went on, 'Ah, it's easy for you to be wise after the event. What would you say if Tom was cheating on you? But, really, If I'd known that it was her money, I wouldn't have taken it, I really wouldn't. I feel so awful about it. I wish I'd listened to you.'

'It's no use crying over spilt milk,' Faith said firmly. Melody's quip about Tom had made her uneasy, and she wanted to bring the conversation down to manageable proportions. 'I'm just relieved that you're out of that relationship. It could have been worse.'

'And the swine has the nerve to keep phoning me! I have a mind to give him back the cellphone. Maybe it's one of the presents his wife sent him from UK.' Melody began to cry again.

Faith sat down on the bed, 'It no longer matters where he got the phone from. Don't try to give it back. Just block his calls and get him out of your life,' she said decisively, mulling over some 'what ifs'. What if Melody had not discovered that Chanda had a second girlfriend? Would she have left him, if she hadn't discovered that he was splashing out his wife's hard-earned British pounds? Didn't Chanda's own salary belong to his wife anyway? Unwelcome thoughts lingered. Melody could easily get involved with yet another married man. She decided to ask, 'What about your university fees? You did say the reason why…'

'Don't remind me, please. My fees will be taken care of. There's more dignity in begging from my father's brothers …' Melody shrugged her shoulders, looking forlorn, '… and they'll make me beg all right.'

'Can't we talk about something else?' The expression on her face forestalled further questioning.

'All right, why don't you get up and wash your face, you'll feel a bit better then. There's water at the moment,' she added with a half-smile. Melody nodded.

Life would go on.

Having suggested that Melody take an aspirin to help her sleep, Faith left the room, resolving at some point to take the discussion further. Foremost in her mind was the risk of HIV that her friend had exposed herself to, although Melody had insisted that she was using condoms to protect herself.

'I'm not stupid. There are condoms and condoms,' she had said flippantly. But Faith still worried, as she occasionally did about herself. Wouldn't it have been prudent for she and Tom to have gone for an HIV test before they became intimate? Or before she switched from using condoms to the pill at his insistence?

What about her mother's wise words about not sleeping with a man before marriage? But what good would that have done for a woman like *mainini* Onai, for instance? Avoiding sex before marriage made no difference to one's lifetime risk of getting HIV. It could only increase life expectancy by delaying the age of infection. When she'd read this, she'd thought that the writer was a cynic and a pessimist. Now she was not so sure. If only life could be less complicated ...

She walked dejectedly down the stairs and back to her room, for some strange reason thinking more about *mainini* Onai's risk of HIV infection than hers or her friend's.

≈≈≈

With no income from the market, Onai found herself under the burden of even greater financial constraint. Waking up each morning to face long, bleak days had become an ordeal. She was perplexed by Gari's prolonged silences and intermittent outbursts of verbal abuse. It also bothered her that he still looked unwell. His eyes were a disturbing yellow and he appeared to have episodes of mild confusion. She wondered if she was the one who was confused, and not Gari. The stress in her life was more than enough to make her so.

As he was getting ready for work the following morning, Gari suddenly started retching. He bent over and held both hands across his upper abdomen. He vomited profusely all over the bed and the floor. The vomit was dark brown, like clotted blood. Alarmed, Onai managed to clean him up and helped him back into bed. His body felt hot to touch, although he was shivering as if cold.

'I think you need to go to hospital *baba va*Ruva. Your eyes are quite yellow and you don't look at all well,' she said gently. When he did not reply, she asked, ' Do you want me to call for an ambulance?'

He turned to glare at her, replying curtly, 'Leave me alone. I want to sleep.' In a gesture that conveyed a clear message, he turned over and pulled the bedcover over his head.

Maddening, random thoughts darted through her mind. Is that how you talk to Gloria? Would you talk to me like that, if I was Gloria? They were silent questions without answers. Ones that she still dared not speak. She was at a loss as to what to do next.

With slow, tired steps, she walked into the sitting room and sat heavily in an armchair. There was hardly any money left in her Lactogen tin under the bed. All she had was a few hundred thousand dollars worth of bearer cheques which would last less than a week.

Thinking of her children's school fees for the following term made her head spin. She leaned forwards in the armchair and rested her head on her arms. Invitations for people to come forward and register for new market stalls had not yet been issued. She had to do something, but what? Spending the rest of the day in a haze of gloom only made her feel worse.

≈≈≈

Gari got up at dusk, looking slightly better. Onai said nothing further, although she thought he looked like a sick man.

After a supper of fried cabbage and sadza which Gari had devoured with surprising enthusiasm, she decided to talk to him about her concerns. She looked directly at him across the wobbly table, cluttered with plates and the remnants of their evening meal.

'Baba vaRuva, I need more money to buy groceries. There's a rumour that there will be a delivery of soap, mealie meal, sugar and cooking oil at the Superstore some time this week. I need money so that I can start joining the queues tomorrow. It may be a while before these goods are available again.'

Gari's jaw slackened and dropped. He looked at her, as if she had lost her mind. 'Why are you telling me this?' he asked coldly.

Onai fought a growing feeling of panic. She worked her hands then placed them firmly on her knees, trying hard to bolster herself.

Plaintively, and she wished her voice sounded stronger, she responded, 'As I'm no longer able to trade at the market, I've run out of money. The children need to be fed. In two months' time we will need to pay school fees. You will remember that the new fees and levies are now three million dollars. I thought we should share ideas about how to take care of our expenses.'

His yellow eyes bored into her and he spoke to her as if she was a delinquent child. 'Do you ever listen to what I say? I've told you many times that our duties are clear-cut. I provide accommodation and you do the rest. Now stop bothering me. I'm going out for a beer.' His dismissal was one to which she was accustomed, but still, it cut her with a renewed sense of rejection, which hurt like an old bruise.

Without saying anything further, Gari washed his hands in the rusty metal dish and abruptly stood up. He buttoned his coat with hasty movements, obviously eager to leave.

As she watched him, she wondered if he was off to see Gloria, and what time he would come back. The Humpty Dumpty clock beamed down at her, showing it was eight o'clock already. Jealousy burned inside her, making her feel ill. The door slammed shut behind him as he disappeared into the night.

When the door banged after him, the children drifted into the sitting room. They found her supporting her head with hands that were wet with tears.

'What is it, Mum? Are you all right.? Please don't cry', Rita pleaded, pulling gently at the hands that were covering her face.

Onai smiled through her tears and quickly wiped her face. She placed her hand on Rita's shoulder and said softly, 'Yes, I'm OK. Have you finished your homework, *mwanangu*?'

'Yes, I've finished,' Rita replied hurriedly. 'But Mum, listen, I have a plan. I can start selling foodstuffs on the streets. We can get enough money for bread, I think.'

'No Rita, it's illegal. You might get arrested. We have to wait until we get a chance to register for a new market stall. I should be able to do that next week, when they start taking application forms.'

'But *Amai*, my friend's mother was saying the licences will take a long time to come through. I heard what father said to you. I want to help. Ruva has to study, so I will go with Fari. He can watch out for the police while I sell. We can go after school and at weekends. Some of my friends are doing it and they're making a lot of money.' It was obvious that she had given her plan a lot of consideration.

While Onai was touched by her daughter's thoughtfulness, she had reservations. How could she let her children take part in something that meant breaking the law? The children were her responsibility, hers and Gari's. It could never be the other way round. She shook her head, and squeezed Rita's hand.

Ruva declared loudly, 'I'm not going to be a part of this.' She glared at Rita who was kneeling next to her mother. 'Count me out!' she snapped at her and scowled fiercely.

'Nobody asked you,' Rita retorted and turned to her mother. 'Please, *Amai*. Its true, that's what a lot of my friends are doing. I really want to help,' she persisted.

Onai felt the stirrings of temptation. She smiled at the determined little face before her with a mixture of unhappiness and guilt. The idea was appealing. If other children were helping their parents that way … maybe there was no harm in hers trying it out. Just for a few days. Even a few weeks. Just until things improved. Bravely, she gave in to Rita's plan.

Ruva looked appalled. She slammed shut the thick General Science textbook which she had clearly been pretending to read. 'Mum! What if they get arrested?' she demanded, her voice loud and cross.

Fari started jumping up and down. He was frantic to have his point heard. 'We won't get arrested! I'll guard Rita and watch out for the police.' He hit against a chair accidentally in his agitation. It toppled over with a loud bang.

'Stop that. Be careful, Fari!'

'I'm sorry, *Amai*. I want to go selling things with Rita. We won't get arrested. I will guard Rita and watch out for the police,' he was almost crying.

Ruva was overwhelmed by popular opinion. There was just enough money for them to make a somewhat less than modest start. Nevertheless, it was a start. The master plan took shape. It was a plan which would work reasonably well, and keep the small family from starving.

≈≈≈

Mr Nzou arrived for his appointment with John promptly at half past eight that evening. He was not wearing his uniform. Casual wear complemented by a stylish denim jacket gave him a sociable air, in spite of his rather intimidating status. Because John was present, Katy felt none of the apprehension that she had previously experienced during transactions. The police officer was quite genial, smiling broadly as he exchanged greetings with her and her husband.

Turning to John, he said, 'So how was your trip down south, Mr Nguni?'

John responded, 'It was fine. It's the terrible developments here which have unsettled me.' Katy stiffened besides him. The words were hardly appropriate. They were almost like a challenge.

Mr Nzou gave an awkward grin, for once appearing discomfited. 'Well, Mr Nguni, some of these measures are quite necessary, otherwise *nyika yedu* will go to the dogs.'

John shook his head slightly, while Katy forced herself to suppress laughter, amazed by the man's words. Otherwise the country could go to the dogs? Well.

Appearing to recover his composure quite quickly, Nzou said, 'I'm afraid I can't stay long. You did say ten thousand rands, didn't you?'

John nodded.

'*Ko ma*US dollars?' Nzou questioned.

'I couldn't get any this time around, maybe next time.' John sounded regretful.

After a bit of haggling about exchange rates, the transaction was concluded. Mr Nzou signed John's notebook while Katy looked on.

'That little notebook is my security. Those signatures could be priceless, one day,' John had told her. With the way things were going, she was glad he had insisted on getting a signature for each transaction. She accepted the money from Mr Nzou and walked into the bedroom.

Conversation between Mr Nzou and her husband floated towards her. Mr Nzou was saying, 'No, don't worry. Nobody will touch you. I will make sure of that.'

John laughed. Rather uneasily, Katy thought.

Again, she heard Mr Nzou's voice. 'Business transactions are now so difficult because no foreign companies want our money. I would appreciate any currency that you can get for me. Even Zambian kwacha. Did you hear that since South Africa tightened border controls, our girls are now crossing over to Zambia in search of the kwacha? The girls over there are out of business because our girls charge so much less!' He laughed.

John sounded puzzled, 'Our girls?'

Nzou responded, 'Ladies of the night, Mr Nguni!' At that, they broke into noisy laughter.

Men! Katy thought bitterly as she packed the bearer cheques into a small box. A little while later, she heard John offering to walk Mr Nzou out.

CHAPTER 17

Onai went back to ordering small quantities of fruit and vegetables for resale from VaGudo. Chubby and cheerful as ever, he had resumed making clandestine deliveries in a concealed, bushy area on the periphery of Mbare. Like all yet-to-be-registered traders, he was playing a cat-and-mouse game with the police.

Onai claimed her own territory in the city centre, selling fruit and vegetables to city workers and people in fuel queues. On days when it seemed as if there were police officers patrolling every street in the city, she took to making door-to-door sales in the high-density townships. One had to be constantly watchful, in readiness to run away should the figures of authority appear, as they did habitually. It was like an intricate game of hide-and-seek.

Youthful officers nicknamed 'The Bike Brigade' were the most feared. Stories were told of how aggressively they cycled after vending mothers, especially those with produce on their heads and crying babies strapped to their backs. The enthusiastic officers had absolutely no patience with such a brazen disregard of the law. Many of their targets had their goods pulverised on the tarmac, before being handcuffed and frog-marched to police stations, so Onai took great care.

Fari and Rita targeted long-distance commuters at the main terminus. Their selected goods were bananas, sweets, crisps, *maputi* and cigarettes. They took to their task with a level of dedication and diligence that sometimes worried Onai. Was this the right way to raise her children? What sort of people was she exposing them to at the bus terminus? And what about Rita, whose presence was bound to stir interest among the bus touts, the *vanahwindi*? She worried that poverty had consumed her sense of right and wrong. Without any pressure being put on her to join her siblings on their vending mission, Ruva had declared, 'I'm not going to be part of this madness. I don't want to get arrested and miss my exams. You can go to prison if you like. The rats and lice can feast on you!'

Fari was amused. 'We will never get arrested because I have X-ray eyes! I can see policemen from a long way off,' he'd declared proudly.

'You don't even know what x-rays are!' Ruva had snapped, irritated. She had adopted a very high-minded attitude to their vending, and seemed not to want to change her position.

Initially, Onai was troubled that Gari barely took any notice when Rita and Fari returned in the evening, and counted out the money they'd made from sales. She longed for him to give them some sign of approval or acknowledgement. Even some indication that he didn't want his children to become illegal vendors, would have been welcome. But he said nothing. Indeed, it looked as if the pattern of their lives was now irreversibly set in this cycle of abuse and indifference.

After a while, his lack of concern stopped bothering her, because life simply had to go on, and so it did. Indeed, for her and the children, it was definitely a bit better than it had been immediately after the market closures and demolitions, because Fari and Rita worked so hard. Onai comforted herself that not only did they seem to enjoy vending, but despite their father, were proud to be contributing to the household.

≈≈≈

Without much enthusiasm, Emily had booked herself in for some locum work in the Casualty Department when her leave fell due. Salaries had not been increased to match the escalating cost of living, so she needed the extra earnings. Better-paying locums at the Avenues and West End clinics had suddenly become more competitive, with older, more experienced doctors being preferred.

Her hospital colleagues had been muttering about a strike to press for better salaries and the improvement of conditions in hospitals, but Emily was not holding her breath. In her opinion, going on strike was a costly, futile exercise that only served to worsen the plight of patients, and harden the attitude of the authorities, if they took any notice at all. Patients died needlessly, until doctors trickled back to work, consciences pricking; their concerns not having been addressed.

Even though she was working with two colleagues and a team of nurses, her first morning in Casualty was hectic. A good number of patients were newly homeless people, who had come in with diarrhoea and chest infections, worsened, no doubt, by overcrowding, lack of sanitation and exposure to cold weather. Every time she thought she should take a break, the queue lengthened as more patients wobbled into the department; or the odd crowded ambulance decanted several people needing urgent attention. Having missed breakfast, by eleven o'clock, she was very hungry.

'Mind if I take a break, Ngoni?' she asked one of the other doctors, taking off her white coat and untangling a stethoscope from around her neck.

'No problem. Once you get back, I'll need one too. It looks like this shift will only get busier.'

Emily stepped into the corridor and looked towards the entrance of the Casualty Department. There were fresh arrivals being led in by a nurse, who was clutching several blue referral letters distinctive of district hospitals.

'Aren't you going, Emily?' Ngoni asked her from the treatment room.

'Fresh arrivals,' she replied grimly and stepped back into the room.

The sister-in-charge took her hand and led her towards the door. 'I have another doctor starting very shortly, so don't worry. I don't want you collapsing from exhaustion. I'm so tired, myself, that if you do collapse, I might just be tempted to step over you!' she teased.

'I wouldn't mind if she collapsed! Maybe I could perfect my basic mouth-to-mouth resuscitation skills on a live …!'

Emily whirled round and interrupted the speaker, 'Oh, Ben! Shut up. We've work to do here,' she scolded her friend who had just walked into the treatment room.

The sister laughed. 'No arguing, please, *vanachiremba,* Dr Sibanda. Just go. I would like to see you back here in thirty minutes, with no missing teeth or eyes!'

The two doctors strolled towards the exit. 'What are you still doing here, anyway? Shouldn't you be at home now, after being on call last night?' Emily asked.

For a moment Ben did not answer, then avoiding her question, he said, 'Let's walk over to the Red Cross canteen. I could do with some Fanta *nemabhanzi.'*

She nodded. 'Sure.' Fanta and fresh buns at the Red Cross Canteen was an enduring favourite from their medical school days when they had come to the hospital for practicals. Back then, before its refurbishment, the wooden shack that served as a canteen had been dubbed Typhoid Centre, but general popularity had won over poor hygiene.

She said 'We might get *mabhanzi*. Not sure about the Fanta, though. Shortages, shortages. And you haven't answered me, why are you still here?'

'I had to do a ward round, and then see the consultant on call to discuss an incident that happened last night.' He was silent for a moment, then he added quietly, 'I almost killed someone last night, Emily.'

Of course, he was joking. He had to be. She laughed, 'The confessions of a would-be murderer! I'm not sure I can stomach them so early in the day…'

'I'm serious,' he sounded anxious.

She sobered up, peering at him. 'What happened?' she asked.

He shook his head and took a deep breath. 'Emergency Caesarean Section last night. We had a power failure. The generator came on for about two minutes, then it crashed.'

Emily froze in her tracks. 'Whaaat!' she squealed and hovered at the edge of the car park.

'Believe it or not, I finished the C-section in candlelight. Nobody could find a free torch. They looked everywhere in the Maternity Department. The anaesthetist was ventilating manually. So she became very irritable, and kept telling me to finish and close up. I've never had such terrible tremors as I did then. I could hardly hold the instruments. Bloody hell, I couldn't even see what I was doing!'

'I can imagine. So you did finish all right?'

'No such luck. I missed an artery, I think. She almost bled to death, out in Recovery. Getting blood to transfuse her was another nightmare,' he said in a dull, defeated voice. 'The consultant had to come in. We took her back to theatre. Fortunately, by then, there was electricity.

It never rains … she had to have a hysterectomy. Now she has one child and no uterus, and it's all my fault. Women have been divorced by their husbands for less,' he said miserably. 'I can't do this anymore. She could have died on me, Emily.' His face was pinched and drawn.

She tried to comfort him. 'Hey, I'm sure you did your best. It was brave of you to continue at all. I would have just walked away in fear!'

He sighed. 'I can't wait to go back to the Medical Wards next month. That incident has totally put me off obstetrics.'

Emily wondered what difference that would make. Each department held challenges of similar gravity, because of critical shortages and frequent high-risk incidents. But pointing that out would only make him feel worse. So she said instead, 'Don't be so hard on yourself. You did your best. By staying, you probably saved her life. Anyway, let's get something to eat. I have to get back to work.'

They crossed the car park and strolled over to the canteen. The place was already swarming with medical students, who had just been dropped off by the university bus. Emily joked, 'Hungry students. That means no *mabhanzi* for us.' She was right. There was no Fanta either. They ended up buying Cascade juice at twenty-five thousand dollars a bottle, then finding a concrete bench to sit on, enjoyed the warmth of late morning winter sun.

Emily's Cascade was refreshingly cold but it had a faint sour taste. She grimaced, tightening the bottle top. 'I think this needs to go into a bin.'

Ben nodded. 'So does mine. Not surprised, are you?' She shrugged. They rose and walked towards a bin.

'I'd better get back to work,' Emily said.

'OK. Can we meet up at St Elmo's for a pizza later this evening?' Ben asked.

'Well, after work I have to go somewhere with Tom to see about a petrol deal, there is hardly anything in my tank. He knows somebody … I'll see you at half-past six, if that's all right.'

'That's fine. If possible, please get some fuel for me as well. I'm not sure how I'll get to work next week.'

'Sure.'

'See you, then.' Ben said, and slouched off towards the Maternity car park, his hands in his pockets.

Emily's eyes followed him. When he wasn't annoying her by making declarations of love, Ben was a very good friend. Matters of the heart were just too far from her mind. 'Ice Babe', the male JDs called her. She didn't care.

He really is worried, she thought, when she realised that he'd walked off without his car keys. She ran after him.

Back in Casualty, her first patient was an eighteen-year-old assault victim. In her company was a fatherly-looking policeman. The young woman had been beaten by her husband for serving him a cold meal of left-over sadza *nemuriwo* from the previous night, instead of a proper breakfast of tea, buttered bread and fried eggs.

She explained to Emily, 'He's always hitting me, *chiremba*. He does not give me enough money to buy the bread, butter and eggs that he wants. And today I could not heat up the leftovers for him because there was a power cut. He hit me with a knobkerrie. The pain in my arm …'

Emily looked sympathetically at the girl's arm. Swollen and bruised, it was probably broken. In a gentle voice she said, 'You did the right thing to report this.' Severely assaulting one's wife over such petty issues was gratuitous and cruel. There was probably more to it than that.

She accepted some medical report forms from the police officer. 'Thank you. May you kindly wait outside while I examine her? I shouldn't be too long.' The officer thanked her politely and stepped outside.

Emily examined the woman and sent her off for an X-ray. As she had feared, it showed a broken radius. Fortunately, it was a minor fracture, which only required a plaster cast. Once the bone was set, Emily briefly counselled her and referred her to Kushinga Women's Project on Seventh Street. The woman promised to go to the centre for counselling and assistance the following day. Increasingly aware that mobilising victims was like fighting a losing battle, Emily found her attitude quite refreshing. She would probably seek help before it was too late.

As she handed over the medical report to the police officer, she said, 'All done. So, do you think we'll meet in court?'

The man threw his head back casually and laughed. 'Mmm, I doubt it, *chiremba*. We do our part, but these women always withdraw charges against their husbands. Very few, if any, ever get to court. How many reports do you fill out, and how many times do you ever get called to court?'

'I've been only once,' Emily replied .thoughtfully 'What reasons do they give you when they withdraw their charges?'

He shrugged. 'To avoid compromising their marriages, of course. A man cannot go on living with a woman who's dragged him to court; a woman who depends on him for everything, for that matter! It would be like living in a war zone.' His laughter was loud, as if all such matters were absurd.

Emily said lightly, 'I sometimes feel that you male police officers always sympathise with the men, the culprits. Isn't it true that many cases don't get to court because you accept bribes from these women's husbands so that evidence gets destroyed and dockets disappear?'

Looking embarrassed, the officer protested, 'Ahh, *chiremba?* How can you say that? Just like you, we are true professionals. We do our job, the rest is up to the women.' Still wearing a sheepish expression, he thanked her and left the room, as if he couldn't get away quickly enough.

Emily shook her head, accepting that just encouraging women to report an assault would never be enough. The problems ran much deeper and demanded a more complex solution. Her thoughts wandered. She could remember women, whom she had attended to in the past ... women who had obviously been assaulted, and whose records had indicated previous presentations to hospital with similar injuries. But, almost typically, most of them denied that they were in abusive relationships. As the police officer had said so matter-of-factly, it was out of a need to protect their marriages. But were such unions ever worth the effort, Emily wondered. Sadly, she acknowledged that nothing would change, as long as vulnerable women found themselves entirely dependent on abusive husbands. Even where economic dependence was not an issue, cultural practices that glorified passivity and subservience to one's husband, despite personal suffering, did nothing to help. She shook her head and glanced at her watch. It was almost time for a much-needed lunch break.

≈≈≈

Onai kept her disgraceful secret to herself until Katy stumbled upon it by chance, and wasting no time, immediately invited her friend to her house for a cup of tea.

But, no sooner had Onai sat down in the kitchen, than Katy confronted her, 'Sahirwa, I saw Rita loitering at the bus terminus this afternoon. I'm not sure what she was doing but she seemed to be attracting quite a lot of attention from the touts. ... whistles, suggestive comments, impertinent remarks ... Ah, those *vanahwindi!* Rita had disappeared before I could ask her why she was there. You should watch out for her, Onai. What on earth was she doing?'

Onai's face burned with embarrassment. 'Fari and Rita ... are vending at the terminus. They're helping me out.'

'They're what?' Katy exclaimed, looking horrified. 'Tell me I've heard you wrong, *sahwira*.'.

'They're helping me to raise money. They're doing a bit of vending, after school,' Onai said hesitantly. Her worries resurfaced.

Katy shook her head and poured out two cups of hot tea. With undue force, she wiped away two drops that had spilled on the linoleum surface. The table squeaked in protest.

'When I saw Rita, I suspected as much, but I hoped I was wrong. Do you know that it's illegal? Why are you taking such risks with your children? Don't you care that your daughter is being ogled by those ... those *mahwindi* at the terminus? You will only have yourself to blame if she gets pregnant! If you needed help that badly, why didn't you tell me? I could have helped you out, Onai.'

Though she had expected criticism, Onai was wounded by the strength of her friend's condemnation and went on the defensive. 'I'll tell you what, I can't survive on your hand-outs, Katy. I have three children. Can you afford to help me look after all of them? What would your husband say? How, if ever, would I pay you back? Do you think I want to be indebted to my friends?' Her nostrils flared indignantly. She pushed away the cup of tea that Katy had poured out for her.

'But Onai, there has to be something else that you can do. Don't send your children out to sell, please,' Katy said, now gentler and less confrontational.

Onai knew her friend was right, but she still felt she had to defend herself. 'Its easy for you to say that, Katy. You don't live my life. You don't have the husband that I've got. Your daughter is grown up. She has almost finished her university education, but I still have a long way to go. *Woda kuti ndiite seiko?*'

'But you *know* that people are being arrested for vending? Maya was locked up for two days last week. Two whole days, Onai. Fine if you want to take that risk, but what about your children? Do you know what happens in those cells?'

Onai sighed, her fighting spirit overwhelmed by sudden lethargy. She looked with longing at the cup that she had pushed away. It was possibly the last sugared tea that she would have in a long time. She lifted it and sipped slowly, but without real enjoyment.

Then, lifting her eyes, she said, 'I know that people are being arrested. I saw Maya yesterday. She was boasting about how she had terrorised the guards in the holding cells.' She gave a forced laugh. 'But please don't question me. For the sake of our friendship, please don't. Do you think I would risk sending my children out, if there was any other way? I think of myself as a good mother. I am a good mother. But we have to survive, Katy. The money that my children have made from their sales has enabled me to pay a deposit towards Ruva's O-Level exam fees. Where else could that money have come from? What better choices do you see for us?'

Katy shook her head and took a deep breath, 'As I've said so often before, I really think your life would improve, if you left Gari. *Asi chii nhai Onai?* How bad must things get before you see that you have to leave him? If he was a responsible father, your children wouldn't have to vend on the streets and Rita would …'

Onai interjected emphatically, 'Katy, please, I beg you. Please, don't interfere. Where would I go if I left Gari? I would simply be homeless, on top of everything else. I know what I'm doing.' Ignoring an urge to leave, she remained defiantly seated. There was still some tea in her cup.

Katy sighed and stood up. She picked up the damp cloth again as if to wipe more unseen drops off the table. Then rolled it up and threw it irritably into a bowl.

'If you think I'm interfering, I'm sorry. But I care about you, Onai. I just want things to get better for you, that's all. Don't you think you should at least confront Gari about his affair with Gloria?'

At the mention of Gloria, a knot of pain tightened in Onai's heart. She had wanted to do just this, but fear of reprisal had held her back. She fidgeted aimlessly with her cup and then gripped the edge of the table to steady her hands. She looked up at her friend and said, 'Let me try and talk to him tonight.'

Katy took Onai's hand in hers and held it fast, 'It will be all right. It must be. At least if you get *nyaya ya* Gloria out of the way you might be able to deal with other issues.'

Onai nodded and said as firmly as she could, 'I will.' With that resolve, she felt the tightness in her chest slackening. As usual, peace was easily restored between the two friends.

Onai had another cup of tea while they chatted, after which she walked home, deep in thought. She wanted, and didn't want, to be free of Gari. In fact, she no longer knew what she wanted, because she was not sure what either option would mean for her children. How could she deprive them of their father? Or deprive herself of her husband? She felt confused. If only she could reclaim her youth, there were a lot of things that she would have done differently.

≈≈≈

Examinations had never been more taxing, and Faith was relieved that she only had two papers to go. It was exhilarating to think ahead; if she passed, she would have a degree in Law. The idea kept her going. The only cloud on her horizon was Tom. Ever since their trip to Victoria

189

Falls that had ended so badly, matters between them had never been quite the same. Tom had taken her questions about his farm, and her reluctance to accept what he'd told her, as a personal insult. She knew that the growing rift was mostly her fault, but she couldn't help it. Their argument about the clean-up operation had made matters worse. Much as she loved him, she wanted to be sure. She did not want to sink into an emotional or moral quagmire just for the sake of marrying a rich man. Besides, as a lawyer, she had a good career ahead of her. All being well, if she specialised in women's issues, she might even make a difference. Were all her years of work and studying worth giving up just to be someone's wife?

Not that she thought Tom would mind her working. Indeed, he'd often joked that he'd be proud to have a lawyer as a wife; and she'd be able to get him out of all his scrapes.

After supper, she trailed after Melody. 'I don't really feel like studying tonight.'

'Great! Neither do I. How about keeping me company while I iron and share a bit of gossip?' They laughed. Melody unlocked the door to her room.

Looking seriously at her friend, Faith asked, 'Is your brother still working for Dombo and Partners?'

'Yeah,' Melody replied distractedly as she cleared her desk of a disorderly array of books and prepared to iron some clothes.

Faith muttered unhappily. 'Can I ask for a big favour, Mel?'

'Sure, anything. We're friends aren't we?' She looked up at Faith, disconcerted by her sudden change of tone.

'What's wrong with you?'

Faith hesitated, 'Could you please ask your brother to carry out a deeds' search on Tom's farm? Please?'

'Why are you sneaking behind his back? I thought we agreed a long time ago that the best thing to do was to ask him directly. Why didn't you?' Melody glowered with disapproval.

Faith sighed. 'I did ask him and he told me that he'd bought his farm, but I didn't believe him.'

'Why ever not?' Melody sounded exasperated.

Faith shrugged. 'Instinct. I'm sure you know, his farm was owned by that white farmer who died ... or was killed ...'

Melody stared at her, surprised. 'And so? What exactly are you getting at? Are you seriously trying to tell me that you think Tom was responsible for the murder of that farmer?'

'Of course not!' Faith was indignant. 'But I find it suspicious that after his family was evicted, Tom acquired the land so quickly.'

Melody frowned. 'That still doesn't preclude the possibility that he bought it. It seems to me you've already made up your mind that Tom did something wrong, so why bother with a deeds' search? Right from the start, you knew he had a farm, this farm. So why didn't you make an effort to find out more about it then? Have you ever been there?'

'Only once. I just couldn't bring myself to go back, although the farmhouse is lovely and Tom is doing so well ... I don't know. I can't explain it ...'

'Ask Emily. She's quite friendly, isn't she?'

'She is, but it would only make things worse because she's so close to Tom. Please, Mel. I just need to be quite certain that he's telling me the truth. If he was involved, I wouldn't be able to live with my conscience. What would getting married to him make me?' She found herself suddenly close to tears.

'A very rich woman, if you ask me,' Melody retorted, then laughed. 'You're too intense, Faith. Just ask Tom to show you the title deeds.'

'I did ask him.'

'And?'

'He shoved some papers under my nose but I didn't look at them!'

'Why ever not?' Melody was frustrated.

'We were having a row and I was too angry to read the documents. Now I'm too proud to ask again. What if they were fakes?'

'Faaaaaith!' Melody's voice rose, 'What's wrong with you? Have you lost your confidence in him to such an extent?'

'Please ...'

'All right,' Melody consented grudgingly. 'Give me the details. I'll need at least two weeks. My brother can't carry out an isolated search in company time. So it will have to be when he has some other searches for clients.'

Faith opened her bag and pulled out a notebook in which she had scribbled the details. 'You're the best,' she said.

≈≈≈

That night, she sat up long after the children had gone to bed and waited for her husband. The latest *sungura* tunes on Radio Two kept her company. Gari came in well after midnight, long after she had decided that he wouldn't come at all.

Predictably, he was very drunk. He gave the sadza *nemuriwo* which she set before him an uninterested glance, making no attempt to eat it. Wondering if Gloria had cooked for him, she braced herself for the inevitable confrontation and blocked his way as he staggered towards the bedroom.

'Please sit down *baba va*Ruva. I want to talk to you!' she demanded, anger fuelling her bravery. If a fight started, she knew that she could easily give him a good hiding because he was so drunk. It was a whole year since she'd dared to hit him back. The last time she'd given him a deep cut on the back of his head with the jagged handle of her pot. At that moment, she felt sure that she could do it again.

He slurred, 'Shit down, shit down? What do you mean you cra-crazy woman? Get out of my way.' He lurched against her, pushing her ineffectively.

She stood her ground, stock-still in the doorway, fury mounting. 'You're not going anywhere *baba va*Ruva. Not before you tell me about Gloria!' There. She'd said it.

To her surprise he broke into loud, drunken laughter, his mouth frothing. 'Groria, Groria, what do you know about Groro-ria! *Heee, Groria wachena!*' His voice rose abruptly into an old song about a girl called Gloria then dropped to mutter a few more incomprehensible words. He swayed drunkenly and slumped against the wall, struggling to keep his eyes open.

How could one have a logical conversation with a drunk? Suddenly deflated, Onai stepped aside to let him into the bedroom. He threw himself on the bed and immediately started snoring, saliva dribbling from the corner of his mouth. Angrily, she yanked his dusty shoes off, removed his jacket and rolled him forcibly under the blankets. With slow tired movements, she undressed and prepared for bed. The chance to extract a denial or a confession had passed. In a way, she was relieved because she had no idea how she could have coped with either.

As usual, her husband's porcine snores kept her awake. She tossed and turned until fatigue dulled her senses. In her drowsy mind, he was hers and he was lying next to her. Because his snores were so familiar, she eventually slept.

≈≈≈

Although he had experienced a lot of unanticipated difficulties, it was finally over. The demolitions had complicated his self-styled ritual, threatening its completion. Sleeping under the dilapidated viaduct had become almost impossible because of recurrent police raids. Twice, he'd come dangerously close to being taken away to a holding camp, together with the other homeless people. He had had to move away from the Jo'burg Lines area to a quieter part of Mbare that was less frequented by police. He had not spotted Tom in Mbare again, and that was fine. Neither had he come across Mai Ruva and her children since moving away. About that, he had mixed feelings.

Now, it was time to return home. Previously, he had been looking forward to his mythical return, but now he was filled with a sense of unease. Living like a vagrant had somehow seared his guilt. It had provided a bizarre but necessary escape from reality with its daily reminders of loss. Because his new life was so strange, he occasionally wondered if this was how people lost their minds; and if this was how losing touch with reality began – placing oneself in a world where everything was unknown. He shook his head. No, he was not mad, whatever the people of Mbare might imply by calling him Mawaya. Going back home would definitely set him right. Nonetheless, because Edith would not be there for him, the future was still daunting, and he had to face it alone, and without his wife. He had to accept her death.

He could not live on the streets forever. There was only one more thing for him to do. He patted the almost empty money belt under his rags. He had, perhaps foolishly, worn it throughout. It seemed a reassuring symbol of his other self. He had only used small amounts to buy toothpaste and soap, after discovering that it was easy to get a quick wash-down at the communal terminus toilets, and had become addicted to this early morning routine. So, having used only part of the money, he still had enough to effect his new plan.

Slowly, he walked along the pavement, looking for a space to sleep. He spread out his newspapers in a small enclave next to the supermarket entrance that other homeless people had avoided. It did not take him long to discover why. The place reeked of stale urine. He rose and gathered his newspapers, cursing loudly. He immediately stopped when he saw a young girl huddled against the wall staring at him with frightened eyes. He walked along the pavement and found another spot. With the images of two women fusing in his mind, he fell into a deep sleep, oblivious of the rats gnawing at his worn shoes.

CHAPTER 18

July was a promising month. With winter approaching a much-awaited end, Saturday was a cool but sunny day. Onai was feeling surprisingly optimistic and this in itself made her more buoyant. It would be another day of undercover vending in the city centre and she was looking forward to making good sales. The fuel queues were longer these days and that meant more potential customers. She was beginning to get used to city vending; even to enjoy it a little.

Carefully, she packed her children's satchels and filled her two baskets with *maputi*, apples, bananas, tomatoes and cigarettes. Impatient, and still excited about spending all day hawking, without taking heed of her repeated instructions to watch out for the police, Fari and Rita sped out of the house.

Onai left Ruva concentrating on her homework and set off on the long walk into the city centre. Far from tiring her, the walk filled her with a sense of purpose. With one basket balanced on her head and holding the other with her right hand, she pounded the tarred road with fierce determination. By the time she entered the central business district, she was panting, but still felt herself to be in high spirits.

She was further pleased when she made brisk sales to hungry men, who were waiting in a fuel queue. Through a mouthful of *maputi*, one of her customers said appreciatively, '*Maita henyu, Amai*. I slept in this queue and I am so hungry. Thank you.' Smiling, Onai thanked him for his payment and moved on.

Further down the queue, were two women in a car, also waiting for fuel. Onai approached the driver's open window, hoping for another sale.

'How are you, *vasikana*? I have some *maputi* and fruits for sale here. Tomatoes as well if you need some,' she said brightly.

The two women exchanged glances. One of them looked at Onai, saying superciliously, '*Imi Amai imi!* Just leave us alone. You're the same women who trade by day and return to these queues as prostitutes by night. Aren't you ashamed of yourselves?' She turned to her friend, 'I thought they'd got rid of these people in Murambatsvina and dumped them in the rural areas! Look how quickly they're back on the streets!'

The other woman curled her lips and laughed derisively. 'No wonder this place is littered with used condoms every morning. *Muchafa neAIDS,*' she said with an accusing glare, then pointed at a battered condom that was flattened on the tarmac.

Onai was momentarily stunned by their unjustified accusations and contempt. Quickly summoning her dignity, she said, '*Vasikana*, I am a respectable married woman. I'm only trying to raise my family in difficult times. Not everyone is living well like you.'

The driver scowled at her and quickly wound up her window. Feeling hurt and diminished, Onai made her way down the road, suddenly wishing to be home. How quickly her mood could change! Swallowing, she squared her shoulders and continued working her way down the queue. They had to live.

By afternoon, all she had in her box was money; lots and lots of notes. Worthless money as people called it, but still, it was better than nothing. Her family would live. It certainly counted as a productive day.

≈≈≈

The house was quiet. Ruva was still concentrating on her books. Onai wondered if she'd taken a break at all. 'How is the studying going, my dear?' she asked, smiling.

'It's difficult *Amai* but I must pass. You know I want to go to university?' Ruva looked at her solemnly. 'Like Faith,' she added.

Onai nodded at her daughter. She looked very serious, hands cupping jaws, elbows sticking out of identical holes in the threadbare jersey that had once belonged to Katy. 'Yes, you did tell me …' She had noticed that her daughter was trying hard to be like Faith. Even the corn-row of plaits in her hair were patterned like the older girl's. Onai was not worried. As an idol for her teenage daughter, Faith was unquestionably safe.

She glanced up at the clock. Humpty Dumpty grinned back at her, almost half-past five. Normally on a Saturday, Fari and Rita would have been back by now. Their earnings would have been counted, and they would be chatting with excitement about their interesting day of under-cover hawking.

'Now, where are those two?' she asked, peering over Ruva's shoulder.

'Not back yet,' Ruva replied distractedly. She continued staring at a text about the mineral-rich Great Dyke of Zimbabwe. Onai watched over her shoulder as she attempted to draw layers of the earth's crust, frowning at the result of her effort, then tearing up the piece of paper.

Onai smiled and moved away, saying, 'I hope they'll be back soon.' She went into the kitchen and placed a pot of water on the hot-plate in preparation for cooking sadza, which they would have with left-over beans from the previous night.

She knelt and spread out a blanket on the cold sitting room floor. With an iron, she worked her way through a pile of creased clothes, taking short breaks to the kitchen to check on the pot. She kept throwing anxious glances towards the door, expecting to see her children bursting energetically into the house at any minute.

By half-past six, it was dark, and still there was no sign of the errant pair. Just as she finished cooking, the lights suddenly went off. Another power cut. It was time to go out and look for her children. 'Ruva,' she said, 'I'm going out to see if I can find Fari and Rita. They should be home by now.' Her daughter looked up at her and nodded worriedly.

Onai walked silently out of the house and marched up 50th Street, armed with nothing apart from a mother's protective instinct.

She peeled her eyes and scrutinised the thick darkness, watching out for any shapes or suggestive movements that might materialise into the missing culprits. None did. She dropped in on Mai Hondo's house, but her children had not seen Fari or Rita all day. She had no luck at Maya's house. She also stopped at Katy's house, but there appeared to be nobody at home. Even John's decrepit Datsun was not parked in its usual corner.

Reluctantly, she crossed over into Tsiga Grounds where groups of the homeless were sitting around blazing fires. None of the children she spotted remotely resembled her two. She approached a group of young men sharing noisy laughter. 'Excuse me, my sons,' she started cautiously. They stopped laughing and turned to look at her.

'I'm looking for my two children, Fari and Rita. Have any of you seen them here?'

'I don't know anyone called Fari, but I know one pretty Rita who lives up on 50th Street. *Mwana akanaka iyeye!* Are you looking for that Rita?' one of them asked. A roguish smile on his face.

'That's her, my son,' Onai replied politely, anger quickening in her belly.

'No, we haven't seen her. But if you find her, please send her this way, will you? She's a very beautiful girl. I wouldn't mind her keeping me warm tonight. The nights are cold out here.' His words dripped with innuendo. Onai felt sick.

The young man's friends slapped him hard on the back in a gesture of admiration. He was clearly their hero. Then egging each other on, they broke into more noisy laughter amidst ribald comments about the beautiful Rita's attractions.

Onai turned away abruptly. Their comments shook her. Had Katy been right? Was this what she was exposing her daughter to? Rita was an innocent girl, a child, but it appeared as if there would be no short-age of men who might think otherwise.

She blocked out the young men's taunts and walked off dejectedly. Where were they? And why couldn't Gari be a responsible husband and father? It wasn't right that her children had to go out peddling on the streets like orphans, when they had a father who should have been looking after them.

Blindly, she walked back home in the darkness. If they had not arrived, she would have to go to the police station to report them miss-ing. She wondered if that would do any good. The perennial police complaint was that there was no manpower, cars, or fuel for them to carry out their normal duties. Just look at how long it took them to start investigating any report. It was surprising that there had been so many of them on the streets at the peak of the demolitions!

On getting home, she almost cried with relief when she found Rita and Fari huddled on the sofa. They were covered in dust from head to toe. They looked miserable and exhausted under the soft glow of candlelight. Rita was hysterical. She scratched her knees, sobbing with agitation. 'They arrested us, Mum. They arrested us,' she cried.

Onai was shocked. Fear gathered in the pit of her stomach. She reached out to take the child in her arms. 'Stop crying, Rita. Please slow down and tell me exactly what happened. Slow down Rita for goodness sake.' She stroked the young girl's back. 'Quieten down, quieten down. You're home now.' But Rita was inconsolable. She continued crying and muttering incoherently.

Ruva said unhelpfully, 'I told you that you would get arrested, but you wouldn't listen. Now you're no better than common criminals. Disgusting!' Onai gave her daughter a look that told her to shut up.

Turning to Fari, she asked softly, 'Tell me, what happened, my dear? Take your time.'

The boy frowned and answered hesitantly.' We were arrested … I think.' He looked doubtful. 'They took our sweets and cigarettes … in the morning. There were so many of us, Mum. They took us away in a big truck. I don't know what the place is called. We spent the day cleaning up the streets and carrying rubbish to a dump.'

'Oh, my poor children, but you're home now. You needn't ever go out again.' As Onai tried to comfort them, she silently castigated herself. All this was happening because of some failure on her part. Why hadn't she listened to Katy? Something didn't make sense. People who got arrested were taken to holding cells. So why had they spent the day on a street clean-up? Surely, this couldn't have been an official police arrest. But as things were nowadays, one could never be sure. There had been incidents when groups of people in the society had given themselves powers not unlike those of the police or soldiers.

Rita's anguished voice cried out, 'He squeezed my breast. He fondled me, Mum.'

Onai felt a sudden rush of anger, 'Who? A policeman?'

'I don't know. He wasn't wearing a police uniform. He said if I told anyone he would come after me.'

Onai was enraged. 'Stop snivelling, Rita! Come on, tell me! Did he do anything else to you? Who was he?' she shouted venting the anger she felt for the man, on her daughter.

'No, he didn't do anything else. I don't know him,' her daughter whimpered, then stopped crying abruptly, startled into silence by the intensity of her mother's rage.

'Would you know him if you saw him again?' Onai asked more quietly.

Rita looked horrified. 'I told you, Mum ... he said he would come after me if I told anyone. I didn't look at him. I can remember the other man who came and shouted at him and told him to leave me alone. He was wearing a red cap and a shirt with many colours ... yellow, red and green ... I can't remember.'

Onai clicked her tongue crossly. Maybe Rita was just afraid. A complaint against a faceless, unknown man would be a waste of time. She didn't have enough confidence to go to the police to report this violation. There was just no way of telling who exactly had molested her daughter. They were lucky, it could have been much worse. They could have been beaten or kept in the cells. Vending was illegal now, after all.

The woman squared her shoulders and sighed, deciding there and then never to send them out again. Another 'arrest' could easily mean her daughter spending time in police custody, incarcerated with hardcore criminals. Stories of sexual abuse in prisons were rife. So she would have to make do alone, without involving her children.

A knock sounded on the door. She frowned and stood up to open it, wondering who could be visiting so late. It was already eight o'clock. Not more bad news, she prayed. She squinted into the darkness and was surprised to see Mawaya on her doorstep. It had been such a long time since he passed by; since she had spotted him competing for food with the stray dogs of Mbare. He moved closer, out of the shadows. He looked the same. Same thin face and same brilliant smile. He clapped his hands. Onai's initial surprise gave way to irritation. Why was he here at such a late hour?

'Makadii, ambuya?' he asked after her health.

'I'm fine, mukwasha,' she replied, making an effort to sound pleasant.

'Rita's husband,' Fari squealed from behind her, miraculously recovered from his ordeal. Onai turned and gave him a stern look. He froze into silence.

Mawaya said, 'Mai Ruva, I've come to say goodbye. I have a small present for you and your family.'

A present from Mawaya, the beggar? Onai was intrigued. She threw a suspicious glance at the Spar Stores bag in his hands and wondered which bin he had picked it from. She didn't want to hurt him with an absolute refusal of the gift. So she played for time, while racking her brains.

'Goodbye? Where are you going?' she asked.

'I'm going back home, back to face my life. Please take this.' He held out the package. When she hesitated, he said, 'Don't worry. I didn't steal it or pick it out of a bin. I bought it. Please take it. It's my thank you for all the kindness you've shown me.'

Onai was surprised. This was the longest speech she had heard from Mawaya. He sounded different, more articulate. But what did he mean about going back home to face his life? He had no home, so what was he talking about? She'd never really believed that Mawaya could be mentally disturbed. Now, she was no longer sure.

He held out the parcel again, his hands shaking ever so slightly. Only because she didn't have the heart to refuse and hurt his feelings, she accepted the package, astonished by its weight. She murmured humbly, 'Thank you.'

He nodded and left immediately. Onai went back into the house and looked into the bag: two litres of cooking oil and a kilogram of flour. Her husband had not bought any groceries in a long time and here was Mawaya buying cooking oil and flour for her family! This was not the way it was meant to be. She sank back into an armchair. How strange that kindness should make one want to weep.

≈≈≈

Faith had spent the afternoon watching a movie at Westgate with Tom. She'd realised again how much she loved him and how much she'd missed him during her exams, which were thankfully now over. That afternoon, they'd managed to recapture some of their easygoing intimacy. She could still sense the slight shadow that hung over them – their last argument, and the fact that his farm was now a taboo subject. She hoped it wouldn't be too long before Melody's brother gave her the information she needed. It was almost two and a half weeks since she'd spoken to her friend about the matter.

As it happened, she did not have much longer to wait. Several days later, Melody told her that her doubts about Tom had been unfounded. Faith was both relieved and mortified.

'It was not completely straightforward.' Melody reported, 'but he did everything by the book.'

'What do you mean?'

'When Mr Johnson was murdered, Tom was in the process of making final payments on the farm. It seems that the sale had been agreed between them for some time. However, soon after the farmer's death, his property appeared on the list of farms that had been repossessed by the government ... and I hear a few bigwigs were eyeing it, as they always do when they spot a good thing. So Tom took the matter to court where, fortunately, he won. So the farm was subsequently taken off the repossession list.'

'I'm so embarrassed, Mel.'

'As well you should be!'

'But, well, the murder was such a nasty business ...' Faith's voice trailed away.

'Look, the whole farm business, the *hondo yeminda*, was often ugly and unpleasant. Only those who were on the farms when these things took place will ever know the whole truth of it all. Not people like you and I who have to rely on hearsay and conflicting media reports. Surely, the issue is that if you love Tom, you should trust him. I think you owe him an apology. You're my friend and I'm not going to let you ruin a great relationship. You don't know how lucky you are. Have you any idea what I would do for a guy like Tom?'

Faith laughed, relieved. 'Educate me, *shamwari*. What exactly would you do?'

'Pledge myself into eternal slavery ... as his slave that is.' Faith smiled and shook her head. Melody continued, 'Seriously, Tom is the kind of man who could be womanising left, right and centre. Girls would be falling over him, but he's obviously devoted to you. Boringly so, in my opinion! Now be a good girl and promise me you'll stop terrorising him about farms, the black market, demolitions or whatever else you two have been quarrelling about. You can't change the state of Zimbabwe by arguing about these things.'

Melody spoke a lot of sense. Faith was relieved. But had she been so wrong to be suspicious? Any good relationship had to be based on shared values. Discussions and arguments about principle were better than silence or indifference.

Faith hugged her friend. 'I'll do my best,' she said, 'but you know me. I find it hard to keep my mouth shut if I think something is wrong. Why else would I want to be a lawyer?'

Melody answered guardedly, 'Well, that's one thing I admire about you, Faith. But in general, I would say try a little subtlety and caution, in case you get caught up in things that you can't handle. Look around and learn. Good intentions are not known to be adequate protection.'

Faith nodded.

≈≈≈

When her husband came in later that night, Onai was already in bed. Again, he was drunk. She got up to serve him sadza and kapenta. He refused to eat, and muttered something garbled about having places where better people served him better food.

Onai was not particularly bothered by his refusal to eat. Her children could have the food for lunch the next day. Fari loved kapenta, although he always took pains to decapitate the small, dried fish before he could eat them, claiming that the heads were too salty.

She didn't tell her husband about the children's alleged 'arrest'. Neither did she tell him about the surprise present from Mawaya.

He looked unwell, his eyes were still yellow, and now he had a slight cough. But there was little point in saying anything. Returning to bed, she soon fell asleep.

≈≈≈

The look of irritation on Mai Ruva's face had been disquieting. He asked himself what he had expected, but he didn't know. Of course, her manner had been appropriate. To her, he was just a beggar. And it was possible that like everyone who called him Mawaya, she thought he was mentally unbalanced. But still, her manner had hurt him. He'd expected more, due to a vague sense that they had a connection of some sort. He couldn't identify exactly what had given him the idea, but it seemed obvious that he had been wrong. Beggars were not regarded as human beings, his experience had taught him this. Why should Mai Ruva have been any different?

He hoped that she had been pleased when she discovered the flour and cooking oil. He hoped too that her children had been happy, especially Rita. Like her mother, she had been kind to him.

He walked back to his sleeping place near Mbare Bus Terminus, immersed in thought, anticipating his return with some apprehension, wondering if his young brother had managed to keep his business afloat. Had it really been worth it?. Yes, he did feel purged, cleansed somehow, at least spiritually. He longed for a good, long bath, a good haircut, and some clean clothes. But he still had to make a huge effort to avoid thinking about how he would cope without Edith. He didn't think he would be able to love anyone as much. Preoccupied, and careless of the road, he didn't see the car until its hot fender rammed into his body. As he passed out, his last thought was that people who drove unserviced cars without headlights should be locked up; and the keys to their cells thrown away. There were just too many bad or drunk drivers on the roads. What they did to themselves was one thing, what they did to their victims, quite another.

≈≈≈

After midnight Casualty became a bit quieter. Emily stood in the resuscitation room and chatted with two colleagues, Ngoni and Tariro. Tariro was still relatively new to the hospital, having only been there for a month. Emily still found it strange that Tari had left a job in the UK, the place where everyone wanted to go, to return to Harare. Maybe there was something she wasn't telling them.

'You're a strange girl, Tari,' Ngoni said as he fiddled with a drip stand.

She laughed, then grimaced, 'If you're going to say what I think you are … Don't start.'

Ngoni continued, 'But I have to. I keep asking myself, why on earth you came back? At first, I thought you must have returned for some incredibly lucky man. But no … I've been watching you, you know.' Here we go, Emily thought, Ngoni with his not-so-subtle advances, his impulse to flirt with every pretty woman.

Tari laughed. 'Why does everyone keep asking me this? And why should a man lurking in the background seem the only sensible reason to return?'

'It's just that most medics are trying hard to get to the UK, to earn forex, work with good facilities, feel that they can do something and make a difference.'

Emily said, 'What can we do here? Everything is stacked against us. So, coming back, just seems like professional and social regression …'

'Emily. This is home. This is where I belong. I wasn't in exile, so why shouldn't I come back? Only yesterday, my sister – *my sister* – said that maybe I was deported, just like the failed asylum seekers !' She laughed.

'I can understand why she would say that. I've been thinking quite a lot about leaving and the UK is my first choice,' Ngoni said. Emily was not surprised. If it wasn't one doctor leaving for so-called greener pastures, it was another.

Tari was silent for a moment, then she said, 'Put it this way, Ngoni. It's not as rosy as people make it out to be. After a while, I just felt that maybe I'd overstayed my welcome.'

'Why? Did you ever encounter racism?' Emily asked.

'Of course! It's very subtle, but everyone knows that it exists. Besides, the support that I received for my training was only a fraction of what my 'home-grown' colleagues were getting,' Tari said as she stretched out her long legs and reclined on a chair in the corner.

'Did you talk to your supervisor about it?' Ngoni demanded.

'I did try talking to one of the registrars. She just said, "Look, the British taxpayer is paying for your education, not you or your country! If you – or anyone else – is not happy with the system, then go home."'

Tari smiled. 'So I decided to stop moaning and come home. True, it's hard here, but I'm coping better than I did there, when I was constantly on the brink of clinical depression!'

'It can't be that bad. From what I've heard, the UK is the most culturally diverse and tolerant society in the world. How do others cope? Foreign doctors are flocking there.'

Tari gave a snort, 'That's part of the problem, too many junior doctors and not enough training posts. You'd be surprised by what people put up with, just to get by. The choice is whether to take it or leave it. I chose to leave it. Which is why I'm here. Any doctor thinking of going to the UK should do some serious research. New policies will effectively crowd out foreign doctors, unless they're Europeans.'

They sat in silence for a while, then Tari added, 'I suppose it's not all bad. No. I met a lot of people who were friendly and supportive. But now and then something would happen which made it clear that I didn't belong, that I was rated a second- even third-class doctor. Those few incidents somehow overshadowed all the good experiences. I knew I wouldn't last ... You have to be emotionally tough, and as I've just said, I was depressed half the time.'

'You're too sensitive,' Ngoni countered 'You over-reacted. I know a lot of people who are doing well over there. Some are almost consultants. I'd have stayed ... '

Tari shrugged, 'That's your opinion ... horses for courses ...'

Ngoni continued, 'True. But look at it this way. Racism is the way of the world. It's only natural. Look at how many countries introduce affirmative action for this or that ...'

Emily murmured thoughtfully, 'Not quite the same.'

Ngoni shrugged, 'Still racism, if you ask me. Everyone looks after their own. It happens everywhere, sometimes in very extreme ways. And talking of extreme examples ... look at what we've done here over the last five years, and tell me if that ...'

Just at that moment, the emergency buzzer went off. The three doctors immediately raced towards the Casualty Resuscitation Room. The emergency team was attending to a woman on a stretcher. There were already too many people around the trolley. Emily hovered in the background, close enough to be of use if required. That was when the man was wheeled in. He looked like a bundle of rags. Reluctantly, Emily moved forward.

Street people. Star patients. The name on the papers would be Mr Unknown Unknown and the medical history would be hopelessly inadequate. He probably belonged on a psychiatric ward.

'Hit-and-run from Mbare,' the nurse who had wheeled him in from the ambulance said. Miraculously, no fractures or other obvious injuries apart from the bruising on his forehead. Possibly concussed. He's a bit agitated. We might need to call the psychiatrists, after he's been assessed by the neuro team.'

Emily picked up the man's card. Sure enough, there it was. Name: Mr Unknown Unknown. Age: Unknown. Address: Unknown. She shook her head. The man thrashed about on the trolley, mumbling unintelligibly.

The nurse smiled tolerantly at him, 'Now calm down, Sir. This doctor would like to take a look at you.' The man seemed oblivious to her words. He continued mumbling. Emily thought she caught something which sounded like 'Piwa', but trying to make sense of his words was hard work, and she was tired.

The nurse raised her eyes. 'They said in the ambulance that he was claiming to be that prominent businessman who disappeared.' She scratched her head. 'For some reason, I can't remember his name. I'm sure you would remember it if I told you the name, *chiremba*. The story was all over the papers.' Emily just shook her head, and peered at the man again. There seemed nothing remarkable about him, just another beggar. She sighed.

The nurse held him steady on the stretcher again and said, 'Calm down, please.' Looking at Emily she laughed. 'Now if I were to count the number of confused psychiatric patients who come in claiming to be this or that minister or the other … well. Ministers!' She laughed again. Emily smiled. Grandiose delusions, they called them.

After X-rays, stabilisation and an appropriate period of observation, the man was moved over to the psychiatric unit where he would get the treatment he needed.

≈≈≈

It was morning when Mawaya woke up. He was confused to find himself in a clean bed, wearing clean hospital pyjamas. His head was throbbing. He looked around. There were more beds with people lying on them. So, he really was in a hospital! For a moment his mind was blank, and then he remembered the car, the impact and the painful heat. Something else niggled at the back of his mind. Tom's sister, the doctor. Had he seen her? She'd seemed so real. Had he been dreaming?

A loud, cheerful woman descended on the ward with a creaking food trolley. Her plump motherly face was wreathed in smiles as she served plates of porridge. At once the ward became a buzz of activity.

The patient whose bed was next to his, came over with his plate. He gave a wide smile and said brightly, 'You are now my only friend here. I think everyone else is jealous of me.'

'Who?' he asked, confused.

The man held a porridge-smeared spoon suspended in mid-air, looking very worried indeed. He dropped his voice to a hoarse whisper, 'Them. They know I'm a minister. Today my salary increment was announced on TV. It's the third time this year, mind you. Tomorrow, I'm getting the latest Mercedes Benz. Maybe I'll throw away the one I bought last year. Maybe give it to my child.' He shrugged, then continued, 'Now, everyone knows that I'm special because it was announced on TV last night. It's all their fault, all these bad things that are happening. It's not my fault, you know. It's them and their … their … gangsters, I think.' The man stopped to scratch his head, then concluded, 'We'll deal with them. They must watch out. They just don't know who we are!'

Mawaya struggled to make sense of what the man was saying, and failed. Then realisation hit him. My God. I'm in a psychiatric ward. Why?

The man was whispering again, his voice hoarse and urgent. 'You have to help me escape. It's like a jail here. I'm sure he'll come at night with a big injection to kill me. He killed someone last night. My Benz is parked outside. It's gold. We can't miss it. Let's go now, Peter.'

His head jerked. His name was not Peter. His name was … Mawaya's mind was blank. Blank. Panicking, he struggled to remember, but nothing … nothing … My God …

The other man scraped porridge loudly from his metal plate and got up, 'I was joking about being a minister. I'm a big fish from the United Nations. I'll put this plate away and come back to tell you all about my peace-keeping job.'

He was smiling broadly again, amused by some secret joke; obviously no longer afraid of the man who was coming to kill him that night.

CHAPTER 19

On Monday morning, Onai left home very early for a day of vending in the city centre. Along Samora Machel, she found a fuel queue that must have been close to twenty cars long. She was both surprised and happy when Hannah, a colleague from previous market days, joined her shortly afterwards. The two women worked their way down the queue, advertising and making sales as stealthily as they could. Where police officers were concerned, one could never be too careful.

Business was slow to start off with. A few frustrated motorists were verbally abusive and quite hostile. They told Onai and Hannah to stop pestering them. The two women continued their business, cheerfully. A few insults could not dent their determination. They had families to feed.

Onai noticed that there were a few women standing around at the top of First Street, evidently looking out for potential customers. Further up was a group of young boys who appeared to be selling cigarettes. This was not good at all. There were just too many vendors in the area and that suggested impending trouble. She was right. A little while later, a truckload of policemen arrived and started chasing the vendors up the road. Onai and Hannah ran as fast as they could, struggling to keep hold of their remaining goods. They crossed the busy street diagonally, weaving their way dangerously between moving vehicles, and continued on towards the Reserve Bank.

In front of the towering building they stopped briefly and leaned against the railing, trying to catch their breath. Just at that moment, there was an ear-splitting bang and a terrible scream cut through the early afternoon air. A street child who had been running away from police officers was flung high into the air by a big truck. Time appeared to stand still in the stunned silence that ensued. While most of the policemen had stopped at the scene of the accident, Onai and Hannah noticed that a few others were still after them. They started running again, along Second Street, then Jason Moyo, towards the downtown area that would lead them to Mbare. They only stopped when they were safely beyond the city limits.

They briefly savoured the respite, then continued walking, That poor child … Onai shuddered. Had he lived? Had he died on the spot? It could have so easily been Fari.

Hannah told Onai that she was ready to give up. 'I no longer have the strength for this. My husband crossed into South Africa. For a whole month, I've heard nothing from him. I'm homeless, I have no money, and my child has stopped going to school. I can't take this anymore. I think I've enough money to go to my parents' home in the rural areas. I hear they don't want us there, but what else can I do?'

Onai did not know whether to encourage her to go or to stay. Life in the rural areas was known to be generally harder. People were barely surviving on food aid. The drought only exacerbated an already desperate situation. Besides, there was a rumour that headmen in the rural areas had been authorised to turn away any displaced people arriving from the towns. She didn't know if it was true, but she knew of at least three families who had returned to town and were once again camping on Tsiga Grounds.

All she could do was to embrace Hannah and wish her good luck. She watched the woman disappearing around the corner and felt sorry for the sweet, kindly soul whose only flaw was her anxious whining. She would miss her. She wondered about the woman's husband. Hopefully, he was not among the unidentified group who had recently made headlines – the men had drowned in the Limpopo River while trying to escape to South Africa.

≈≈≈

At Mbare shopping centre, Onai stood in a corner and counted the money from her sales. She had three hundred and fifty thousand dollars in her pouch. She took another twenty minutes to count the notes again; just to be sure. There were just too many five hundred dollar cheques. It was amazing that people still used them, when one bill couldn't even buy a few sweets.

Her earnings for the day were enough to buy a kilogram of chicken and some brown rice, or seven loaves of bread. She sternly told herself to stop comparing everything to the cost of bread. What she had in mind was so much more important, and the atmosphere would have to be just right. She had to do this. The idea had been developing for some time; after her argument with Katy, it had slowly dawned on her that even her friend saw her as a victim. This realisation had come as a shock. She had been too worn down by circumstances to do anything but try to circumvent and survive them. Now, she felt she was going to act. Almost irrationally, she had no doubt that an exceptional meal of rice and chicken would make Gari more approachable. Then they could talk openly about their marriage and, as a couple, how to manage the school fees.

She was ready to compromise about the bedroom situation, if Gari consented to have HIV tests. She had denied herself the basic needs of her womanhood for too long. Sharing that intimacy willingly again, and without fear, would be good. Gari would only have to meet the necessary requirements of being a husband and father; and she was fully prepared to meet him half-way. If her plan worked, there would be no need to mention Gloria at all. The idea pleased her. Allowing her imagination free rein enabled her to picture a day when her life would change for the better, with Gari by her side.

The small grocery shop was almost empty. Thankfully she didn't have to queue, because chicken and rice were luxuries. The young woman working at the till was familiar in a vague sort of way. She smiled broadly when Onai came forward to pay for her groceries, 'It's me Mai Moyo ... Chenai.'

Onai stared at her blankly.

'I was Sheila's friend. We met once. I was standing by your gate with Sheila,' she said, her manner now rather more subdued.

Onai looked at the girl enquiringly, then recognised her. This was the girl who had told her about a delivery of sugar and cooking oil at Parktown shopping centre several weeks before. It all seemed so long ago.

'I'm sorry, Chenai. I didn't recognise you. How are you? Are you no longer working in Parktown?'

'Not any more. I got a better job here ... at least it's supposed to be better,' she chuckled and tried to explain. 'It depends on how you look at it, Mai Moyo. At Parktown, I did the shelves and my hands grew sore changing price tags every few hours. Prices have been rising that fast, you know,' she giggled. 'Now that I'm doing till-points, my hands are still sore, but this time, it's from counting millions of bearer cheques.' She laughed again, as if life was one great joke.

Onai found herself smiling. The girl lowered her voice and spluttered, 'I hear they're going to buy money-counters for us ... you know, like in the banks.' Her voice rose, fuelled by amusement, 'Ridiculous, isn't it?'

Onai nodded, still smiling, then asked, 'How is Sheila, by the way? I haven't seen her since she was taken to the holding camp. Have you seen her?'

The smile on Chenai's face was instantly replaced by a look of horror. Her words tumbled out, 'I'm sorry, Mai Moyo. I thought you knew. Sheila died a week ago.'

Onai's eyes stung. 'I had no idea at all. *Nematambudziko*, Chenai.'

The girl accepted her condolences, and said, 'I saw her a few days before she died ... I didn't realise she was so close. Her relatives were not interested. She had been taken in by the church. She spoke very highly of you.'

Onai shook her head. 'If I'd known, I would have visited her myself.'

Chenai frowned. 'She said something about wanting to give you an apology. She wouldn't tell me what it was about, though. In the end, I felt that maybe she was just confused.'

Onai remembered how agitated Sheila had been the day her shack was destroyed. She had apologised for some wrongdoing, but had refused to disclose any details. As far as Onai knew, Sheila hadn't wronged her in any way. She said as much to Chenai, then asked, 'What about the baby?'

Chenai sighed. 'She was taken in by the nuns at an orphanage in Epworth. Like I said, her relatives are not interested. But I've heard that police officers demolished the orphanage a few days ago, because the church had built it without council approval. So I really don't know where the baby is now.

'Sorry, Mai Moyo … I can see my supervisor throwing me some evil looks. She doesn't like us talking to customers. Let me run your groceries through. It's been good meeting you.'

Onai nodded and paid. The tinkle of Chenai's girlish laughter floated towards her as she left the shop. She walked home sadly, wondering about Sheila's baby, and her apology from the grave.

≈≈≈

Gari had not been disappointed by the outcome of his meeting with the human resources manager. His retrenchment had been confirmed but the severance package was not bad. Eighty million dollars, the man had said. Gari was lucky. Silas had been offered only fifteen million, but then, he wasn't a section manager. The most junior general hands had barely made it past five million.

Gari felt elated. In six weeks, when the company was due to make its move to South Africa, he would get all of eighty million dollars. A myriad of possibilities stretched before him. He had to share this good news with someone. Gloria was just the person. He passed by her lodgings on his way from work.

As he'd expected, she was quite pleased by the retrenchment package. 'Remember what you said about not having money before? Does this mean that we can now get married?' she asked, wrapping her arms around him, her smile sweet and seductive.

Gari answered readily,' *Chaizvo*, darling.' He did not see any reason why not. Onai had made up his mind for him. Onai or Gloria? It was not a difficult choice. Throwing Onai out completely was bound to cause problems, so he would take Gloria as a second wife. Traditionally, that was acceptable and no one would criticise him. In fact, with a second wife as young as Gloria, he would be the envy of a lot of men. If Onai did not like the idea, she was free to leave. He chose not to think too much about Gloria's past. She was now exclusively his.

'When will we get married?' she wanted to know.

Gari coughed and scratched his head. 'We can decide the date later, *mudiwa*. You have to trust me.'

'Gari! We have been talking about marriage for a long time, but so far, you've done nothing. I want a guarantee,' she demanded.

'But *dhiya*, I'm giving you my promise. Is that not enough? Let's talk about this some other time, please,' he pleaded, planting playful kisses on her lips. He was in the mood for making love, not war.

Gloria tossed her braids petulantly. 'It's not enough for me. I don't live on words. I want action. You have to show me that you're really serious.'

He gave a slight cough and cleared his throat. 'Tell me how? How else can I make you believe me?' He said, eager to please the woman he loved.

She explained what she wanted. Gari was initially doubtful, but Gloria was quite persuasive. Finally, he warmed to her suggestion. All things considered, it was a reasonably good plan.

≈≈≈

With great care, Onai prepared the meat the way she knew her husband liked it … deep-fried in oil and seasoned with chillies. She added spoonfuls of peanut butter into the boiled rice, stirring and mixing the pot slowly. It would be their best meal yet.

Just after seven o'clock, the food was ready. Onai wondered if she should serve her children, in case Gari was late home again. Suddenly, she heard a deep cough; then his loud voice came through as he opened the outside door into their sitting room. Thankfully, he had decided to come in early, so her calculated efforts would not go to waste. With a bit of luck, he would be sober and they would have their first civilised conversation in ages. Everything would work out just fine and Gloria would be condemned to the recesses of history, where she deserved to languish. Onai had a very good feeling about the outcome of the evening.

With an affectionate smile on her face, she walked into the sitting room to welcome her husband. At the connecting door, she stopped in her tracks and froze, unable to move, or utter a single word. A guttural sound escaped from her mouth. Her girls immediately rushed to her side. Following right behind Gari into the crowded sitting room was a beautiful young woman – Gloria herself! Onai stood open-mouthed, slowly absorbing the incredible scene unfolding before her. It was unreal, but within seconds she'd grasped the reality.

Gloria thrust her well-shaped bosom forward and teetered into the sitting room on stiletto heels. Her multitude of colourful bracelets clattered loudly as she plumped up the cushion on Onai's favourite chair. She sat down daintily, then crossed and uncrossed her legs unnecessarily, as if undecided about how she wanted to sit. Her mini-skirt strained and threatened to ride the whole way up to her hips, flaunting enviably smooth skin.

She was a young woman who combined vulgar sensuality with an air of alluring seductiveness. It was easy to see why men would be attracted to her, like flies to cow dung. She fluttered her lashes and tossed her cascading braids, some of which had fallen gently over her face. She looked at her open-mouthed audience, as if expecting them to break into a round of spontaneous applause.

Gari threw himself into the seat next to Gloria. 'Sit down, all of you,' his countenance daring anyone to do otherwise. Then he coughed and cleared his throat.

Onai continued to stare at Gloria in confusion and anger. She could have dealt with a confession from Gari; she might even have accepted, as her due, another assault. But not this. The idea of having to confront Gloria in her own house, had never crossed her mind. It was beyond the range of the possible. Now, suddenly, she felt skewered by an outrageous and grotesque present. She could not bring herself to obey Gari's abrupt order to sit down. She remained rooted to the spot, frozen with shock.

'I said, sit down!' Gari barked. Rita and Ruva shuffled uncomfortably and perched on the chair nearest to the kitchen door. They looked suspended; almost as if they were poised to take to immediate flight.

Onai had no choice except to squeeze past Gari and Gloria so she could reach the single unoccupied chair in the room. She had been relegated to the least popular chair – in her own house! Her face smarted with humiliation and suppressed rage.

Gari took Gloria's expertly painted hand in his. She leaned towards him languidly, fingers curling possessively over his arm. Gari appeared to gloat, but he did not carry it off very well. The illness seemed to have taken something out of him. He coughed again, holding his hand across his chest for what seemed to Onai like an eternity. Her perception was distorted and she felt light-headed.

Gari sat back, and addressing no one in particular, he asked 'Where's Fari?' He swept yellow, penetrating eyes over his daughters.

Ruva stiffened and looked away. Rita wilted under his glare. She recoiled, a look of confusion and fear on her face. In a voice that was scarcely above a whisper, she mumbled, 'I don't know.'

'Address me properly, and look at me when you speak, you stupid girl!' her father roared.

She flinched, and with involuntary disobedience, stared not at him, but at her bare feet on the floor. Onai's heart went out to her. She wanted to touch her, to shield her. Her children did not deserve this.

'I'm sorry father,' Rita murmured again. Gari shook his large, shaggy head in exasperation.

Onai stared blindly at the blue wall facing her. The streaks on the wall appeared to be in slow, illusory motion. A fat cockroach darted in front of her. At that moment, she envied it its obvious freedom. She was in chains and her life was falling apart. Her gaze shifted from the cockroach to the cheerful Humpty Dumpty clock. She looked away. The words that she wanted to scream were stuck in her throat.

Gari put an arm around Gloria's sloping shoulders, and continued speaking. 'Anyway, it doesn't matter that Fari's not here, you can tell him the good news when he comes. I'm sure you all know *mainini* here?' He looked at them with raised eyebrows, as if searching for some sign of acknowledgement. None was forthcoming.

'I've brought her here today for a formal introduction. I'm going to take her as my second wife very soon.' He spoke casually, letting the cruel words sink in slowly. The girls huddled together on the sofa, disbelief and fear written on their faces. Onai wanted to reassure them that it was all right. But it wasn't, and she couldn't speak to them. Not yet.

Gari coughed and held a hand to his mouth. His careless monologue continued, 'I expect her to move in next week. She will share the main bedroom with me. Anyone who is not happy with that can move out.' The last statement was directed at Onai, who still sat in motionless shock. She opened her mouth to speak but the lump in her throat would not budge. The feeling of nausea became a bitter taste of bile in her mouth.

'Did you hear what I said, Mai Ruva? This is your *mainini*. I want you to welcome her into our home.' He leaned back on the sofa and looked at her. His words reverberated and floated across her like an echo, disturbingly unreal. Hot tears stung her eyes.

Gloria looked very smug. A confident smile lingered on her lips. Probably in an attempt to break the interminable silence, she drew in a deep breath. Well-rounded breasts looked as if they might burst from her clinging body-top. She caressed Gari's hand and raised it towards her lips. Onai was not sure what Gloria was about to do, but one thing was clear in her mind. She did not want her daughters to be subjected to any more of this vulgarity. Without warning, she sprang up in a blazing fury. She grabbed a handful of Gloria's braids and rammed a clenched fist into her face. The force drew a spurt of blood from Gloria's nostrils and she keeled over backwards.

The attack was so unexpected that the girls and Gari did not move until Gloria emerged from her near-faint with ear-splitting screams. In the next instant, Onai felt Gari launching himself upon her, struggling to haul her off Gloria's writhing form. The girls pulled at him ineffectually, shouting and crying as they did so.

Onai was like a woman possessed. In the pandemonium that followed, Gari managed to drag her off Gloria. She fell onto the floor and looked up to see the flash of a knife in his hand. Her daughters screamed. The door burst open and Onai caught sight of Fari rushing in. He hurled his small body at his father, hands raised aiming to wrestle the suspended knife from his father's grip. He ricocheted from the impact of their collision and fell violently against the wall. The knife fell from Gari's grip and grazed Onai's shoulder before clattering onto the floor. Gloria continued to wail loudly and unrestrainedly.

≈≈≈

Outside, a loud, inquisitive crowd had gathered to witness this dramatic and very public show of domestic strife. The buzz of their voices drifted towards Onai. Katy and Maya had materialised from nowhere. She heard Katy pleading, 'Please *baba va*Ruva, forgive her. Please don't hurt her.'

The two women managed to shield her from Gari's ferocious attack, but not before they received a few blows themselves.

'Get away, all of you,' Gari bellowed at the throng through an open window. His mouth frothed, spraying a shower of saliva over Onai, who now sat slumped below the window. His lips curled back in a snarl and the muscles in his neck stood out like taut wires, as he shouted through the window, 'Bastards!'

Putting a protective arm around the sobbing Gloria, he said to Onai, 'You'll be sorry about this. I'm going to fix you, do you hear?'

She looked at him through blurry, streaming eyes. Her throbbing upper lip felt tight and engorged. So exquisite was the pain in her jaw that she could not open her mouth to speak. She had not managed to utter a single word since Gari had walked in with this mistress.

Furiously, he spat, 'I thought I would show you some consideration and respect as the mother of my children. I thought I would at least give you notice about Gloria moving in. You don't deserve even that! She will move in today, this very night. I'm going to help her pack. When we come back, I want to find you gone. I swear, I will kill you if I find you here.' He wiped the blood off Gloria's face with a handkerchief and led her to the door.

The two lovers made their exit and disappeared into the gloom of night. Onai heard jeers, then Gari's angry voice yelling, 'Get away, all of you. What are you looking at?' Then the voices and taunts faded. The show was over.

≈≈≈

Katy glanced at Maya with irritation and suspicion. She looked like someone enjoying herself. As if sensing Katy's ungracious thoughts, Maya walked to the window and shouted after Gloria, 'Bitch!' She moved to kneel by Onai's side. 'Don't cry, Onai,' she said.

Katy ignored her and took command, telling Ruva to bring a bowl of warm water and a towel. Still looking bemused, Ruva quickly obliged. Rita hovered uncertainly near her mother. Fari sat near the door like a guard.

Katy accepted the towel from Ruva and soaked it in the bowl of tepid water. She squeezed it and applied it to Onai's face with great care. Gently, she wiped the blood away. Onai flinched with pain and grimaced as the towel made contact with raw, bruised flesh. The numbness around her jaw eased a little. Perhaps it was not broken.

'You have to leave now, Onai. Come with me. You can stay at my house while you decide what to do next; but we have to make a report of this assault at the police station first,' Katy urged, when she had finished tending to her friend's injuries.

'No, I can't,' Onai shook her head slowly, as if to deny what had just happened.

'But why?' asked Katy, her voice rising with frustration. 'Surely I don't have to convince you that your life is in danger. Come away with me, please.'

'What would be the point of reporting him? He'd kill me if I do.' Relieved that Onai was able to speak, Katy felt a mixture of pity and anger. Would her friend never act? Although Onai was in a dreadful situation, it was not one without hope. She could get help. She was a talented woman. But, first, she had to take action; she had to go to the police. She had to leave Gari. She had to do something constructive with her pain. Katy sighed, 'Look, I understand how you feel. But the fact that he pulled a knife on you should make you realise that your home is no longer safe. Imagine what could have happened if the knife had found its mark.'

'Oh Katy, you don't know what you're asking me to do. My children will starve and ...'

Katy interrupted firmly, 'No, your children will not starve. Where do you expect to take them at this time of night, anyway? Gari is their father and he has an obligation to look after them. You have to sort out your own life, first.'

Maya paced the floor restlessly. Her ample chest heaved as she jabbed a finger at Katy. 'I can't believe I'm hearing this! Are you encouraging Onai to desert her marriage? You, who claim to be her friend? Where is the pride in being a woman, if she cannot fight for her man?' Maya was at her most confrontational. 'Who are you, anyway, to just barge in here and tell her to leave her husband? An affair never means the end of a marriage. Maybe this is just the wake-up call that Onai needed to put her house in order!' She spoke at the top of her voice.

Katy answered her levelly. 'If a man is disrespectful enough to bring his mistress into the marital home, then he is worthless. *Worthless*. I think Onai …'

Maya interrupted her rudely. 'What do you know about it? You've brought that husband of yours down to his knees with every love potion under the sun. Everyone can tell that you rule him. The man has no balls at all!'

Katy breathed fire. 'How dare you, Maya? How dare you? What has my marriage got to do with you? Is this the moment to insult me with your opinions? There are children here. Mind your tongue! Can't you see that this is no time to be fighting? We have to help Onai. I'm taking her with me, no matter what you say. Will you kindly leave *now!*

Maya looked at Onai, as if expecting support, but she silently averted her eyes. Maya was left with no choice and departed, slamming the door behind her.

Nonetheless, Maya's intervention seemed to have focused Onai' mind, and she agreed to leave with Katy. Her children looked horrified. Rita was the first to break down, 'Please don't go,' she cried. Fari started crying too. Katy could see that Ruva was struggling to be brave.

Onai drew them close to her and whispered reassurance, 'I'll come back. Everything is going to be all right. I'll be back soon, I promise. And, anyway, I'll only be with your *maiguru*, just down the road. You can come and see me tomorrow. Your father won't hurt you, and in a few days time I'll be back, or we'll sort something out.'

'Really?' Ruva answered, her expression one of utter disbelief.

'Really,' Onai affirmed. 'Everything will be all right.'

Katy nodded approvingly. She helped Onai to pack her bag and they left. 'Remember to have your supper,' Onai said. She couldn't bear the thought of Gloria eating her way through the lovely peanut-butter rice and chicken. 'Ruva, make sure you all eat!' She hoped the food would give them some comfort, as they were still in tears.

≈≈≈

Katy said that Onai could stay with them until she calmed down, and thought through what she was going to do next.

Onai sighed, emotions still raw with pain and confusion. 'Maybe I should go to Zhombe to collect Chipo, Gari's sister. She might be able to help as she seems to have some influence over him.'

'No, there is no rush to go to Zhombe. Stay here for a while. Let's think things through. Maybe you should get some advice … at least go to the Kushinga Project … if you won't go to the police.'

'I don't know, Katy. And what about John?' Onai asked anxiously.

'Don't worry about him. He's going to South Africa in two days' time.'

When John returned home, Katy took him aside. After a few minutes he came back into the sitting room, 'Katy has explained everything to me. I'm sorry about what has happened. You're welcome to stay, Mai Ruva.'

Onai expressed her gratitude. They hardly spoke as they ate supper and watched the latter half of the evening news. The exercise to demolish markets as a means of flushing out criminals, and getting rid of trading places which had become a health hazard, was still continuing. As the reporter intoned, this would pave way for more orderly, more hygienic trading in crime-free zones.

Also in progress was the continued demolition of illegal shacks that were being rented out as homes. The shacks were reported to be blighting the urban landscape and overburdening the city's infrastructure.

The government had pledged a large amount of money to build decent accommodation for the homeless. The next report was about demolition of illegal homes in the U.K., which were said to belong to people referred to as Travellers.

Onai wondered about its relevance. Propaganda, maybe, 'If they can do it there, why can't we do it here?' But were the situations really comparable? Were there any truly homeless people in the UK?

She did not know much about the country. Katy had recently told her that one pound equalled fifty thousand dollars on the black market. She also had a vague idea that people with family in the UK were living a relatively good life. Nowadays, the status of most families hinged on who had the greatest number of relatives abroad, and who received gifts and money from them. '*Tine mudiaspora* in the family,' had become a declaration of well-being.

By ten o'clock, Onai was physically and emotionally exhausted. Too much had happened in one day and she badly needed to sleep. Katy had made up a bed for her in Faith's room. She gave her some Paracetamol for the headache and antiseptic to put on her bruised mouth before she slept.

Onai lay on the bed, willing herself into unconsciousness. She burned with jealous rage against Gloria. She imagined Gari lavishing her with presents, while their children starved. She saw Gari and Gloria entwined in a tight embrace, Gloria enjoying the tender intimacy that should have been hers by right.

A frenzy of emotions swirled in her head. Hadn't she driven Gari into Gloria's arms by persistently asking him to use condoms? But there had been no other choice. How had everything backfired so quickly, despite her good intentions? The river to which she had run in an attempt to extinguish the flames licking at her feet, was the same river in which she was now drowning. She had a multitude of regrets, not least. the sheer futility of a life spent with Gari. What had it all been for? Was she now going to lose her children as well? And why, oh, why hadn't she challenged him about Gloria before?

Jealous rage gave way to a pain so intense that it seemed to tear her heart to shreds. She felt it rise, filling her mind and destroying her sanity. She hugged the pillow tightly and buried her face in its softness, weeping bitter tears.

The Paracetamol gradually took effect, her headache eased and she drifted slowly into troubled half-sleep. There was no comfort in subconsciousness. She had an unpleasant dream about her mother giving her a stern lecture on the virtues of being a good wife.

CHAPTER 20

Some time during the night, Onai suddenly awoke from her troubled sleep to what sounded like Ruva's voice. She sat up in bed and realised that Ruva was indeed beating on Katy's front door and calling out for her. John and Katy got to the door at the same time as she did. 'Please *Amai, maiguru*, come home. Father is vomiting blood. Please, come. He has to go to hospital,' the distraught girl cried.

John turned to Onai, 'I'm sorry, I can't take him to hospital. There's no fuel in my car.' Katy asked him to ring for an ambulance immediately. Led by Ruva, the two women raced down the street and round the corner to Onai's house.

Gari had collapsed on the bedroom floor, and was vomiting blood. Gloria was standing helplessly by the door in a pink, filmy nightdress; elaborate frills accentuated an already prominent bust. As they arrived, she recoiled against the wall, looking like a frightened little girl and quite unlike the feisty young mistress who'd invaded Onai's home so brazenly. Before anyone could say anything, she flung a blanket over her shoulders, grabbed a small case and ran out into the night. Nobody tried to follow her.

Onai pushed her children into their bedrooms and ordered them to stay there. She just couldn't believe what was happening. Was there no end to trouble? Katy helped her to tend to Gari as he lay limply on the floor. They cleaned him up and lifted him onto the bed. He avoided their eyes and did not speak. Onai wondered whether it was out of embarrassment, but concluded generously that it was because he was so unwell.

They positioned him carefully on the bed so that he wouldn't choke on his vomit if he was sick again. Then they sat and waited. The clock ticked away loudly and Humpty Dumpty continued to beam incongruously from his perch. John had phoned for an ambulance at one o'clock. By three o'clock there was still no sign of it. While they waited, Gari vomited once more, large clots of dark blood.

John spoke apologetically, 'I'm very sorry, Mai Ruva. If it wasn't for these fuel shortages, I would have taken him to hospital myself. What kind of ambulance service have we got now? This is an emergency, and they're still not here!'

'Well, you can blame the diesel shortages or whoever is responsible for bringing fuel into the country.' Katy made a half-hearted attempt to provide reasons, the excuses they all knew too well. There was always something to blame.

Onai didn't comment. She just wanted an ambulance. Any kind of rationalisation was of no value at such a critical moment. She sat on the bed and clasped her hands across her knees, rocking herself gently backwards and forwards.

At five o'clock an ambulance finally arrived. By then Gari was weak, incoherent and barely conscious. There were three other lifeless-looking patients in the vehicle. There was no room for Onai to sit by her husband's side. She and Katy would have to take the long walk to the hospital.

When they arrived later that morning, they found Gari on the crowded Medical Ward. He looked frail and vulnerable. His breathing was shallow and rapid. An oxygen mask covered the lower half of his face. He was hooked up to a blood transfusion and a second drip of clear fluid. It was difficult for Onai to believe that he was the same man who'd shown so much aggression less then twelve hours before.

The doctor on duty led her into a small office behind the nurses' station. 'Your husband was very lucky to have arrived here when he did. He'd lost so much blood, he could have died.' Onai nodded. He looked at her from above his glasses and continued. 'He drinks a lot of beer, doesn't he?' Onai nodded, still wordless.

'Well, there are quite a few things going on. The preliminary blood results show that his liver is not working properly. I suspect he has alcohol-related liver cirrhosis. He's been bleeding from a stomach ulcer, which might have been caused by too much alcohol. The bleeding seems to have settled, but we have to keep a close eye on him. On top of all that, he has a chest infection.'

Onai continued nodding silently, not quite understanding what he was saying about Gari's liver problems and beer. However, she did realise that her husband's condition was very serious. Her heart raced uneasily.

The doctor went on, now sounding regretful. 'I've requested a chest X-ray and a hepatitis screen. I still need to do further tests that unfortunately aren't available at this hospital.'

'So, what does this mean? I mean, what will happen to my husband?'

'I see that your husband has no medical aid. If you raise about thirty million dollars, I can refer you to a private hospital in town. Everything that needs to be done will be taken care of, including more tests, plus medication.'

'I'm afraid I don't have any money, *chiremba*,' Onai said. 'Can we not be billed by the private hospital, and pay later?'

'I don't think that's possible. The private clinic that I want to refer you to offers tests and treatment on a cash payment basis only. Unless, of course, one has medical aid. I hope you understand that there's nothing more I can do. I'll transfer him to the high dependency unit for supportive treatment; and, of course, we'll hope for the best.' He handed her a prescription to buy some intravenous medicine.

'This is a prescription for a very strong antibiotic. It should be available at any QV pharmacy in town,' he said. Onai accepted the scrip and left the room to join Katy.

'Don't you also want to be seen in Casualty, Onai?' Katy said. 'You look unwell and your face is a bit more swollen today. It seems a pity to waste the opportunity, now that we're here.'

'Don't worry. I'll be fine. I still have some Paracetamol,' Onai responded quietly. Being seen in Casualty would mean another bill, and she had no money. At that point, Gari's medical treatment took precedence. She parted ways with Katy and started on the long walk to town. If she walked fast enough, she would get there around nine o'clock, go to a chemist and return to the hospital well before lunch.

≈≈≈

'Hi Ben! Good morning. Why are you looking so glum? Night-shift is almost over. Let's go for a cup of coffee. My flask is downstairs,' Emily said cheerfully as she poked her head into the tiny office.

He looked up with a tired smile. 'Hi Emily. Yes, you're right! Only one hour to go before hand-over. I wouldn't mind a cup of coffee, thanks.' He rose and followed her slowly out of the ward.

'So what's with the long face?' she asked as they walked down the corridor towards the staircase.

He shook his head. 'I've just attended to this man from Mbare. He was bleeding from a possible gastric ulcer and he's going into liver failure. He has raging pneumonia, and I can't rule out TB. I have to order more tests, he needs IV antibiotics but the wife was telling me that she has no money. I gave her a prescription, anyway.' He was silent for a minute. 'When I became a doctor, I really thought I would be in the business of saving lives. Now I'm so disillusioned. What are we doing here?'

Emily gave a snort and linked her arm through his. 'Welcome to the real world, my friend. It's the story of my life.'

'Well, I'm tired of having this kind of conversation with my patients' families. Of watching their disappointment when I explain that we have limited resources. I'm beginning to feel as if my contribution to the patients' well-being has diminished to nothing. Zero.'

'Don't we sound gloomy this morning! Is this the first time you've realised that we can't do much for our patients?' Emily laughed.

'Well, no, but there was something about the woman, the wife of my patient …'

'Doctor, doctor! That's so unprofessional. You can't be ogling your patients' wives. Whatever happened to medical ethics? Perverts like you should be struck off the register!' Emily tried to lighten his mood.

'You know that's not what I mean, Emily,' he said, then took a stab at his favourite subject. 'You know you're the girl of my dreams. I am waiting for you …'

'Oh, Ben,' she laughed again. 'I love your flattery, you know that, but I'm just a dream …'

He grimaced. 'One day … Anyway, going back to this woman, she seemed so concerned …'

'Which would only be natural,' Emily shrugged.

'Yes. But she had swelling and bruising on her face. I suspect she'd been assaulted by her husband. Apparently he was well last night. Maybe they had an argument and the stress led to his collapse ...'

'Abused women. I see them all the time. They never volunteer information. All they'll ever say is they 'walked into a door', had an 'accident with a table'... They know you know, but *aiwa*, they won't talk. They're too demoralised to see clearly. A few modules should be included in our training about how to handle all these frustrations. But, cheer up. I'm sure we must have saved a few lives overnight.'

'Yeah, right! After my scare in Obstetrics last month, I really thought the Medical wards would be better. No such luck. This place is a nightmare,' he said bitterly.

Emily just smiled and said, 'You'll live! You're just tired. Forget the patients. Let's have coffee.' She pushed open the door of the doctors' rest room.

≈≈≈

In town, a white-coated pharmacist took the prescription from Onai. The lenses of his glasses gleamed and distorted the size of his eyes as he peered at her. She was not surprised by his scrutiny. She knew it was because of the bruises on her face. The doctor at the hospital had also given her an odd look, as had various other people whom she'd met on her way into town.

The pharmacist tapped something into a computer and looked at the screen with marked concentration. She shifted restlessly on her feet, wondering why he was taking so long. Finally, he looked up at her and smiled. Yes, they had the drug in stock, he told her. She would need two million dollars to pay for a full week's course.

Onai didn't have the money. She slipped the pink paper into her pocket and tried hard to think of an option. None was immediately obvious. Asking Katy was out of the question. Even if her friend had the money, how on earth would she ever pay her back? She just couldn't take on any more debt. Neither did she want to strain a valuable friendship.

So she trudged back to the hospital and ruefully informed the sister-in-charge that she had not been able to buy the medication. The Sister told her that it was all right. They would give Gari an alternative, although it was not the best antibiotic for his type of infection. Onai wondered what was the point in having a hospital if it couldn't even provide drugs for patients in emergency situations.

Later that afternoon, Gari was moved into intensive care. His condition had deteriorated.

CHAPTER 21

Faith had excelled in her exams, obtaining one distinction and passing the rest of her subjects with no less than class 2.1. The university graduation ceremony was scheduled for September. She was ecstatic. Ruzvidzo and Partners had signed her on as an intern. She was due to start work at the beginning of August.

Tom was pleased for her, and proud too. Now that the anxiety of waiting for results was over, it was time for a serious discussion about their plans for the future. He'd had a lot of time to think, when Faith was studying, as they hadn't been spending most evenings together. Being a man who was used to getting his own way, he'd been perplexed by Faith's rather ambivalent attitude to marriage. He'd also been somewhat dismayed by what he decided to call her passionate morality. In his view, the former should be kept for the bedroom, the latter for church. And yet, he also knew that this was the voice of his cynical self, a self he didn't much like, but one which would have certainly come to the fore had he married a rich Borrowdale *musalad*. He'd flirted with enough of those to convince him that he wanted to make his life with someone rather different. Faith was intelligent, sparky and warm. She cared about people and ideas in a way that reminded him of his younger self. He recognised that the down side of this would be occasional arguments like the one they had had over Murambatsvina, but taking the long view, he felt sure that this was a difficult moment, in a difficult time. A born optimist, he felt sure the economy would improve and then everyone's life would be easier.

He was, though, both offended and irritated by Faith's attitude towards his farm. She simply had no idea of how long the whole process had taken, and of his intention to do the right thing. That the farmer had been killed amidst so much negative publicity, had shocked him, and made him very reluctant to talk about it. Had he not been reasonably thick-skinned, he would have been hurt to think that Faith so distrusted him, that she was prepared to believe the worst.

In all other respects, they had got to know each other well over the last two years. She would come round, he was sure, if he was patient, and didn't lose his cool. Still, it was a test; and on several occasions, he'd nearly lost his temper completely. But, as his father always said, 'the truth will out'; and in some ways, as he'd liked and respected Mr Johnson, he was glad that at least Faith hadn't adopted the safe, knee-jerk response that because he was a white man, his death wasn't of any significance.

≈≈≈

Now, Faith's exams were over, she had done well, and he was going to take her out to dinner to celebrate. They would begin the next stage of their relationship in style. He was prepared to compromise; in fact, since their argument, he'd begun to think that a longish engagement would be just right for them both. He didn't want to hustle her unwillingly into marriage.

The softly-lit dining area at the Sheraton Hotel was crowded, as it was Friday night. The air was full of conversation, laughter and the tinkle of cutlery and glass against a background of muted music. Tom, mellowed by good food and wine, felt happy and relaxed in her company.

As they ate, Faith surprised him by suddenly blurting out an apology. 'I'm sorry I've been suspicious about your farm.' She paused briefly, then looking intently at him, she went on, 'Don't take this the wrong way. I know I've been anything but receptive, but I would really like to know how you came to own the land …'

He put the cutlery down and raised his hand in protest, 'Not again, Faith … Please, not tonight …' He felt tension rise in his belly. Surely she wasn't going to spoil the evening. It was too much …

'Please don't misunderstand me. This isn't about me interrogating you, or having prejudices, as you've implied. It's just that we've never really been able to discuss this without quarrelling and I just want you to share with me …' She bowed her head..

Tom sat back in his chair and took a sip of water. 'It's a long story.' He looked around warily, lowering his voice.

'I have all the time in the world,' she said gently, and wiped the corner of her mouth with a napkin.

'But the restaurant closes in two hours!' he joked, some of his tension easing.

She frowned, looking a bit anxious. 'But we can always …' she began.

'Goodness, what's happened to your sense of humour?' He smiled at her but Faith didn't return his smile.

'I suppose you're right. I should have taken the time to tell you all about it, but to be honest, as long as you were so suspicious and critical, it was easier to steer clear of the subject.'

'I know, and I'm sorry. Perhaps we can put that behind us now?'

Tom nodded and explained how after his father's death in 2001, he had inherited a substantial amount of money from his estate. Through a friend, he had heard about Mr Johnson, a farmer who was about to leave the country. The man had been keen to make a quick sale of his farm in Darwendale. He made no bones about having had enough of the tensions surrounding the land, and what he had referred to as the growing propaganda against white farmers.

Tom told her that he had been impressed when he went to view the land and had immediately started making arrangements to purchase it. However, just after the payment had gone through, the farmer had been murdered in his home, and his family brutally assaulted in what had been widely reported in the papers as a burglary. His wife had fled abroad with her children, soon afterwards. Tom had been left holding the receipts – and no title deeds. Then, the farm had been listed for acquisition in the resettlement programme.

'That can't have been easy,' Faith interrupted briefly.

'That's an understatement, *mudiwa*. I was devastated. There was talk of me being given my money back, but I wasn't sure I would get it at all – the Johnson family had no obligation to pay me back, and frankly speaking, nobody did, considering the way acquisitions were going. Besides, inflation had more than doubled property prices. So, even if by some miracle I had got my money back, I couldn't have bought a house in Budiriro with it! And I don't think you'd want to live there.'

Faith laughed, showing perfect, white teeth. Something stirred deep within him. How could he have even imagined living without her?

'So what did you do?' she asked.

'Against my mother's advice, I took the commission to court. I wanted to get the farm de-listed and I wanted the title deeds to be processed in my name. Fortunately Mrs Johnson agreed to come back into the country as a witness.'

'That was brave of her. And of you …'

'Believe me, I didn't feel brave at all. I was scared stiff, a paranoid wreck! I worried about Emily's and mum's safety. For a long time, I went around looking over my shoulder all the time because I had the strangest feeling that I was being followed. I was even scared to drive, in case my brakes failed …'

Faith burst out laughing. He smiled, 'You can laugh all you like, but my fears weren't unwarranted. For some reason, that farm had generated a lot of interest and you wouldn't believe the number of people who were waiting to take over … some of them quite influential.'

'I suppose it's understandable. Darwendale is a prime agricultural area,' Faith said thoughtfully.

'Anyway, the trial took place. I had a very good lawyer, a Mr Pfende; you probably know of him. He's brave, clever and very clear. And we were lucky to have a strong independent judge. The defence were weak; they'd lost some of their papers, and really they didn't have much of a case.

'So the judgement fell in our favour.

'Surprisingly, I not only got the farm, but I've been allowed to work on it in an uninterrupted way. Maybe it's because my father was a businessman who gave a lot of help to the party during the struggle … maybe … It was a horrible period, but well … all's well that end's well. Four years have shown me that I can make it as a farmer.

'Of course, I still occasionally have this fear … that someone might target me and hound me off the land.'

'Could that happen?'

'My dear, nothing surprises me anymore. Absolutely nothing. That's the reason why I've tried my best to be active, getting involved in all these TV programmes about new farmers. I'm not just an attention-seeker, you know. I'm actually a very calculating man!' He laughed.

Faith was silent for a while. Tom sipped his wine and watched her. Finally, she said, 'It seems ridiculous, doesn't it? We've been going out together for over two years, now. We've spent hours in each other's company, and yet I … we … have allowed this episode, which after all has only taken you about fifteen minutes to tell me, to nearly drive us apart. I know it's mainly been my fault. I was suspicious. I remember reading about the murder in the papers. I didn't take time to go to the archives and read the back issues of the newspapers when I might have understood a bit more … and my suspicions made it difficult to talk about …' Faith took a sip of Tom's wine and pulled a face. 'Ugh. At least I think I've learned something about the value of trying to be honest …'

'You're not the only one,' Tom replied quietly.

They looked at each other as if a burden had been lifted.

In the relaxed and somehow safe atmosphere of the restaurant, Tom told her of his earlier fears about their relationship. Admitting that he loved her and did not want to lose her, was a humbling experience. He had missed their easy companionship, their discussions and, of course, their intimacy. He was sincere in hoping they could put all the strain of past weeks behind them and look forward to the future.

Now, more than ever, he was aware that Faith was an asset, the kind of girl he would be proud to have as his wife. She was beautiful and intelligent, and they shared a compatibility that he had not shared with any other woman, even Nyaradzo, to whom she bore an uncanny resemblance.

As usual, remembering Nyaradzo stirred up feelings of deep regret. He was ready to settle down, and this time he was determined to do it right. There would be no room for slip-ups. His foolhardiness had cost him his little daughter, Shamiso, as Nyaradzo seemed to have vanished off the face of the earth since leaving for the UK. One day he'd tell Faith all about that. And sooner than later, he thought.

His mother was now constantly on his case. She wanted to see her son married and settled. She wanted grandchildren. She wanted a daughter-in-law who would look after her. Her own desires and her ambitions for her son, went hand in hand.

'So what's your game-plan?' He smiled at Faith.

'Well, like I've said, I'm looking forward to my internship and finding my way into a career that involves women and the law.'

'And where do I fit in this grand scheme?' he asked lightly, hoping she would be the first to bring up their previous discussion about marriage. He half-feared hearing more declarations about how much she had to do for her parents before settling down.

She smiled, suddenly enigmatic. 'Well, it all depends …'

Tom didn't push her. 'Mmm, how about corporate law? Who knows, I might need your services when I build up my business empire! Women and the law … what a waste! Tssk …' he clicked his tongue, teasing her.

She immediately became serious. 'A waste? Not in my opinion. Sometimes I feel the workings of society are designed to benefit men, at the expense of women of course. I really want to be in a position to help disadvantaged women. Which reminds me, I should talk to Emily about volunteer work at the Kushinga Women's Project …'

'Are you out to start a feminist war, or what? If Emily recruits you, then I'm a dead man! What is it with you girls?' Tom protested.

'Huh! Typical male chauvinist! You'd only need to be a woman for a day to understand. You'd need to have seen what I've seen the women in Mbare experiencing … Maybe you also need to have known my *mainini* Onai,' Faith toyed with the remains of her cheesecake. Would Tom ever really understand? How could such a kind generous guy be so oblivious? Maybe it had to do with his upbringing. Wealth protected you from knowledge of the painful and ugly. Would he, could he change …?

'Is your *mainini* still with her husband?' he enquired. He had heard so much about her from Faith that he felt as if he knew her.

Faith put her spoon down and shook her head slowly, reflecting on the gravity of the situation. 'Of course she is. And in my opinion, things are only getting worse.'

≈≈≈

For a whole week, Onai trudged to and from Mbare to visit her husband in the ICU. None of his immediate relatives turned up, although she had sent word to both his sister and brother. Because bus fares had recently gone up, yet again, she concluded that they were probably still looking for money to travel to Harare.

That week, she went to Cola Drinks Company to inform Mr Taruvinga, Gari's manager, about his hospitalisation. The man was very understanding and came to visit Gari with two other workmates. Acknowledging the gravity of the situation, Mr Taruvinga invited Onai to his office; he told her he had something important to discuss.

She was surprised to learn that Gari was due for retrenchment. Involuntarily, she expressed her ignorance about the pay-out he was due to receive. The manager looked astonished at her response, but he didn't probe. Instead, he asked, 'How are you going to pay the hospital bills? Apparently, your husband never signed up for our company medical aid scheme.'

She swallowed and shook her head. 'I really don't know. As it is, I've been struggling with prescriptions. The hospital has said they will give us a bill when he's discharged.'

Mr Taruvinga nodded sympathetically. 'Get in touch when you receive the bill. We'll arrange something.' She thanked him and left, feeling greatly relieved.

Sometimes, Katy accompanied her to hospital, and on a few occasions, she dragged along a rather unwilling Ruva. She had no idea how to deal with her daughter's silent antagonism towards her sick father. Talking seemed to make no difference. Because of Rita's sensitive disposition, she thought it best not to take her just yet; at least not until Gari's health improved. Fari would not be allowed in, because he was considered too young.

It was a physically and emotionally draining week. The hospital's dreariness, the heavy smell of illness and the air of despondency surrounding patients and visitors alike, only aggravated her low spirits. It

237

was a place that inspired no hope, especially as Gari's health appeared to be deteriorating. He lay immobile on the bed, connected by several tubes and wires to beeping machines, drifting in and out of consciousness.

On the seventh day, he seemed more responsive. The doctor spoke to Onai again. He was optimistic about her husband's general condition. Gari looked at her and blinked, his dry lips moving slowly and silently. She patted his hand, and smiled. Cold fingers curled around hers feebly. Her pulse quickened in response to his touch. This was the closest they had been in a very long time. Surely, after all this, their marriage would get stronger. Concerns about Gloria now had the inconsequential feel of a storm in a teacup. Coming so near to losing him, had reversed her earlier decisions. As his wife, this was her rightful place. She smiled at her husband again, feeling happier, the stress of the previous week lifting. Hope once again began to lift her spirits.

On the eighth morning, she found Gari's bed empty and neatly made up. He had probably improved further during the night and been transferred out of intensive care. The ward sister greeted her cheerfully and led her into a small office. She was a matronly woman with an air of efficiency. The crisp, rather formidable uniform did not detract from the warmth on her face. She made Onai sit in a comfortable chair and explained that Gari had slipped away peacefully during the night. They had not been able to contact her because there was no telephone number for his next of kin.

Onai received the news with disbelief. No, *Gari could not be dead.* She still needed another chance to talk things through with him, another chance … The muscles of her face worked, and moved her lips, but she was unable to speak. She found herself wanting to tell the ward sister that she had it wrong. Gari couldn't possibly have simply slipped away *peacefully.* He had been so full of life … so brutally aggressive. How could he have slipped away peacefully?

Why had he left her when they were so close to improving their marriage? Hadn't his fingers curled around hers only the day before? Hadn't that been a sign that he needed her, wanted her? She tried hard to summon grief; she wanted to cry for her husband, but the tears that were expected of her didn't come.

'Will you be all right, my dear? Have you come here with somebody?' the nursing sister asked in a low, concerned voice.

Onai shook her head. 'No, I'm alone. I think I'll be all right. Thank you, sister.'

The ward clerk offered his condolences and handed her a bill for five million dollars. Onai registered the huge sum with dismay, suddenly reminded of her own hospital bill.

'But how can it be so high?' she asked him despairingly. 'There is no way I can pay this.'

'Intensive care is expensive, Mrs Moyo,' he said sympathetically. Onai knew that most patients in the hospital were poor like herself, otherwise they would have been at the Avenues Clinic, or some other private hospital. Was this one running on debt, then? She shook her head. Maybe Gari's company would pay. But hospital bills and finances were not what she should be thinking about. Her priority was to break the news to her children, and the rest of the family.

≈≈≈

For Onai, the first day of Gari's wake passed in a haze of headaches. Katy was a constant presence at her side, supporting her and making sure that she had something to eat. Faith also came as soon as she heard the news. Gari's siblings, Toro and Chipo, arrived with their families later that evening. The relatives wailed loud and long into the night. Their lamentations escalated with each new arrival; their displays of grief briefly interrupting the stream of mournful songs and drums. Onai's emotions were confused. She wanted to mourn her husband, but when she searched her heart, she found only anger, disappointment and a real sense of having been cheated by his death.

≈≈≈

Onai's mother, MaMusara, arrived the following day from Chiwundura, with members of her extended family. To Onai, it seemed as if everything had spiralled out of control. There was none of the privacy for which she craved, but of course funerals were like that. There were

239

people everywhere. Her home no longer felt like her own. Even the toilet was constantly in use. It was as if she had been dispossessed. Her bedroom had been taken over by Gari's relatives, who wandered in and out freely. Furniture had been moved out of the house so that more people could be accommodated indoors. She worried about thefts and breakages but there was nothing she could do about it.

She still could not cry, despite making a conscious effort to do so. As she said to her mother, and later to Katy, she felt as if her reservoir of tears had long run dry. Her eyes were heavy, and felt gritty with lack of sleep. VaHondo's widow clung to her shaking, as she wept. Onai had the feeling that the woman was crying because Gari's death had brought back painful memories of sudden loss; but also because she enjoyed the drama and the attention that she received as she wailed her bitter tears.

Faith dutifully took her *mainini's* children under her wing. They cried constantly, like many of the female relatives. Mourners marvelled about what a strong woman Onai was and how well she was coping. Trust me, you don't want to know my true feelings, she thought miserably, but she accepted their condolences and comments with good grace.

Gari's sister, Chipo, had no such kind thoughts or words. 'One day you'll tell me what you did to the son of my mother. How can a man vomit blood?' Taut muscles stood out on her scrawny neck as she shouted at Onai. The mourners around them shifted uncomfortably. Chipo's words insinuated that Onai had murdered Gari using witchcraft.

Onai bit back a counter-offensive. The funeral could easily turn into a platform for confrontations and accusations regarding the manner of death. Customarily, for every dead person, there was at least one alleged witch. Onai was in no mood to engage in such wrangles, so she walked over to the fireplace where her neighbours were cooking large pots of sadza for the mourners.

She spotted Maya hovering close by, obviously waiting for an opportunity to pick up something that could be twisted into gossip. In all probability, she had already mentioned Gloria to Gari's relatives. She wondered if somebody would bring up the issue. Glancing towards the seated men, she spotted Chipo and Toro in deep conversation, their heads suspiciously close together. Watching them, she felt a sense of foreboding. Trouble was looming. She braced herself.

≈≈≈

Onai did not have money to buy a coffin and engage the services of a funeral parlour. Neither did Toro, Chipo or their cousins. Funeral contributions from friends and family had all gone towards feeding the large gathering of mourners. Thankfully, Gari's firm paid for the funeral expenses. Mr Taruvinga again asked to see Onai at his office, this time to discuss the balance of what the firm owed Gari.

The worst moment for Onai came when she had to accompany male relatives and the undertakers to collect Gari's body from the hospital mortuary. The shelves were full, and bodies littered the floor. A mortuary attendant had warned them about a malfunction in the refrigeration system, but nothing could have prepared Onai for the overpowering stench of decomposing flesh. She gagged as she stepped over bodies, her eyes looking wildly around for her husband. Much to her relief, after only ten minutes, they found Gari's body. He was lying on the floor in a corner, cold and rigidly still.

≈≈≈

Finding a burial place was complicated. The nearest cemetery was reported to have filled up, due to the frequency of AIDS-related deaths. Empty gravesites in the second nearest one had all been bought up for future burials. They ended up burying him at Mbudzi, just outside Harare. Fortunately, his company again stepped in and provided transport.

At the graveside, Gari's oldest uncle, nicknamed VaSolo, was given the honour of the first speech. He stood up slowly and took off his hat to show respect for the dead and the living. After clearing his throat, he addressed the gathering. He launched into an elaborate speech about Gari's attributes. After a lengthy pause, he went on, his voice now shaky. 'An untimely death has robbed me of my brother's first-born

241

son, in a way, my own son. Baba vaRuva's life has been snuffed out, leaving his children as orphans, his young wife as a widow. No amount of words can express the grief that I feel today, as we lay him to rest.'

He turned towards Onai's direction saying, '*Muroora*, as the most senior man in the Moyo family, I pledge that we will be here for you and the children. You are still our daughter-in-law, a wife of the family. The children are ours.' Onai bowed her head, not reassured by the seemingly kind words, contemplating their deeper meaning. Surely they did not expect her to be 'inherited' by Gari's brother? Well, she would have none of it!

VaSolo sat down, amidst ululation by Gari's nieces from the extended family. They had the important role of lightening up the atmosphere and diffusing funeral tensions. So far they had done well.

In the same vein, speaker after speaker sang Gari's praises, and showered him with accolades. The proverb, 'every dead man is a good man', could not have been more true. Katy had difficulty in recognising the person they were describing, and wondered how Onai would cope with the bitter irony of so much acclamation. In death, Gari became a hero, as had so many before him.

After his body had been lowered into the ground, Onai and her children, followed by other relatives, threw in handfuls of freshly-dug soil into the grave. To Onai this act seemed doubly symbolic. She was burying a long, sad chapter of her life. She still hadn't cried.

≈≈≈

John prepared to leave for South Africa after Gari's burial. He was surprised when Katy said abruptly, 'By the way, I'd almost forgotten to tell you that I packed some condoms for you.'

He stiffened and turned round to face her. 'Condoms? For what reason? Don't you trust me?'.

'I do trust you but I also know that you meet a lot of young women on your trips. I'm sure they throw themselves at you in droves.'

John grimaced inwardly. She was right in one respect. Border posts were crawling with prostitutes of all shapes, sizes and ages. Beitbridge had its fair share. Some of the girls were barely pubescent but they were still capable of fulfilling any man's wildest fantasies; as John knew from his acquaintances. For a lot of men, the thrills were so breathtaking that the cost was irrelevant – so self-indulgent were they that the threat of HIV diminished to just something that happened to other people.

Sleeping with a prostitute was something that John had done at a much younger age, well before the advent of AIDS. In his mind, that made him a better man than most. He would never expose his wife to HIV, or any other infection. So the condoms were not necessary. He did not tell Katy about his 'loose association' with the girls that she was so concerned about; neither did he tell her how well-known he had become for providing safe and affordable passage into South Africa.

'Even if they do throw themselves at me, it doesn't affect me, Katy. I'm not that kind of man. I don't sleep around,' he replied with quiet dignity.

'Maybe one day you will be tempted, and when that time comes, I would like you to be prepared. There is AIDS out there, John,' Katy said dispassionately. John shook his head. Why was she being like this, and why this sudden fixation with AIDS? Was it because one of his colleagues had recently died of the disease? Or could one of the boys from work have said something out of turn?

He took a deep breath, keen to avoid a quarrel during his last few hours at home. 'Fine, I'll take them if that will make you happy. I'm sure the boys will be glad to have them,' he responded, in an equally detached tone. His travelling companions would be glad to have free Protector condoms, all right.

≈≈≈

Long after John had gone, Katy mulled over one of the hardest things that she had ever done – packing condoms for her husband. She trusted him, yes, but there was always a niggling suspicion that one day he would stray. Cross-border truck drivers were known to be in a high-risk group for contracting HIV. Of everything that she had heard on the news, that was one of the few things she was inclined to believe. The condoms in his bag gave her a sense of security. She would sleep well in his absence.

Any other woman would have told her that her mind was unhinged, and that she was sanctioning infidelity. She chose not to see it that way. These were not times when one could rely on naïve assumptions and sit back complacently. One always had to be on guard. Out of her own volition, this was her way of protecting what she held close to her heart.

Asking her husband to use condoms within their marriage would, of course, have been taboo. Getting the female condom for herself was equally out of the question. Either implied a breach of trust, and undermined John's status as her husband. She didn't want to imagine the possible repercussions. Somehow, packing condoms for him didn't seem to carry the same implications. It was a subject she would have liked to discuss with Onai, but despite their closeness they had never talked about what went on in the bedroom with their husbands; sexuality remained an almost unmentionable subject. Katy sadly acknowledged that this lack of transparency probably did more harm than good, where communicable diseases, like AIDS, were concerned. She sighed, remembering her *tete's* words of advice when she got married. Her father's sister had told her to accept that men had needs that could not be fulfilled by one woman. Animalistic needs that drove them to seek out other women. *Tete* was of the opinion that it did not matter if a man strayed, as long as he always returned home. Even in those bygone days, when AIDS had not been an issue, Katy had been sceptical of her *tete's* advice.

That evening as she sat alone, she made another difficult decision. She would go for an HIV test. And maybe when the dust in Onai's life had settled, she would persuade her friend to go for one as well. Which woman was not at risk? At least for now, Onai's risk had died with Gari. That is, if she wasn't infected already.

≈≈≈

Onai's mother prepared to leave for her home in Chiwundura the day after Gari's burial. Before she left, she made Onai promise to visit her with the children during the school holidays. The Moyo family did not leave with the rest of the mourners. The following morning, they gathered in the sitting-room to share out Gari's personal effects.

According to tradition, Fari was the heir, being the first-born son. However, he was given Gari's old blue shirt whose front was riddled with holes. Onai watched bitterly as Gari's good clothes were shared out among the Moyo men, amidst noisy jokes about who deserved to get what. Scuds of opaque beer that were being passed round seemed to have oiled vocal cords and transformed the previously sombre atmosphere into a bizarre party. The men were drunk and voluble; the women fittingly taciturn, but watchful of the proceedings. Through their menfolk, there was potential for material gain.

'At least I will have some money for the children,' Onai thought with relief. There would be money in Gari's account, including the balance of the redundancy package that he had been due to receive.

Gari's uncle, VaSolo, had just one more thing to say. He addressed Toro: 'I now leave you in charge of this young family. Every home needs a man to be in charge, so you must take this very seriously. As we have agreed in the *dare* one year from now, we will hold a ceremony to bring our son's spirit back into his home.'

Turning to Onai, he went on, 'That is what we have decided, Mai Ruva, *muroora*. Everything else will be resolved next year, including *nhaka*. We have all agreed that we want to keep you in the family.' Onai was dismayed by the murmurs of agreement that accompanied his words. She could already see that she would never be free.

Toro's lecherous eyes swept over her, a suspicious half-smile on his lips. His wife, Shungu, gave him a murderous look. Onai wanted to reassure the younger woman that she was not interested in her husband. The Moyo men could wish as much as they wanted, but she would not be inherited. Come one year from now, she would name Fari as her 'protector'. It was customarily acceptable for any woman who didn't want to be inherited to take such a measure. That would show them!

Toro and his wife did not leave with everyone else. Toro called Onai and her children to the sitting room, later in the afternoon. He gave a little cough before he spoke. '*Maiguru,* now that my brother is buried, we need to plan how we are all going to live.'

Onai feigned naiveté. 'We will be all right, *babamunini*. You do not have to come here to look after us. If I have any problem, I will send word out to you *kumusha*,' she said gently.

Toro laughed. His wife gave him a strange look. 'You do not understand, *maiguru*. You heard what *babamukuru* VaSolo told us, I'm now in charge here. I can't balk my responsibility, so I will move in here, with my wife and children, and we can all live together as one big family. I can't run two separate homes in these difficult times.'

Sincerity had never been one of Toro's strong points, and Onai could see right through him. She would have none of it. 'No, *babamunini*, I don't need you to look after me. I'm not a child. Besides, this house is too small for all of us.'

Toro sprang up in a rage. 'How dare you challenge me? What gives you the authority to talk to me like this … without respect?' he spluttered, his face dark with anger.

She stood up, anticipating an assault, ready to hit back and defend herself. She had taken enough from Gari, and she wouldn't allow a repeat cycle. Her children cowered behind her. Shungu also stood up, as if ready for combat.

Toro shook with anger, jabbing at the air in front of Onai with a finger. 'You disrespectful, stupid woman! Get out of my house now, and take your snivelling children with you.'

At his words, Onai's courage abandoned her. Could he really throw her out of her home? What had she done? She slumped back into the chair, suddenly afraid. Her children started crying. *'Babamunini!* You can't mean that! Please. Where do you want me to go with the children, *nhai babamunini?'*

She shrank backwards when he raised his hand as if to strike her. His wife placed her baby on the floor and sprang between them. She begged, 'Please, *baba vevana*. This is not the time to be fighting. Please, you are frightening the children.'

He shrugged and sat down, clearly struggling to control himself. 'How dare you challenge me in front of the children? I want you out of here, immediately!' His male pride wounded, he was harsh and unfeeling.

'Please, let me stay here, for a while at least. Ruva is registered to write her exams in November,' Onai begged, with increasing desperation. She would never forgive herself if her words had cost her children their home. Her eyes stung: tears that she had failed to weep for Gari rolled down her cheeks. She lacked the energy to wipe them away.

Toro was unmoved. She watched him stroking his shaggy beard in a manner so painfully reminiscent of Gari that again she wanted to lash out and scream. She averted her eyes in affected humility, which she hoped would soften his heart.

He spoke harshly. '*Maiguru,* this house belongs to the Moyo family, and you have shown me that you do not respect us. You dared to talk to me as if I need your permission to live here. Next, you will be bringing your boyfriends into our home … insulting my brother's memory!'

She was stung by his cruel accusations. 'Please don't do this to us, *babamunini.* I was never unfaithful to my husband and I'm not planning to bring any boyfriends here. Have pity on me. These are your children, too. They carry your name, your totem. You're now the closest they have to a father. Please,' she begged.

Toro threw her a hostile glance, 'How will they respect me when they have witnessed you talking to me so disrespectfully? You are now wasting my time, Mai Ruva. Just take your clothes and leave with your children.' His face was uncompromising, his words final. Spittle had collected at the corners of his mouth.

Onai looked with pleading eyes at Toro's wife. Shungu was now cradling her gurgling baby. Making no effort to help, the younger woman looked away, thrusting an engorged teat into the baby's mouth. The child immediately fell quiet and began to suckle hungrily.

Onai knew that Shungu wouldn't help her. She probably couldn't wait to move to the city. Life in the rural areas was getting worse by the day. Perhaps she needed a break from the hard labour of tilling unproductive land; a break from queuing for food donations.

Ruva and Rita stared vacantly at the floor. Onai couldn't comfort them because her own need of solace outweighed her ability to give any. Fari begged his uncle for permission to take the Humpty Dumpty clock. Toro's face puckered into a scowl. He glanced irritably at the clock hanging on the wall, it's face smiling broadly as if to cheer up Onai's family.

He pulled it abruptly off the wall and shoved it into Fari's waiting arms.

'One other thing, before you leave, *maiguru* – can I have my brother's bank card?' he asked. Numbed by a sense of despair, Onai dug into her battered handbag and handed the card over.

Toro snatched it unceremoniously. 'I have the death certificate, so don't try to collect any money from his workplace. I'll do that myself next week.'

Onai nodded silently, resigned to this sudden turn of events. She knew that there was no way Toro would spare any money for the children when he was throwing them out of the only home they'd ever known. She had lost everything. Although Gari had paid a full bride price, their marriage had never been registered. What rights did she have to anything? Who could she approach for help? Would talking to Gari's manager, Mr Taruvinga, who had been so kind at the funeral, help? The Moyo family had made it very clear that as a woman, a widow, she had no rights to take any independent initiative. A multitude of regrets swamped her; not least the sheer futility of a life spent with Gari. This ending was a mockery of her immense effort to tolerate his every injustice, just to keep her marriage intact.

≈≈≈

Katy promptly came to her friend's rescue and took in the destitute family. They would be terribly crowded, but there was no immediate alternative.

'What will John say? He left only yesterday and here we are, descending on his home. When is he coming back? What about Faith?' Onai asked anxiously.

'Don't worry, I'm sure he'll understand. He's not back for another three weeks, anyway. I'm crossing the border to meet him in Messina at the end of next week. I'll explain everything then. Faith is starting her new job next week. She's moved out to share a flat in town with her friend, so you can make use of her room.'

The two women talked late into the night, trying to plan a way forward.

Katy suggested that Onai should take Fari and Rita temporarily to Gari's sister in Zhombe until the issue was resolved. Knowing Chipo's true colours, Onai had qualms about taking her children there.

'We can't ignore the fact that these children carry the Moyo totem. You can't alienate them from their blood relatives, Onai. What if they develop problems in the future that need traditional rites?'

Onai nodded. 'Yes, you're right. I doubt Chipo will welcome us, though. I'm really not looking forward to facing her. Besides, there's her husband to consider.'

'If she won't have them, she might be willing to talk to the father figure in the family, that VaSolo, and ask for intervention. You might be allowed back home. And if VaSolo is a just man, he will make sure you get the money from Gari's firm for the children. It would be good to resolve the issue without the courts getting involved. As I said, you can't afford to alienate these children from their father's family.'

Before they slept, they had agreed that Onai would travel to Zhombe the following morning. If Chipo refused to have the children, she would proceed to her mother's home and leave them there until things improved. Ruva would have to stay in Mbare because of her O-level exams.

CHAPTER 22

All night, Onai had tossed and turned, acutely sensitive to every nocturnal sound. As a result, she woke up feeling tired and with a dull headache. The day had a depressing outlook and she felt like conceding defeat and crawling back into bed, never to wake up again. However, life had to go on.

She took a cold shower that made her shiver violently, but left her feeling more refreshed and alert. Rita and Fari had a quick wash while Katy prepared breakfast. They ate hurriedly and prepared to leave. Because of the fuel problems, arriving early at the terminus was the only way to increase their chances of getting a bus.

Katy looked worriedly at Onai and said, 'I know this is hard. Losing both a husband and a home can never be anything but hard. For a while, things might even get a bit harder, but remember that I'm here for you. You deserve happiness, *shamwari*, and I'm sure one day things will be just fine.' Onai nodded, not trusting herself to speak. They were only words. How could her friend know what the future held?

Katy pressed a wad of money firmly into her hand and assured her that she wouldn't have to pay it back any time soon. 'Let me know how you get on. I'll keep an eye on Ruva until you return. I've phoned Faith and she's quite happy to come and keep her company when I go to Messina.'

Onai bit her trembling lower lip. 'Thank you. I don't know what I'd have done without you.' They were words that she'd said many times before, words she hoped that Katy might one day say to her.

'If I can't be here for you, then I wouldn't be worthy of calling myself your *sahwira*.' Katy replied sincerely, then added, 'I'm sorry, I can't accompany you to the station. Mr Nzou insisted on coming to pick up some foreign currency early this morning, so I have to wait for him. I think he'll be here shortly.'

Onai brushed the apology aside and gathered up her bags to leave. Her friend's capacity for kindness was a great comfort.

≈≈≈

Onai and her children left Katy's house and walked in silence to the terminus. They strained their eyes in the early morning mist and struggled with their bags. Onai found it disconcerting to see how normal everything looked. Life was going on as usual. The world did not care about her plight. Nothing had halted in sympathy. As if it would, she sighed wearily, adjusting the strap that was cutting into her shoulder. The clean-up operation's continuation was just a matter of course. The roadsides were littered with mounds of wood, brick and mortar debris, pitiful remains of demolished homes and market stalls. The garbage that had gone uncollected for months made the Mbare landscape even more unsightly.

As they walked, she caught glimpses of small family groups lying on top of mounds of rubble that had once been their homes. All they had as protection against the cold, were thin blankets and plastic sheeting. In the open space next to the terminus, she saw a gaunt woman sitting next to a dying fire, together with a toddler and small child of school-going age. The way she sat, with her shoulders hunched forward, head drooping from a slender neck, reminded her of Sheila. But Sheila was dead. At that moment Onai found enough optimism to count herself very lucky. She was not one of the women spending their days and nights with their families exposed to the cold winter weather.

Early-morning commuters hurried towards the bus terminus with purposeful strides, each of them focused on walking to outpace the others. The later one arrived at the terminus, the higher were the chances of not getting transport. In this race, the only ones making slow progress were the elderly, the unwell, the very young, and those who were manoeuvering piles of bedding and furniture in pushcarts.

Onai was dismayed to find the place already teeming with throngs of people, many looking anxious, even desperate. Most of them sat next to heaps of all their worldly belongings and waited for transport to the rural areas or wherever else they hoped to make another home. Unlike the customary bustle of traffic, there were only a few buses in sight. It was obvious that fuel was still in short supply. The buses seemed overburdened with bicycles, beds, and other furniture stacked on their lug-

251

gage carriers. At least two were fully loaded, and the engines were being warmed up in preparation to leave.

The little family stood in the cold and waited patiently for the bus to Zhombe. Rita clung to her mother for warmth and Fari sat down on one of the larger suitcases. His enthusiasm for anything that moved on wheels was blunted. He just sat, hugging his knees, not saying a word. He did not venture out to take a closer look at the buses as he would have normally done.

Thankfully, a bus soon arrived, and touts were calling for passengers to Zhombe via Kwekwe. Onai pushed and shoved energetically with the other frantic travellers. She was among the last to get in. She secured some seats at the back and they boarded.

A few people who had too much luggage, especially those with furniture, were told brusquely that they could not be accommodated on the bus. They would have to find private transport.

'This is not Biddulphs Removals. Why don't you people ever learn?' one *hwindi* shouted angrily at a woman who was pleading not to be left behind. She had secured a seat and all she required was for the young man to allow her bed onto the carrier.

Onai watched sympathetically as the woman gave up her seat and alighted. She knew that private transport would cost less at least five million dollars. None of the stranded men and women would be able to raise such large amounts of money because they were either unemployed or vendors whose market stalls had been closed. It would mean more days of uncertainty and more nights of sleeping out in the cold.

The slightly muggy interior of the bus was a welcome reprieve. Onai squeezed her hands into the hollows of her armpits in pursuit of warmth and comfort.

The bus left Harare at a breakneck speed that was maintained for most of the journey. By half-past nine, they were in Kwekwe. Off the main road towards Zhombe, the bus ride was extremely bumpy and uncomfortable. The dust road was pot-holed and littered with small rocks. In places, the wear and tear of erosion had carved irregular gullies. The damaged road inflicted a cruel abuse of its own on the decrepit vehicle whose smooth tyres already looked prone to accidents. The bus creaked disturbingly as it moved. She hoped they would not have a breakdown before reaching their destination. Nobody else on the bus looked concerned, so she imagined that they would be all right.

≈≈≈

Onai's first stop was at the rural shopping centre close to where Gari's sister lived with her family. The once vibrant shopping centre looked deserted and dilapidated. A few chickens wandered aimlessly on the dust-brushed veranda of Peter's General Stores. The entrance was littered with a scattering of droppings. A sullen young man stood at the door, frowning slightly, as if daring them to approach and ask him to shift himself.

Onai thought of buying half a loaf of bread for her sister-in-law then surmised that there would be none in the shop. There hadn't been any bread in the city shops for at least a week. She would have to go empty-handed and risk Chipo's displeasure. Her sister-in-law was generally an unpleasant woman, and the thought of meeting her was disheartening. She led the way towards Chipo's homestead, their *pata-patas* squelching on the sandy road.

She could not figure out how to open the sturdy metal gate. She pushed against it, hoping that it would automatically open. The noise attracted a scrawny dog which half-limped and half-ran to the gate. It had an unhealthy, dull pelt. Barring their way, it bared its teeth and gave a high-pitched bark that sounded more like a strangled yelp. Rita moved closer to her. Fari stared warily at it.

'Get away, Shumba, *voetsek!*' Onai shouted at the dog in a loud voice sounding braver than she felt. But the dog continued to snarl menacingly and did not back off.

An authoritative male voice boomed, *'Aiwa* Shumba! Get away!' At the voice of his master, the wretched dog immediately retreated, limping off hurriedly at a tangent, tail between his legs. He hung his head as if he was contrite at being caught threatening visitors so shamelessly. Onai felt a flood of relief. In his prime, Shumba had been a real menace who had guarded the homestead with aggressive loyalty.

Chipo's husband emerged from behind the lofty chicken-run. His muscular frame was clad in his trademark blue overalls, which were worn out at the knees. A bright yellow monkey-skin hat sat on his head. Onai noted that his beard was speckled with grey, his face lined. How fast the years seemed to have gone! They were all ageing.

'Greetings, *Mama*.' He clapped his large hands resoundingly in salutation and approached her. He opened the gate easily and relieved her of the heavy bags. Onai smiled at him and returned his greeting. He led her and her children into the yard, keeping a respectable distance as custom demanded.

They followed him into the mud-plastered thatched kitchen where Chipo was preparing a meal, possibly a late breakfast. None of her children were to be seen. They had probably gone to school. Onai and her children entered the dim interior and sat deferentially on a goatskin mat behind the door. A bright fire was burning. Warmth immersed Onai. She was happy to be indoors, but the feeling didn't last long.

Chipo looked surprised to see them, before assuming her usual hard mask. She frowned and looked pointedly at the children and their bags. Rita cowered under her steady gaze. No sooner had they exchanged brief, obligatory greetings than Chipo hurriedly asked, 'Is everything all right?'

'Yes, everything is fine, *Tete*,' Onai responded carefully.

'So what brings you here?'

Onai gave a sigh and stared at the floor. It looked as if it had been freshly polished with cow dung that morning. Her mind flitted back reluctantly to Gari's brother and the unpleasant events of the previous day. She couldn't find any non-inflammatory words that would adequately explain the turn of events.

Chipo's husband broke the heavy silence by offering his condolences as he had not managed to attend the funeral. Onai accepted them, politely. Once again, an oppressive silence descended.

Her sister-in-law wiped her face with the back of her hand, then stood up to readjust the cloth that was hanging loosely from her waist. With her *chitenge* now tightly wrapped around her, she looked like a long, malnourished reed. She bent down to stir the thick porridge in the pot. Adding more maize meal to the simmering mixture, she concentrated on her task as if whatever was in the pot was a matter of life and death. Onai's discomfort grew. She wished she could be anywhere but in that stifling kitchen.

Chipo's husband took out a discoloured bottle from the depths of a pocket at the front of his overalls. He emptied some snuff onto his left palm. Sniffing loudly, he drew it into his nostrils, then gave a satisfied grunt. Chipo's gaze swept scornfully over his hunched form. He replaced the container in his pocket, apparently unaware of the disdain on his wife's face.

Onai shifted her eyes to the fire, still remembering the manner in which Toro had thrown her out of her home. The flames were beginning to falter. Tendrils of smoke rose from the logs. Her eyes stung and watered. She coughed as the acrid wisps thickened and permeated the room. Rita shifted uncomfortably next to her.

Chipo puffed out her cheeks and blew vigorously at the wavering flames. They immediately sprang to life and a few sparks flew dangerously towards Onai, jolting her back from the unpleasant memory of yesterday. Finally, she summoned enough courage to speak of Toro's cruelty. '*Babamunini* Toro has forced me to leave the home, *Tete*. He says his family is moving in. We've been chased out of the house with nothing, apart from our clothes.' The words caught slightly in her throat.

Chipo's husband coughed deeply and rose from his three-legged stool. He lingered for a moment, then left the room.

His wife said nothing. She pursed her lips and pushed the logs together, even though the fire was already burning brightly. She stirred the porridge again, without obvious need. After a considerable silence, she launched into a lengthy speech, 'You must have done something to make my brother throw you out. Frankly speaking, I'm not surprised. Things get round, you know. I heard that our brother vomited blood before he died. That was very disturbing. I also heard something about the second wife he'd decided to take because he was not happy with you. His death was very convenient for you, wasn't it?'

Onai looked at her sister-in-law, dazed. She had at least expected a word of sympathy, not another accusation about Gari's death. She leaned forward on the goatskin mat and bowed her head, blinking back tears, wanting her distress to be private. She would not give Chipo the satisfaction of seeing how upset she was.

'I had nothing to do with my husband's death, *Tete*. You can go to the hospital and talk to the doctors.' Resentment rose, and she struggled to retain her composure. When Chipo did not respond, she said, 'These are your brother's children. Won't you at least help me with ideas about how to look after them? We are now homeless.'

Again, there was no response from her putative hostess whose face was creased with obvious displeasure.

Onai sighed wearily. 'I was also hoping that you would talk to the fathers of the family on my behalf so that this issue can be resolved peacefully. *Babamukuru* VaSolo pledged at the funeral that the children would be looked after, but as a *muroora*, I cannot approach him directly. I want to go back to my house, *Tete*.' She spoke earnestly, hoping that Chipo would find it in her heart to assist her in some way, however small.

'What do I care about VaSolo ? He's just a stupid old drunk. You know I don't talk to my uncles since my own father died. I'm surprised that you would even think of the house as yours. Gari inherited it from our father. Toro is next in line to inherit, so he has done nothing wrong by asking you to leave! We don't want you bringing your boyfriends into that house, tainting my brother's and our parents' memory.' Chipo was almost shouting.

Onai had no idea why the accusations about boyfriends were being aired again. She objected. 'Please, *Tete*. I have no boyfriends, and no intention of having any. You know I wouldn't. The fact is I need your help. I'm worried about my children because ...'

'Huh,' Chipo interrupted rudely. 'I know nothing about what you would or would not do. And I can't help you. Had you been a better wife to my brother, we'd be having a very different conversation right now! Maybe my brother would still be alive.'

Onai realised that any further pleading would simply be twisted and used against her, or that she would be perceived as weak and malleable. She rose from the goatskin mat with as much dignity as she could muster, and gathered her children and their bags together. 'I see I was wrong to believe that you might pity the children of your brother, now that they have no home. So we shall manage on our own.' She spoke as clearly as she was able and was glad that her voice, low and level, gave no hint of the anger, hurt, rejection and despair that clutched at her heart.

She felt a pressing need to get away from this hard, scornful woman. She would take her children to her mother. If they left now, they would arrive in Kwekwe in time to catch the late afternoon bus to Chiwundura.

Surprisingly, her brave words did nothing to provoke her sister-in-law any further. 'I'm making sadza. Stay and have some,' Chipo ordered abruptly. For a fleeting moment, Onai thought she might have misheard. Was this a peace offering? She didn't know. Whatever it was, it was too little and too late.

'Thank you, *Tete*, but we must leave,' she murmured, not wanting to stay a minute longer than necessary. Besides, she would not be able to stomach the food after Chipo's verbal attack.

'Suit yourself. I won't beg you to stay. I'm sure you can find your own way to the bus-stop.' Her sister-in-law was back to her old spiteful self. Onai walked out of the kitchen with her children, her head held high. Never again, she vowed. Never again, would she leave herself so open to anybody's mercy.

Chipo's husband helped them to carry their bags back to Peter's General Stores. Fortunately, the bus arrived only five minutes later. It sprayed sand over them and pulled up several metres from the designated stop. They had to run after it. The conductor gave Onai an impatient glare as he grabbed her largest bag and heaved it onto the carrier. She waved goodbye to Chipo's husband, and paid their fares. The children stared out of the window as if they were looking at a wasteland.

≈≈≈

When she arrived at her mother's homestead later that afternoon, Onai was relieved to find her at home. She was busy watering her small vegetable garden. She was with Wanai, her youngest niece, who now lived with her and helped around the compound. MaMusara placed the water carrier down and rushed to the gate to embrace them.

'*Kwakanaka here ku*Harare?' she asked with concern, as soon as they sat down in the mud hut that served as a kitchen.

'Everything is fine in Harare, *Amai*.' She had decided against mentioning her eviction immediately. She didn't want to find herself breaking down in front of the children. Her mother looked at her with disbelieving eyes, but thankfully did not press her further.

Later, after an evening meal of sadza and sour milk, Wanai and Onai's children went to sleep, leaving her sitting by the fireside with her mother. MaMusara's lined face looked very troubled. She pushed back the headscarf that had slipped over her forehead; her knobbly hands trembled.

She probed gently, 'My daughter, I know something terrible has happened. Why are you here so soon after the burial? It's not right for you to leave home just after your husband's burial. It shows lack of respect to your in-laws, and indeed to your dead husband. Have the Moyos already finished all the rituals?'

Onai cleared her throat and stared blindly into the fire. 'The men of the family shared out Gari's clothes yesterday morning, and then left. They said everything else would be discussed a year from now, according to custom. *Babamunini* Toro and his wife stayed. He took *baba va*Ruva's bank card and asked me to leave, *Amai*. He said the house now belonged to him.'

Tears streamed down MaMusara's face as she heard about her daughter's callous treatment at the hands of her brother-in-law. 'I'm sorry, Mai Ruva, *mwanangu*. I never imagined that things would turn out this way.'

Onai shook her head, slowly. 'Neither did I. *Kunenge kurota*. But if it's a dream, when will I wake up? As *Tete* Chipo has refused to help, I think I will have to take this up in the courts when I go back to Harare. I have no marriage certificate, but there must be a way. If we lose the house, the children must at least get something – even if it's only Gari's pension contributions.'

MaMusara objected vehemently. 'The courts my child? That's not the proper way of solving such issues. You will only create bad feelings between your children and their relatives. They will be outcasts from the Moyo clan.'

'But *Amai* ...' Onai began, once again feeling panic rising. 'What else can we do?' Her mother was echoing Katy's words. Who would give her the support that she needed to pursue the matter? 'We ...'

Her mother interrupted. 'No, my child. I cannot agree with the road that you want to take. These children belong to the Moyos. For that reason, you have to accept whatever your *babamunini* has decided. Anything else will only cause bad spirits to rise up. If the Moyos disown these children, there will be no end to your problems. Who will marry off your daughters? Who will guide Fari into manhood? Instead of inviting antagonism, I would rather you start a new life for your family. You're strong enough.'

Onai took a deep breath. She couldn't understand why her mother was being so superstitious. Did she have no idea how traditions were breaking down, or simply being abused, especially in the towns? But maybe she was right about her starting a new life. Hadn't she been craving independence? Right now, though, the price of emancipation seemed too much to handle.

She spread out her hands in front of the fire, 'You're right, I need to go back to Harare to look for a job. Can I at least leave Fari and Rita with you for a while, please?'

Her mother was quick to say, 'You do not have to ask, *mwanangu*. I will be glad to have them here until you settle down.'

'It's only a week or two before schools break for the August holiday, but I'd still like to have the children registered. It could take me some time to sort things out.'

'Do you think the local school will take them in at this time of year?'

'I really don't know, *mwanangu*. We'll have to find out tomorrow. I'm sure something can be done.' Her mother seemed more sympathetic, and Onai was glad that she had resisted the desire to argue. She took her mother's hand and squeezed it. It was good to be home. 'Maybe,' she thought, 'I'll talk to Faith. She'll know if there is any chance that going through the courts might help me.' The thought cheered her.

≈≈≈

The following morning, Onai was pleased when she secured a place for Rita at the local high school, barely a stone's throw away from her mother's home. Half an hour later, she found herself at the adjacent primary school, sitting in a small, airless office and facing a very young headmaster.

He shook her hand firmly and introduced himself as Mr Dube. She looked at him doubtfully. He was worryingly young. How could he teach, let alone head a school? To her surprise, he was a very courteous and patient listener. She explained that, if possible, she would like to enrol her son at his primary school. Circumstances beyond her control had forced her to take her children away from Harare.

He looked at her regretfully. 'I'm afraid that I can't offer you anything at this point. As you might know, we've recently had a great influx of displaced people coming in from the towns. At the most, our classes should take forty pupils but, as it is, the three classes in your son's grade already average fifty. Why don't you try St Patrick's? They have both a primary and a secondary school on one site.'

'But surely, accepting just one more little boy won't cause a problem? Please.'

'I'm afraid it will. I've already risked my job by stretching the Ministry's regulations on class size. I'm really very sorry.' He was polite and sincere.

Onai remained seated. She lacked the energy to drag herself out of the chair and embark on the long walk to St Patrick's.

As if speaking to himself, Mr Dube went on softly, 'Things are so hard nowadays. We're short of desks and chairs, books and stationery, even chalk … everything! Sticking to recommended class sizes is the only way of maintaining some semblance of standards, and even that doesn't seem possible.' He gave a nervous laugh.

'Even now, I'm trying to compile a list of children who need food hand-outs from the donor agencies, which are sometimes allowed into the area. So far, it looks as if all the Grade One pupils are in need. It's going to be a long list. A typewriter would help. But no! Such facilities are not to be had in a rural school, or perhaps in any school that requires state funding!'

Onai nodded sympathetically, thinking that if she listened, he might enrol her son. The young man continued, cataloguing the problems he faced. 'Less than half of the children have paid school fees, but the term is already coming to an end. I'm sure we're going to have a large number of drop-outs next term. Yesterday, two Grade Seven girls fainted during assembly, probably from hunger. One of the two, a thir-teen-year-old girl, is looking after her two younger sisters; both her par-ents died of AIDS. A thirteen-year-old heading a household!'

'It's very sad,' Onai responded sympathetically. While she was not unfamiliar with such disquieting stories – they existed in Mbare – she had simply not thought about the rest of the country. Mr Dube said, 'I think I can save you a walk to St Patrick's. Let me phone the headmas-ter to find out if they can take your child.'

'Thank you,' Onai said gratefully.

He lifted the receiver to his ear then exclaimed, 'I'm so sorry ... I'm so absent-minded. I'd forgotten that our phone is out of order. We've been waiting more than a week for it to be repaired. I'm afraid you'll have to walk there.'

Onai thanked him for his time and left. It was still morning. She might just be able to get to St Patrick's before the offices closed for lunch.

≈≈≈

Both Fari and Rita were subsequently enrolled at St Patrick's. It seemed more sensible to keep them together. As the term was almost over, they were not charged any fees for the few days that they would spend famil-iarising themselves with the school. It would take them about an hour to walk there. While she was relieved that they would continue with their education, Onai fussed and fretted. How would they cope with walking such long distances? In Harare, their school had been only fifteen minutes away from home.

Her worries lessened somewhat when she realised that there were several other children in the area who attended the same school. Two of them who lived next door were older girls in the fourth form. MaMusara called them over and they quickly made friends with Rita.

A group of boys came to play with Fari. His descriptions of the bus terminus where he'd been an undercover hawker, earned him great admiration. His new friends appeared to be even more impressed when he told them that he had once been arrested.

Watching him thriving in his circle of new friends, Onai smiled. It would not be such a lonely walk for her children. She decided to stay in Chiwundura for a few more days while they settled in. The break was doing her good, she would be better able to face Harare's challenges.

≈≈≈

Faith's relationship with Tom seemed better than ever before, as the bond between them strengthened. Passing her exams and getting a job had boosted her self-confidence, and made her feel less dependent, less afraid to be herself. When Tom brought up the question of marriage again, she felt none of the pressure that she had felt previously. She knew exactly what she wanted and she wasn't afraid to tell him. Working for a year would give her enough time to concentrate on her parents, who'd invested so much in her education. She also wanted to experience life as a single, independent woman; something that she had always admired in Tom's sister, Emily.

At her suggestion, Tom had seen the wisdom of a year-long engagement.

'But we must have an engagement party,' he'd insisted.

'Oh, do we really need to?' The thought of meeting a lot of Tom's family all at once for the first time, made Faith feel unexpectedly shy.

'Of course. Otherwise my mother will never believe that I'm serious about settling down. I think it's high time both of us were introduced formally to each other's families.'

They discussed the pros and cons for a while, finally agreeing on a December date. Faith felt slightly anxious. She still had to tell her mother about her new plans. Her *tete* would be tasked with informing her father.

≈≈≈

Her friendship with Emily was also thriving. Although she had not yet signed up as a member of the Kushinga Women's Project, the idea of joining a march against gender violence at Emily's invitation was quite appealing. The event had been arranged by the Project, and supported by a number of other women's groups. It was a disappointment, though not a surprise, that a request for TV coverage had been ignored. The publicity would have gone a long way towards helping the cause.

Tom didn't hide his disapproval. He warned the two young women that the authorities were highly suspicious of any gatherings, anything that resembled a protest. So-called 'peaceful demonstrations' often tended to turn violent because the riot police invariably suspected the worst and descended upon the marchers, even when they were only carrying peace placards or roses.

Faith laughed, trivialising his concerns, 'But it's only a peaceful march to promote awareness about the evils of gender violence. It's not political at all!'

'Not political? So when have women's issues not been political?' Tom was exasperated. 'Have you forgotten that more women than men cast votes in any election? Just think of that … Rumour has it that next year a bill will pass through parliament, which will see men languishing in prison just for ordering their wives to make them a meal! Of course, there's a bit of a paradox there, but the timing could be just right,' he concluded mysteriously, as if he would always know more than they did.

Emily clicked her tongue and Faith arched her eyebrows, shaking her head at his attitude. How typical!

Undaunted, Tom smiled quirkily at them, saying, 'I hear the bill will include that contentious issue of marital rape!' He shook his head in a comical manner and snorted, 'Marital rape indeed!'

'Oh, shut up, Tom! I find it very disrespectful of you to be making fun of serious issues even if you're just trying to provoke us. In my opinion, that bill is long overdue. It's going to address some very serious concerns regarding gender violence. What would you say if a drunken husband forced himself on me!? You can stuff your theories about timing and paradoxes,' said his sister crossly. 'Women are the care-givers in every society. Doesn't bearing so much of society's ills and burdens entitle them, at the very least, to some respect and protection? These issues are only political because you men don't have a clue about democracy and certainly not in a home!' She turned to Faith, 'I hope you're listening carefully. This is the man you've agreed to marry – and he doesn't think there is such a thing as *marital rape!*' Her voice rose as she looked at Tom questioningly. 'Got you there!' she thought smugly.

'As for the march, we had a similar one in April and we had no problems. All we're going to do is walk through the streets with our banners, handing out leaflets. We only want to raise awareness. I think the authorities only react to what they see as political dissent. Don't forget we have the implicit support of several women in parliament.'

'You think so, do you?' Tom replied ominously. 'Why don't they join you on your march, then? Try telling an irate riot police officer that your march is not political and see if he listens. Have you forgotten what happened to those women who were marching peacefully 'under the umbrella of love' on Valentine's Day? Were they politically motivated? I think your definition of what is and what is not political is pretty narrow, to put it mildly!'

'Mmh …' Emily conceded. 'But this march is different. Permission has already been granted. Besides, I'm sure we'll have a police escort,' she added stubbornly. Faith nodded vigorously. Tom remained openly sceptical, but the two women, who were fast becoming friends now that they were to be linked through marriage, paid no heed to him.

≈≈≈

On Friday afternoon, several hundred women assembled in front of the Town House and set off as arranged. Faith was slightly concerned that there was no police escort, as had supposedly been organised. Crinkling her nose, Emily said, 'I'm not surprised, or bothered. One gets used to such things.'

After they'd walked for a few metres along the sidewalk of Leopold Takawira Street, riot police suddenly appeared, and the march collapsed into a chaotic debacle. As they ran along the street with the other women, trying to escape from armed officers carrying tear-gas, Faith wished they'd listened to Tom. Conspicuous in their Kushinga slogan-bearing T-shirts and red caps, hiding away was an impossible feat. Sweating bodies pushed and shoved, arms and legs flailing. Motorists hooted impatiently as they tried to make their way through the mass of demonstrators. Both Emily and Faith received baton-stick blows before being manhandled and jostled into a police truck, together with a lot of their shouting, outraged colleagues.

At the central police station, they were charged with public disorder and inciting violence, and then locked up in smelly, overcrowded holding cells. Later, they were taken in small groups to an office where they were asked to sign admission-of-guilt forms and pay fines. Furious, both Emily and Faith protested.

'*Imi vanasisi*, I have no time for your histrionics. If you want to be difficult, I can become even more so and lock you up, good and proper,' the police officer said. Both young women stared at him defiantly.

His colleague assented, 'Just lock them up. *Vanoda kuwonererwa*. Who do they think they are?'

At that moment, Tom strolled in. 'The minute I heard about this, I knew I'd find you here. Maybe I should've let you spend a night in the cells.'

'You tell them!' one of the officers egged him on.

Tom continued, 'That would teach you. I warned you. You girls really ought to be careful about what you get yourselves involved in.' He sounded rather smug and self-satisfied that he, the man, was coming to their rescue.

'Don't rub it in!' Emily and Faith chorused, unrepentantly. Reluctantly, they signed the forms and allowed Tom to pay their fines, leaving a lot of their fellow demonstrators still protesting. 'I'll ring the office as soon as we get back, just to make sure that our lawyers are on their way,' said Emily. 'We should also try to get a doctor to see them. Several of the women were beaten quite badly; our bruises are only superficial. Right now, they're so angry, they may not realise that they need medical attention.'

'Well, do what you like, but remember that next time it might not be this straightforward. I'm sure neither of you wants to have a criminal record. For the sake of your careers; if nothing else.'

Faith decided this was not a moment to argue. She was learning to choose her moment. As a lawyer – if in no other way – she felt the experience had been useful. She understood much better what activists were up against and how the police seemed to have little respect for anyone daring to make a statement.

She linked her arm through Emily's and, changing the topic, said, 'I was thinking … there's somebody, I'd like you to meet. Can I refer her to you at Kushinga?'

'Who's that?'

'My mother's friend, Mai Ruva. She's … she's … her life has been a … well, I'm not sure what to call it. She's just been … kicked in the teeth so often that I wonder how she finds the strength to continue. Everything seems ranked against her. Now, her awful husband has just died. In the long term, this might have provided some relief, since he used to beat her up and have girlfriends, but now she's been thrown out of her home by her in-laws. I want to help but I think I'm too emotionally involved to be of any use; anyway, I have no experience.'

'Of course, I'd be glad to help. Quite often when I'm tired and think of quitting or when – like now – I feel we're just beating our heads against a brick wall, I remember that sometimes we do make a difference. At least, to particular individuals in particular situations.

'I was talking to a friend, just the other day. She's on leave from a hospital in the US. They have everything they could possibly want in terms of health care, but she's also dissatisfied – not financially of course – but in comparison to Zimbabwe, she said all the issues seem so ephemeral: should one switch off life-support after someone has been brain dead for four years? How does one deal with an obese ten-year-old? Should thousands of dollars be spent on a single operation, when people in the third world don't even have Aspirin?

'So, I'd be pleased to meet your mother's friend if you can persuade her to come to Kushinga. Often such women are so dejected that they won't or can't even ask for help.'

'Or realise that they need to,' Faith interjected. 'Anway, thanks so much. I understand that she is in her home area now, with her mother, but I'm sure she'll be back soon, and I'll try to arrange a meeting. I'm sure she'll be open to advice. There are so few choices open to her.'

'Women's issues!' interrupted Tom. 'Will you two ever stop talking or am I just the driver?'

'Ah, today you're just the driver. You have to be useful for something!' Faith said, laughing.

'Well, if that's the case, then I'm not making any effort to get you out of custody next time you get yourselves arrested!'

'OK. OK! You win. We are grateful. I'm relying on Faith to make you just a little more aware of the real issues. You might laugh at us, but we wouldn't need to march at all, if you men weren't such chauvinists!'

'Peace. Peace.' said Faith laughing. 'I think it's time we all went for a long, cool drink.'

CHAPTER 23

Because of the previous year's drought, water was scarce and much sought-after. Even the little girls and boys had a vital role to play. Onai would spot them proudly carrying two-litre containers of water from the village borehole. The thirsty earth had sucked dry most family wells, reducing them to pathetic puddles; the rainy season was eagerly awaited.

The food situation was no better. Because of the state of affairs in the rest of the country, shortages were naturally more acute *kumusha*. Sadza was every family's dream. On occasion, it proved elusive. At other times, it was realised only as a part of a very basic meal, with none of the meat or vegetables that would have normally have supplemented it. To her surprise, Onai found herself enjoying sadza, with roasted *madora* preserved from the previous rainy season. As a young girl, she'd found the task of harvesting the fat, squashy worms from mopane trees revolting. Now, they were a delicacy.

Onai and Wanai joined a gathering of women waiting to receive free maize meal brought in by donors. A police presence stood by ready to subdue any disturbances. Onai listened as the woman in front of her whispered salaciously about how certain officers would take the food, meant for starving families, for resale in town. There were murmurs of agreement.

Another woman laughed, her voice muted, 'And to think they're our keepers! It's an open secret that some of them are shameless thieves. Speaking out is not safe, you never know what might happen.' She swayed to and fro as she spoke to lull the fretful baby on her back to sleep. Onai was doubtful. How did they know? Had any of them witnessed officers stealing food packages? One needed to have faith that society's custodians were worthy of their role. She desisted from taking part in the conversation, needing to hold on to her residues of hope.

A few hostile remarks were also exchanged about the people who'd arrived from the urban areas after their homes had been destroyed in the clean-up operation. In theory, their presence meant less food for the villagers. Onai hoped nobody would order her out of the queue.

Her mother had hinted at how political hostilities had infiltrated the shaky food distribution structures. Occasionally, people from one political party or the other had been ordered out of the queues. Political affiliations of people from town were generally regarded with suspicion. Thankfully, nobody ordered her away; she concluded that it was out of pity, as most people knew that she had been recently widowed.

Nonetheless, even with a police presence, allocation of the bags of maize meal became a complicated, disorderly affair. The women were unruly, pushing and shoving in their desperation for food to feed their families. Wanai and Onai each managed to walk away with a ten kilogram bag of maize meal. It was a cheap, not very palatable variety. However, this was not the time to be choosy about what one ate. As long as something was edible, and as long as it assuaged one's hunger, it was more than perfect.

So the week wore on, each day merging into the next. Onai shared ideas with her mother about how she could try to improve life for her children. Despite a wealth of good ideas, none of them seemed immediately feasible. Each required what seemed like large start-up capital, and Onai had no money; neither did her mother, who had anyway sold her cows to fund Onai's sewing course.

The relative peace of these few days also gave her time to reflect on her life with Gari; and their first few years together, a time when their lives had been full of promise. Less frequently, but with pain, she remembered their last years together. Strangely, she occasionally missed the sense of belonging that had come from being his wife. He had obviously loved her when they were first married: where had that love gone? She had no answers. Gari was the only person who might have had answers, and he had refused her the respect of any discussion.

Looking to the future, she was almost overwhelmed by fear. Was it possible that her life would continue in the same unrelenting cycle of suffering? So it had been for Sheila; so it was bound to happen to people like Mawaya, and others who'd been reduced to begging on the streets of Mbare.

≈≈≈

The man was impatient and confused. Why didn't anyone believe him? He was exhausted from the sheer effort of talking to people who were unreceptive and as impenetrable as a brick wall. He was tired of being coerced to take tablets that only made his mind groggy, his tongue heavy, his mouth dry, and his vision blurry. Even the comedy of the man who imagined himself a minister of state one minute, and a UN envoy the next, were wearing his patience thin. He longed for home, and for his old routines. In a way, even the streets of Mbare had seemed better than this. He'd been free to roam as he pleased, and he'd connected with some kind people, like Mai Ruva. He knew he wasn't insane, but he had to find a way to convince them, otherwise he would be trapped in the ward forever.

That morning, a medical student came to talk to him. She asked him a lot of questions, all the while scribbling his responses on a pad. His narration about losing his wife – though he couldn't remember her name, which was unfortunate – and then turning to the streets of Mbare in his grief was met with barely concealed disbelief. He didn't really care. He felt proud to have answered most of her questions well. He just couldn't remember his name or anything else about himself. He couldn't tell her that he was called Mawaya. He somehow knew that was not his proper name. No, surely it had been just a nickname that he'd been given on the streets; one that implied he was mad. But he knew he wasn't. Until he remembered his real name, he would think of himself simply as a man; never again as Mawaya.

After a while, the student led him into the consultant psychiatrist's office where she presented Mr Unknown Unknown as 'her case'. The consultant was a middle-aged man with heavy jowls and a paunch that strained against his shirt. Mr Unknown listened to the consultant and his student talking about him, as if he wasn't there. He heard the alarming phrases: occasional 'grandiose delusions', 'clinical depression'... who wouldn't get depressed in such a place? Why did they automatically think he was delusional, when he was only trying to tell them about himself?

After the student had finished presenting 'her case', the consultant turned to him. 'So what is it that you do again, Mr Eh …?'

He answered confidently, 'I own a car import company. You could say that I'm the managing director.'

'That's great. Which company would that be, then?'

Another blank in his memory, the man threw a sheepish glance at the consultant, who stared back with patronising tolerance, bending his head to write something on a sheet of paper. Raising his eyes, he asked another question. 'Where do you live?'

'I have a house somewhere in Borrowdale.'

'What is the address?'

'For some reason, I can't remember, but I swear, I really own a house in Borrowdale.' How he could make the doctor believe him? The consultant nodded condescendingly. Mawaya was infuriated, but then he thought, my God, what if his family thought he was dead, would they have sold it? Why hadn't this occurred to him before? He felt desperate. He had to get out!

'What was your name again?' the doctor asked. It was a trick question, asked as if he'd already answered it before. It was also a very basic question that any two-year-old could answer. But the patient hesitated; he just could not remember.

The consultant bent his head again and quickly scribbled something. 'And your wife …?'

The patient was getting angrier. 'I've already told her about my wife!' he snapped, pointing at the student.

Turning to the student, the consultant said, 'Well done. That was an excellent case history. I've prescribed an alternative drug, one which I hope will make him less drowsy and give him fewer side effects.' The student nodded proudly, as she gathered a sheaf of papers from the desk.

Suddenly the man sprang up, bristling with rage. 'Why are you talking about me as if I'm not here? Why won't you believe me? I'm not mad, I don't need your bloody tablets. Just let me out of here!'

The consultant stood up and said reasonably, 'Now calm down, Sir.'

But the man wouldn't listen. He grabbed the edge of the table and shook it violently. 'I will not calm down! Let me out of here!' he yelled. The medical student froze in the corner, her eyes wide with fear. The consultant cowered from him, then reached out to press a buzzer on the wall.

Angrily, the man screamed, 'I'm not an animal. Why are you acting as if you're afraid of me? I just want to be let out of here! I'm not going to attack ...' he did not finish. Suddenly the room was full of people grabbing him, restraining him.

He struggled, trying to escape, looking wildly towards the door that was between him and freedom. As he thrashed about, he hit his head against the wall; the fog in his head seemed to lift, his memory cleared. At that very moment, he felt a needle-prick. Then a sudden lethargy and drowsiness overwhelmed him.

≈≈≈

Behind the main house lay three unmarked graves. Onai had long intended to erect tombstones for her father and her two brothers. The dream had not died. One day, she would do it, once she'd saved up enough money. She took a hoe and dug out the weeds around the graves, then carefully cleaned up the area with a grass broom.

Her mother found her engrossed in the task. '*Waita,* Mai Ruva. Thank you. That was long overdue,' she said, a distant look in her eyes.

Onai nodded, smiling. Her mother joined her, and the two women worked companionably side by side, each immersed in memories. Onai's thoughts drifted not to Gari, but to Mazwi and Mashoko ... two names with related meanings for her twin brothers who'd been 'as alike as two buns'. The pattern of their lives had been similar. They had shared the same contagious enthusiasm to succeed, leaving Chiwundura for Harare. They had been devoted to their little nieces, Ruva and Rita, showering them with presents and spoiling them shamelessly.

It appeared that they had done well in the city, or so Onai thought, until she discovered that their jobs at Harare's Sheraton Hotel had been an elaborate pack of lies. Too late, she had learnt of their decadence, drug dealing and whatever came with it, including the woman who had been their joint girlfriend. She was the woman who had apparently given them HIV: if they hadn't given it to her. Onai was only too aware of female vulnerability. She'd been so shocked by the reality of their lives that she had kept most of the details to herself, to avoid hurting her mother. She would never know what had driven her kind, ever-smiling brothers into a life of deception and crime.

Mashoko and Mazwi had eventually returned to Chiwundura to die. Her widowed mother had nursed them lovingly, right until they died, within hours of each other. That was the day Gari had finally allowed Onai to visit them. Death had failed to separate the two brothers who did everything together. Onai sighed. How she had loved them, and still missed them.

MaMusara's melancholy voice broke into her thoughts. 'Never for a moment did I imagine that I'd outlive any of my children.'

Onai could not find suitable words of comfort. With the advent of AIDS, many elderly parents outlived their sons and daughters. Many grandparents had been left with the demanding task of raising orphans, when they should have been the ones to be looked after in their twilight years. At least her mother had escaped such a predicament when her brothers died, because they'd left no children, or none that any of them knew of. Onai shivered.

MaMusara bowed her head, her eyes wet with unshed tears. With slow movements of her gnarled hands, she adjusted her loose headscarf. Onai wanted to take those hands and massage them, to ease the stiffness from the joints.

She said slowly, 'One day, I will have a tombstone erected on each of the three graves, *Amai*.'

Her mother replied quietly, 'You do that, *mwanangu*. You do that.' Onai nodded, with complete understanding. Her mother's pain could only be appreciated by someone who had borne a child. Yes, she would erect the memorials one day. She had no thoughts of doing the same for her husband.

On her fifth day in Chiwundura, Onai took a long walk to a nearby hill. It was the place where as a young girl she had gathered wild fruits with her friends and played lively games in the grass and among the rocks and trees. It was the place where, as awakened adolescents, they had shared dreams about the rich men they would marry; the exciting lives they would live.

It had all been unrealistic and illusory, except for Stella, who had found a rich man to marry. She was now said to be working as a nurse in the UK. The house that she had built for her parents, just across the road from MaMusara's, could have competed with any house in Belvedere, the suburb where Onai had always wanted to live. The homestead even had electricity. Why not? Stella was earning the mighty pound. Irrelevantly, Onai wondered whether electrified homes in rural Chiwundura would also experience power cuts like those in Harare.

She breathed in deeply, trying to blunt the intensity of envy that Stella's good fortune had aroused. 'If only I could get a proper job, and earn a regular monthly salary!' she said to herself. There were so many things that she wanted to do for her children, her mother and herself. Just thinking about her mother's cows, which she still had to replace, filled her with remorse.

She saw her chances of finding a job dwindling. With each poverty-riddled year, colleges and universities churned out increasingly large numbers of job-seeking hopefuls. More and more of them graduated with aspirations and certificates, only to be confronted with the failure of unemployment. At a similar rate, people were being laid off work, as companies closed down, or moved to neighbouring countries. Being realistic, Onai had no idea how she would ever find a job.

Wallowing in despondency and self-pity, she walked up the hill, the blustery air catching the folds of her long dress, and almost dragging her down. At the top, the air was calmer, less restless. Her agitation eased. She found a flattened rock and sat down, watching the twilight as the sun dropped over the horizon. Deep shades of red and pink painted the skyline. Onai hugged her knees and sat quietly for a long time, alone with her thoughts, bathed in the vivid colours of nightfall.

She remembered how ardently Gari had wooed her; and her mother's disappointment when she'd put on hold her plans to go to college. By then, she'd already been pregnant with Ruva. More painfully, she remembered her own disappointment, once it became clear that Gari's exciting promises had been without substance. In no time, she'd become an impoverished housewife, hence her stall at the market. She recalled the escalating domestic violence, never greater than when she'd insisted on doing that dressmaking course, years later.

Sitting on the hilltop, she cried her first tears for Gari; for their love that had failed to withstand the challenges of marriage; a love that had withered too soon, leaving her with the worst possible memories. Her body shook with violent sobs, and she was relieved to be alone. When her tears were finally spent, she wiped her face and turned again to look at the young night sky with a hardened resolve. While she could not stop day from turning into night, she could at least prepare for its coming. At that moment, she found strength in the acceptance of everything that she had lost.

Feeling better, she clambered down the hill. Allowing her grief an outlet seemed also to allow her to dream of a future. The children would all be all right. Fari was very bright. He would do well at school and maybe go to university, as would Ruva. Maybe Ruva would become a doctor like the young woman at the hospital; or a lawyer, like Faith. Rita would probably make a very good wife and caring mother. Thoughts of her children made her smile. Yes, it was time to return to Harare to prepare for their future..

≈≈≈

Katy was annoyed with her husband. John's trip meant carrying company goods to Beitbridge, where he would pick up another load bound for Johannesburg. Knowing this, Katy had wanted to meet him in Beitbridge and she failed to understand why he had insisted on meeting her in Messina. While she waited for him there, she sold the expensive bedspreads and upholstery covers that she'd bought cheaply from an unfortunate woman whose sewing shop had been demolished. She managed to earn a modest amount of rands from her customers. When John arrived, he gave her groceries and another five hundred US dollars before proceeding to Johannesburg with his load.

He had seemed distant, edgy and impatient to leave. He hadn't let her

275

sit in the truck, as he normally did. Katy was infuriated. She wondered if he was having an affair. Their encounter had been too brief for her to confront him or to explore that possibility. Good thing I packed those condoms, she thought crossly, wondering if he'd been using them at all. She hoped he'd be home for Faith's graduation, as he'd promised.

Her bus ride back to Zimbabwe was largely uneventful, save for a few hassles at Beitbridge border post where customs officials were searching people for foreign currency. Arriving home in Mbare the following day, nothing had changed; homeless people drifted hopelessly in search of shelter; piles of rubble remained strewn all over the place.

'Good afternoon, Katy. I haven't seen you in such a long time!' Katy turned at the sound of a familiar voice. It was none other than Maya. She was dressed in a tent-like green dress that swept the ground. Her double chins wobbled happily, and she had a suspicious glint in her eyes.

Katy was not at all pleased to see her neighbour, but she had no choice except to pause. It was obvious that Maya had something to say. The problem was that when Maya had something to say, she was a serious liability.

'Hello, Maya. How are you? How's the trading?' Katy attempted a friendly tone and succeeded. She hoped a small exchange would suffice, and she would quickly be able to continue home. She was in no mood to listen to any gossip.

'Oh, you know me. I'm doing ever so well. It's been tough trying to re-register for the market but after endless queuing I got my licence last week.' She winked at Katy and giggled like a schoolgirl. 'I had to make some special friends at the offices, though. These days things only move if you are connected to someone. Otherwise, you have to pay.' Katy nodded. It was common knowledge.

'My new stall is right in the city. Getting there is the only difficulty, because of the transport problems. The rest is easy. I'm starting to get regular customers; and I really like the place. You wouldn't believe the profit I've made this week alone,' Maya gushed, glowing with pride.

Thank God for small mercies, Katy thought to herself. If Maya's stall was in the city, then maybe their paths would cross less frequently. She smiled. But before she could get away, Maya placed her heavy hand on her shoulder. 'Hey, I've been wondering about Onai. Do you know where she is?' she asked in a hushed voice. The folds of her large dress fluttered in the afternoon air, exaggerating her size.

Reluctant to discuss the details of her friend's life with this woman, Katy pretended not to have heard the question and, instead, asked her how her husband was.

'Mazai? Oh, he's fine,' Maya answered, and then waved a sagging arm dismissively. 'It's Onai that I really want to know about. How is she? Did she really go to Chiwundura? I've seen that child of hers around … that Ruva. She's all clammed up. Won't tell me where her mother is. Is it true that she's now staying at your house?'

Katy opened her mouth, but clearly Maya was not waiting for an answer. She rushed on, 'The other day somebody said Onai might have jumped the border into South Africa. I found that very funny. Of all people, Onai crossing illegally into South Africa! Ha ha! She wouldn't know how to scale the high fences, let alone survive for a single day beyond the border!' She made a gurgling noise and broke into loud gales of laughter.

Despite her rising annoyance, Katy could hardly get a word in. Tired of the one-sided conversation, she said a hasty goodbye. Maya was still talking as she turned on her heel.

Just at that moment, a metallic grey Nissan 4x4 drove past, gleaming proudly in the afternoon sun and raising a thick cloud of dust in its wake. Katy recognised the driver as Mr Sibanda. Sitting beside him was her daughter, Faith. Neither of them appeared to have seen her standing by the roadside with Maya.

'There's that Mr Sibanda, the farmer who's always on TV. My niece works for him at his flower shop in town,' Maya announced knowledgeably.

'The things that these rich men do! I wonder who he has in that car. She looked very young. These thoughtless girls! They would jump into bed with any man who has a car and a bit of cash!"

Katy was tempted to laugh. Clearly, Maya hadn't recognised Faith. She made another excuse about needing to get home quickly, as she was tired from her long trip. They would talk some other time.

'Any time, my friend. You know where to find me. Any time,' Maya said, smiling broadly.

≈≈≈

Faith and Ruva didn't hear the knock. They were engrossed in a drama on television. Mischievous Gringo was up to his antics again, fuelling a fight between his employer and his promiscuous wife. The couple were close to murdering each other, while Gringo jumped up and down excitedly in the background.

The girls were both startled when Faith's mother walked in. They quickly relieved her of her bags and exchanged greetings. After her mother had had a shower, and some tea, Faith told her that she and Tom had though a lot about their marriage plans and decided that it would be best to have a formal engagement for a year.

'We'll have a party,' Faith said. 'Tom is very keen. He wants us to announce our engagement to the world. He feels that this is the only way his family will think he's being serious for a change.' She chuckled.

They're not the only ones, thought Katy, though she spoke more diplomatically, and this time without any reservations. 'Your young man sounds serious. I'm sure your father will also be pleased, as long as the Sibanda family do everything according to custom. If you intend to have the party in December, you must get your *tete* involved, and as early as possible.'

'I will do that, *Amai*. Will father be back in time for my graduation next month?' she continued, concerned, as one thought led to another. She too had recently noticed a change in her father – a slight reticence, almost a sheepishness at times.

'I'm sure he wouldn't miss it for anything,' her mother reassured her.

Faith smiled. Life could only get better. 'I talked to Melody on the phone today. She's appointed herself my chief bridesmaid and she's already talking about what she's going to wear to the wedding – a year away!'

Her mother laughed. 'How is she?'

'She's all right, just struggling to raise the university fees for her final year. They start in a few weeks. I think she'll be OK.' Then turning to Ruva she suddenly said, 'I hope you will agree to be one of my brides-maids, Ruva? We'll probably have the wedding in August next year, if all goes well.'

Ruva stared at her, openly surprised. 'Really? You're asking me? I have … I have nothing to wear,' she stammered in her excitement. She looked down at her faded frock. And then at her bare feet resting on the floor.

Faith noticed. 'Of course you won't be wearing that dress, you funny girl! We'll get you a proper bridesmaid's dress. And some matching shoes,' she added light-heartedly. Inwardly, she chastised herself for her thoughtlessness. She should have long ago offered Ruva all the clothes that she no longer wore. Rita as well.

'Me, a bridesmaid? Really?' Ruva pushed the chair aside and threw her arms around Faith. With no warning, she started crying; harsh, anguished sobs. Katy and Faith looked at each other and tried to console her. Faith didn't know exactly why Ruva was crying, but she knew that the girl had more than one reason to do so. What touched a mother, invariably left a mark on her children. She wondered when *mainini* Onai would return. She really wanted to persuade her to make an appointment with the Kushinga Project. She felt sure Emily would be able to help.

CHAPTER 24

Onai's chosen date of departure coincided with the children's last day at school. She got up as usual and prepared cornmeal porridge for them, using up the last spoonfuls of sugar. Fari toyed with his porridge and pretended to eat, while Rita simply refused her food. Onai tried hard to cheer them up with promises that she would return soon.

'When you come back, will you take us back to Harare with you?' Fari demanded.

It was the question Onai had been dreading. The truth was she didn't know; but she was sure he would weep if she said as much, so she replied, 'Of course, we'll all be together in Harare, before too long ...' She forced herself to summon hope, because without it there was no point in even trying. Rita just stared at her, suspicion in her eyes.

'Rita. Rita! We're late. Hurry up and let's go!' a clear voice rang out in the morning air. Onai looked out to see two girls waiting by the gate. With their final goodbyes, she stood by the door and watched her children walking away, wishing she could hold them close to her heart and never let them go. The sight of their small frames hanging back behind their friends, as if unwilling to leave her, etched itself into her memory.

At midday, Wanai and her mother accompanied her to the bus-stop. From the window of the bus, she looked out at the rural landscape as they passed through it. The earth was barren and dry. Now and then, clouds of dust would spiral into whirls, typical of the dry and windy month of August. The trees stood bare, stripped of their leaves during winter. It all seemed so desolate, that she closed her eyes and tried to sleep, resting her head against the window.

Some time later, she was jolted awake by angry voices. The bus had stopped at a police roadblock. Sacks of maize were being thrown off the carrier, and into a police truck. Onai looked out of the window, confused. A road sign indicated that they were twenty kilometres from Norton. A few of the passengers got out to watch the spectacle. Onai remained seated.

'What's happening?' she asked the young man sitting next to her.

'They're confiscating the maize that people are bringing with them from the rural areas. They don't want them to bring maize to town. It's illegal,' the young man explained.

'But why?' Onai asked, surprised.

The young man shrugged. 'All maize is now supposed to be sold to the Grain Marketing Board.'

To Onai's still sleepy mind, it didn't make sense. Maize meal was in short supply in town, so why were people obliged to sell it to the GMB if they needed it to feed their families? People frequently complained that the money paid out by the parastatal was never enough to buy maize in similar quantities from private traders in town. She shook her head. A lot of things no longer made sense.

Looking out of the window, she heard a woman pleading with one of the police officers. She was crying, 'Please don't take my maize. There is no mealie meal in town. My children are starving. Please.' The man simply turned his back on her dismissively and started a conversation with one of his colleagues. The distraught woman re-entered the bus, still weeping.

When all the sacks and containers of maize had been confiscated, passengers were ordered to get back onto the bus. The vehicle was waved through. For the rest of the journey, a debate raged about the maize confiscations. The woman in the red dress complained bitterly, waving a piece of paper in the air. 'They gave me this receipt and told me to go to the GMB to get payment for the maize they've taken. How much will the GMB pay me?' Her voice was shrill with bitterness. Heads shook and voices rose. Nobody knew exactly how much she would be paid.

She held out her hands. 'These hands ... these hands worked hard, tilling the land and planting those mealies. But now I'm not allowed to use that maize to feed my own children!' Her voice rose higher. 'Why?' she demanded.

There was no shortage of answers from the other passengers. The debate deteriorated into wisecracks and mockery of the authorities. Onai tried to sleep but there was too much noise, and her hard seat had become increasingly uncomfortable. The window rattled noisily against her head. She sat up straight for the rest of the journey, dry-eyed and morose.

Mbare was much the same as it had been when she left. Small heaps of broken furniture, and bricks and mortar remained a constant symbol of the destruction of people's lives. Increasingly, rubble and dirt seemed a permanent fixture, as the household rubbish collections had become few and far between, and the council seemed to have no sense of responsibility.

She crossed the newly open space next to Fari's former school. A mound of decomposing vegetables and other perishables, the remnants of yet another demolished market, lay decaying on the ground. A swarm of flies hovered over them. The stench was unbelievable. Holding her breath, Onai scurried past.

Only a few years previously, dumping anything on disused land would have been considered an offence that warranted the payment of a fine. The present piles of rubbish were an eyesore, as well as a health hazard. But it seemed as if no one cared. For the ordinary citizen there were issues of much greater concern: where the next meal would come from, and where one would sleep the following night.

Walking towards Jo'burg Lines, she had to strain her eyes to see where she was going. The few tower lights were off: another blackout, another evening of load-shedding. Faint candlelight illuminated the windows of the houses; it would be an early night for most people. And for those who hadn't known there would be no electricity, and had not bought firewood for cooking; it would be another night on an empty stomach, most people having long shelved their paraffin stoves, as paraffin was just as hard to find as other fuel.

She took care to avoid walking down 50th Street. An encounter with *Babamunini* Toro or his wife was the last thing she wanted.

≈≈≈

She was pleased to find Katy already back from Messina. Faith was also at home. As usual Ruva was trying to study for her exams, this time by candlelight. Onai worried that the poor light would damage her daughter's eyesight, but she made no comment, not wanting to discourage her, so soon after her return, . She went outside with Katy and began cooking since she was so much better at handling a sadza pot on an open fire than either Katy or Faith. After the meal, they sat by the fireside and roasted groundnuts while they talked.

'Faith has some good news for you. I thought it would be better for her to tell you herself because she also has a request to make,' Katy said, nudging her daughter.

Onai looked enquiringly at Faith who said excitedly, 'I'm getting engaged soon, *mainini*, and we hope to have a wedding next year.'

'*Makorokoto,* Faith. This is good news indeed!' And Onai was pleased, although she wondered if Faith wasn't a bit young to be getting married. What was she? Twenty-four? Well, maybe she was old enough. At that age, she herself had already had two children.

'And Ruva here has agreed to be one of the bridesmaids!'

'Please don't say no, Mum,' Ruva said, her eyes shining with pleasure.

'As if I would!' Smiling, she turned to Faith, 'Thank you for asking her.'

'I just have one small request, *mainini*. I hope you will say yes …'

'What is it?' Onai was mystified.

'I would like you to make me a dress to wear at our engagement party. I've seen a really beautiful dress in a South African magazine, and I've set my mind on it. Father still hasn't found a buyer for the sewing machine, so please could you make the dress for me?'

Onai shook her head doubtfully. 'I don't know what your mother has been telling you about my dressmaking skills, but let's have a look.'

Squinting in the firelight, Onai scrutinised Faith's choice in the magazine. It was an elegant, long dress with a low cleavage. Without a doubt, it would look wonderful on the young woman, who had the bearing and the looks to carry it off.

However, the idea of making it was more than a little daunting. She had never attempted anything so sophisticated. The bodice detail was exquisite, but intimidating. How would she manage, and without a pattern? She looked uncertainly at Katy and Faith's expectant faces.

283

'What if I make a mess of it?' she asked.

'If you do, which I doubt …' Faith smiled again, '…then Tom will just have to take me to South Africa to buy one. I can't find anything that I like here.'

'All the way to South Africa, just to buy a party dress? Your Tom must be a rich man!' Onai exclaimed.

Faith smiled shyly, 'Not really rich; just all right, I think. But yes, he said he'd take me if I can't find what I want here. It seems quite wasteful, so I'd rather you made the dress for me.' Hesitant, Onai demurred. But Faith and Katy laughed at her. Finally she agreed and promised to begin work as soon as they had the material. They made a plan to look for fabrics at a few of the better shops in town, Onai reiterating that she hoped they wouldn't regret it.

A little while later, Faith and Ruva went to bed, leaving the older women chatting by the fire. Katy regaled Onai with tales of happenings at the border post. 'It's now so much harder to bring foreign currency into the country. Can you believe that this man wrapped his rands tightly in a small plastic bag, and swallowed it; then had a few drinks and forgot all about it, until he'd emptied his bowels in a pit latrine at the border post? You should have heard his lamentations!'

Onai couldn't help laughing although the story sounded apocryphal. How could you swallow a small plastic bag?

As Katy said, the rest of her trip had been unremarkable, apart from one incident. Acting on a tip-off, a customs official had insisted on strip-searching cross-border traders for undeclared foreign currency. Some of her unfortunate travelling companions had had their rands confiscated. A few had spoken of being stripped, poked and prodded in private places, but providence had smiled at Katy. She'd been right at the end of the queue, and before they reached her, word filtered through that the officers had to hurry up as congestion was rapidly building up.

'Well, that was a lucky escape!' Onai marvelled. 'It must be risky, though.'

'It is, but how else would I survive? This is what I do. For as long as it gives me a living, I'll continue. John says he no longer wants me to go to the market, but we still have to raise money to pay off the Mabelreign stand; and there will be more problems and expenses once we start building.'

Onai said she hoped her friend would be more careful.

Katy laughed. 'Don't forget *ndinodealer nemashefu!* It's very useful to know important people. Assistant Commissioner Nzou would never let us get arrested.' She spoke with confidence.but Onai was doubtful.

Katy continued, 'There's nothing to stop you from getting a passport, now. You could go on shopping trips to Botswana or South Africa. You can never go wrong with electrical goods, because most people can't afford to buy them from the shops here.'

Onai stared at the dying fire. Somehow going to South Africa on shopping trips no longer held such appeal. 'You know what I would really like to do, Katy?' she looked up and asked her friend.

Shaking her head, Katy prodded the fire, trying to breathe life into it.

'I would like to get a dressmaking job. My training has to be worth something.'

'Why don't you start applying then?'

'Once I'm settled, I will,' Onai said.

'But, first, your most important priority is to apply for a market-stall licence. And since you say your mother is against you going to court to get Gari's money and your house back, why don't you try the council housing list? Houses are being built for the people whose homes were destroyed in May and June. They're calling it Operation Garikayi.'

Onai's hopes rose. 'Really? But do you think they'd put me on the housing list? My home wasn't destroyed.'

Katy shrugged. 'Look, Onai, just give it a try. The worst that could happen is that they refuse your application.'

Onai nodded. She would certainly try. A house was what she needed; a house for herself and her children. By the time she went to bed, she had a plan for the following day, and she felt much better. She would be very busy; and she reminded herself that at some point she wanted to discuss the court procedure with Faith. Before she finally decided to do what her mother had asked, she needed to know what the options were.

~~~

The next morning, Onai made an early start for the municipal offices. Registering for a market stall was her top priority. Even at that early hour, the place was already swarming with men and women, a sea of faces expressing sadness, lethargy, despair and aggression. A few children were also present, acting as 'placeholders' in the queue for their parents. Still, there was no comfort in numbers. She was on her own, and she knew it.

There was hardly any talk as the crowd waited. Now and then, the near-silence would be broken by the wail of a restless baby strapped to its mother's back. The offices opened at eight o'clock, but the queue was served at such a slow pace, it seemed as if there was no movement at all. The crowds swayed and murmured subdued complaints.

By mid-morning Onai felt very hot, despite it being only August. The young man in front of her kept furiously typing messages on his mobile phone. After a while he took a call. He seemed to be arranging a deal involving sugar and cooking oil. Onai sighed. It seemed as if survival itself had become dependent on who you knew and what deals you could pull off.

After a further two hours, the young man suddenly turned to face her. *Notorious B.I.G!* was written across the front of his T-shirt in huge italics. 'So do you have your police clearance with you?' He asked her rather abruptly.

She suspected that his question came from a desire to break the monotony, rather than genuine interest. Shaking her head, she was not sure what he meant. 'Police what?'

First the young man looked incredulous, then delighted by the depth of her ignorance. 'Police clearance. Are you telling me that you don't know about police clearance, and you've been waiting here all this time?' His mouth gaped, revealing yellow teeth and a pierced, stud-bearing tongue.

Onai shook her head again, trying to contain her alarm. The young man tugged at his baseball cap, and took a deep breath. In an over-bearing manner, he slowly explained that in order to register, she would need a police-clearance document.

She looked up at him doubtfully, until he waved a copy of his own clearance certificate in her face. She realised that she had wasted the whole morning: six long hours. Discouraged, she walked slowly away, debating whether to go to the police station or straight home.

Still, in one respect, she was relieved to leave the queue: her bladder was so full, it felt close to bursting. She looked around for a public toilet. There was one near the bus terminus – a small, filthy room, reeking of excrement. A discoloured notice declared that the toilets were cleaned regularly. Holding her nose, she entered. Needs must.

Sweating, hungry, and with a parched throat, she trudged on to the police station. Unbelievably, another long queue awaited her. It wound out of the front door, right along the wall, and turned the corner where, fortunately, the building threw a long, cool shadow. She was grateful to be in the shade at last.

Zimbabwe was surely a nation of queues. What was the joke? 'We have high IQs,' Onai smiled to herself. Very soon we might progress to sign-posted queues: registration queue, bread queue, petrol queue, sugar queue, cooking-oil queue … Her weak attempt at humour made her feel slightly better.

She waited patiently. Bureaucracy at its worst. The early afternoon became progressively hotter, and by 3.20 when she suddenly found her-self out of the shade, the heat was unbearable. Her wide-brimmed straw hat served no purpose at all. Sweat trickled continuously down her face. She was dizzy and longed for a drink of water, but she dared not leave the queue for fear of losing her place.

At long last, she managed to complete a set of confusing forms. Her fingerprints were taken by a sour-faced man who gripped her hand with unnecessary force. When she winced, he snapped at her impatiently.

'Eh, eh get a hold of yourself, woman. We're not here to play games!' She disliked him instantly. Why were people in civic office so rude and unfriendly? Normally, she might have explained away such rudeness – they were after all at the other end of these long queues. Instead she wondered if he hadn't pulled in enough bribes and took the liberty of swearing at him silently, not without a little malice, safe in the knowledge that he did not know what was running through her mind.

Her answers to questions about any criminal history that she might have were brief and polite. Her mind flitted to Fari and Rita who had been 'arrested' in June while on their secret vending mission. Was their 'arrest' on record? Would it count as criminal history and permanently blight their future?

When everything was done, the officer informed her that the clearance report would take a week or more. Onai was appalled. She had hoped to start trading within a few days of getting back to Harare. How could she afford these constant hurdles? It seemed that everything possible was being done to delay and demoralise people, to undermine their every endeavour to help themselves.

She glanced at her watch. It was nearly closing time. There was no time to go and enquire about the new houses on offer under Operation Garikayi, a name that promised good living. Was it just another of those promises whose fruition always fell short of the many voluble declarations of intent? She hoped not. Her life now depended on this rebuilding exercise. She slunk behind the tall building and found a quiet spot to sit down before embarking on the long walk back to Mbare.

A tall, dark-skinned, police official sauntered out of the building. He wore a smart uniform with multiple epaulettes, marking his seniority. His bearing was immaculate. The creases on his trousers looked as sharp as a knife. His shoes were shone to a high polish.

He was talking authoritatively into a mobile phone and did not appear to have seen her at all. Gesticulating for emphasis, he said, 'I told you to bring them in. If you found foreign currency on them, and they can't account for it … just bring them in … Isn't this what I told you to do?'

There was a lengthy pause as, tapping his foot irritably, he listened to the reply. Then he said, 'Look, we have to teach these criminals a lesson! They're destroying the country's economy, don't you see that? We can't have people selling money on the streets, I repeat......we can't have people selling money on the streets. They're stealing business from the banks. Why do you think the banks are collapsing? It's because of these criminals ... Huh? ... No way. Those are my orders, right? Just bring them straight here. I will deal with them personally.'

He slipped the phone back into his pocket and took a long, slim cigarette from an expensive packet. Lighting up, he took a leisurely pull, blowing tendrils of smoke high into the air.

His mobile phone rang noisily. 'Assistant Commissioner Nzou here... That's brilliant. Five hundred US dollars you said? ...Well, I can't thank you enough ... yes, usual story, I can't get any forex from the bank. Its maddening, isn't it? Well... ' He broke off and listened again, taking another slow pull of his cigarette.

'Well, you can say that again. What's a man to do in these terrible times? Let's meet at the usual place ... eight o'clock tonight ... yes ... I'm so sorry but it has to be at night for obvious reasons ... thank you, thank you. I appreciate your help. Bye.' He put the phone back in his pocket. The irony of the situation was not lost on Onai.

The man stubbed out the cigarette and turned round, as if to look for a bin. Onai was sitting on the edge of a bench, right next to the bin. Her gaze met his eyes, which swept over her dismissively. She was a nothing. A nobody.

'What are you staring at?' he shouted, then strode back into the building, slamming the door behind him. Onai flinched. The injustices of the world had rarely seemed more present.

≈≈≈

Later that evening, she mentioned the incident to Katy, then asked her, 'Are you certain that it's safe to deal with this police officer? Like I told you, he was giving somebody an order to arrest people who had been caught with foreign currency. Are you not risking too much?'

Katy was nonchalant. She laughed. *Iwe,* don't worry. Don't you know, the law has two sides? One applies to us ... the people they deal with; the other applies to ordinary people, people without contacts, connections or money to pay bribes.' She laughed again. 'And like John says, this assistant commissioner will be the man to get us out of trouble, if we're ever threatened with arrest.'

Onai was unconvinced. Her friend seemed to be playing with fire. Didn't she know that there was no honour among thieves? And when it came to survival, the weaker thief would always lose out!

≈≈≈

Her next priority was to get onto the list of beneficiaries for Operation Garikayi. At seven o'clock the next morning, she found herself in yet another queue, this time at the municipality office. When, it was finally her turn to be served, she stepped forward anxiously. The female officer, who was chewing gum, looked at her disinterestedly. Studying her manicured hands as if they were the most interesting feature in the world, she tossed a stream of questions at Onai: 'Are you a displaced person? If so, were you living in one of the shacks that were demolished? What was your address?'

Onai felt unsure which question to answer first.

'I have no previous address to give with respect to the demolitions. I've become homeless because my brother-in-law evicted me from my house when my husband died last month,' she said, hoping that she was not automatically disqualifying herself.

The officer looked at her hands again, scrutinising her red, claw-like fingernails. When she spoke, her voice came across in a jaded monotone. 'No, we are not giving homes to widows or people in your circumstances. This is a project to tackle the plight of the genuinely disadvantaged – people who were being housed in illegal shacks by crooked home-owners – not the likes of you.'

The officer brushed aside some hair extensions, which had fallen over her face, and continued in the same flat monotone. 'I suggest you go back to your brother-in-law and talk things over. You must try and resolve your differences within the family, instead of wasting civil-service time. This is not a court.'

Onai shifted on her feet and dropped her gaze to hide the fury in her eyes. There was no point in annoying this powerful goddess. She felt the beginnings of her first headache in two weeks. Her lips quivered, 'Please help me, my sister. I really need ...'

'Eh, eh, excuse me, I'm not your sister. Now, move aside and stop wasting my time,' the officer interrupted rudely, invigorated by a mixture of impatience and annoyance. She glared at Onai with cold eyes.

The older woman gave up. Already the officer was waving her aside with a slight movement of her slim hand. She gestured for the next woman in line. Onai moved slowly away, her legs tired and heavy. She crossed the large room towards the door. Just as she was about to make her exit, she heard a deep, friendly voice. 'My sister, can I talk to you?' She turned and saw a cheerful, rotund man gesturing towards her from behind a counter. She stopped and looked at him, enquiringly. Nothing stirred in her memory. He was a total stranger.

'My sister, I would like to help you. Please come this way.' He smiled kindly at her. She took in his jolly face and friendly eyes. Maybe he really could help. She stepped forward through the low door on the counter.

He led her silently along a dim corridor to a small corner office. Pulling out a chair for her, he faced her across a desk littered with untidy piles of paperwork, and the remains of what might have been his lunch – chicken bones from Nandos. Onai resisted the urge to create order on the cluttered desk, and waited for him to speak.

He interlaced his chunky fingers and laid them on the edge of the desk. His voice dripped with compassion. 'My name is Mr Boora. My dear sister, I am very touched. I could not help overhearing what that girl said to you. It is very sad when a woman is so cold and insensitive to the predicament of another. I really feel sorry for you, and I believe I can help. Could you explain again what it is that happened to you, my sister?'

Onai heaved a sigh of relief. Finally, here was a considerate somebody who was prepared to listen to her difficulties with the sympathy that she deserved. She started speaking, hesitantly at first, then her voice grew stronger as the man nodded and smiled reassuringly at her, gently encouraging her to go on.

'Oh, my dear sister,' he began, laying emphasis on the word 'sister'. 'I fully appreciate your problem. I think I can help you, but I'm sure you will understand that it's not easy. No, not easy at all.' For a moment his face bore a deeply tragic look, as he reiterated the great degree of difficulty.

Comprehension dawned; Onai realised what a fool she'd been. The man obviously wanted a bribe. Nobody did anything for free anymore. Why should she expect him to put himself out for her, a total stranger, when people often expected payment in return for carrying out their normal duties? Even if she had the money, she wondered how these matters were conducted. Should she offer him a bribe outright? Stories were told of people being arrested for offering bribes. What was she supposed to do?

She raised her eyes; he was still looking at her. With an effort, she steadied herself. 'I'm not sure if I'm expected to make a payment. If so, I'm very sorry, Mr Boora. I have no money at all. Perhaps we could have an agreement whereby I pay you at the end of next month. I would greatly appreciate your help; I need to get onto the housing list as soon as possible, because I'm in such a desperate situation.'

To her surprise he slapped the desk delightedly and burst out laughing. It was a harsh, uncomforting sound. 'Oh, my dear sister! *Sisi veduwe!* What makes you think everything comes down to money? You don't have to pay me at all. We can come to a small understanding. No? Just the two of us.' He smiled intimately and laughed again.

Onai looked at him in astonishment; not wanting to understand what he was alluding to. She felt sick. Her heart raced. She willed herself to stand up but her legs had gone weak and felt incredibly heavy.

Suddenly, Boora walked round the desk, and bending over her, wrapped his arms tightly around the upper half of her body, and clutched her bosom. Onai froze with shock. She felt his hot breath on her face. He smelt of cigarette smoke; acrid and overpowering, worse than Gari's cigarette breath. Then his dry lips were crushing hers, his hands groping her lustfully, in places where she had not been touched in a very long time.

She remembered something vague … a lesson on self-defence from a TV programme years ago. She stood up quickly, focused all her strength on her right knee, and rammed it forcefully into his bulging manhood, as she pushed him away with both hands. With a guttural moan, he recoiled, then slumped against the wall, his hands on his groin.

She shoved the door open and ran along the corridor. A man tried to stop her in the passage. '*Amai*, what's wrong? Can I help you?' The concern in his voice sounded genuine enough, but Onai pushed past him without even looking at his face. She'd had enough. She ran out into the warm sunshine and embraced her freedom.

Why, why, why … she asked herself, as she walked home, shaken and disappointed by the outcome of her long day. It wasn't as if she weren't trying. She was. As usual, her mind returned to Gari and the long series of mistakes and failures. She was too tired to fight back; but to look at things from a more positive perspective: she had survived, she had three lovely children, she had good friends, she was a skilled dressmaker …

As she slowly strolled along, observing the variety and colour of life, she began to feel a little more optimistic. She would not allow herself to give up. With a determined lift of her head, she braced herself: there had to be a way. Though she had no money, she didn't completely rule out having to pay a bribe. That was the way of life. But never would she demean herself by offering sexual favours.

On the periphery of Jo'burg Lines, Onai noticed someone she thought was Maya, though she was at least one and a half times the size of the woman who she'd last seen only a few weeks before. Some people seemed to thrive in times of hardship, greedily sapping up the reserves of those around them. Maya, without a doubt, was one such person. Her skin was glowing and she looked incongruously prosperous and happy.

Onai thought of turning back but it was too late. Their eyes locked across the road. Maya lumbered towards her, her outsized basket overflowing with vegetables – no doubt for sale the following day. With great ceremony, she set her heavy basket down on the dusty roadside.

Onai knew that she was meant to notice the basket, and acknowledge it as a sign of Maya's success.

'Am I so pleased to see you, Onai, or what?' Maya enthused. Her voice sounded surprisingly genuine.

'Hello Maya,' Onai forced a smile.

'I always knew you would come back! Like I said to Katy only last week, you should register for a market stall and start trading again. It doesn't matter that you're now homeless. You can always camp at Tsiga Grounds with your children. Even if the police send you away, you can come back. People always do. Besides, the days are so much warmer now. Sleeping in the open won't be that hard ...'

Maya's words were as unbelievable as they were absurd. It was plain that she wanted to see Onai and her children continuing to suffer. Onai looked directly at her neighbour. 'Yes, I'm now in the process of registering for a market stall; but I will never take my children to live out in the open. Very soon I shall have a home of my own.' She threw Maya a determined look.

Maya was oblivious. She prattled on, 'Onai, are you crazy? How can you, of all people, talk of having a home? Where would you get the money from? Are you hiding a secret lottery win from me, then? I hear they win billions these days!' Her laughter sounded cruel.

Furiously, she broke Maya's laughter. 'Look here, Maya! I don't have to stand here, listening to your rubbish. What's wrong with you? Just get a life, will you! Stop interfering with mine!' She strode off, towards 49th Street, her head held high, leaving Maya open-mouthed in shock.

≈≈≈

At home, Onai sat on the small veranda with Katy. The sun was setting and a gentle, early evening breeze displaced the heat of the day. One of the nicest things about staying with Katy, Onai thought, was that they often seemed to be drinking tea (with sugar!) and eating biscuits.

As they sipped their tea, Onai told Katy all about her difficult day. She wondered if she should report Boora.

Her friend was not sure. 'It depends how far you want to take it. It would be your word against his. A man like that is probably a smooth, well practised operator. He'll have his contacts and his defences securely in place.'

Onai nodded. For all she knew, he might even have given her a false name, but would she be able to pick him out of a hundred men. She'd never forget that chubby face and those leering lips. She shuddered.

Katy was not too bothered by the dismal outcome of Onai's day. 'What you need to do is to go to the Kushinga offices,' she said. 'I was talking to Faith about this only the other day. She thinks her boyfriend's sister, who works there, might be able to help you; or at least give you some advice. I'm sure Faith wanted to talk to you about this herself.'

Onai nodded, admitting that she had heard of the organisation and the work they did. Their main focus was the promotion of equal rights for women; but they also helped those in difficult domestic or social situations. She remembered that she'd once even considered approaching them for advice when Gari had been at his worst, but she'd never done so. Why? A moment's reflection reminded her that it had been Maya's gossip.

Maya had a distant relative, whose marriage had broken down after she foolishly got Kushinga involved in her problems. Maya claimed that the organisation was run by a group of divorcees, intent on persuading women to get divorced. The irony of it was, however, that these so-called 'liberated women' were rumoured to be having affairs with married men.

Onai, who had been very depressed and easily swayed at the time, had allowed Maya's forthright opinions to discourage her.

Katy couldn't help laughing as she listened to the warped version of the organisation's activities, which Maya had given Onai.

'Trust Maya to say something like that! Really, that woman should be hanged!' The two friends shared a burst of guilty laughter, imagining how ludicrous Maya would look hanging from a gallows.

'Sorry, that was a joke in bad taste.' Katy said, still laughing. 'But on a more serious note, I think you'd be wise to go and see them. Faith says it's an organisation where professionals – lawyers, doctors, whatever – give their time voluntarily. If they can't help you, at least they might direct you to somebody who can. Legal advice would be useful if you decide to pursue your rights to the house, or to Gari's company pension.'

Onai shook her head, thinking of Gari's brother with distaste. No, she didn't want to return to that house. That time was over. But she did need the money for her children, and would be glad to have it; as long as Toro had not somehow claimed it as his own.

CHAPTER 25

Tapiwa Jongwe looked and felt better. He was no longer sure what had worked – his brief stint as a psychiatric in-patient, or his self-styled ritual of *kutanda botso* on the streets of Mbare. He often thought of Mai Ruva, the woman who had always had a little food to spare and some kind words for him. She had never made him feel like a beggar. He wondered how she'd fared during the clean-up operation. At least she has a home, he thought.

His family had been pleasantly shocked when they were called to the hospital to see the man who was claiming to be their relative. After five long months they had lost hope that he would ever return. They'd concluded that he'd committed suicide following his wife's death, but felt they should wait a year before doing anything about his affairs.

His parents came all the way from Nyanga to stay with him while he recovered. His father talked of taking him to see a *n'anga*.

'I'm sure what you endured was very difficult, my son. However, when such things happen, there is usually a reason for it. In our culture, the commonest cause is evil spirits. It's possible somebody is directing such spirits towards our family. Do you think people are happy that you are so successful?'

Tapiwa had laughed. 'No, *Baba*. I don't need a *n'anga*. I just need to rest and I'll be all right.'

The old man was offended. 'You young people think you know it all, *nhaika*? You'll see that I'm right.' But nothing would change Tapiwa's mind.

His mother fussed over him and fretted about him being so thin. He laughed at her concerns and assured her that he'd gain weight in no time, teasing her that being slim was generally healthier than being fat. 'Tssk … You don't expect me to believe such nonsense! You were meant to be strong and healthy with a big stomach, just like your grandfather, who was the first-ever businessman in the clan!'

In order to achieve his release from hospital, Tapiwa had agreed to continue with the medication prescribed by a psychiatrist at

Parirenyatwa Psychiatric Annexe, where he'd been transferred as soon as his identity came to light. It had been a small price to pay for having his real identity accepted, even if some of the medics still quietly held their suspicions.

His return also caused waves in business circles. Man back from the dead, his associates teased him. His friend Tom was sympathetic but found great amusement in the extreme measures he'd taken. '*Kutanda botso!* You're not serious, *mudhara*. Besides, you did it all wrong! And how could you, of all people, have lasted a single day in Mbare? You're a walking miracle!' he'd laughed, slapping his friend on the back.

'Well, I did. But don't make fun of me, please. It hasn't been easy, you know.' Tapiwa was slightly affronted by his friend's hilarity.

Tom was immediately contrite. 'Sorry, *mudhara*. You know me, I like to joke about everything. Anyway, it's very good to have you back.'

People around him had quickly learnt that he did not want to talk about his experiences, though they would have been fascinated to hear them. They let him be, and he got on with the business of settling into his former routines. Not that they'd ever be quite the same again. Nonetheless, the ache of loss had diminished a little, and it did feel good to be home. For the first three weeks, he did nothing except eat, and go through his company's accounts. It was hard work. Being away from the business for so long had made his mind rusty. He acknowledged that his brother had done an excellent job.

There was just one final thing he needed to get sorted, Edith's bridal shop. His friends said he should just close it down, but he had other ideas. He wanted to keep Edith's memory alive, and the shop had given her so much pleasure, and allowed her creativity to flourish.

≈≈≈

August passed quickly and before she knew it, it was September. Graduation day came and went. Faith was relieved that her father had taken leave from work to attend. She had sensed some tension between her parents, but she hoped it was nothing serious. It was still two and a half months before the engagement party, but because Tom had planned a big event, there seemed to be a lot to do.

'I really don't know why we have to do all this and invite all these people. It's not a wedding, you know!' she'd protested, feeling rather overwhelmed and balking at the cost.

Tom had joked, 'There's nothing small about me, my dear. You might as well get used to it!' His enthusiasm was infectious, so she swallowed her misgivings, and the more she became involved, the more she began to look forward to the party.

Saturday was a special day for them, the day she would take Tom to her father's sister for a formal introduction. She sipped a Coke while she waited for him in the Wimpy in Westgate. On her intern's salary, this was one place that she could afford to take him out for lunch. He was running late and she wondered whether they'd have enough time to eat before driving out to her *tete's* home in Darwendale.

As she glanced at her watch, she saw him walking across the restaurant towards her. He threw himself clumsily into a chair opposite her.

'Sorry I'm late. I had a hard time with the travel agents.' He smiled apologetically, slightly breathless.

Faith's eyes twinkled. 'You're doing it again ... that's so unfair,' she returned his smile.

'What?'

'It's that smile of yours ... Even when I should be angry with you ... I can't. Not when you smile at me like that!' she exclaimed half joking. He gave a relieved laugh.

'All right. I'll try hard to look a bit sorry for being late.'

'No. Don't ever change. I love you just the way you are.' A waiter brought over their food. 'I took the liberty of ordering for you. I hope you'll be fine with this,' she said apologetically.

Tom looked at the mixed grill, 'Are you a mind-reader or what? But let's eat quickly. I can't afford to keep your *tete* waiting!'

'I agree. She's one particular old lady. ... So, when do you leave?'

'Next week Wednesday. I would've wanted to travel on the Sunday flight.'

'Why ever not?'

'Only BA has seats on Sunday and they're not accepting local currency. I don't have six hundred pounds on me.'

'That much?' she was shocked.

'It is indeed. Could be cheaper if you make an early booking,' Tom unfolded his table napkin.

'Anyway, I hope everything works out for you this time.'

The young man gave a confident smile. 'I'm sure everything will go just fine, this time. My only worry is that the plane will run out of fuel in mid-air ... or it will be diverted because a VIP needs to be dropped somewhere ... A flight that's supposed to take approximately nine and a half hours could easily end up taking twenty-four. As they say ... there's no hurry in Africa.' He laughed.

'You're exaggerating ... '

'But, seriously, I've no doubt I'm striking gold this time. Blooms.com was a big let-down but Florals Inc. have already said that they like my products. Flowers are great business abroad. This trip should see a contract signed ... and, well, a few other technicalities sorted out. I should start exporting at the beginning of next year. Things are looking up for us, *dhiya*. ... By the way, has Mai Moyo begun work on your dress yet?'

'She only got back from Chiwundura a few weeks ago. I expect her to start working on it soon. She's just been busy trying to obtain a market licence. She doesn't seem to be having much luck getting onto the housing list for Operation Garikayi. I must talk to her seriously about seeing Emily or somebody else at Kushinga ... I've just been so busy at work.'

Tom nodded. 'It's a difficult time for a lot of people who lost their homes. I hope she'll be OK. I'm just not sure why you seem so bent on her making the dress for you.'

'Well, first, I'm sure she'll make it just the way I want it – after all she's known me since childhood – but I also think it will give her confidence – and other clients. After all, if we don't give her an opportunity, who will? I know you might prefer to buy the perfect article, but I want to do something for my *mainini*. Besides, if I'm right, it'll give me so much pleasure. ... By the way, did you manage to visit Tapiwa? Where had he disappeared to?'

'I think my dear friend is a bit mad. He was talking about *kutanda botso* … '

'Why? Isn't that something people used to do ages ago if they'd wronged their mothers?'

'Precisely. It's a little bit different … and very confusing with my *shamwari*. If you remember, he just disappeared after his wife was buried. Then he materialised at the Psychiatric Unit at Harare Hospital last month. Personally, I think grief made him lose his mind, for a while anyway … he blamed himself, you know.'

'But why? I thought his wife died in a car accident.'

'Edith was running an errand for him when the accident happened. She was pregnant …'

'Poor man,' Faith murmured.

'I'm still worried about him. Something about him is different. Listening to him talking about *kutanda botso* as if it were the most logical thing in the world, gave me the impression that he might have gone a bit nuts. I mean Faith, *kutanda botso* is something that we read about in historical novels. Who in their right mind would do this today? I pointed it out to him that he hadn't gone about it correctly, anyway.'

Faith stared at him contemplatively. 'Who are we to question what he decided to do? Or whether doing so actually shows that he'd lost his mind? Not everyone copes with grief in the same way. Some people behave as if nothing has happened, while others buckle under the weight of sorrow.'

'I suppose you're right. He's still on some medication, I think. He was lucky his brother was there to keep his car import business running. Those guys are loaded because they don't sell only to individuals, but to large companies as well. They're among the lucky few whose businesses still get an official foreign currency allocation. Otherwise they'd have gone bust a long time ago.' Tom sounded almost envious.

'Is he still insisting on re-opening his bridal-wear shop?'

'He is. I just can't understand his obsession. I think he should just close it down. But he won't hear of it. He says he wants to keep the memory of his wife alive. Very sentimental. It was her shop, you know?'

Faith nodded. 'He must have loved her very much.' 'He did. Anyway, my offer still stands. If you can't get the dress that you want here, I've told you that we can fly to Johannesburg to look around. Nothing about me is sub-standard. And that includes my future wife's clothes,' he winked at her.

'Don't be such a show-off, Tom!' she scolded lightly, 'But, thank you for the offer. It may sound silly, but I just have this strong feeling that my mum's friend can do it. She's quite good.'

'Whatever you say, Your Majesty,' Tom teased. 'Let's eat up and make our way to Darwendale. I don't want to upset your *tete* or I might find myself with no bride!'

≈≈≈

Soon afterwards Faith made time to talk to Onai about going to the Kushinga Project. 'They're professionals, *amainini*. Everything you tell them will be kept in the strictest confidence. They work with lawyers who specialise in issues regarding women, so this is definitely the right place for you to go. My friend Emily has already told me that you qualify for free legal aid, which will come in handy when you make your claim on *babamunini's* estate.'

Onai asked slowly, 'So we could end up in court … fighting my husband's family for the money?'

Faith smiled, 'I wouldn't use those words. You would only be claiming what's rightfully yours. I'm not so sure about the house,though, if you say it belonged to *babamunini's* parents.'

Onai nodded. 'Yes, the title deeds are in their names. I never imagined that I or my children would inherit it, but then I never thought they'd turn me out. I'd be grateful for the money, but the thought of a confrontation in court is putting me off. The other day I was talking to my mother about how doing this could result in my children being alienated from their blood relatives … the people whose totem they carry, *PaChivanhu,* that could only lead to disaster. The more I think about it, the more I feel I should just concentrate on rebuilding my life and aim to get onto the housing list for Operation Garikayi.'

Listening to the older woman, Faith was dismayed. 'But you can't just give up because of these cultural beliefs that, in my opinion, serve no purpose except to worsen the suffering of women and children. Why do you think your children will be alienated because you've claimed for them what's rightfully theirs?'

Onai shook her head. 'I hear you, Faith, and I do appreciate your concern. But believe me, these traditional values can't be taken lightly. You're speaking more from a point of view *yechirungu*, but you will understand when you're older.'

'OK, I don't think I can convince you on this one. Maybe Emily will succeed. Promise me that you'll go and see her on Thursday.'

'Of course I will. I'm sorry if I sounded ungrateful. Everything is so confusing. But, yes, I will go and see your friend.'

≈≈≈

Onai went to Kushinga Women's Project the following Thursday afternoon. The reception was spacious and furnished in a modern way. She asked for Miss Sibanda, Faith's friend. A tall, smiling receptionist directed her to a cool, inner office towards the back of the building.

There was a young woman in the office. Onai was convinced that she knew her from somewhere. She introduced herself as Emily and welcomed Onai, offering her a cup of tea. Although she couldn't normally resist one, Onai thanked her and declined the offer. The day was too hot. She asked for some water instead. It came in a tall glass within minutes.

The young woman sat herself opposite her and said pleasantly, 'Faith has told me a bit about you. Now, how can I help?'

Onai cleared her throat and explained her situation. She recounted the recent events and her fears about her children in Chiwundura, who were now having to walk long distances to and from school. She described her loss of earnings, her homeless state, and how desperate she was to find somewhere decent to live so that she could bring her children back to live with her. The young woman listened attentively. Onai was a little breathless when she finally came to the end of her story.

'If you like, I'll refer you to one of our lawyers who can help you recover something for your children from your husband's estate. Would you like that?'

Onai shook her head, saying emphatically, 'No, I would rather go on the Operation Garikayi waiting list. I don't want anything from my husband's estate. It would only make things worse …'

'May I ask why you feel that way?'

She drew a deep breath. 'It's difficult to explain, but I would like to be independent of my husband's family. Besides, if I engage lawyers, there would be too much hostility and I can't alienate my children from their relatives …' Her voice trailed away. She was unsure how the argument she had repeated so many times would sound to this young woman. Faith had obviously not been impressed.

Emily gave her a strange look and said thoughtfully, 'Operation Garikayi is meant for those who were displaced during the demolitions. I agree that you are technically a displaced person, even though you were not directly affected. What I'm not sure about is whether you would qualify as a beneficiary. Have you tried going to the municipal offices to register?'

'I did,' Onai replied. She told her about her encounter with the young female officer who had treated her with contempt, and about the man called Boora who had made an indecent proposal.

Emily's face darkened. 'This is not acceptable. Would you like me to take it up with the city council?'

Onai hesitated. She had a brief moment of indecision. If she pressed charges and caused trouble, she would probably compromise her only chance of getting registered at all. 'Not really. I just want to get on to the housing list, that's all.' She would not let herself engage in confrontation. There was just no need.

Emily asked Onai for a physical description of the man, in case she had been given a false name. Onai opened her mouth. The words lingered, then tumbled out unwillingly. She gave the most accurate description that she could think of. 'I really don't want to cause trouble,' she said anxiously. 'In my position, I can't see that it would do any good.'

'I wouldn't dream of causing problems for you. Just write down your full contact details and I'll see what I can do. Are you able to come back here on Monday? I won't be here, but I can leave a message for you at the front desk.'

'Yes, I can come in on Monday. Thank you very much,' Onai took the proffered pen and wrote down her details. When she finished she looked up and asked, 'I'm sorry to ask, but, are you a doctor? You look so much like the girl who attended to me when I was in hospital several months ago.'

'I'm a doctor, yes. You know, I had the strangest feeling that I knew you from somewhere, but I didn't want to say anything out of turn. I hope your life will improve very soon.'

Onai nodded. 'I hope so too.' It felt good to come across somebody who was showing so much genuine concern.

'I'll do my best to help you. Don't hesitate to come here if you need any more advice, Mrs Moyo. I'm only a volunteer but we have many professional people who can assist you. If you want to see me specifically, I'm usually here on Thursday afternoons. I look forward to seeing you again.'

Onai thanked her and left. Hope was once again nudging at her mind. Who knew what tomorrow might bring?

≈≈≈

On her way home, she passed the New Start Centre offices. A bright orange sign depicting the rising sun invited people to come forward for free HIV tests. She knew that being married to Gari had put her at considerable risk; and, deep in her heart, she knew that she should go for a test. But now, she had more important things to think about. Above all else, getting somewhere to live with her children. What she did not know would not kill her.

When she arrived home Katy was fiddling around with the sewing machine, trying to figure out how the more advanced functions worked. Onai sat with her, explained things and tested out the embroidery stitches on some fabric.

'I hope John isn't still thinking of selling this machine. I'm beginning to like it. Maybe you can teach me how to make duvet covers and cushion covers that I can sell?'

Onai thought it was a good idea. Time was what they had a lot of. She promised to take Katy through the basics. Duvet covers were not that difficult. Certainly, nowhere near as complicated as making Faith's dress.

Katy suggested that while Onai waited for her licence, she should apply for a passport. Buying goods from South Africa for resale would boost her income. Onai was not so sure, but she accepted a loan from Katy for an urgent passport application. And a few days later, armed with photographs, they went to the passport officer to submit the application. The passport officer told them regretfully that the document would be ready in three months, at the earliest.

'But why? We have just paid the fee for an urgent application, haven't we?' Katy asked.

'That's right. If you had paid the standard fee you might have had to wait six months, or even longer. There's no paper in the country to print passports. No ink either, hence the delay,' the man explained apologetically. The two women left, not believing how fast things seemed to be deteriorating. Passports were the latest casualty. They wondered what would be next.

There was nothing more to do apart from waiting for Onai's various applications to go through. She had mastered the art of waiting. While she waited, she began working on Faith's dress. The 24th of December was now just over two months away. She studied the pattern carefully, and took Faith's measurements. Almost with dread, she cut the fabric,. What if she got it wrong? Faith's reassurances that if the dress was not perfect, she would buy one in South Africa only threw her into a flurry of panic. How embarrassing that would be. She would have to get it right, no matter what.

Ruva stayed up at night to study for her forthcoming O-levels. Onai sat up with her and worked on the dress. Occasionally she would glance up at her daughter's face puckered with concentration, and wonder what it was that drove her. She hoped sincerely that Ruva would pass her exams and go on to do A-level. She would have to find the fees somehow. She did not want her daughter to end up as a vegetable vendor. Her children's lives had to be better than her own.

≈≈≈

One afternoon Toro's wife, Shungu, passed by Katy's house. Onai was surprised to see her. She looked drawn and somehow thinner. She also had a raised scar forming a ridge that ran down one side of her face. It had not been apparent at Gari's funeral. Onai wondered if Toro was abusing her.

Her sister-in-law declined the invitation to come indoors, hanging back on the doorstep. 'No, I can't come in. I'm in a hurry. I thought I would just drop off these letters that came for you sometime ago.' She thrust several envelopes into Onai's hands. Onai wondered who could have written to her. Shungu hurried off without another word. Onai and Katy exchanged glances.

Onai frowned. 'What odd behaviour! She looked upset about something. Maybe urban life has not lived up to her expectations,' she said as she opened the letters while walking back into the house. They were demands for payment of two hospital bills: her own and another for Gari's stay in the Intensive Care Unit.

She drew in a deep breath and leaned against the wall, 'I've had nightmares about these bills. I kept hoping the hospital would forget. False hope! What am I going to do, Katy? It says here they will forward my name to debt collectors if I don't pay up. Could they get me arrested, do you think?'

'There is nothing you can do about it now, Onai. Let's keep focused. If they do send debt collectors after you, we'll take it from there. Try not to think too much about it now. After all, what good can that do you?'

Onai felt growing anger. It was unfair that she had incurred the first bill after Gari had assaulted her. It was even more unfair that he had died … leaving her with this colossal bill from his stay in the ICU. If only he'd treated her better … she wouldn't have minded being obliged to pay the bill. She wouldn't have minded at all. If only …

At that moment, she wished for so many things that were out of her reach. She rested her cheek against the window and stared outside. The ground was littered with dry leaves and scraps of paper. She watched them as they blew around in the dust in a frenzied little dance, spurred on by sharp bursts of blustery air. Even they had an indefinable but free existence that appeared superior to hers. She bleakly turned away from the window. When would life get better? When, when, when?

CHAPTER 26

On Monday, Onai picked up a note from Emily at the Kushinga Women's Project. The message was for her to go and see a Mr Ndlovu at the municipal office. He would process her application and put her on the list for housing beneficiaries. Onai could hardly believe it. She hurried away, hoping that Emily had not left the message in error. When she arrived at the offices, Mr Ndlovu said he'd been expecting her. He led her into an airy room with comfortable chairs. He spoke politely and took down her details. She was initially suspicious of his manner. After her encounter with Boora, she half-expected him to pounce on her, or to present her with an indecent proposal. It did not come.

Her suspicions were dispelled when he said, 'I'm sorry about the incident with one of our officers. We're dealing with him. It has been recommended that he should leave his job … yours was not the first reported incident.'

Hardly believing him, Onai could only nod. Mr Ndlovu advised her that, all things being well, she would be given a house by the end of November. Onai thanked him profusely, briefly overwhelmed with relief. But too much had gone wrong in her life for her to accept a change in fortune without a premonition that it might not last; so the shock of delight was tempered by moments of anxiety.

≈≈≈

As she walked home, she wondered … maybe she could celebrate by indulging in some small pleasure; perhaps some soft, new underwear. She laughed aloud at the absurdity of the idea. A group of schoolchildren stared at her and hurried away.

'Underwear,' she thought again. How ridiculous! She dismissed the thought but it stubbornly resurfaced. Beautiful underwear, indeed! Hers was not the kind of life that could indulge in such useless extravagances. What lay beneath her dresses was not anyone's business. She shrugged and wondered what had come over her.

In the distance, she spotted the bright red and white uniform of a

Lyons Maid ice-cream vendor. There was a rush of saliva in her mouth. She knew immediately how she would celebrate. She would allow herself just the pleasure of buying a milky ice-cream cone. It had always been her favourite. Even Gari had known that. In the early, heady days of their romance, he had wooed her with ice-cream and sweet words.

Her mouth watered. She looked at the vendor again. He had stopped at the traffic lights ahead, waiting to cycle across the busy intersection. She approached him uncertainly, her conscience beginning to prick.

The man ignored her for a moment. She noticed how he deliberately pulled down his red cap, and carefully pretended to check something in the refrigerated box at the front of his bicycle.

Brightly, she asked him for a vanilla cone. 'Fifty thousand,' he said abruptly and made as if to start cycling across the road. Onai held the money out to him. He accepted it with a barely concealed look of surprise and, almost reluctantly, handed her the cone. She registered his manner and smiled to herself. Today, she did not care. She had her ice-cream and nothing would spoil her pleasure, not even this man's contempt. Hurriedly, she tore off the transparent covering. Her lips savoured the delectable softness. She closed her eyes briefly and swallowed hard. A frisson of enjoyment coursed through her body as she relished the sweet coolness. Her skin tingled. She walked home to share her good news with her friend.

≈≈≈

That evening, Faith stopped by for a fitting. The deep yellow silk, clung and flowed around Faith's young body as if she were indeed a flower in spring.

'Oh, thank you, *mainini*. I knew you wouldn't let me down,' she said happily.

'Well, don't thank me too much before I've finished or you might have to eat your words,' Onai said doubtfully, but with a sense of pride. The result of her efforts had surprised her.

'I don't have any doubts at all. Not when it's looking so good already. I can't wait to see what it'll look like when you've stitched in the trimming on the bodice. I really think you could earn a good living from dressmaking, don't you think so, *Mai?*'

Katy looked up from her crocheting and smiled.

'You tell her, Faith. Every time I praise her, she looks as if she's going to bite my head off. She just doesn't believe me.' Katy lifted the duvet cover that she was working on and appraised the effect of her crocheted trimming.

'*Mainini*, I can showcase this dress for you, and maybe you'll find work. Just finish it and we'll see.' Faith's eyes glowed.

How could the girl imagine she could find her a position on the strength of just one party frock, when she had failed to do so through conventional applications and interviews? Onai shrugged, wondering why Faith seemed so excitable. But then, she was becoming engaged to one of Harare's most sought-after bachelors, who was throwing a huge party in her honour.

≈≈≈

Emily was pleased when Mrs Moyo arrived at the Kushinga offices on Thursday afternoon.

'Good afternoon, Dr Sibanda,' she said warmly.

'*Masikati,* Mrs Moyo. But why Dr Sibanda? Call me Emily, please. So, how did it go?' she asked, smiling.

'I've just come to say thank you. My application was approved. My new house will be ready by the end of November,' Onai replied, a note of wonder in her voice. 'I still can't really believe it, but I want to thank you.'

'You're most welcome, Mrs Moyo. Mind you, it's only a two-roomed house,' Emily cautioned.

'I know and it doesn't matter at all. I just need a roof over my head, a home for my children. Two rooms is so much better than being homeless. How can I ever thank you?'

'You don't have to, Mrs Moyo. This is why we're here. I'm glad we're able to be of some help, and I hope you'll be reunited with your children soon.'

'I hope so too,' Onai said brightly and thanked her again before leaving. Emily felt a glow of satisfaction to have made such a positive difference to somebody's life.

Just that morning, a grateful patient had brought her a live chicken as a thank you present for treating her baby for pneumonia. Emily smiled at the memory of the bird squawking at the hospital reception, and the look on the orderly's face. It was these seemingly little things that gave her second thoughts about leaving the country. Working abroad was financially rewarding, everyone realised that, but what she also knew was that she would never get as much job satisfaction, or such an opportunity to make a real difference to the lives of people, as she would in Zimbabwe. Slowly, she was learning to make do with the few available facilities, so as to give her patients the best she could. Now, more than ever, she appreciated that in order to continue enjoying her work, she had to remember that medicine was indeed a calling, and not just a route to financial success. Besides, the more she became involved with the women's movement, the more convinced she was that Zimbabwe was where she belonged. Ben did not seem too pleased, but they'd not yet made any firm commitment to each other and time would tell.

For now, the fulfilment that came from satisfying real needs eclipsed the frustrations of waiting in a fuel queue or giving a patient a prescription that they couldn't afford.

She glanced at her watch. Ben would soon be coming to pick her up.

≈≈≈

John returned from South Africa on Friday evening. He did not talk much about his trip. It was as if he was purposefully avoiding the issue. 'Your daughter works very hard,' he commented to Onai as they had their evening meal. Onai glanced at Ruva and smiled.

'That she does. I'm sure she'll get straight As,' declared Katy.

'I would like that, *maiguru*, but I don't know if I'll succeed,' Ruva replied wistfully as she toyed with her sadza. Onai looked at her closely. The stress of preparing for her O-levels was affecting the child. She'd hardly eaten anything.

'You mustn't overwork, Ruva. You've done your best. As the exams get closer, I don't think you should have any more late nights.'

Ruva protested, 'But I still have some subjects to cover. I'm not yet ready for the first paper.'

'Let's see. If you carry on like this, by the time you sit your exams you'll be too exhausted to do justice to anything you've learnt.'

'What course would you like to study at college, Ruva?' John sensibly changed the subject.

The girl looked up shyly. 'Journalism,' she said without hesitation, looking at her mother as if seeking approval. Onai's mind was blank.

'Bad choice. Don't even dream about it,' Faith said as she carefully moulded a portion of sadza, and popped it into her mouth.

'But why, *sisi* Faith? I like the idea of journalism. I think it's an exciting job. I would travel all over the country, interview important people – maybe even the President. I would write for newspapers, appear on TV…'

Katy interrupted, 'I agree with Faith. I think journalism is a bad choice.'

John nodded. 'Certainly,' he said.

Ruva's face fell, confused and hurt that all the adults had responded so negatively to a dream that she'd been nurturing for months.

Faith explained. 'Just look at how many journalists have been arrested over the last few years. Why would you want to have a career that's so unsafe, especially for a woman? I'm sure there's something else that interests you; something safer. Besides, you'd always want to report what you see, and not what someone told you to see. If you do that, then you're as good as dead!'

Ruva's jaw dropped in alarm.

'Faith!' exclaimed Katy. 'There is no need to be so over-dramatic. You're frightening the poor child. Don't worry Ruva. She's just teasing.'

Faith turned to the stricken girl and smiled sweetly. Ruva did not return her smile. 'I really want to be a journalist. I'll do my job well. So I don't think I will get arrested,' she insisted.

Seeing her daughter's distress, Onai asked, 'Surely, it's not that bad?'

John said cryptically, 'Just think about it, Ruva. Think about it really hard.' He would not elaborate.

Katy tried to cheer Ruva up. 'You're a very bright girl, Ruva. Why don't you think about nursing?'

Onai found herself unable to contribute to the conversation. She'd always hoped Ruva might one day go to university. Did they offer a degree in journalism? Was it really such a risky profession? She had never really thought about what her daughter might do, she'd only prayed that she would not have to become a vendor. With her A-levels still two years ahead of her, she wondered whether the discussion was not more than a little premature.

John nodded at Katy. 'I think nursing is a good idea. At the moment it's the fastest ticket out of Zimbabwe. Every day, nurses are leaving for the UK, America, and even Australia. You will be assured of a good future if you study a course that will enable you to travel.'

Onai said, 'But wouldn't she have to go into a youth training camp if she's to be considered for nursing school?'

Katy sighed. 'I'm not sure. But you could be right. All the rules have changed haven't they?'

Faith agreed. She looked at Onai. 'If I were you, I wouldn't let Ruva go to one of those camps. Remember that girl who caused an outcry when she claimed that she'd been gang-raped?'

'Was she telling the truth?' Onai asked and raised her eyebrows.

John said, 'Well, nobody was arrested, so we'll never know. Anyway, there are many other girls who've been to the camps, who haven't claimed that they've been raped. So it might just have been a one-off incident. Women do get raped, even in their own homes, you know.'

Onai was not as dismissive. Her maternal instinct came to the fore. 'Well, I won't let Ruva go to one of those camps. *Nekufashaira kweAIDS* everywhere. Why would that girl lie?'

Faith murmured, 'Who knows? What I know is that there are serious food shortages in those camps, just as in the colleges, the prisons, and even the hospitals …'

'OK, OK,' John interrupted impatiently. 'We all agree that Ruva is not going to a youth training camp. Maybe she should just join the thriving dressmaker's club here,' he attempted a joke. 'Or find a job in a supermarket, so that we won't have to join the food queues!'

Faith said, 'Well, anyway, she has plenty of time to think about it. I'm sure she'll pass her O-levels with flying colours and go on to do her A-levels, so there's plenty of time for her to think about a choice of career or of study. There's no need to think about the camps at this stage.'

Onai nodded thoughtfully, and everyone tucked into the last of the sadza.

≈≈≈

After she and Ruva had washed the dishes, Faith gathered up her handbag and books. Tom was waiting for her somewhere up the road, successfully back from his trip to the UK. She was looking forward to the time when he would meet her family openly. He had now met her *tete*, her father's sister. There would have to be a formal lobola ceremony – probably some time after the engagement party. Her *tete* had promised to proceed quickly with the formalities, so that there would be no awkwardness at the party. John could be a stickler for traditional custom, and Faith was his only daughter.

Indeed part of Faith's anxiety about the huge party was that it was not traditional and would almost certainly be the very first time their respective parents met. Would they like each other? Coming from such different backgrounds, would there be gossip? None of her anxieties seemed to bother Tom at all. All he'd said was, 'Culture is not static. If we can embrace white weddings, why can't we have engagement parties?'

She spotted his car in the shadows near the corner and increased her saunter to a brisk pace.

≈≈≈

As they were preparing for bed, Ruva said, 'I don't want to go and live in another country, Mum. Why should I have to? I want to live here in Zimbabwe. Must I really take a course that will enable me to leave? Must I really go to nursing school?'

'I honestly don't know, Ruva.'

Her daughter frowned. 'I can't work in a hospital. I hate hospitals. They smell horrible … they smell of death,' she concluded emphatically.

Onai nodded. Her own recollections of hospitals were morbid. And, yes, they did smell of death and detergent, a smell that seemed to linger around her, long after they'd buried Gari.

'Everyone is leaving … doctors, nurses, teachers, accountants, engineers … everybody! Why is everyone leaving? Who is going to be left here to do their work?' Ruva asked gravely.

Onai could not answer her. Her own life had never afforded her the opportunity to leave. It had simply not been an option. She envied her childhood friend, Stella. The pounds that she earned as a nurse in the UK had certainly taken her family to a higher level in society. Unlike nursing, dressmaking was not a fast ticket out of Zimbabwe.

'Maybe just you and me will be left here,' she finally replied and laughed. Ruva did not see the funny side.

≈≈≈

Onai awoke to the sound of long-awaited rain pattering on the asbestos roof. By late morning, the rain had stopped, the sun was shining and the air smelt fresh and earthy. Everything looked clean and washed. Young children played in street puddles and moulded animal shapes and dolls from thick mud.

The rain brought hope and possibly good fortune because that afternoon, Onai was finally issued with a vending licence. She was assigned a stall at the old Mbare market place. The market had been quickly and roughly touched up, but it looked a bit cleaner. It also appeared less crowded. There were no beggars lurking about and no street children waiting for the perfect moment to pounce and grab fruit. She appreciated the cleanliness of her surroundings. Her neighbouring stall holders were all new to her but she quickly made their acquaintance.

She expected to see VaGudo, the large, blustery farmer who had previously livened up market mornings, but he didn't come. One of the women informed her that he'd been involved in a car accident, which had left him paralysed. The front wheel of an oncoming bus had come off and bounced onto his windscreen, causing him to lose control of his truck. Market days would never be the same without him.

Onai wondered how many times she'd heard of accidents resulting

316

from burst tyres. John had recently joked about the huge amount of money he'd had to spend on just one tyre – ten times more than the car itself had cost. The same applied to other spare parts. As a result, a lot of vehicles were simply disasters waiting to happen: death-traps and moving coffins. But it didn't seem as if anyone bothered. 'It's life,' was the fatalistic comfort people offered each other when someone died. She felt very sorry for VaGudo, she was going to miss his warm, blustery good humour, and she wondered how he would survive.

Onai knew that it would take a while for her regular customers to grow in number. She planned to throw herself vigorously into ordering and selling, keen to make as much profit as possible. She wanted to pay Katy and John for her upkeep. Sending money to her mother for Fari and Rita was another priority. Being in a position to earn money once again gave her a fresh taste of independence and a sense of renewed optimism.

Everything was slowly starting to fall into place. The shortages and the endless queues didn't bother her so much, now. They had become a way of life, even entertaining social events. Didn't one pick up the latest information about anything and everything in a food queue? Didn't one enjoy the greatest number of laughs?

She found serenity in acceptance and realised that she had not had any of her terrible headaches for several weeks. In small, but nevertheless important ways, her life was improving. The only thing which would surely have completed her happiness was to have Fari and Rita back with her.

CHAPTER 27

There was a loud knock on the front door at around six o'clock the following evening. 'Police! Open up!' Ruva looked up from the book she was reading. Katy and Onai froze. John looked uneasily at the door and stood up. His legs felt weak.

He looked around for an escape route. 'Police!' a different voice was heard through kitchen door. John cursed the burglar bars on the windows. There was no way he could get out.

'We know you're in there. Open up now!' Katy stood up. John nodded at her. She opened the door. Four male officers barged in. One of them waved a piece paper in the air.

'Search warrant! We have reason to believe you're dealing in foreign currency. Everyone stay where you are, while we conduct our search,' he barked. They all stared at him in stunned silence.

One officer stood guard while the others combed the rooms, rummaging everywhere, and turning everything upside down.

After some minutes, the man who'd been searching the main bedroom came out holding John's coat. Digging into a pocket, he brought out a thick wad of South African notes. John knew he was holding at least five thousand rands – the money that Assistant Commissioner Nzou should have exchanged that very morning for Zimbabwean dollars. Why hadn't he come as they'd arranged? He looked down.

The officer gave him a triumphant look. 'This is exactly what I was looking for. Now, tell me, do you have paperwork from any bank, South African or Zimbabwean, to explain how you came to have this money?'

John swallowed and shook his head. 'Handcuff him, guys!' the officer ordered and threw the wad of notes to his colleague, saying, 'Take that as evidence,' Katy sprang forwards.

'Do you want to come along, too? I will book you in as an accomplice if you like,' he snarled.

Katy stepped back. Onai put her arms around her friend's trembling body.

As John was led away in handcuffs, he turned to Katy and mouthed, 'Nzou'.

The officer pushed him roughly out of the house, 'Let's go.'

≈≈≈

They left the women in shocked silence. Katy turned to Onai. 'I've always feared this would happen. What am I going to do, now?' She was close to tears.

Onai was at a loss for words. She managed to say, 'Ring that police officer, Mr Nzou. As your business partner, he should be able to help you.'

'I think I'll do that.' Katy picked up the phone. With fingers that were visibly unsteady, she dialled. After a while, the receiver pressed against her ear, she redialled. This and three further attempts were fruitless.

She turned to Onai. 'His phone keeps going to voice-mail. Faith isn't answering her phone either.'

'Don't worry, my dear. We'll try again in the morning.'

'No. I think we should just go to the police station first thing tomorrow and find Mr Nzou. Talking to him face to face might be the only way.'

Onai was not so sure. What if he refused to co-operate? Could he not turn around and arrest them for interfering with the due process of justice?

That night, Katy and Onai hardly slept, their minds anxious and restless.

≈≈≈

Assistant Commissioner Nzou's head was splitting. He stared at the final demand for a loan repayment lying on his desk. It couldn't get any worse. All his accounts were in the red, and he still hadn't paid his workers their October salaries.

Just thinking about Tsikamutanda infuriated him. The man was a crook and a liar of the worst order. None of his so-called charms had worked. The man had bled him dry of foreign currency, wooing him with assurances that his business would flourish, and he would be promoted to Senior Assistant Commissioner by the end of the year. But his business was now on crutches and his name had not been put forward in the last round of promotions. There was even talk of him being transferred to Gweru! What was that, if not a demotion?

The phone on his desk rang, breaking his train of furious thoughts. The tone indicated an internal call. He lifted the receiver with annoyance. It was only five minutes past eight. Who could be ringing him so early in the morning?

It was the new secretary, the bright, breezy woman who was so enthusiastic that it was annoying.

'Good morning, Sir. I have two visitors for you in reception. Shall I show them through?'

'Who are they?' he asked irritably.

'Your sisters, they said.' The young lady sounded doubtful.

Nzou swore under his breath. His only sister had died in 1988. So who were these women? He would see what this was all about.

'Show them in,' he barked.

A few minutes later there was a timid knock on his door.

'Come in!' he bellowed. To his surprise, it was Mrs Nguni and a woman who looked vaguely familiar. He struggled to place her and failed.

He gestured the women towards two chairs and asked them to sit down. Shaking their hands, he asked, 'Now how can I help you?'

Mrs Nguni gave a troubled sigh. 'My husband was arrested last night for foreign currency dealing. I was hoping that you could help me by getting him released.'

Nzou frowned. Then he laughed. 'Now, whatever gave you that idea? I'm a man of the law, Mrs Nguni. I can't just get your husband released if he has committed a crime. The law has to run its course.'

Mrs Nguni rose furiously. The other woman pulled her down. She sat down with a thud, looking him in the eye. After a brief, charged silence, she spoke in a cold voice, 'Whose law are you talking about? Are you not in this together with my husband? The rands they found in our house is the money you should have collected yesterday morning. I'm sure there is somebody who would be interested in getting such information.'

The man leaned back in his chair and regarded the two women. A nerve twitched in his right hand. He picked up a pen and tapped it on the desk.

How dare she? He desperately needed to lash out at her … at anything. Instead, he laughed shortly, 'Are you threatening me? Look here, Mrs Nguni, do you know who you're dealing with? I'm a senior police officer, and you are a nobody … or rather … you're the wife of a criminal. Who would anyone believe? You or me? Now stop being so foolish. Remember, I could have you arrested for being your husband's accomplice.'

The teasing pleasantness with which he had previously related to her had gone. She angrily stood up again. Her friend followed suit.

'I'll leave you with just one thing to think about. Over the last six months, I have had six transactions with you. I have receipts signed by you, written in your own handwriting. Think about that. You know where to find me,' she trembled as she spoke and walked towards the door.

Nzou suddenly felt deflated. The threat was real. He knew a few people who would be happy to see him fall. 'Wait,' he said. The two women hovered uncertainly. He lifted his phone and dialled, making a great effort to suppress his anger.

'Hello? Who is the member-in-charge on duty today? Mafa? Tell him I want to speak to him now … Is it you, Mafa? Did you have anything to do with arrest in Mbare last night … John Nguni, that's him,' he forced himself to laugh, trying to appear as if this was a perfectly normal conversation.

He listened as Mafa explained how the arrest had been effected. 'You ordered the arrest?' He made a pretence of sounding incredulous. 'Well, that man is my brother! I want him out of there this very minute … No, no, no … you don't treat my family like this … at least you should have informed me, before you moved in. You can't treat my brother like a common criminal … Fine, apology accepted, but be very, very careful in future. Yes … Now. And give him back his money … No. You don't need it as evidence because there is no case,' he slammed the receiver down.

He glared at the two women. 'Now get out. You got what you wanted.' Mrs Nguni gave him a triumphant look. You're never going to get any more business from me, Nzou thought angrily.

≈≈≈

At the holding cells, an officer called Mafa opened John's cell and glared at him. 'You are free to go because apparently you are my boss's brother. Brother, huh? You two are as alike as a baboon and a donkey!' he snorted contemptuously, and handed him his South African rands.

John accepted the money with surprise. Katy had done it! Mafa spoke. 'It's not over yet. They don't call me Mafa for nothing. I will get you, somehow. You've been smuggling people across the border too, haven't you?'

John's heart raced. How could he know that? Mafa leaned closer and glared at him with bloodshot eyes. 'You and that assistant commissioner brother of yours are going down together.' He laughed loudly.

'Your so-called brother has been running the department like his personal business for years. And I'm going to nail both of you. For your own information, there are a lot of honest people within the force … and we are going to get you and your brother. Just wait and see!'

John recoiled. He brushed past Mafa and rushed out of the building. There was no transport at the terminus, and he did not have time to waste, so he chose to sprint all the way back to Mbare.

≈≈≈

Raised, angry voices came from the main bedroom. Onai's stomach filled with anxiety. For the first time since she'd known them, she heard Katy and John arguing. Thankfully, Ruva had gone to school. She sat on the sofa and supported her head with trembling hands, willing Katy and John to stop. They didn't. The voices grew louder and angrier. What a mess, she thought. What a dreadful mess and what terrible timing too.

≈≈≈

'I have to go Katy, please!' John insisted. 'I'm lucky to have gotten out at all.' He threw his clothes hurriedly into a suitcase.

Katy was crying. 'What about your job? What about our plans? What about our daughter's engagement party? You have to be there, John. Don't break Faith's heart. She has put so much into this celebration.'

'Katy, you have to understand, and Faith must also understand, that I won't be any good to you if I'm in jail. Let me go to South Africa. I'll

322

try to come back later, once things have settled down. If I can't do that, I'll just have to look for another job, and stay there for a while.'

'What about me, John? Are you just leaving me … leaving our marriage?'

'No, its not like that. Please understand me, Katy. They want me for something else that I've been doing … something that I can't tell you. So, I am not over-reacting, I must leave.'

'What did you do, John? Please tell me so that I can try to make sense of this!'

'I can't.' John was adamant.

'I'm your wife, John. *Mukadzi wako*. Since when did we start having these secrets? I notice things, you know. For the last few months, you've been acting strangely. Are you running off with a girlfriend? What did you do, John? Whatever it is, was it worth all this trouble? How could you?' she blazed at him.

A look of anger flashed across his face. 'How could I what, Katy? And what girlfriend are you talking about? Everything I've ever done has been for you and Faith. We needed money for Faith's fees, to pay off the stand, to start building. Do you really think that working as a driver could give me the large sums required for foreign currency dealing? Where did you think I was getting all those dollars from? Or didn't you think at all?'

'Oh, John, if I'd realised you were doing something very illegal, I would have asked you to stop. We could have found another way to raise the money.' Katy shook her head in despair. 'But please don't go. Mr Nzou got you released, he's a powerful man … he'll help us. Please don't go,' she begged.

John slammed the suitcase shut and looked at her. He shook his head. 'Forget about him. He's probably going to be arrested, too. I really have to go. I promise, I'll be in touch soon.' He gave her a quick embrace and ran out, leaving her weeping on the bed.

Onai tried to console her. But no words could alleviate the pain.

≈≈≈

Faith came home late that afternoon. She was frantic. 'I had a phone call from father. He's at the border post in Beitbridge. The connection was bad … what happened? He sounded very upset.'

Katy explained. Faith was shocked.

'It was all for us. He said it was all for us, whatever it was. I wish I'd known,' Katy kept repeating sadly.

Faith was alternately perplexed, infuriated and embarrassed. How would Tom and his family take this? How would she survive the embarrassment of having a father who was officially a criminal, and on the run? She loved her father, she really did, but at that moment what she felt for him was more like hatred.

≈≈≈

It was, however, just as well that John left when he did. That evening, police officers came looking for him. He was wanted for leaving the holding cells unlawfully, and also in connection with some shady deals for which a just-suspended Assistant Commissioner Nzou was being investigated. No other crime was mentioned, so what had John been talking about? Katy hoped that it was something less serious than foreign currency dealing.

When she was taken away by the police for questioning, she denied any knowledge of her husband's foreign currency deals. The officer called Mafa gave her a number to phone if her husband made contact. John was said to be a crucial witness in the case against Nzou. The officer hinted that he would get off with a very light sentence if he co-operated. Katy did not believe it. She scrunched up the piece of paper on which Mafa had scribbled his phone number and threw it into a bin.

'I've lost faith in the justice system, Onai. What guarantee do I have that this officer is telling the truth?'

'I agree. There's no way of knowing. Life holds no guarantees. But what will you do if John does not give himself up? I wish I could help but I don't know where to begin.'

≈≈≈

A week passed before John plucked up enough courage to phone Katy. He knew she would be upset. 'Why haven't you been in touch, John? I've been so worried. The police have been here twice. They've been asking for information about where you are. What are we going to do, John?'

'I'm sorry, *mudiwa*. I just thought that I should lie low for a while. I'm safe here in South Africa. I just need time to think things over.'

'When are you coming back?' His wife sounded close to tears. He hated her tears.

'I don't know, Katy. Maybe I could look for a permanent job here and we can take it from there. Maybe …'

She interrupted, *'Chii?* How can you be thinking of looking for a job in South Africa? Have you forgotten about Faith's engagement party next month?'

John sighed. Katy didn't know half the story. He wondered if he should have told her. Foreign currency dealing was one thing. Trafficking young girls across the border was another, more serious crime. He did not enlighten her. 'I won't be there for the party, Katy. Just go ahead without me. I'm very sorry.' He could almost feel her disappointment and pain down the telephone line.

'But John …'

'I'm sorry, Katy. I have to go, I've run out of air-time,' he lied to end the possibility of more accusations and pain.

He had to meet up with a fellow Zimbabwean man who had advised him to lodge a claim for asylum. 'But isn't that difficult? I'm not really an asylum seeker. I just need to be able to live and work here with no immigration problems until certain issues at home have been resolved,' he'd said.

The man had laughed. 'Its not difficult. *Hazvidi hope, chete!* If your claim is not real, all you have to do is to cook up a grim tale of persecution. What might be difficult is putting together the evidence, but I have connections at home who can put together authentic documents to support your claim. They can even be backdated. If you're willing to pay, everything will be simple, *shasha,'* he had said convincingly.

But, of course. Didn't everything come down to money? For his freedom, it was worth a try. He would deal with Katy's rage later.

≈≈≈

Faith was tense and anxious all day, and when Tom arrived to see her that evening, she started a blazing row that was based on a sneaking suspicion. 'You're ashamed to have my parents as your in-laws, aren't you?'

He averted his eyes and did not answer.

'Don't deny it, I know you're ashamed. I can see it in your eyes. But guess what? I am proud of my parents and I don't care what you or anyone else thinks,' she fumed.

'What exactly do you want me to say, Faith? Do you want me to say your parents have done nothing wrong? If that's what you expect, well, I'll have to disappoint you.'

'But can't you see that it's the system, Tom? It's the system that is turning good people into so-called criminals. My father is a good man. If my parents sold foreign currency, it was because they identified a need in the economy and capitalised on it. It's a struggle to survive, Tom. Don't talk down to me. You know nothing about struggling to survive,' Faith, alone all afternoon, had worked herself up into a rage of anger and shame, and needed a scapegoat.

'No, Faith. If one does things that are expressly against the law, that is a crime. It doesn't matter how much you try to disguise it. Facts are facts. You can't hide behind poverty, or whatever else, to excuse breaking the law. I feel for your parents, sure I do, but I can't take your side on this.'

'And if my father is a criminal … so are you! You also buy foreign currency on the black market. If you're such a hypocrite, just go to hell and leave me alone!' she shouted, banging the door in his face.

She collapsed on her bed in tears. How could everything be going so horribly wrong just before their engagement? She wondered if he would consider cancelling the party. The thought threw her into a panic. She swallowed her pride and called him to apologise. He didn't answer.

In the morning she was relieved to wake up to his coded knock on the door. They had both had time to reflect, and both felt a need to apologise, but they regarded each other with a certain wariness.

Altercations such as this spoke of some deeper, more fundamental, difference in their world view.

≈≈≈

The days seemed to fly past and before they knew it, it was November. Onai was worried because Katy was distracted and irritable. She was frantic when John didn't phone, and even more frantic when he did. Onai worried about Rita and Fari in Chiwundura. She worried about Ruva who moved around the house like a listless shadow, worn out by the stress of exams. Even though she had only two more papers to go, she refused to take a break. But she worried about her friend most of all. Katy, who'd always been her rock, was falling apart. Onai found it hard to give comfort and support, when she still needed so much herself.

'What if the police have a means of eavesdropping on our telephone conversations? Maybe they can trace the calls back to where he's living now,' Katy said.

Onai doubted it. She tried to reassure her friend, but it was as if the woman had made a conscious decision not to be comforted. The police had stopped by on two further occasions. That alone had thrown Katy into increasing panic and left Onai feeling even more helpless.

Sergeant Mafa had been unexpectedly courteous. He had taken the time to give Onai and Katy a concise education about the merits of co-operating with the police. Onai was slowly beginning to feel that she could trust him, but Katy was adamant that she had long lost faith in the police. 'Justice is something that can always be twisted to suit the needs of those in power. I doubt that there will be any for John. If you ask me, I have a feeling that Nzou is going to get away with this. John will be the one to rot in jail.'

'I understand your fears, Katy, but I'm not sure this is a situation where doing nothing is the best option.' Onai had become aware that even in desperate straits, it was possible to act, and that this alone helped one to feel that one was regaining control of one's life.

'I don't think so,' Katy replied. 'Without being able to talk properly to John, without knowing what Sergeant Mafa is really thinking, I could just make everything worse, and John would never forgive me. We'll just sit and wait.' Katy answered sadly. ...'Did I tell you that John is thinking of applying for asylum in South Africa?'

Onai looked up, 'What?'

'Yes. And that means he won't be able to return.'

'But why?'

'Why? Because he thinks that if he comes back, he'll rot in jail. What am I going to do, Onai? If he becomes a refugee, it will be the end of my marriage. I can't move permanently to South Africa,' Katy said despairingly.

Onai sighed. What had begun simply as a means of fending for the family was fast deteriorating into something worse. What if his false asylum claim backfired? What if he got deported?. She took Katy's hand, trying to offer strength, while simultaneously trying to draw strength from her friend.

Later that afternoon, Faith arrived for the final fitting. She was accompanied by her friend Melody. Onai was pleased to note that Katy immediately brightened up. They all admired Faith as she paraded around the room in the finished garment. Onai was pleased by the results of her effort. Not in her wildest dreams could she have seen herself making such a beautiful dress, with such a perfect fit. Faith twirled round, almost bumping into the table.

'Careful, *shamwari*, careful,' Melody said, pushing the table aside. 'We don't want you ruining your dress!'

'As if I would!' Faith laughed. 'I love it. I just love it! Thank you, *mainini*.'

'Now let's talk business,' Katy said seriously, looking at Onai.

'What business?' she asked.

'We'd like to offer you a payment for making this dress,' her friend said.

Onai laughed, genuinely surprised by the offer. 'I've enjoyed it and not for a moment did I expect payment. Your family have done so much for me.'

Faith protested, 'But, *mainini*, you have spent so much time and effort, that I would like to pay you. Please let me.' Katy nodded, but Onai was firm.

'You've already paid me by being so supportive, and by taking me and

Ruva in. No. No. I couldn't accept money.'

'All right, let's make a deal. Could you make something for mum as well? And maybe the bridesmaids' dresses, early next year? I want everything to be ready well before the wedding. But this time, for a fee. I'll check current dressmakers' rates in town and pay you the same. Please?'

Onai was happy to accept the offer. 'I would have done it for you anyway, but since you insist, I will take payment for the other garments as I make them. The wedding is still a long way off and I can take my time.'

Katy smiled with appreciation. 'Thank you, *sahwira*.'

≈≈≈

The girls talked excitedly to each other about also getting orders from their friends so that Onai could increase her earnings. The older woman laughed, wondering whether Katy would continue to let her use the new machine for her own business.

Later that week, she took Katy's measurements and started working on a *bou-bou*. 'I want you to look like *vamachidengaira chaivo*, the queen,' she said.

≈≈≈

In the absence of John's regular contribution, the grocery supplies started running low, so Katy and Onai took every opportunity to join the food queues in town. They had to stock up enough for the inevitable worsening of the situation in December. Onai also had to send groceries to Chiwundura for her mother and her two children.

As Katy said later, the one day which made her lose hope that things would ever change was their Saturday spent queuing in town. On the strength of a rumour about possible sales of cooking oil and mealie meal at OK Store, they went to the shopping complex at five o'clock in the morning, more than three hours before opening time.

Onai was pleasantly surprised when Hannah joined them in the queue. She was even more surprised to note that Hannah was heavily pregnant.

'*Wakadii,* Hannah? When did you get back from *kumusha*?'

'I returned from the rural areas two months ago. Life out there was worse for me. My son now stays with my sister in Darwendale and I'm renting a room in Ardbennie. I think I told you last time we met that my husband went *ku*South. Once he gets a job, he'll come back for me.'

Onai exchanged glances with Katy. John was struggling to get a job, yet he knew so much more about South Africa than Hannah's husband, who was probably an illegal border jumper. Onai had doubts about Hannah's husband coming back for her. Not anytime soon anyway. That was the story in a lot of families. For whatever reason, the men tended not to come back for their wives and children. A few had even drowned in the Limpopo while border-jumping. Others had fallen prey to crocodiles. She thought of John and felt sorry for her friend. What would happen to them?

'I managed to get onto the housing list though, Hannah continued, which will help because it might be a while before *murume wangu* comes back for me.' It was as if she was trying to exonerate her husband for abandoning her when she was pregnant. Onai and Katy nodded in unison. 'But I think it will be a long time before any of us get to live in those houses,' she added.

'Why?' Onai asked her sharply. As far as she knew, her own house would be ready the following week. At least that's what she'd been told. She realised that what with everything else, she'd hardly given the matter any thought. Why hadn't she gone back to the municipal office to check? She'd have to do so soon.

Hannah dropped her voice. 'I heard that the soldiers and the police are getting first preference for the houses that are nearing completion. The real displaced people will be lucky if they are housed at all.'

Katy shook her head. 'You can't say such things, Hannah, not when you have no hard facts. It's very alarmist,' she said sternly.

Hannah was instantly penitent. 'It's something that I heard, that's all. A rumour,' she muttered sullenly.

Onai suddenly felt tense. If the rumours were correct, her efforts might all have been in vain. How silly she had been to hope that everything would be all right. She pulled herself together. Mr Ndlovu had assured her the house would be hers, and why should she doubt him? She took a deep breath; anxiety would get her nowhere.

They stood lethargically in the early morning sunshine and waited patiently. But by eleven o'clock the heat was overpowering. Katy left the queue briefly to get some drinking water from a tap at the nearby bus terminus.

'I feel faint and dizzy,' Hannah said weakly. She turned and moved away from the queue in slow motion. Onai rushed to her side and helped her to sit down on a patch of dry grass. People turned to stare.

Katy ran quickly over to them. 'Is everything all right?'

Onai replied, 'I think so. She's just feeling faint.'

'Here, drink this water, Hannah. It's too hot. Let's sit in the shade. Onai, can you go back to the queue? The groceries will be coming out any minute. We don't want to lose our place in the line.'

'All right, *shamwari*. I think Hannah should go home, though.'

Katy sighed and nodded.

≈≈≈

After about fifteen minutes Hannah felt well enough to get up. Katy carefully helped her stand and indicated to Onai that they were leaving. Her friend made as if to leave the queue, but Katy motioned her to stay where she was. Somebody would have to buy the sugar and cooking oil. There was no point in all of them going home empty-handed.

Katy supported Hannah as they walked to the bus terminus and joined another queue. The sun beat unremittingly down on them. The crowds continued to swell as they waited, their hope of transport slowly fading. After a full hour with no sign of a bus, they decided to walk.

It was a long, slow walk with occasional stops to give Hannah a rest. When they got to her lodgings, she was feeling no better. She refused Katy's offer to proceed to the hospital.

'No, I can't do that. I still owe two bills from when my son was poorly in the winter, after spending so many nights in the open. I can't afford another bill. I'll just have a nap. I'm sure I'll be fine when I wake up,' she said dispiritedly.

'Promise me you'll go to the hospital if you don't feel better. Think of the baby you're carrying, Hannah. You will, won't you?'

The woman gave an unconvincing nod. Katy left for home, knowing in her heart that Hannah would not go to the hospital, even if her condition got worse. Katy wondered how she could help all her friends. Each day saw them a little worse off. All they had was each other. However, there was a point when 'having someone' would not suffice … their needs were too great. She was too close to that point, and she feared that Onai was as well.

≈≈≈

Onai arrived home shortly after five o'clock. She was empty-handed, both the mealie meal and the cooking oil had run out before it was her turn to be served. Katy looked at her dust-caked feet with disbelief. 'Don't you tell me that you walked from town too!' she exclaimed.

'I did,' Onai smiled as if amused. 'You know, this is getting to feel quite normal. In fact, it is normal. No transport, no bread, no sugar, no mealie meal, no cooking oil, no soap and no …everything. *Saka?* It's not a big problem. It's life, Katy. If the day ever comes when I can get transport to and from town, or have enough money, or can walk into a supermarket and buy what I need without having to queue, well, I'm not sure how I would cope! Who knows? I might just die from excitement!'

The two tired friends laughed as only two township women hardened by poverty could do. Humour and resilience were their only weapons in a situation that would have otherwise crushed them.

Recovering herself, Onai quickly asked after Hannah.

Katy shook her head. 'Not too good, but I think she'll be all right. She refused to let me take her to hospital because she owes them a lot of money.'

'Bills, bills, I try to forget mine but I know I'll be getting a reminder soon. Maybe I'll be the next to get arrested,' she laughed again. Katy shook her head.

Onai continued, 'It's hard, isn't it? Poor Hannah. I hope her husband will come back for her soon.'

332

Katy frowned. 'I doubt it. So many families break up because the men go south and never return. When I think of John, it worries me too.'

'If you talk like that, I'll lose hope,' Onai said, 'You're so much stronger than me that I can't bear the thought of you admitting that life is too hard – even for you ...'

'I do try to be positive, Onai. I honestly do. But we can't deny that our lives have got worse. It doesn't make me feel good that John is in hiding ... that he now has a criminal record. I could easily have one, too. I just feel like we've been cornered into living in a way that I never could have imagined,' she replied softly.

Onai felt a lump in her throat. It seemed that laughter and tears were so close to each other, they might have been the same thing. Nonetheless, she did not want to see Katy's tears. Crying was something she did, not Katy.

Suddenly pulling herself together, Katy lightened up. 'Faith wanted me to give you a message about her dress. Unfortunately, the phone got disconnected and I didn't hear all she said, but she'll stop by on Wednesday to collect Ruva. You can talk then.'

'I hope the seams didn't come undone or something.'

Katy laughed, 'Don't be silly. Think, instead, of what you've achieved over the last two months ... Faith's dress, mine in the making, and you've secured an order for four bridesmaids' dresses!

'I'm almost reconciled to the fact that John won't be with us, but our relatives have promised to come, and I hope you'll be there with me at the party.'

Onai looked at her. 'Of course I'll be with you. It's the least I can do, after you've been such a friend to me.'

'No,' Katy said. 'All things considered, I should be thanking you ...'

'If you like we can fight about it,' Onai teased. Katy shook her head. She took her friend's hand and squeezed it in a gesture that embarrassed them both. They walked to the kitchen. It was time to start preparing the evening meal. It would be cabbage and sadza again. How reassuringly normal that was!

CHAPTER 28

After some more reflection, Katy went for an HIV test. Uncertainty had made her decide against telling Onai, though she knew that she would need her friend's support if she tested positive. As it turned out, she'd had no need to worry, but a chance sighting of a figure from Onai's past on the way home rekindled her fears for her friend.

'Guess who I met today?' Katy asked Onai, the inflection of her voice suggesting something significant. Onai looked up from the ironing board and immediately stopped rearranging the folds of the long dress she was making for Katy.

'Who?' she asked warily.

'Gloria.' The word fell from her lips like a curse.

Onai's heart contracted. She had effectively blocked out memories of her husband's mistress. Now they were being thrust upon her.

Katy spoke again. 'She looked very unwell.'

Onai made no effort to reply. She understood the implications.

'Have you ever thought of having an HIV test, *shamwari?*' Katy continued more gently.

For a moment, Onai held the garment suspended in mid-air, then she placed it back on the ironing board, and slowly turned to face Katy, 'No, I'm too afraid of what I might discover.'

'But I think you should – because of Gari … and because of his relationship with Gloria. Perhaps it's better to know one's status than to live in the dark, especially now that one can apply for the government's *chirongwa chema*ARVs.'

'But it's always said that this programme only caters for a limited number of people – just over a tenth of those who need the drugs. Remember, Sheila couldn't get any, although she was so ill.' Onai attempted to shift the focus, trying irrationally to justify not being tested. She was unhappy to find herself being forced to confront her fears yet again. From time to time, she had considered having a test, but summoning up the courage to actually do so was another matter, and with so much else on her plate, it had been easy to push the idea to the

334

back of her mind.

Her anger with Gari flared again. Even now he seemed to be reaching out for her from beyond the grave. Would she ever be free of him? Hospital bills, the effects of his abuse on her and her children, the possibility of HIV...

Almost expecting a negative answer, she asked Katy, ' Would you be brave enough to go for a test?'

'I've just been for one ... I'm sorry I didn't tell you ... but you know how it is. The results were negative, though I'll need to go for a repeat test in three months' time.'

Onai stared at her. The colourful material in her hands fluttered to the floor. She picked it up hastily. 'But why did you go for a test?' she asked, shocked by this unexpected revelation.

'Because I don't know what John gets up to when he's away from home,' Katy replied with a calmness that disconcerted Onai.

'But John seems so ... loyal ... so caring. Don't you trust him?'

'I'm afraid I don't completely. You know that long-distance truckers are said to be a high-risk group. I can't just ignore that ... I even packed condoms for him the last time he went on a trip.'

Onai's mouth hung open. 'But Katy, isn't that like giving him permission to sleep with other women?'

'No, I don't think so at all. It's the least that I can do to protect myself, though it might not be enough. It does comfort me to know that I'm clear. Still, when he returns, I'll ask him if we can go for tests together. I should have done it a long time ago, but I never had the courage. You know what men are like.'

Onai shook her head. She couldn't believe that John might be unfaithful to Katy. Their marriage had always seemed a perfect union – at least from the outside.

Onai's face was a picture of disbelief, and Katy said irritably, 'Oh, my dear, don't be so naive; or is it just that you are an incorrigible romantic? You know you only need to sleep with a person once to contract HIV. John, or whoever, only needs to slip once ... and how many men are like him? Most are constantly tempted by women who are not their wives. They see it as their birthright! They even argue that it is a part of their culture.' Her laughter had a bitter ring to it. 'As if the tradition of polygamy has anything do with today's multiple partnerships! How many friends or colleagues of ours have died because their husbands saw temptation and couldn't resist.'

Onai nodded. She knew what Katy said was true. These issues had never been far from her mind but anxiety had always deterred her from voicing them. Women were always blamed, but it was the men who played around, boasting of their prowess; or complained that women put temptation in their way, as if they had no will or morals of their own.

'How much better it would be ...' Katy continued, 'if we women were able to negotiate with our men about everything related to our sexuality without starting a war? Why should protection and birth control become a battlefield?'

'Maybe we lose our eligibility to negotiate when our men pay *roora* and our parents are happy to accept it. Aren't we taught that we must always submit? Why, my own mother has told me that getting beaten is a woman's lot. She can't expect otherwise. When father was alive, he used to ...' Onai's voice suddenly broke. She raised her hand as if to wipe away the expression of pain that had appeared on her face. Then, clearing her throat, she concluded, 'Anyway, how many parents will support their daughters if they want a separation or divorce?'

'Yes, and look what happens. Their daughters die and they're left bringing up the grandchildren!' Katy said sharply.

Feeling acutely aware of her vulnerability, Onai didn't answer. She rearranged the long garment on the ironing board and resumed her task. It was time for her to face up to her fears. 'I'll think about having a test sometime soon,' she said quietly. And she did think about it. For three days her mind dwelt on nothing else. What if she tested positive? Treatment was a lifelong commitment, but access to drugs was not guaranteed. She thought again of Sheila, who had failed to get onto the list for ARVs. Affording private purchase was a dream. So what would happen to her, if she tested positive?

Onai handed her papers to the clerk at the reception desk. He glanced at them as if checking for her name. 'Good afternoon, Mrs Moyo. How can I help you today?' he asked politely and gave her a bright smile.

'Good afternoon,' she replied. 'I've come to confirm whether my house is ready. I was told that keys may be ready for collection this week.'

He nodded, walked over to the computer and tapped the keyboard with nimble fingers. He stared at the screen and stroked his beard. Onai looked anxiously at his still profile. When he came back, he was no longer smiling. 'I'm afraid there's a small problem with your application, ma'am. Everyone is supposed to pay a deposit of fourteen million dollars. There is no record of you having made any payment at all.'

Onai took an involuntary step backward. 'Fourteen million dollars! But I thought the accommodation was free! There was nothing about a payment … I mean, nobody told me about one!'

The man laughed. 'Free accommodation? Is there anything for free these days? I wonder where you got that information from, Mrs Moyo.' He glanced at some papers. 'We sent a letter to your address on 50th Street, Jo'burg Lines, Mbare, explaining about the deposit.' He looked at her again, this time with genuine surprise and something that could have passed for compassion.

Toro or Shungu had probably received the letter and not bothered to deliver it to her at Katy's house. Onai wanted to explain to him that 50th Street was her old address, but there was no longer any point. She heaved a sigh, not knowing what to think; not knowing what she would do next. The end of this particular journey was too far removed from anything that she had anticipated. How dared she have hoped? How dared she have allowed herself to feel happy, even to dream. It was like challenging destiny to crush her again.

'So what does this mean?'

'Well, for a start, the homes should be ready by next March …'

'March? But I was told November …'

'Yes March. Surely you must understand the delays, Mrs Moyo.

There's a shortage of building materials in the country. If I were you, I would pay the fourteen million dollar deposit as soon as possible, to avoid further problems. In the meantime, we will keep you on the list, but I warn you the pressure for these houses is increasing every day. '

Onai rose, mumbling her thanks. She gathered her documents together and left the office in a daze. Fourteen million dollars! How could she pay that kind of money? Where on earth would Hannah, or any other homeless person, get that kind of money? Even teachers and nurses only earned ten million dollars a month!

She dropped heavily onto a bench outside the building and held her hands to her face. Years of suffering had not made her resistant to pain. She felt it like a deep, physical ache. She was tired of poverty, tired of life, tired of everything that trivialised her best efforts.

Katy found her slumped on the bench, weeping. 'What is it, *shamwari*? Please stop crying and tell me what's wrong?' Through a tide of tears and sniffles, Onai explained the situation.

'I'm so sorry, Onai. What can I say? Wipe your tears and let's go home. There has to be something we can do.' Katy took her friend's hand and led her away from the building. For a short distance they walked in silence.

After a while, Onai said, 'What am I going to do, Katy? What about Fari and Rita? I promised them that they would be back with me before Christmas. It's already November … but that man was talking about March … How will I cope until then? I can't live with you forever.' She was right.

In Katy's mind, words of encouragement seemed wholly inadequate. Her friend needed so much more than words. She had lived on words for too long. She needed something positive to happen, something positive to sustain her. 'Try not to worry, Onai. And don't you blame yourself for anything. You've done your best under awful circumstances. It might be difficult for your children to understand this now, but they will later. Let's go home and we'll think about what to do next.'

'I'm sorry, Katy. I didn't mean to cry. It was just such a shock … coming at a time when I thought everything was falling into place.

…But what about you? Did they say you can start building soon?'

Katy blew out her cheeks and frowned. 'No such luck, my friend. Just before John's arrest we made what I'd understood to be the last payment. Today, they told me we need to pay another thirty million before we can start building. Apparently, over the last two years, the land sold by the council has been wrongly priced … I wonder why a 'wrong price' always means that we have to pay more! I really wish John was here to help me make sense of all this …' Her voice faded into a silence broken only by the thud of their feet on the ground.

'Apparently I should be grateful that our land is not being repossessed. Some people have actually had their stands taken over in the last few months, because they couldn't afford the top-ups.'

'I can't believe that …'

'Well it's true, my dear … It doesn't make sense to me either. Considering everything, I feel I'm living in a madhouse, and I'm sure I'm not the only one'

They walked back to Mbare. Neither woman could see the faintest promise of hope on the horizon. The heavy clouds that had been gathering all afternoon released a sudden downpour. Drenched, Onai allowed her tears to fall again, but no amount of rain could wash away the hurt.

≈≈≈

Faith, Tom and Melody drove to Tapiwa's house in Borrowdale. Tom had to collect some fuel that would be used to help ferry people to the party, as the venue was a short distance out of Harare; on a route not normally served by public transport. The fuel stations were once again dry and some of the invited guests had expressed concern that they might not be able to make it.

They found Tapiwa waiting impatiently just outside his gate. 'I was about to leave. What took you so long?'

Tom laughed. 'Sorry. I'm travelling with *magero!* They had to freshen up their make-up or do whatever it is that women do.'

Faith and Melody exchanged glances. Male patronage!

Tapiwa led them across the large garden to a shed where several twenty-litre containers of diesel and petrol were stored.

'One hundred and forty litres for you,' he smiled, looking rather pleased with himself.

Tom slapped him on the back and said, 'You're the man, Tapiwa. Thank you very much. I think we can fit only four containers at the back of the car. We'll come back for the rest later.'

Faith was curious. 'Where did you get all this fuel from.?'

He glanced at Tom and smiled evasively, 'Well, this is Harare. There are always ways and means.'

Melody and Faith exchanged another look.' Catching it, Tom said, 'Go on tell them, *shamwari,* otherwise they'll harass me all the way home!'

Tapiwa explained that one of his friends had got the fuel as a government-subsidised allocation for public transport operators. Like so many others, he preferred to park his buses, drain the fuel off, and sell it on the black market. He was making a lot of money and saving his vehicles from wear and tear at the same time.

'And, of course, the poor people who need public transport are the ones to suffer,' Melody said with raised eyebrows.

Faith nodded, 'And we wonder why things only get worse. There's just too much dishonesty nowadays.'

Tapiwa looked guilty. So did Tom, but he managed to say, 'Hey, don't torment my friend. How else would we have managed to get so much fuel? It's not his engagement you know!'

Melody made another face. 'I suppose you're right.'

As they loaded the containers into the back of Tom's 4x4, Faith suddenly said, 'I just don't know why people are so passive. How can they put up with the shortages, the queues and all the corruption, when it means that their hard-earned money is going into the pockets of a few very rich people? Who would've thought that by now teachers, nurses and most of the civil service would be living below the poverty line? Things have to change!'

Tom was quick to answer. 'Come off it, Faith. This is the real world. People... well Zimbabweans anyway ... admire the wealthy, they aspire to be rich themselves, they like to think there are people like us, who can hold their own anywhere in the world.'

Melody nudged her friend and looked at Tom as she spoke, 'I agree that things have to change. But I put it to you … what "people" are you talking about? Isn't change your responsibility as much as the next person's?'

Faith rolled her eyes dramatically. 'The fact of the matter is that the underprivileged cannot …'

≈≈≈

Tapiwa laughed. 'Lawyers, lawyers. Where do you pick these women from, Tom?'

'My misfortune!' Tom drawled.

'Tapiwa! Tom!' Melody shook her head in mock disgust. Couldn't they have a serious discussion without Tom and his friend slipping into this buffoonery?

Faith tugged at Tom's shirt, 'This man sometimes bewilders me. He can be so principled, so moral, so caring about the people that he loves, and yet almost amoral when it comes to the poor and underprivileged. I suppose you just think of them as a sort of indistinguishable mass, much like the socialists did when they talked of the "masses".' She paused reflectively, 'After all we've referred to squatters as "rubbish".'

Tom's jaw dropped. Melody burst out laughing. Tapiwa wagged a finger at the young woman, 'No need to be quite so provocative, Faith. I'm sure you'll realise soon enough that some of these issues have no solution; well, not any time soon …'

Faith would have none of it. 'But …'

Melody interrupted. 'We can't win this, *shamwari*. Can't you see who we are up against …'

Faith interrupted hotly, 'No, I will not …'

Tom said, 'Oh come off it, *mudiwa*, before you totally contaminate Melody with your extreme ideas. You and Emily are as alike as two peas in a pod. You want to change the world for the better, but you want me to make the money so you can live in comfort while you do it.'

'TOM!' Faith exclaimed.

Her look of complete outrage made him laugh.

'Come on. The world won't change in a day. Let's be on our way. I've got to get back to work ... make a bit more money ... employ a few more people ... but first we have to get to Mbare, and we're late already.'

Tapiwa turned to Faith, 'Have you confirmed my appointment for Saturday?'

She shook her head. 'No, but we're going to see her now. Don't worry, I'll make sure she's there on time.'

'Thank you.' Turning to Tom he joked, 'If you don't come to collect your fuel, I'll sell it off. Your guests will just have to walk.'

'Don't you dare ...'

'As if I would! But *mudhara*, all this for an engagement party! I wonder what the wedding will be like?'

'Too right,' said Faith. 'I've told him over and over again that he's overdoing it.'

Tom laughed heartily. 'You ain't seen anything yet! They don't call me Mr Harare for nothing. And a man only gets engaged once!'

'Huh! I don't know about that!' Faith retorted.

'Certainly not a Zimbabwean man,' Melody joked, 'Not with all these "small houses" all over the place.'

'Now, don't tempt fate!' Tom wagged a finger at the two young women. 'Are you trying to provoke me?'

Tapiwa smiled as he waved them away.

'Doesn't it bother you sometimes?' Melody asked Tom.

'What?'

'That we're now existing as semi-criminals ... in the sense that ... there's so much fraudulence. I can't believe public transport operators would sell fuel that has been subsidised by the government ...'

Faith interrupted, shaking her head, 'I've become quite used to living with double standards. I should know better ... but Tom has taught me well,' she laughed.

Tom said, 'Well, as I always say ... life is all about survival of the fittest. Rules can be twisted to suit one's needs ... at least that's how things feel right now. But, seriously, one thing does worry me. When the economy does recover … if it ever does … will we recover enough honesty to maintain economic order; or will we continue to operate as, to use Melody's phrase, "semi-criminals"?'

Faith muttered, 'Frankly speaking, we'll need a miracle.'

'I think you might be pleasantly surprised,' Tom answered. 'I believe there are a lot of people who would prefer to operate honestly, people who still have moral values – and not just this God blesses the rich nonsense – people who will be relieved to work within the law … if we ever get back to such a situation.'

Faith interrupted. 'Hey, the situation is bad, but it's not that bad … At least if you believe that people have the ability to change their own lives, rather than just assume fatalistically that somehow the future will improve of its own accord.'

'Sure,' said Melody, 'but right now we're all just petty criminals and at least for me it makes it worse if we pretend otherwise. We may as well call a spade a spade. Otherwise we won't even know right from wrong.'

Not easy, Faith thought. There no longer seemed to be a clear distinction between the two, at least where economic activities were concerned. Looking at it from another angle Faith realised that Melody had learnt something profound from her broken relationship with Chanda … and so she smiled at her friend in agreement.

With a strong smell of fuel in the car, they drove silently to Mbare, each wrapped up in their own thoughts.

They were disappointed to find that only Ruva was at home, but decided to wait.

≈≈≈

When the two women arrived wearily back in Mbare, they were greeted warmly by the youthful party. Onai was startled to see Tom in her friend's house, then she remembered that he was now welcome to visit openly as the formalities were now in progress.

'Where have you been? We've been waiting and waiting!' For someone who'd been kept waiting, Faith sounded rather upbeat. Coming in from the rain, Onai found the cheerful atmosphere almost surreal.

351

The two older women changed into dry clothes and came back into the sitting room. Faith said animatedly, '*Mainini,* my dress and all the work you've done … I've told Mr Jongwe all about you and he wants to offer you a job. A full-time job, *mainini.'*

Melody nodded. 'It's true.'

The eyes of the two young friends were alight with pleasure, as they stared at Onai, waiting for a reaction.

Katy was the first to react, gripping Onai's hand, 'Oh, I'm so happy for you, *sahwira!'*

Onai looked from one face to the other. 'Really?' Faith's words filtered through her mind. Hers was a life of guaranteed misfortune. Faith couldn't be right. If she were, something was sure to happen that would wrench the opportunity away from her.

She swallowed, 'Did you tell him that I have no recent work experience? Are you sure he really wants … me?'

Tom's cell-phone rang. Excusing himself, he made his way out to the car.

Faith grinned. 'I'm absolutely sure, *mainini.'* She lowered her voice, 'And guess what? He wants to meet you on Saturday at Meikles Hotel to have a chat about the job.'

Meikles Hotel? She'd never been to any hotel in her life! Faith pressed a wad of notes into her hands. 'Here's a small present from me and Tom. You're not walking into town on Saturday. Get yourself a taxi. Eleven o'clock. Now don't be late, *mainini.* And mum, please take her to the hair salon. She'll have to look the part. Her big-Afro hair is definitely so last-century!' They all laughed.

Except Onai. She hugged Faith tightly. It was just too much of a shock, especially as it came so soon after her huge disappointment.

≈≈≈

After that everything seemed to happen with lightning speed, as if in a dream. Early on Saturday morning, a completely transformed Onai stood before Katy and nervously submitted herself to a rigorous inspection. Her thick Afro had been straightened and styled to accentuate her features, making her look years younger.

Katy looked at her with open admiration and gasped, 'What a difference a good hairstyle can make! You look beautiful, Onai. I hardly recognised you! *Kusageza shamwari!'*

Onai laughed and peered at her reflection in the mirror with a pride that she'd never experienced before. Vanity felt as if it could indeed be a virtue. She had the strangest feeling of having been liberated by her new look ... yes, liberated. That was exactly how she felt. It was exhilarating.

'And the dress! It looks so much better on you than it does on me. I think I should just let you keep it,' Katy marvelled as Onai twirled round for further scrutiny.

Katy was right about the dress. The light green fabric clung to her upper body and fanned out gently over her wide hips. She was suddenly a woman and not a frump.

'You look wonderful, Onai. I wish you the best and I'm sure you'll get the job. Too bad you are not looking for a man today.'

Onai's cheeks burned. 'Please don't tease me, Katy. It'll only make me more nervous.'

Katy laughed. 'Well, you're going out there and you're going to convince this man that you are good enough to work for him!'

Onai suddenly sat down in a chair and held onto the armrests. She looked at her friend. 'I should thank you for being so supportive. It's... a wonderful surprise and it's all because of you and John, Faith ... it's ...' She squeezed Katy's hand and the two women embraced.

≈≈≈

A loud car horn blew outside. It was Onai's taxi. The promise of sweet autonomy beckoned. She walked out, trying to remember when she had last been in a real hired taxi. If ever. Possibly ten and a half years before, when Gari had come to collect her from hospital after Fari's birth. She wondered what he would have thought if he could see her now. She would never know. But she had a distinct feeling that he would not have been happy for her. She shoved thoughts of him out of her mind. He was the past.

Before meeting Mr Jongwe, she needed to calm down. So she asked the taxi driver to drop her off at the corner of First Street, a leisurely ten-minute walk from the hotel. She paid her fare and walked slowly alongside Africa Unity Square, appreciating the cool shade of the trees. Jacaranda blooms floated gracefully onto the violet carpet on the sidewalk. She trod softly and closed her eyes briefly, savouring the beauty of the afternoon. This was the splendour that she had looked for, and which she had not found, when she had come to Africa Unity Square in winter.

She emerged from the shadow of the trees to feel the warm sun playing lightly on her back. She took pleasure in the sensation and crossed the wide road into the lobby of Meikles Hotel. With a newly-acquired confidence, but still drawing in a deep breath, she walked calmly into the hotel.

Her eyes darted around the large reception area. It was obviously a busy day. Most of the tables on the raised dais of the cafe were already occupied. Closest to the entrance was a group of smartly-dressed young women who were sharing animated conversation. For a moment Onai appraised them. Their girlish laughter drew glances from the other guests. The girls seemed unconcerned. They were young, carefree and probably came from rich families. Maybe they were celebrating something. As far as she could see, there was only one man sitting alone. He seemed to be staring directly at her. Could he be Mr Jongwe? He looked much too young to be the man on whom all her hopes were pinned.

They exchanged looks, and he got up and began walking towards her. 'Mrs Moyo?' he asked. With a relieved smile she nodded. 'When two strangers are waiting for each other, they always meet,' he said reassuringly. 'Come and sit down and have a cup of tea, won't you – and a scone? Meikles are internationally famous for their cream scones!' He smiled almost mischievously and Onai wondered if he could really be serious.

Mr Jongwe was strikingly good-looking, she reflected, cautioning herself for the obvious impropriety of her thoughts. She walked towards him on slightly unsteady feet, shook his proffered hand and was instantly rewarded with a wide, genial smile. Something about the smile seemed very familiar. Metaphorically shaking her head, Onai concluded that her imagination was playing tricks.

They sat down. Mr Jongwe raised his hand and a waiter came forward to take their order. Tea and scones for two.

'So you are Mrs Moyo, the dressmaker who has made Faith's lovely party dress that Faith's told me so much about?'

'Yes,' Onai replied briefly, trying to keep a ring of pride out of her voice.

'As Faith might have told you,' Mr Jongwe had plunged straight on, 'I have a bridal shop in town.' Onai nodded, not trusting herself to speak just yet. 'My late wife's shop...' his voice trailed away for a moment. 'I had to close it down for a while. And now when I want to re-open it, I've had problems getting a good dressmaker. I had one briefly, but she went off to South Africa, leaving me with her two assistants who don't seem to know much beyond ...assisting.' He laughed and shook his head.

Onai nodded smiling.

'I was impressed by what Faith told me, and the fact that she's known you for so long. She has a lot of confidence in you ... Do you think you'd like a job in a bridal shop? The conditions, of course, would be subject to discussion.'

Onai didn't hesitate, but she said honestly, 'I have no work-related references. Since I completed my course several years ago, I haven't worked at all that is, until I began to make the dresses for Faith and her mother, for this big party they're having.'

'That's all right. Faith told me something like that. But from what I hear, I have no doubt that you're the right person – talented, hard-working, honest ... besides, I'm quite desperate for a replacement,' he laughed

Onai relaxed a little. She was glad he had a sense of humour.

The conversation was quite different from anything Onai could have imagined. It was almost as if he was placing her on an equal footing; almost as if they were old friends.

Their tea arrived. Unusually, Mr Jongwe poured, but Onai felt it was not her place to offer to do so. As he passed her a plate, he said, 'Excuse me for prying, but can you tell me a little bit more about yourself. Apart from what Faith has told me, I know very little. I've had a few good friends in Mbare, so I'm interested. I know many people there are having a hard time.'

Onai found it easy to talk to him. He seemed genuinely to understand. She told him about being a vegetable vendor at the main market in Mbare, about her dressmaking course, and her disappointment at not finding a job. He kept nodding, and so she went on to tell him about being widowed and her struggle to get a home for her children. When she saw him frowning, her cheeks burned with embarrassment. There had been no need for her to tell him so much. He'd probably just let her continue talking out of politeness.

She was relieved when he said, 'I'm afraid my life is not as interesting or challenging as yours has been. I run a car import company. I'm just trying my luck with wedding dresses. My late wife was doing an excellent job and she loved it. It's sentimental, I know, but I don't want to let her down.'

A cautious silence fell as they negotiated their scones heavy with jam and cream, both conscious of possibly having said too much too quickly. It was broken when Mr Jongwe said, 'Going back to the job… the starting salary would be fifteen million dollars a month plus accommodation. Of course, your pay will be adjusted depending on how everything goes. There is a two-bedroomed house on my premises in Borrowdale. The workshop is right next to the house. You will, of course, have two assistants working with you but they won't live on site. I have the full contract here for you to take away.' He patted a slim leather folder, 'How does that sound to you?'

Onai could only nod. Maybe this was a dream. Fifteen million dollars! Even a teacher earned less than that! She felt a lump in her throat and swallowed hard.

He went on. 'I feel the shop has a lot of potential. White weddings are very popular, you know. Why, even couples who've been together for years and have grown-up children, are having them now. But we can discuss all this in more detail later.'

Onai nodded again. Mr Jongwe passed her a big envelope. 'Don't look at it now. Read it carefully when you get home, and if everything is all right, we can both sign it. Give me a ring on Monday. I'll be at the office all day. My business card is in the envelope.'

Onai did her best to appear composed but her heart was beating and she longed to get home to share this wonderful news with Katy. She was going to be what she had always wanted to be, and not just any dressmaker, but one in a bridal shop. She would be the magical hands behind Bridals Direct on First Street.

'Do you have any special requests at all?' Mr Jongwe asked before he called for the bill.

Onai thought of her children. Would he let her move into the house with them? She was not sure if she could ask. Would she jeopardise everything if she did?

Then she said shyly, 'Would it be possible to have my children live with me on the premises?'

'I'd taken it for granted that they would. It shouldn't be difficult to arrange because the house isn't occupied at present.'

And with that, they made the final arrangements. Once the contract was signed – and Mr Jongwe was adamant that no good business person would sign such a deed without reading it closely first – Onai would move into the house at the end of the week, and begin work the following Monday.

Before they parted in the foyer of the hotel, Mr Jongwe said slowly, 'One last thing. When I was going through a difficult time in my life, there was one person whose kindness kept me sane. Now I think it might have been your sister. You look so alike. You reminded me of someone when I first saw you, but it has taken me a little while to work out who it might have been.'

'No,' replied Onai, puzzled, 'I don't have a sister …'

Mr Jongwe gave her a rather strange look, 'Oh, dear. I'm always making this sort of mistake, seeing likeness where none exists.'

He held out his hand, 'Goodbye, Mrs Moyo. It's been a pleasure meeting you. I look forward to seeing you on Monday to sign the contract.'

Onai gave a small bob as she shook his hand.

In a moment, he'd gone and she was left standing on the steps of the hotel feeling as if she had been transported into another world.

≈≈≈

That evening, the two friends discussed the practicalities of Onai's move, the party and all the work that still needed to be done in time for the wedding. To imagine a future beyond the next day with both hope and excitement was a rare indulgence and one they relished. But when the headiness was over, Katy said, 'I haven't told you that Mr Mafa was here while you were in town. He's insisting that John should turn himself in. They promise to drop the other charges against him – though he refused to tell me what they are. Now, it's just the foreign currency dealing that they want him for, and it seems that they're determined to use him to trap Nzou.

'Mr Mafa seems quite sincere, and I'm beginning to believe him. The difficulty is going to be to persuade John. He's so afraid of being thrown in prison, and with good reason. But the alternative is for him to live in exile. And what will happen to me? All I wanted was to educate my daughter and build a home. I never thought it would turn out like this.' Without any warning, Katy burst into tears. Onai held her. It struck her that the intensity of the sorrows and now the joys of the last few weeks and days, had been more than anyone could bear without release. Perhaps this was the reason why they seemed to be doing a lot of crying. After all, there was a lot to cry about.

≈≈≈

When John phoned that evening, he said he'd withdrawn his asylum application. It was all too complicated. Asylum applications took a long time to get processed, and during that time, he wouldn't be allowed to work. There was always a risk of deportation if one worked illegally. Besides, he was beginning to understand the resentment that so many

South Africans felt about Zimbabweans, who so often seemed to get the best jobs.

Hard truths had prompted him to seriously consider returning, and he knew his company still wanted him. Katy, in her turn, tried to explain Mr Mafa's promises, and his determination that if John was willing to appear as a witness against Assistant Commissioner Nzou, then the charges against him would be dropped or minimised. Her husband promised to think hard about coming back home.

CHAPTER 30

The workshop was a large airy room partitioned into three working areas. Its windows opened out into a garden flooded by the morning sun and the bright colours of summer flowers: white and purple petunias; deep orange geraniums, and others with which Onai was unfamiliar. When she'd moved in the previous evening, she hadn't been aware of being surrounded by such loveliness. This was the dawn of her new existence; and it seemed beautiful.

Across the garden stood Tapiwa Jongwe's house. Never had Onai been anywhere near such an impressive home. It still surprised her that her employer was so humble. What had her grandmother said? Something about real manners being those where no one felt any discomfort. But it was more than manners that she was thinking about, it was a question of equality … we're all born equal until someone gives us a dirty look … that was true. Many people did try to raise themselves on the backs of others. But it didn't have to happen that way.

She turned her gaze away from the window, back into the workshop – her own workshop and quite unlike anything she could have ever hoped for. There were four good sewing machines in the large room, and three flat-topped working tables, each with a brass tape-measure fixed along one smooth edge. Four ironing boards stood in a row against the wood-panelled wall, next to well over twenty rolls of soft, beautiful fabrics.

She opened the cupboards and drawers, trying to familiarise herself with everything in the room: rolls of lace, boxes of beads and seed pearls, pattern books, pins and scissors. A few unfinished wedding dresses hung in one cupboard together with two that had been completed. It was obvious that her predecessor had been a truly skilled dressmaker.

Onai shook her head. Only five days ago, she had been industriously peddling her vegetables at the market, for a pittance.

Suddenly, from the next room she heard Rita's voice. 'But *why* can't I be a bridesmaid? Why?'

'Because you can't, that's why. Faith chose me, not you,' Ruva's voice was adamant and not a little smug.

Rita's voice dropped, 'If I can't be a bridesmaid, please ask Faith if I can stay at her flat until the party. Please?'

'You only came from Chiwundura two days ago. You have to stay with *amai* for a while …'

'You're just too bossy. I can ask her, you know!,' Rita replied hotly. Onai listened to the exchange with amusement. The events of the last few months had changed them all. They'd all done a lot of growing up. Even sweet, docile Rita was now beginning to stand up to her older sister!

The issue was resolved when Faith and Tom arrived with Melody. Faith suggested that they could do with Rita's company at her flat, where Ruva would be staying until the party. Rita shot a triumphant-look at her sister who in turn made a face.

Onai put an affectionate arm around Fari's shoulders as they watched them all drive away. She went back into the house to prepare lunch for her son. While he had his food, she cut herself a large chunk of melon. She watched the news as they ate. There was an item about an Assistant Commissioner Nzou who had been arrested for soliciting bribes, dealing in foreign currency, and arranging for his partners in crime to be released from remand prison. Onai was surprised.

She remembered going to meet Mr Nzou with Katy, threatening him with exposure until he agreed to arrange John's release. But how incredible that he should have been arrested! The man had acted and spoken as if he was above the law. Justice did exist after all. When she'd left Katy's house, her friend had seemed so much happier, after all the stress of the preceding weeks. John would be coming back home to testify against Mr Nzou in a trial that was now a hot topic of conversation. In exchange, he'd been promised leniency. It was sad that he would miss his only daughter's engagement party, Onai thought, but on the other hand, he probably didn't want to take the risk of spoiling the event by finding himself in prison. Faith would have been devastated, and how would Tom have coped? The young man's affiliations and principles were something of a mystery. It was a tough time for her friends, but she felt sure that they would weather it. Her attitude to what was possible had shifted; she no longer simply expected the worst.

After the news, Onai sat at her desk and waited for her assistants to come in. They had to make a work plan for the busy months ahead.

While she waited, she wrote a letter to the hospital's accounts department. She would pay a third of the money she owed at the end of January, and the remaining balance over two months. She apologised for the delay but explained that she had had no previous means of paying. She advised them of her change of address, in case they needed to contact her again. It felt good to have her own address again. The contrast between her past and her present being was something constantly in her mind, as if reality itself had turned on its head.

≈≈≈

A knock interrupted her thoughts. Surprised, she walked to the door to find Emily and a young man on the doorstep. Pleased, she said, 'Come in, come in.'

Emily walked in, smiling. The young man followed.

'We'd just stopped by to see Tapiwa, but he's out, and I heard from Tom and Faith that he'd offered you a job, and that you'd moved in. It's a small world,' she laughed. 'So before we left, I thought we should greet you. I hope we're not intruding.'

'Oh no. Not at all. Please make yourselves comfortable,' Onai replied, leading them to some chairs in the sitting room. 'Can I offer you a Mazoe?'

'No thank you, Mrs Moyo. We're not staying long. Meet my good friend and colleague, Ben.'

Onai smiled at the young man and dipped a small curtsey, an instinctive gesture that showed the respect dictated by tradition. Ben grinned and stretched out his hand as they exchanged greetings.

Onai sat down, and turned to Emily. 'I'd really like to thank you for the help you gave me. In the end, of course, because my new job came with accommodation, I didn't need the house ... a good thing really, as they wanted an up-front payment, which I didn't have ... but still, I'm so grateful to you.'

Emily made a dismissive motion with her hand. 'Nonsense. I was only too pleased to be of help.'

Feeling a bit self-conscious, Onai said, 'At a time when so many doctors are leaving the country, I'm glad that we still have people like you, people who still care, despite the difficulties …'

Emily inclined her head. 'It's a funny thing. Often I'm tempted to leave, to go away, to work somewhere with proper amenities, proper salaries, but being able to make a difference, a real difference to just a few people's lives through my work at the hospital and the work that I do for Kushinga Women's Project … the satisfaction that I get from it all is what makes me want to stay. In England, in Australia, I'd live a comparatively pampered existence, but this is what I really want. And if I weren't there to do the job, someone else would be. Whereas here …' Her voice faded. She looked towards Ben as if seeking affirmation. In that glance, Onai recognised something. Ben's response confirmed her supposition.

'But no doubt you'd like me to get a job here with the World Health Organisation!'

They all laughed.

≈≈≈

Onai felt more keenly than ever before that her destiny was now in her own hands and that at last her children stood a chance of being able to fulfil themselves. She would do her best for them. They would not be oppressed by a system beyond their control. She looked out of the window and smiled to herself.

GLOSSARY OF WORDS

(Unless otherwise indicated all words, if not abbreviations, are in Shona or are Shona neologisms)

aiwa – no

amai – mother/Mrs/honorific for older woman

ambuya – grandmother/mother-in-law/common term of respect for a mature woman

asi chii nhai? – but what is it?

asi tashaya nyaya here? – don't we have anything better to talk about?

asi – but

baba – father

bhururu – friend

chaizvo mukwasha – yes! son in-law

Chaminuka – an eminent historical figure who prophesied the coming of the white man

chii chitsva? – what's new?

chiremba vakuru chaivo – senior doctor indeed

combi – commuter omnibus

dhiya – my dear, my darling

ET – emergency taxi, euphemism for combi

Gloria *wachena!* – Gloria, you're smart!

haiwa – no

hakuchina – there is no more of that

hakusi kupenga ikoko? – is that not madness?

handidi ngozi pano! – I don't want avenging spirits here!

handiende – I won't leave

haurevesi! – you're not serious!

hazvichinje! – nothing will change!

hesi vasikana! – hie ladies!

heyi – hey!

hondo yeminda – war for the land

hazvidi hope – you have to be jerked up

imi amai imi – you woman you!

364

inini chaiye miriyoneya! – me being a millionaire!

iwe – you

iwe neni, tichagara mushe – you and me, we'll live comfortably

iwe mwana iwe! – you child you

izvozvi! – now!

izvozvo – that

kana muKwayedza? – even in *Kwayedza* (a vernacular newspaper)

ko maUS dollars? – how about the US dollars?

kugomera uripo chaiko, mwanangu – its about persevering whilst you're there my child

kumusha? – to the rural areas?

kuora chaiko! – definitely rotten!

kupi? Ari kupi Shelia? – where? where is Sheila?

kusiri kufa ndekupi? – which way doesn't involve suffering

kutanda botso – a ritual of begging and accepting public insults undertaken when a child wrongs his/her mother beyond verbal apology

kutenga mari yako – buying your own money

kwakanaka here kuHarare – is everything all right in Harare (at home)

mahobho – security guard

mahumbwe – a children's game

mahwindi – touts

mai/Mai – mother/Mrs

maita henyu – thank you

vamwene – mother-in-law

maiwe, maiwe! – mother, mother! (exclamation of surprise or shock)

makadii? – how are you?

mambokadzi – queen

manyepo chaiwo! – definite lies

mapositori – members of the Apostolic church

maputi – roasted maize grains

marooro – bride wealth

mashura chaiwo! – bizarre incident

maswera sei? – how's your day been?

matomati, mazai pano! – tomatoes, eggs for sale here

*matsotsi e*Harare – (petty) thieves of Harare

matsotsi haagerane – there's no honour among thieves

mbanje – marijuana

mbira – a traditional thumb piano

mimvuri – shadows

mudhara – old man

*muchafa ne*AIDS – you will die of AIDS

mudiwa wake – his/her lover

mukwasha – son-in-law

mumusha – in the home

mutengesi chaiye – a real traitor

mwana akanaka iyeye – that child is beautiful

mwanangu/ vanangu – my child/children

ndatenda – thank you

sahwira – a close friend, usually of the family.

ndezvake izvo! – it's his own look out!

*ndi*Emily *iyeye* – that's Emily for you

*ndinopika neguva ra*Amai vangu vakafa – I swear by my dead mother's grave

ndinotenda – I thank you

ndiri kurwadziwa – I'm in pain

ndiri shasha pakusona! – I'm good at sewing!

ndiudzei – tell me

ndiyo Zimbabwe *yedu* – that's our Zimbabwe

ndizvo – that's it

ndoshandira mhuri yangu vakomana – I work for my family

nemabhanzi – with buns

nematambudziko – let me express my condolences

nemuriwo – with vegetables

nyama yekugocha! – roasted meat

*nyaya ya*Gloria – Gloria's case

nyika yedu – our country

pabva gondo pamhara zizi – replacement of something by another less good

*pa*Chikurubhi – at Chikurubi (a local prison outside Harare)

pata-patas – slippers/flip-flops